The Way Back Home

Freya North is the author of 13 bestselling novels which have been translated into many languages.

She was born in London but lives in rural Hertfordshire with her family and other animals, where she writes from a stable in her back garden. A passionate reader since childhood, Freya was originally inspired by Mary Wesley, Rose Tremain and Barbara Trapido – fiction with strong female leads and original, sometimes eccentric, characters.

Her fourteenth novel, *The Turning Point*, will be published in 2015.

In 2012 she set up and now runs, the Hertford Children's Book Festival. She is a judge for the CPRE Rural Living Awards, and also an ambassador for the charity Beating Bowel Cancer.

To connect with Freya and hear about events, unique competitions and sneak previews of what she's writing, join her at www.facebook.com/freya.north, @freya_north or log onto www.freyanorth.com to find out more.

Praise for *The Way Back Home*

'Brimming with emotional drama and packing a huge twist, this story will keep you guessing until the very end' *Heat*

'I was gripped from the start and raced through to the end in one long sitting'
Sara Lawrence, *Daily Mail*

'A lovely read that keeps you anticipating a twist that is nicely unexpected. . .I couldn't put it down'
Sarah Broadhurst, Lovereading.co.uk

'A very telling and enjoyable take on contemporary life' *Woman and Home*

'If you like emotional family dramas with a twist you'll love this' *Daily Express*

'Freya North has given us another poignant tale – you won't be able to put this one down' *OK*

'An intriguing tale that keeps you absorbed from cover to cover.' *Candis Magazine*

'It is a story of reflection and redemption - a tender tale that seems to have come from the very heart of this author' *New Books Magazine*

'Packed with love, lies and drama'
Woman Magazine

Acclaim for Freya North

'*Secrets* will make you smile, sigh and cheer as this story proves love can be found in the most unexpected places' *Sunday Express*

'Darkly funny and sexy – literary escapism at its very finest' *Sunday Independent*

'The novel's likeable central characters are so well painted that you feel not only that you know them, but that you know how right they are for each other. . . the beauty of the North Yorkshire countryside contrasts convincingly with the bustle of London' *Daily Telegraph*

'Freya North has matured to produce an emotive novel that deals with the darker side of love – these are real women, with real feelings' *She*

'A delicious creation . . . sparkling in every sense' *Daily Express*

'A distinctive storytelling style and credible, loveable characters. . . an addictive read that encompasses the stuff life is made of: love, sex, fidelity and, above all, friendship' *Glamour*

ALSO BY FREYA NORTH:

The Way Back Home

FREYA NORTH

HARPER

Harper
An imprint of HarperCollins*Publishers*
1 London Bridge Street
London SE1 9GF

www.harpercollins.co.uk

This paperback edition 2015
1

First published in Great Britain by HarperCollins*Publishers* 2014

A catalogue record for this book is available from the British Library

ISBN: 978-0-00-746228-5

Typeset in Meridien by
Palimpsest Book Production Ltd, Falkirk, Stirlingshire

Printed and bound in Great Britain by
Clays Ltd, St Ives plc

In loving memory of Hannah Berry 1983-2013

Beautiful, funny and brave. We miss you.

www.beatingbowelcancer.org

When I was . . .

When I was born there were already other children at Windward. None was beyond toddling age and, as such, we were grouped together pretty much like the clumps of perennials in the garden, or the globs of paint on a palette in one of the studios, or the music which drifted from the top rooms – discordant notes that, as a whole, wove together into a quirky harmony of sorts. We were who we were, the children of Windward – a little ragtaggle tribe further defining the ethos and eccentricity of the place.

I wasn't born in a hospital. I was born at Windward but I wasn't born in my home. I was born in Lilac and George's apartment with Jette assisting my mother, ably helped by all the other females there at the time, whether permanent or itinerant, mothers or girls, lesbians, lapsed nuns and even an aged virgin. I know all about a woman called Damisi who was visiting at the time though, it seems, no one really knew where her connection lay. She was a doula, apparently, and I know the story off by heart – how she had all the women breathing and bellowing to support and inspire my mother to relax. It worked – I know I was as easy a birth as it's possible to have, slipping out into the Windward world to a backing track that was practically a bovine opera. Some of the other children heard – how could they not – and often, they mooed at me. I didn't mind – it seemed my own special herald. However, when I first heard a similar sound emitted by a cow it scared me senseless.

When I was five, Louis, who was always very old but never seemed to age, hosted my birthday party in his apartment. We didn't know he knew magic. He took pennies from behind all our ears – it was probably the first time any of us had coins of our own. He gave me a piggy bank to keep mine in – to start saving the pennies, he explained. I thought I had to save the coins from some fate that would otherwise befall them.

When I was ten, my birthday party was a disaster. I'd been at the local school for three years, been to the parties of my classmates – pink and proper, simultaneously joyous and lively and yet fastidiously organized. That's all I wanted – a party like that. A neat cake with the right number of candles. My parents got it wrong. There were only nine candles. Someone – probably my mother – had put a tenth one in, but had decided that it was incorrect. Ten? That's wrong. That small dent in the beige icing of my lopsided, inedible cake was to me a sinkhole of indifference. It struck me then that perhaps not everyone loved everyone.

When I was fifteen –

When I was fifteen something terrible happened.

CHAPTER ONE

Oriana

To Oriana, it seemed so small. So ridiculously and unnervingly small that she felt compelled to rub her eyes. It had to be an illusion – the truer, more sensible, more realistic proportions would surely be reinstated after a good blink. But there it was still, nestled in a fold of land which looked soft enough to be made of fabric. Like biscuit crumbs in a scrunched napkin, there was the small town outside which she'd grown up. She pulled the hire car in to the verge. She didn't want to get out, she wanted to avoid familiar smells that might make it seem real. She didn't want to hear anything that might say well! welcome back, duck. She wanted to believe that she had no history with this mini place and no need of it. It looked silly, being so small. Not worth a detour. Certainly not worth a visit. Not worthy, even, of a drive right through. This wasn't Lilliput. This wasn't romantic. This was Nowhere. Nowhere, also known as Blenthrop, Derbyshire. The worst thing about this bastard place striking Oriana as being so small was that it made the rest of the world feel so vast. And suddenly she felt isolated, acutely alone and terrifyingly far away from the place she'd called home for so many years, the place she'd left only the previous day. God Bless America, she said under her breath though she knew she'd never go back.

Driving to her mother's house was easier because she'd never lived there. There was little to recognize, nothing to flinch at; she was unknown and that was preferable to intrusive welcomes and waves, however warm and well meaning Blenthrop folk might be. The further she drove from her childhood home, the longer the space she could finally create between her ears and her shoulders. As she relaxed a little, the car seat felt more comfortable and her headache lifted. Really, jet lag had nothing to do with the tension and now that the anxiety had dissipated, Oriana let the genuine tiredness billow over her the way her mother used to waft her duvet when she was a little girl, giggling in bed waiting for it to land. They call it a comforter in the United States, she thought. My mum's gone all sheets and blankets because she says it makes the bed look 'properly made'. My mom – the all-American girl who's now as small-town English as they come.

The tiredness, the tiredness. Should she pull over? Half an hour left to Hathersage. Open the window. Turn the radio up another notch. Drink Coke. Pinch yourself awake. Pinch yourself that you really are here again, eighteen years on. Kick yourself, wondering if it's a stupid idea, really.

*   *   *

Oriana's mother didn't know what to do. Her daughter was sleeping and though she'd told her mother not to let her, under any circumstances, what was Rachel to do? Her daughter, wan and sunken-eyed, too thin. Rachel looked in at the front room. Oriana was curled embryonically into a corner of the sofa, her hands tucked tightly between her thighs, the tips of her socks hanging limply a little way off her toes; the heel of her right sock was twisted to her ankle, as if her shoe had wanted to cling onto her feet. Her hair looked lank and flat and her lips were chapped. She wasn't wearing earrings. She'd spilled something on her top. This wasn't jet lag, Rachel sensed. This was exhaustion.

Rachel had done that trip back to America often enough since she herself emigrated from there aged nineteen. She knew well that, though jet lag made you feel discombobulated, it didn't make you look like *that* – how Oriana had looked on arriving an hour ago. When Rachel had opened the door to her daughter, she read in half a glance all the unrevealed secrets and sadness that had slipped unnoticed between the lines of her sporadic emails. On her doorstep, Rachel saw how the crux of it all was suddenly writ large over Oriana's face, her general scrawniness. The details, however, remained concealed. She was shocked. How could she have known nothing? She was ashamed that, once again, a mother's instinct had failed her.

'I'll give her another ten minutes,' Rachel said, unsure.

'That'll make it forty winks,' Bernard said. 'I'll be

popping out now. Just round the block.' And he kissed his wife who, just then, really did love his habit of explaining life with sayings and clichés. Bernard Safely. Had ever a person had a more appropriate surname?

'Two shakes,' Bernard told her though they both knew that his walk around the block would take far longer than two shakes of a lamb's tail. She watched him through the bubbled-glass panel of the front door as he walked away. The distortion made him appear to have no bones, amorphous as jelly. Her ex-husband, Oriana's father, referred to Bernard as spineless. Through the warped glass, he did indeed look so. Rachel felt disloyal. She rarely thought about Robin these days. She supposed she'd have to, now Oriana was back, even if she didn't want to. She'd see him in her daughter's crooked smile, her high cheekbones, the way her gaze darted away while she talked but focused fixedly on whoever spoke to her. Father and daughter both had the ability, without realizing it, to make one feel simultaneously inconsequential and significant.

'Oriana Taylor,' Rachel said quietly and then, in a whisper, 'Oriana Safely.'

It didn't flow. It didn't work. It would never have worked. She'd always be Oriana Taylor, daughter of Robin. *The* Robin Taylor. Would they mention him? She and her daughter had managed for eighteen years to skirt issues as if they were dog mess on the pavement.

* * *

Malachy

An ex-girlfriend had described it as *Saturn Returns*. Malachy hadn't a clue what she meant. That dream you have, she'd said, you might not have it often but it'll always recur – like *Saturn Returns*, with similar cataclysmic fallout. It makes you introverted and horrid to be around.

He'd ended the relationship soon after. She was a bit too cosmic for Malachy and she talked too much anyway. If he had the dream, the last thing he needed was a load of astrobabble bullshit. A warm body cuddling next to him, soothing him, taking his mind off it – that's what he required. Saturn Returns. She never knew that a prog-rock band of that very name had formed in his childhood home, exploded onto the music scene for a couple of years in the late 1970s and then finally imploded back at the house in 1981. He never told her, even though the band had jammed in the very place where Malachy currently lived.

Last night, the dream had once again hijacked his sleep, apropos of nothing. In the woods, with his brother Jed, their teenage bodies of twenty years ago encasing their current souls. They were out at summer dusk, shooting rabbits. A large buck running away, stopping, turning and facing him. Delicate eyes and soft silver pelt conflicting with the anomalous fuck-you gesture of lope-long ears rigid like two-fingered abuse. Malachy pulled the trigger and smelt the saltpetre and heard the harsh crack and felt the kick and experienced the extreme pain as half his world went dark.

He'd often wondered whether the rabbit was some kind of metaphor. He'd tried to analyse why in the dream he didn't shout for help; why his brother was there only at the start. And he never knew whether he killed the rabbit, the little fucker. The pain cut the dream short, always. And he always woke up thinking, but it didn't happen like that, *it didn't happen like that*. And he'd be cranky and introverted for a good while after because he knew that he'd much rather it *had* happened like in the dream.

Stupid dream. Malachy left his bed and showered. Dressed, he snatched breakfast, yesterday's post in one hand, toast in the other. What he really wanted to do today was write his novel, not go to work. Business was slack this time of year – early March, thick frost, too cold for tourists, too close to Easter for more hardy holidaymakers; too close to Christmas and Valentine's and Mother's Day for locals to fritter any more of their money. The irony was Malachy could very well *not* open the gallery because, after all, he owned it – but the fact that he owned it compelled him to keep it open, never take time off, never get sick. Tuesday to Friday, 10 till 6. Saturday 10 till 5. Summer Sundays 11 till 2. Closed Mondays. If the gallery was as quiet as he anticipated, he'd work on his novel from there today. He left the apartment, glancing guiltily at the house. He ought to do the rounds, really. He hadn't done so for a couple of days.

Paula de la Mare waved at him, before she hopped into her car, belting down the drive. Malachy followed, absent-mindedly creating acronyms from

8

the letters on her car's registration plate. At the bottom of the drive, she turned right, taking her girls to school. Malachy followed her a little way before joining the main road into Blenthrop.

Some idiot had dumped litter in the doorway of the White Peak Art Space; yesterday's chips lay like flaccid fingers in the scrunch of sodden paper. He rummaged in his satchel for something suitable like a plastic bag. Phone. An apple. Slim leather diary (he refused to use his phone for anything other than calls). A tin of pencils, a spiral-bound notebook and a flashdrive. He had no plastic bag. The toe of his shoe would have to do. He shoved the takeaway detritus into the gutter and opened up the gallery.

It was always the weirdest feeling. It never diminished and it engulfed Malachy the moment he entered. The immediate stillness and quiet of the space contradicted by the undeniable sensation that, up until that very moment, they'd been alive; the paintings, the sculptures. If he'd turned up a minute earlier, or sneaked in through the back, he was certain he'd have caught them at it. Now, as every day, they were just figures frozen into their canvases, others quite literally turned to stone, bronze or, in the case of Dan Markson's work, multicoloured polymer. It was like the characters in his novel – Malachy sensed they existed without him but whenever he returned to the manuscript, he found them exactly where he'd left them.

In the gallery, he straightened a couple of frames and adjusted the angle of a spotlight that was glaring off the glass of a watercolour. There were few emails to respond to and within the hour Malachy felt justified in inserting the flashdrive and clicking on the folder called 'novel', selecting from within it the file called 'novel10.doc'.

'Tenth draft in only fifteen years.'

He said it out loud, with contrived loftiness, laughed and took the piss out of himself, receiving the abuse well. All residual effects of the dream had gone, the details were forgotten. Until the next time.

* * *

Jed

None of his girlfriends knew this, but whenever Jed had sex in the morning, he always had Ian Dury playing in his head. He'd grown used to the soundtrack. It wasn't a distraction and it didn't irritate him; it was a brilliant song after all – as sexy in its funk as it was funny in its lyrics. It had started with Celine. She had been French, intense and passionate, and when she'd purred in his ear in the middle of his sleep, *wake up and make love with me*, that's what kicked it all off.

Jed knew his current relationship was on the way out; from fizz to fizzle in eight months. It had been as awkward as it had been depressing last night, to be the only non-conversing table in a packed and buzzing restaurant. They checked their phones, ate, gazed around the room, checked their phones again, eavesdropped on other people's conversations and barely looked at each other. Fiona went to bed when they arrived back at his flat. I'm tired, she'd said, as if it was Jed's fault. He'd sat up late, finishing off the red wine he'd opened the night before, even though he'd forgotten to put a stopper in it and it really didn't taste very good. Jed had thought, I'm too young to be one of those couples that go out for dinner and don't speak. And then he thought, I'm too old to be frittering away time on a relationship like this. I have a headache, he thought, collapsing into bed and drifting to sleep before he could remember to kiss her goodnight let alone check she was even there.

But he woke, horny. It was natural, chemical. Ian Dury was goading him to have a proper wriggle in the naughty, naked nude. He sidled up to Fiona, his cock finding the soft dale between her buttock cheeks to nestle in. Unlike Ian Dury, however, it wasn't lovemaking he wanted. Just a fuck. She moved a little, her breathing quickening as he ran his hand along her thigh, up her body, a squeeze of her breast before venturing downwards and between her legs. She was warm and moist and she let him manoeuvre her so that he could work his way into her from behind. No kissing. She had a thing – paranoia – about morning breath, which initially he'd found charming, then irritating but today just useful, as he didn't want kissing and eye contact. He just wanted to come because soon enough she'd be gone.

She dumped Jed in a stutteringly over-verbose phone call that lunch-time. It's not you, it's me. I just need some space. Let's just be friends. It's fine, he kept saying, I'm fine with it. I agree. If something of such little substance was finally over, it really didn't warrant this level of analysis or justifying. Don't worry, he told her, don't worry. I feel the same.

'You feel the *same*?' She sounded affronted, as if her self-esteem was dependent on him being crushed.

Jed sensed this. 'I mean,' he qualified, 'if you're *sure*. Take all the time you need.'

'I'm sure,' she said.

'OK,' he said, 'OK.' And for her benefit, he dropped his voice a tone or two. 'Take care,' he said.

'You too,' she said. 'Friends?'

'Friends.'

He had too many of these 'friends' with whom he had mercifully minimal contact. None had truly made the transition from girlfriend to friend. None had even re-formed into useful booty calls. Ultimately, none meant that much to him because none was the one who got away. He hadn't seen her for such a long time, not since she moved to America a decade and a half ago.

CHAPTER TWO

Nine o'clock. Oriana felt pleased with herself. Apart from a vaguely recalled period of wakefulness in the small hours and despite the nap that her mother had tricked her into taking the previous afternoon, she'd slept through the clash of time zones and she'd slept well enough for it to feel truly like morning. There was no need to count the hours backwards and figure out what the *real* time was. She accepted that nine in the morning, GMT, was now the true time in her life. She looked at the dressing gown her mother had laid out for her. It was white towelling and had the crest of a hotel embroidered in navy on the breast pocket. My mum has become one of those people who actually *buy* the hotel robe. She didn't know whether she should laugh or cringe at this. She did know she'd rather get dressed than put the thing on. This wasn't her home and it wasn't a hotel and she wasn't comfortable mooching about in borrowed towelling robes. She opened the bedroom door and listened hard. The house appeared to be empty but still Oriana padded quietly, self-consciously, along the corridor to the bathroom. She thought, this is the type of carpet I fantasized about as a child. The colour of butterscotch and as softly dense and bouncy as a Walt Disney lamb. And the bathroom itself; warm, bright and spotless, with hotel toiletries placed neatly on the sink *and* the bath – additional prerequisites of her childhood dreams. And yet she could not remember her mother ever yearning for such things.

Showered and dressed with her hair in a towel turban, Oriana made her way downstairs. Stairs that don't creak or groan, she mused, make one feel light and dainty. When she was young, her father had called her Fairy Elephant – such was the inadvertent noise she'd make even crossing the hallway of her childhood home. It was only when she was at the base of the stairs that she realized she wasn't alone in the house. From behind the glazed door leading into the kitchen, she could hear the radio tuned low to something middle of the road. It must be Bernard. Had it been her mother, the volume would have been high on a talk show and Rachel would be joining in, or, as Bernard would have described it, having her tuppence worth.

'Morning.'

Bernard looked up from the crossword and a mug of tea. He smiled his uncomplicated smile. 'Good morning, love,' he said. 'Breakfast?'

Last night, Oriana had been too tired not to feel sick after a couple of mouthfuls and prior to that, she'd only snacked on the plane.

'Yes, please.'

'What would you like?'

She looked blankly around the kitchen. She had no idea, really.

'Toast and tea?' Bernard suggested. 'Poached egg?' He could hear hunger in her inability to decide. He chuckled. 'Sit yourself down – have a look at six across.'

She couldn't concentrate on crossword clues and watched Bernard at the stove. 'I had a special poaching pan,' she said, 'in America.'

Bernard had a spoon, a saucepan of boiling water and a perfected technique.

'Fancy that,' he said, his tone genial.

Poached to perfection, Oriana thought, as she tucked in.

'More toast?'

Oriana nodded because Bernard's toast was cut into triangles, buttered thickly and placed in a toast rack. The taste was as comforting as it was delicious. English salty butter and builder's tea. She had to concede that some things just didn't travel well across the Atlantic.

'What do you have for breakfast,' Bernard asked, 'over there?'

Oriana wondered why he was using the present tense. Being tactful, probably. She'd told them both last night that she was back in the UK for good or for whatever. She shrugged. 'I used to just grab something,' she said, 'from a stall or a bakery, on my way to work.'

Bernard filled her mug with a strong brew the same colour as the brown teapot. He used a tea strainer. The tea strainer had a little holder of its own and the teapot was returned to a trivet on the table. He did like things just so, Bernard. Oriana knew that in itself was what had attracted her mother to this ordinary, gentle man. Her father placed used tea bags on windowsills and tore into loaves of bread with his hands and teeth. Her father once told her that plates were for the bourgeoisie.

'You take your time,' Bernard said and she knew he meant way beyond her eating breakfast at his table. 'Your mother'll not be long.' And he returned to his crossword, instinctively knowing when to pour more tea, when to glance and smile. Privately, they both reflected that they liked this time, just the two of them. They'd rarely had it. They barely knew each other. Rachel, who could have been the conduit, had kept them separate.

After breakfast – and Bernard had insisted she went nowhere near the washing-up (plenty of time for that, love) – he sent Oriana out for a walk, explaining painstakingly the route around the block. His pedantry with directions had infuriated her when she'd been a teen. Boring old fart. Mum – he's such an *old woman*! Now, though, she liked it. It was one less thing to think about – which way to go – because in recent months which direction to take had consumed her entirely. Today was a day just for putting one foot in front of the other, for allowing the sidewalk to turn back into a pavement, for acknowledging that driving on the left was actually right, for accepting that cars were tiny and the traffic lights and postboxes were different, more polite somehow, and that this was Derbyshire, not San Francisco, and that was the end of that.

* * *

'Where is she?'

'She's out for a walk – just round the block. The Bigger Block. I told her the way.'

'But round the block doesn't take an hour, Bernard, not even the Bigger One, not even when your knee's playing up.'

'She'll be fine.'

'Something's happened to her.'

'Here? In Hathersage?'

'Not here in Hathersage, Bernard. Out there – *over there*.' Rachel gesticulated wildly as if America, her own homeland, was an annoying fly just to the left of her. 'Something happened,' she said. 'That's why she came back. That's why she looks the way she does.'

'Well,' said Bernard, 'she had a good breakfast. You can't go far wrong on a full stomach.'

Rachel rolled her eyes and left the house.

The cacophony of tooting and the screeching of tyres tore into Oriana's peaceful stroll.

'Get in, honey!' Her mother was trying to open the passenger door while leaning across the gearstick, buckled as she was by her safety belt and hampered by her capacious bag on the passenger seat. Rachel now had the door open and was lying on her handbag.

'Oriana – get *in*.'

For a split second, Oriana actually thought about sitting on top of her – if the urgency in her mother's voice was anything to go by. But Rachel had managed to straighten herself and hoick the bag into the back by the time Oriana sat herself down.

Her mother was agitated. 'You can't take an hour to walk around the block!'

'Can't I?'

'No!'

'No?'

'No! *Not* without telling someone you're going for a *long* walk.'

She's serious, Oriana thought. She's utterly serious. All those years when she didn't know where I was and didn't care what time I was back.

It was so preposterous. Surely her mother could see that? However, the irony appeared not to have confronted Rachel. But there again, Rachel had reinvented herself and parcelled away the past when she'd left Robin for Bernard. The car radio was on and Rachel bantered back vitriolically at the callers and the presenters, having her tuppence worth, all the way home.

CHAPTER THREE

'I thought I'd come this weekend.'

'Good morning, brother dear. Alone?'

'Yes,' Jed told Malachy. 'Alone.'

'You're on your own, then? Again?' Malachy looked at the phone as if Jed could see his expression which was playfully arch.

'Yes,' Jed laughed at himself. 'Again.'

'Which one was it?'

'Fiona – the lawyer.'

'Did I meet Fiona the lawyer?'

'No,' Jed said. 'We were only together about eight months.'

'Jesus – have I not seen you for eight months?'

'Piss off – of course you have. I just didn't bring Fiona to the house, that's all.'

Malachy considered this. But there was no pattern to which girlfriends Jed brought home. Sometimes it was girls he wanted to impress, other times it was girls he wanted to unnerve, as if their reaction to the house was the ultimate litmus test.

'Fine,' said Malachy. 'It'll be good to see you.'

Mildly frustrated with Jed for making him late setting off for work, Malachy cursed his brother under his breath. Not that he was expecting any clients. But still. He had standards and opening times and a novel to write and a business to run. And, now, his younger brother descending on him for the weekend. Which would mean long nights and bottles of wine and philosophizing and reminiscing and arguing and irritation and laughter. Malachy jumped into his car, noting that the de la Mares had long since left on the school run.

* * *

Oriana looked at her phone, deflated. The number she'd rung was unobtainable – the fact that it still had a name ascribed to it made this seem all the more blunt. How could she not have known that Cat had changed her number? Oriana tried the number again and then chucked the phone on the sofa in frustration before slumping down and reaching for it again as if giving the gadget a third and final chance.

Rachel pretended not to notice. 'Do you want to use the proper phone?' she asked, referring to the landline. She and Bernard shared one mobile 'for emergencies' and it rarely left the drawer of the desk in the hallway. If it was mobile, how could it be grounded and trustworthy?

'I was just trying Cat,' Oriana said, 'but I think she's changed her number.'

'And she didn't give you her new one?' Rachel employed extravagant indignance on her daughter's behalf but it backfired.

'If she'd given me her new number, I wouldn't be phoning her old one.'

Bernard looked up, aggrieved, and immediately Oriana regretted her snappiness.

'Sorry.'

She vaguely recalled a mass-text from Cat with a new number a few months ago. She'd been on a stolen weekend with Casey, just outside Monterey, in their favourite fish restaurant, the sides open to the sea, a breeze from the surf bringing an ephemeral saltiness to the food. She remembered being so in the moment, so desperate for no interruption, for time to slow down, for the day to stretch and belong only to them, that when the text came she glanced at it and discarded it.

'Sorry,' she said to her mother and, privately, to Cat.

'I thought she was living in the US too?'

'She was – Colorado – but she came back about a year ago.'

'You could phone Django,' her mother suggested, but they both knew how the phone could ring at Cat's uncle's place and he might answer it, if he felt like it, or not, if he didn't. Usually, he'd rage across the house simply to bury the phone in the sofa cushions to shut the damn thing up.

'Seven, four, nine,' Oriana chanted, 'six, eight, two.' Django McCabe's phone number was one of the few still inscribed into her memory. She'd known it from a time long before SIM cards made memorizing numbers outdated and pointless.

'He's poorly, you know,' Rachel said, 'from what I've heard.'

Oriana thought, I could always drive over there – I loved Django. But she didn't want to. When one had lived away from one's roots for so long, returning always revealed such an unexpected acceleration in the ageing of those left behind. Her mother. Bernard. They always looked so much older than she anticipated. And Django – whom Oriana remembered so vividly and fondly as robust and larger than life – she simply didn't want to see him shriven and ill and aged.

Facebook. In recent weeks, she'd stayed sensibly away from Facebook much as she'd avoided Alice Trenton in the school playground – the cool girl, the mean girl; get too close and you're trapped. Facebook was similar, thrilling and oppressive in equal measure. The choice was between Django and Facebook. The former brought with it intimacy, the latter intrusion, and Oriana wanted to steer clear of both. There again, Facebook afforded her invisibility. She reached for her iPad which, at her behest, Bernard had gingerly had a play on the night before, his index finger out rigid while his remaining fingers and thumb were scrunched into a fist, as if merely pointing at the screen might deliver an electric shock.

Facebook. She signed in. Sixteen trillion notifications and a newsfeed jammed with peculiar app suggestions and people she hardly knew gloating about virtual farms and aquariums and poker games; photos of babies and smiling and beaches and the wild and wacky times that apparently defined everyone else's lives. She typed in 'Ca'. And sure enough, up came 'Cat McCabe' but, just above her, 'Casey' too. He was minute, his photo hardly recognizable at this size. Do not click on 'Casey'. There is no need and there is no point.

With the iPad on her lap, Oriana pushed her hands under her thighs and stared and stared at the screen until the wave of nausea passed and she felt her breathing regulate. She should have unfriended him. She was aware that, if she did so now, he probably wouldn't even notice. She clicked on Cat and sent a message.

I'm back in Derbyshire – call me! I can't find your new number xxxx

A little white lie on Facebook was so pale it practically didn't exist.

Bernard announced he was off out for a stroll. It was only when Rachel cleared her throat for the second time that Oriana realized there was something brewing.

'Cup of tea, Mum?' Clever.

'No. Not now.' It wasn't tea brewing. Rachel appeared awkward and spoke fast. 'I was saying to Bernard last night how lovely it is to have you home. And we both want you to know you can stay as long as you like and take all the time you need – you know, to find a job and your feet and somewhere to live and what it is that you want to do.'

'Thank you.' It suddenly seemed prudent to sound genuine, guileless. But from Rachel's penetrating stare, Oriana knew she saw right through it.

Oriana felt irked. Four days in the last five years, a similar average over the past eighteen years, and already she's had enough of me. 'What you mean is, it's been nice seeing me but you think I should get a job, ship out and get on with it.'

Rachel tutted. 'Honestly – why must you be so defensive?'

Oriana thought, I've got to get out of here. Then she thought, but I have nowhere else to go. 'I'm sorry,' she said and it wasn't to apologize, it was to qualify. 'It's just it sounded like you don't want me here.'

'It's not that,' her mother said, 'but I really don't know what you're even doing here.'

For years, Oriana had felt better about her relation-ship with her mother by believing, quite categorically, that her mother had been in the wrong. Now it was obvious that in this current situation, Rachel was actually quite right. 'Why *have* you come back?' she asked. 'Why give up a charmed life? What happened to Casey – I'm assuming you guys are through?'

Oriana sighed and shrugged as if it was no big deal and just a tiresome topic. 'It was time for a change,' she shrugged. 'It was hard for a while – but I've moved on. And I don't really want to talk about it.'

'And you're OK?'

'It was my call. I'm *fine*.'

'You're sure?'

'Look at me!'

'You're thin.'

'Thin's good! I'm fit.'

'You're too thin – for you.'

'Nonsense. I eat like a horse – you've watched

me! Two poached eggs and toast for breakfast. Seconds at supper. Bernard's "nice biscuit" at regular intervals throughout the day.'

'You look like you've been in the wars,' Rachel said in Bernard's voice. Her transatlantic accent might have been tempered by four decades of Derbyshire, but some phrases would simply never suit her.

'Mother, I'm *fine*,' Oriana said. 'Casey is fine too. We're still great friends – but I had to come back. You know – work, tax, stuff. And I'm thirty-four.'

'Time waits for no man.' Rachel channelled Bernard again. She felt irritated. Her daughter had just said emphatically, convincingly, that she was fine. The thinness, the paleness – perhaps that was just how Oriana in her thirties was meant to look. 'Now you're back – for good – will you go see Robin?'

The name hung like a dead man on the gallows, and silent, loaded looks swung back and forth between mother and daughter.

'Now you're back – you ought to.'

'Why would he even know that I'm back?'

'He doesn't. He wouldn't.' Rachel paused. 'But this isn't a holiday, a flying visit. You have a duty.'

Oriana had to take a moment. A knot of accusations and retorts were loaded onto the tip of her tongue and aimed dangerously at Rachel. She bit it.

'You don't keep in touch? At all?' Rachel said.

'You know I don't. You know that.'

'I just thought—'

'Well, *don't*.'

'You're a lot older now, Oriana – and he's not getting any younger.'

'What's that meant to mean?'

'It means—'

'Have *you* seen him?' Oriana made the notion sound just as preposterous.

'No – but that's different.'

'How so?'

'He's your father – for all his faults, he is still your father.'

How long? When was the last time? Oriana rifled through fading memories, their chronology confused, as if sifting through a disintegrating pile of documents.

'Louis Bayford's funeral,' Oriana said.

Her mother paused. 'That was the last time I saw him, myself. But you didn't stay. You left straight after the service. You disappeared. He never knew you were there.'

Nor did Malachy or Jed. Oriana plucked at the seam on a scatter cushion. That funeral. Five years ago? Six? She had sat at the back of the church, away from everyone, hiding down into her coat, fighting the urge to stare at the backs of their heads, Jed and Malachy; praying neither would turn and see her. She couldn't even remember seeing her father there.

She'd left as soon as she could – to avoid him not so much as them.

CHAPTER FOUR

The doorbell had never worked and the knocker had fallen off many years ago. There had been a cowbell once – but that was now by the hearth because Django McCabe found it the perfect surface off which to strike Swan Vestas when lighting the fire. A bitterly cold March day meant knocking on the old wooden door was not an option – even in balmy weather, bare knuckles on dense wood was a painful thing and, because of the door's thickness, pointless anyway. So Oriana did what everyone did, what she'd always done – she opened the perennially unlocked door, stepped inside and called out knock! knock!

It was Cat's suggestion to meet here, at the old house. She told Oriana that Django was ill though you wouldn't know it. That it would do him good to have a guest, that he'd cook up a storm in her honour. Their phone call had been brief, excited, fond. The arrangement had been made for today, Thursday, a week to the day of Oriana's return.

'Knock knock?'

Django appeared, resplendent in Peruvian cardigan and citrus yellow corduroys. His hair was the colour of gunmetal and platinum and his beard was in a goatee, styled to a rakish point. On his feet, the clogs Oriana remembered so well. She had the strangest urge to run to him, to hold on tight, as if she'd just imbibed a Lewis Carroll potion that had hurled her back to childhood. From the kitchen came drifts of Classic FM, something manipulatively rousing like Elgar or Vaughan Williams. Also, wafts of an olfactory clash of ingredients. Everything about Django McCabe, about his household, was centred on the happy collision of seemingly disparate elements. It was a thoughtful serendipity. It was unbelievably genuine. In America, when holding court amongst her friends and telling them of her crazy technicolour upbringing, Oriana had shamelessly appropriated many of the details from here and transposed them to her home at Windward.

'Oriana Taylor,' he marvelled, taking her hand with great reverence. 'Oriana Taylor. Well, heavens to Betsy.'

'Hey, Django,' she said and she felt as if she was ten, or seven, or fourteen. The slab stone floor underfoot, the peculiar and lively smells from the kitchen, the creak of the house, and the balding kilim in the middle of the floor. It was familiar and a comfort because while her life had gone on regardless, all this had remained just as it should be.

And then Cat appeared with a beaming smile and arms outstretched. 'Oh my God, *Oriana*!'

'Oh my God, Cat – you're pregnant!'

There'd been no need for apologies or excuses or even explanations for the silent months. Their friendship had never lapsed, it had simply loitered where they'd left it whilst time had flung forward.

'So,' said Oriana, 'it *can* be done.'

They were curled at opposite ends of the sagging Chesterfield sofa.

'Yes,' said Cat, 'you have sex at the right time and bam! baby on board.'

'I meant the move back to the UK?' And, just momentarily, the gleam left Oriana's eyes.

'Are you not back for good, then?'

'For better, for worse,' Oriana shrugged.

'It's amazing how fast you'll settle back into the groove. And Casey?'

Being evasive with her mother was one thing. With Cat, it was unthinkable.

'No.'

'No?'

'No more Casey. But it's all fine – bless him.' She was rattling off the words like a mantra. 'Moving back here is the best thing I could do for him too. I mean, I know the United States is huge – but there's space and then there's distance. Sometimes, you need more than merely miles to move on. Sometimes you need time zones.'

'And you're OK?' Cat pressed, because Oriana's voice had been expressionless. '*Really* OK?'

'I am *dandy*.' But still Cat was regarding her. 'We'd come to the end. It was my call.'

'When?'

'A while back,' said Oriana. 'Well, three, four months.'

'Poor Casey though, having left his—'

'I need a glass of water, a cup of tea.' Oriana had both in front of her but her mouth was suddenly dry. If Cat could just leave the topic while she went to fetch a drink. 'Want anything?'

'More space!' The baby was wedged under her ribs. 'How's your ma?'

'Suburban,' Oriana said, returning. 'You wouldn't believe it.'

Cat shook her head. 'I haven't seen her for years. No one has. I still find it bizarre – how she traded one life for another so diametrically opposed. How is Boring Bernard?'

Oriana flinched at the moniker they'd given him as teenagers. 'Do you know, he's just – *normal.*'

Cat thought about it. 'I suppose we confused normal with boring.'

'That's because both of you grew up not really knowing any *normal* people,' said Django, suddenly appearing with a wooden spoon that appeared to be covered in sweet-smelling tar. 'Which was a blessing and a curse. For my part, I apologize. Come on, lunch.'

The kitchen. How she'd always loved the McCabes' kitchen. Despite the size of her own childhood home, Oriana's family kitchen had been pokey. And it had been underused. As unconventional as the McCabes' household had been – three young girls living with their eccentric uncle – it had always felt fundamentally stable to Oriana. And Django – as bonkers and outspoken as he was, he always put food on the table. The ingredients were peculiar, but mealtimes were sacred; they sat down as a family to eat. Throughout her life, she'd often arrived there hungry and wanting. And she'd always left nourished.

'Is that cannabis?' said Oriana.

'No – but I used quite a lot of oregano. And a splash of Henderson's Relish.'

'Not in the dish,' said Oriana, '*there*. On your windowsill.'

They all regarded the plants. Cat rolled her eyes.

'Medicinal,' Django defended himself. 'Your husband's the doctor, Catriona – he's done research.'

'You could get busted!' Oriana said.

'I *am* busted,' said Django. 'I have cancer. Prostrate.'

'Pro*state*,' said Cat quietly.

'It's very slow growing,' said Django rather proudly. He tapped at the bowls in front of them. 'Now look – eat up. I've been experimenting. If Tabasco is hot enough to blow your socks off, just imagine what it can do to cancer cells. They thought I was a goner. I've proved them wrong.'

This was a home where discordance was joyful, where love and hope provided the bedrock for whatever was dumped on top. Oriana felt more settled than at any other time since her return.

'And will you be visiting Robin now you're back?'

'Unlikely,' Oriana said.

'So why did you return?' Django pushed.

'Sorry,' Cat said to Oriana, under her breath. But it was fine.

'It was time.' She shrugged, paused, continued quietly. 'Some things came to an end. Job. Lease. Other stuff.'

Django liked her ambivalence. He wasn't very good at ambivalence and he admired it in others.

'Can't be easy, living where you're living.'

Oriana shrugged. 'It isn't.'

'Seconds,' said Django and it wasn't a question. He gathered the bowls and took them back into the kitchen to refill. Cat excused herself and disappeared upstairs.

Alone at the table, Oriana thought about her mother. She didn't doubt that the woman cared about her, in her own way which could be detached and could be dramatic and was always self-centred. But she knew and her mother knew that the Hathersage house was no place for her.

'Here.' Cat returned with the local paper. 'Just look at this.'

An apartment at Windward was up for sale.

'That's the last place on earth I'd live,' said Oriana.

'You couldn't afford it anyway – they go for a fortune, these days.'

They peered at the pictures which, though in colour, were grainy. The main one was of the house – obviously taken during the summer months. There were four smaller photographs of interiors. Oriana considered them for some time.

'I'm not even sure which one this is,' Oriana said. 'No one had a hi-tech kitchen like that when I was there.'

'It's Louis', isn't it?' said Django, back.

'Is it?' said Oriana, grieving for Louis anew.

'Look.' He jabbed a finger at the final photo. 'Where's that then?'

The girls looked.

'The oriel windows,' Oriana said, 'right at the top. But it can't be Louis'.'

They read the details.

'How on earth did they make *three* bedrooms out of his apartment?' Oriana read on. '*Two* bathrooms, one en suite?' She looked up at Cat and Django. 'I loved it when it was Louis'. It was my place of choice for tea. It was always so genteel.'

Django laughed. 'Fabulous old queen.'

Oriana turned to Cat. 'Do you remember – after school – going for toast and to do homework at his kitchen table because it was so much quieter than downstairs?'

Cat looked at the details anew. 'I can't believe that this is Louis' place. And yes, of course I remember.'

'I practically lived there during exams,' Oriana said.

'Well – between Louis' and ours,' said Cat.

'Two bathrooms and three bedrooms,' Oriana marvelled again.

'Crivens,' Django murmured at the guide price.

'Will you visit?' Cat asked.

Oriana looked at her with exasperation.

'I meant Windward,' Cat said cautiously. She thought about it. It hadn't been so long ago that she and Django had been estranged. However temporary it had been, it was hideous at the time. Oriana looked tired. Behind the smile and the teeth-whitening and Bobbi Brown cosmetics, it took an old friend little time to detect a degree of emotional exhaustion.

'What's the point? I haven't spoken to my father

in years. I rarely heard from him before that anyway. And I don't know anyone there any more.'

It was only after Oriana had left, when Cat and Django were reviewing her visit, that they realized none of them had mentioned the boys. Not once. Not even when poring over the details of the apartment that had come up at Windward. The Bedwell brothers. Malachy and Jed. And Cat wondered whether they, like Robin, were dead to Oriana too.

CHAPTER FIVE

The front door was never locked but Jed was always acutely aware how nowadays, Malachy's was one of only three dwellings whose front door remained resolutely unlocked. Nearly all the other apartments in the old house had new security systems and even burglar alarms. Still, along the Corridor – running subterraneous through the house like a hollow crooked spine – the internal doors joining it were unlocked. That had been the very point, back at the end of the 1960s, when the pioneering group of artists and writers and musicians had rented Windward. There was to be flow, Windward ho – ideas and creativity, triumphs and failures, music and colour, characters invented and real – into and out of the rooms, through the windows, across the seasons, during the days and nights. Now, with only two of the original seven artists still living there, Windward was a quieter place. Apartments were much changed. White-collar people lived there now, quietly, privately. Music, if it could be heard at all, came in faint, civilized drifts from radios and sound systems, not resident musicians. Colour these days was polite Farrow & Ball, rollered to a perfect chalky finish; not Winsor & Newton oils squeezed direct from the tube and daubed in a glistening cacophony of hues. There was a distinction between day and night now, between your place and mine. These days, residents wouldn't dream of entering without knocking.

Nowadays, Windward was sedate, like a peaceable old uncle whose youthful tattoos were hidden from view. Cars were either German coupes or four-wheel drives and were parked neatly, herringbone style. Not Jed's, though. He parked as he'd been taught, when learning to drive at Windward – askew on the gravel like a skate on a turn. Malachy knew this wasn't in defiance of the residents' association standards, it was because Windward was still home to Jed. He couldn't distinguish between the Windward of his youth and the place today. And he didn't understand the importance of compliance, because there'd never been rules back then and there'd been harmony. Whenever Jed arrived, his car was flung as if he simply couldn't bear to be in it a moment longer. Into his childhood home he'd barge, rolling into his older brother's life, shedding bags, heading for the purple velvet sofa. Into it he'd collapse and sigh as if Bear Grylls himself would have been hard pressed to make light of such a journey home as Jed's. Really, it should have irritated Malachy, but instead it always slightly amused him. Jed's return to Windward was akin to that of an adventurer walking through the front door, having spent years exploring the wilds of somewhere far-flung and dangerous. Namely, Sheffield, forty minutes' drive away.

'Hey!' said Jed.

Malachy was finishing off a paragraph on his laptop. Jed waited until his brother closed the lid on his work.

'The novel?'

Malachy shrugged. He stretched and smiled. 'Beer?'

'Music to my ears,' said Jed. He was now sitting with his arms outstretched as if he had beautiful girls nestling to either side. 'I'll get it,' he said, energized by the thought, springing up from the sofa. He went to the kitchen and took two bottles of beer from the fridge. He noted that apart from beer, there was butter, unopened cheese and a lot of Greek yoghurt in the fridge. And not much else. He looked around. Blackening bananas. Washing-up. The cap was off the Henderson's Relish.

'What's up with the cleaner?'

Malachy took the beer and had a sip. 'I don't have a cleaner any more.'

'I can see,' said Jed. 'But why not?' It was one luxury Jed would cut corners elsewhere in his life rather than relinquish.

Malachy shrugged.

'What can your girlfriend think?' Jed said, now noticing a general dustiness.

Malachy shrugged again. 'I don't have a girlfriend any more.' He paused. 'My girlfriend was my cleaner.'

Jed feared his beer might come out his nose. 'You were shagging the cleaner?'

'No,' Malachy protested. 'Well – yes. But don't say it like that – it cheapens it. And she wasn't "the cleaner" – she was Csilla.'

'Was she a girlfriend who tidied up – or a cleaner who became a girlfriend?'

'The latter,' said Malachy.

Jed started chuckling. 'I'm sorry. It's just my cleaner is called Betty and she's a hundred and forty and has whiskers.'

'Csilla was twenty-four,' said Malachy. 'Hungarian, with a physics degree and a Lara Croft figure.'

'Fuck,' Jed murmured, impressed. 'You've certainly shafted yourself – your house is a mess and your unmade bed's empty.' He was starting to notice that Malachy was shrugging a lot, not in an acquiescent way, but with apathy. 'What happened then? Did she no longer tickle your fancy with her feather duster?'

Malachy watched his brother laughing. He'd humour him, he decided, as he went back to the kitchen to fetch another beer. 'She stole from me,' he called through.

From the silence which ensued, he knew he'd wiped the smile off Jed's face. He sauntered back, whistling; gave his brother another bottle and then sat himself down in their father's Eames lounger and put his feet up on the footstool.

'Fuck,' said Jed. This was awful. 'What did she take?'

'Nothing in the end – because I intercepted it. I knew something wasn't quite right but I couldn't work out what. So I left for the gallery with a kiss on the cheek – then returned an hour later hoping to catch her so we could talk. Actually, that's a lie. I returned hoping to catch her at it – at *something* –

red-handed. Like in a bad film.' He paused. 'I laughed at the thought of finding her with some young buck, in flagrante, to justify my hunch. Instead, I found her and some sleazy-looking bastard loading up stuff into packing boxes. Our stuff – Dad's.'

'Fuck.'

Malachy looked at him. 'You're a bit impoverished when it comes to expletives, buddy.'

'Shit. Wish I'd known.' Jed thought, Malachy's going to shrug now. And Malachy did. 'A thought – did you continue paying her once she was your girlfriend?'

'*Caveat emptor*?' said Malachy.

'It's just – out of the two of us – when it comes to girlfriends you're always so much more –' Jed struggled for the right word. 'Discerning.' He wanted to say cynical.

'I reckon it was a long-held game plan of hers,' Malachy said, as if it was just one of those things.

'Wouldn't anyone have seen? Seen Lara Croft trying to make off with your things?'

'You forget, Jed – it's not like it was. People live here but they don't work from here. During the day, there's rarely anyone around. Paula's in and out – but she's not in the main building. And the two who are still here – they're old.'

Jed thought for a moment. Even now, whenever he returned to Windward, he still liked to think it was all caught in a time warp, that everyone would be here, that everything would be just so. That he'd arrive and all would be preserved and someone would be playing bongos and an electric guitar would be searing from upstairs and people would be painting or being painted and everyone would be the same. No one would have left. They'd all be there, for him. As they had been. Jed blinked back to the present. This was Windward now. His parents had lived in Denmark for many years and rarely came over. There was only him and his brother and this faded, dusty place that needed a bloody good scrub.

'So – you'll be on the lookout for a new cleaner then,' said Jed. 'I should imagine.' He wanted to perk up. He wanted to lighten the load. He didn't want to appear rude. Poor bloody Malachy.

'Yes,' said Malachy, 'I reckon I am.'

'And a new girlfriend,' said Jed.

'From now on I'll have either one or the other but not both at the same time and certainly not the same for both.' Malachy thought about it. About Csilla. 'To be honest, a cleaner enhances my life more, anyway. I need one more than I need a girl-friend.'

'It's not about need,' Jed said quietly. And Malachy remembered how much he liked it when his brother went quiet and wise and thoughtful and astute. It was as though he leapfrogged Malachy and became the older sibling, despite being almost three years younger.

'By the way,' said Malachy, though it led on from nothing, 'I'm not having the operation.'

Jed squinted down his beer bottle, as if trying to read meaning into the last slick of foamy liquid the way a fortune teller might with tea leaves. 'Oh yes?'

'Yes,' said Malachy.

'Is that wise?'

'It's not unwise,' Malachy said. 'It's not life and death. It's something else I don't need. I said no more operations and I meant it. I'm too old to be vain.'

Jed thought quickly about his brother's fixation with only wanting the things he needed. He no longer saw it – that which made strangers flinch when they saw Malachy; children stare and point. That which made some people approach and question Malachy quite brazenly; curiosity outweighing manners and decorum, voyeuristic fear putting paid to tact and basic sensitivity. And then Jed thought, despite everything, my brother is still the better-looking one, the bastard.

'Do you want to come in to the gallery with me tomorrow?' Malachy asked, rummaging for the Indian takeaway menu. He deftly folded it into a paper aeroplane and sent it across to Jed, where it nosedived and landed just at his feet.

Jed perused the menu though neither he nor Malachy ever veered from their choices. They both still gave the menu much attention, as if it was rude, disrespectful, not to at least say pasanda and okra and fjal out loud.

'The usual.' Jed launched it back at Malachy where it curved off and glided some way before crashing in to the piano.

'So,' said Malachy. 'Are you coming to the gallery tomorrow?

'Er – no,' said Jed as if he'd considered it. 'It's been a busy shitefest week.'

'Some of us *also* have to work weekends, you know.'

'Some of us have our brother's flats to tidy up and clean,' Jed countered, nodding at the fallen menu as if it was a case in point.

'You don't need to do that,' said Malachy.

And Jed said, 'I keep trying to tell you – there's a meaningful distinction between need and want. I *want* to do it.'

His younger brother was mothering him. It should have irritated Malachy. Somehow, it didn't.

'I might pop in,' Jed said, because around him, he could see what was needed and he could tell that it was what his brother wanted.

CHAPTER SIX

At first it had been the emails, perforating Oriana's return to Derbyshire and compromising the water-tightness of her claim to be content to leave and happy to be back. Skype she could blank, having disabled it on her iPad. But FaceTime – she could no more ignore that than she could answering the door when she knew the caller had already seen her inside. It was almost worth switching allegiance from apples to blackberries. Oh for the days of the brick, she thought, glancing at her mother and Bernard's hefty shared mobile phone whilst looking at her iPhone with a mixture of loathing and anxiety as it attempted to beam Ashlyn into her mother's front room.

Over the sea and far away. Whatever the weather. Wherever you may be. Across time. At any time. A superfast highway. It's a small world and you can't hide. Good morning! It's afternoon. It's raining and cold. It's warm and breezy. We miss you. I don't want to know that.

Oriana had even deleted the photos which defined the contacts in her phone. If it just read 'Ashlyn', surely the request could be ignored, rejected more easily than if Ashlyn's face, smiling and genial, accompanied such an invitation.

Ashlyn would like to FaceTime. Decline. Answer.

'Oriana,' said her mother, 'aren't you going to answer that?' She said so in her 'beggars can't be choosers' tone of voice that implied her socially deprived daughter ought really to invite any interaction into her life, even if only virtual.

'Too late,' said Oriana. But she was too late to switch her phone to silent before Ashlyn was trying again. Her mother raised her eyebrow. Bernard had two clues left in the crossword which were stumping him and the sound of the blimmin' phone was a distraction. Not that he'd say so.

'Oriana,' said her mother; it wasn't a question this time and Oriana felt herself diminish into her teenage self again. God – I've got to get out of here. Move. Leave.

Finally, she accepted Ashlyn's call. She left the sitting room and went to her bedroom, the phone attempting to connect. She knew that Bernard would love to see it do so, to marvel at the technology, at this friend of Oriana's who could bring San Francisco into his front room in Hathersage. But Oriana didn't want them to meet, she didn't want the crossover, she needed separation and privacy. She sat on her bed and Ashlyn, frozen in a particularly unflattering moment, gurned her way into the room fresh from breakfast in San Francisco. She had a different hairstyle. In the three weeks since Oriana had last seen her, Ashlyn had become chestnut brown, not blonde, and mid-length flicky, not long and straight.

'You look amazing,' said Oriana, holding her handset so that she wasn't entirely in shot.

'Excuse me?'

'You look amazing!' she repeated.

'I look amazing?' Ashlyn peered close to her phone as if trying to hear better. 'Is that what you said?'

'Yes,' said Oriana. And only then did she realize how quietly she was talking. She felt uneasy talking any louder. She wasn't in the comfort of her own home, nor the neutrality of a hotel; she was in her mother and Bernard's house. This was borrowed space compartmentalized by paper-thin walls. She was in their spare room. It suddenly struck her that nowhere on earth did she have her own bedroom any more. She watched Ashlyn, could see the bay in the background, thought of the room over there that had been hers, now the realm of someone else who might have painted over every last vestige of Oriana.

Ashlyn on a sunny Friday morning. Oriana knew exactly what she'd just had from the bakery for breakfast and how it tasted. The aroma of the coffee. The feel of the paper bag. The scrunch and dunk as she tossed it into the trash can. The sensation of the cool spring air ascending from the bay being dissipated by the sun's warmth. Long sleeves – but sunglasses, too.

She thought back to her own lunch – breakfast now an irrelevant memory. Egg sandwiches made by Bernard, eaten with Bernard and her mum in the kitchen. Celery sticks in a pint glass filled with a little salted water. A bowl of cherry tomatoes. A bottle of salad cream. Soft white bread that stuck to the roof of the mouth. A cup of steaming builder's tea. And non-stop talk about what's for tea. Friday night – fish supper. Bernard had been talking about it since elevenses. I like haddock m'self, he'd said. And your mother – she's for the fishcakes. We both like a buttered bun and these days we share just the one portion of chips. (He'd patted at his heart, to qualify.) But you have what you like, love, whatever you like. Oriana had tried to say that just then with celery fibre caught between her teeth, she couldn't possibly decide what she might feel like that evening. But that had only encouraged Bernard to list all the fish on offer which, to Oriana, might well have been all the fish in the sea.

'Cod!' she'd shouted to shut him up. 'I'll have cod and chips, OK?' She'd ignored her mother staring sharply at her, she'd turned away from Bernard whose expression revealed the brunt of her retort.

'Don't feel you need to decide now,' Bernard had said gently, as if it would be kinder just to pretend Oriana's snappishness hadn't happened. 'Gerry might have a nice piece of hake. Or even plaice. Now that's a nice fish – and he'll do that in breadcrumbs, not batter.'

'Cod.' Oh my God. 'Cod's good.'

'Well, cod it is then. And will that be a medium or a large? Or you could have the large with a medium chips. Or we could have a large chips between the three of us. And another buttered bun.'

Fuck the chips. Sod the cod. Stuff your stupid buttered bun. I don't bloody know. I'm halfway through my lunch! Why would anyone want to know what they're going to be ordering for their tea?

However, Oriana had said nothing. She'd smiled through gritted teeth but the short, sharp exhale had cut through to Bernard like a blast of a cold, ill wind and she'd seen how he'd been taken aback, hurt even, though he'd kept his polite smile up and had rounded off the conversation with a little anecdote about cod being so last year and coley being the new black. And she'd felt appalled that, even at thirty-four, in this house with her mother and Bernard, she was helpless not to revert to a bolshie teen. Life was going backwards. That wasn't the idea at all.

'Oriana?'

Ashlyn. Right here, now, in this room. Perhaps she thought the call had frozen; Oriana's thoughts had rendered her motionless.

'Hey,' said Oriana, suddenly remembering to look up or all that Ashlyn would see was her bowed head with roots in need of colour or a good shampoo and condition at the very least.

'You OK, babe?'

Oriana attempted to peer at her.

'You sound kind of remote and you look kind of –'

'Shit?'

'No,' Ashlyn laughed and, inopportunely, her face suddenly froze into a grimace. Her voice, though disembodied, came through and hit Oriana squarely. 'You look kind of – wide-eyed and lonesome.'

Even in the tiny thumbnail of herself in the top of her screen, Oriana couldn't dispute it. Wide-eyed and lonesome. Like the lyric to a country-and-western standard.

'I'm still jet-lagged,' Oriana said feebly, wondering if she'd been freeze-framed like Ashlyn. She hoped so – her friend wouldn't see through the lie.

Ashlyn was back in motion, slightly jerky, but still herself. She didn't seem to have heard Oriana. Instead, she'd flipped the viewfinder and was treating Oriana to a panorama of the bay. Oriana flinched.

'Homesick?' said Ashlyn.

'A little.'

'So, tell me – what you been up to? You working? You been going down memory lane? Caught up with your old buddies? You been back to that old house of yours?'

Oriana thought of Windward; how the place had so quickly become the stuff of legend to her circle in California. She'd used it as a way to win friends and impress. She'd never lied. The tiniest of details were drawn from life, every daub of colour, every line from a song, every name, every event – they were all true. The only dishonesty had been the tone of voice she'd used to narrate these vignettes of her childhood and youth. She had transposed the veracity and complexity of her original emotions into a panoply of perpetual, carefree happiness. Details which might smudge or darken the picture were left out. As far as any of her friends were concerned, Oriana had been blessed by a halcyon upbringing during which she'd been nurtured by a group of artists who were as loving as they were eccentric. She was admired, envied, for having grown up in the quirkiest place in the world: a commune which made the heyday of Haight-Ashbury seem positively suburban. And Woodstock downright dull. Yes, Jimi Hendrix played Woodstock – but he had stayed a month at Windward. Tell us more about Windward, Oriana! Tell us the stories you've already told. Again – tell us again. Rod Stewart wrote 'You're in My Heart' there? Seriously? From the top room – the one with the turret? Ronnie Wood forgot to leave? Gillian Ayres painted the walls? Tom Stoppard stayed for a summer, Faye Dunaway for the winter? How cool is that?

'You been back to Windward?' Ashlyn was saying with an expansive grin. 'Has it changed? Who's still there? Can I FaceTime you when you're next there? Do it from the iPad – you can give me a virtual tour.'

'I haven't been back,' Oriana told her.

'You *what*? Why not?'

'Not yet,' said Oriana. 'But funnily enough I'm going there tomorrow.'

* * *

Tomorrow is now today. Yesterday, after medium cod and chips, and a buttered bun she had only a bite from, Oriana went to bed early and didn't mention her plans – if she didn't say them out loud, she could still change them. Even at the last minute she could entitle herself to a turn of heart and no one would be any the wiser. She might feel like seeing Cat instead. Or going to Meadowhall and browsing the shops. Perhaps a day trip to Manchester, to see how it's changed.

'May I borrow your car, Mum?' The tang of malt vinegar on yesterday's newsprint paper still lingered in the kitchen, counteracting any appetite for breakfast. 'For the day?' she qualified. 'May I borrow your car for the day?'

Rachel scoured her daughter's face but it was Bernard who read it first and knew instinctively what to say.

'That'll be fine, won't it, Rachel?' he said, down-playing any need for qualification.

'Why?' said her mother. 'Where are you going?'

Bernard, though, stepped in quickly again. 'We said we'd take the Vauxhall to Wakefield, didn't we? We'll not need Your Car.'

They had the two cars. His was called the Vauxhall. Rachel's was called Your Car. He looked at Oriana. 'We're off to visit the Bennets,' he said, with a quick complicit smile. He turned to his wife. 'Oriana can take Your Car.' He turned back to Oriana. 'You take your mother's car, love. You're on the insurance – you may as well get your premium's worth.' He put a lump of sugar into his mug of tea and looked at his wife again. 'It's a good idea. It gets her out and about a bit. It's a lovely day. We don't want her to feel obliged to join us – on our trip to Wakefield. In the Vauxhall.' He looked at Oriana. 'And much as I know the Bennets would love to meet you – well, sitting around listening to us old folk gab – it's no place for a young woman on the first Saturday in April. A fine one at that.' He paused. Glanced from

Rachel to Oriana while both women stared at him, stunned that he could be at once so subtle yet conniving.

'You take your mother's car,' said Bernard a final time, 'and have a nice day out.' And, by the way he finished his tea, tapped both hands down on the table and declared well now! the matter was resolved and no further information or discussion was required.

Even in the car, Oriana knew she could change her plans and simply turn up at Cat's. Or go shopping at Meadowhall. Or reacquaint herself with Bakewell. Belper. Baslow. Eyam. Anywhere. Or just turn round and go nowhere. And yet no one, apart from Ashlyn, knew she was visiting Windward. She could just go there, drive in, drive out. Never step out of the car. No one would be any the wiser. A secret journey. And so she set off, travelling south, retracing the route she'd journeyed three weeks before.

She concentrated on the road, on the sound of the engine, the milometer racking up, the petrol gauge barely moving – dear little car. Would she turn right and go to Blenthrop? Perhaps just park in the car park and sit for a while? She drove on. Or – she could pull in just here, in the lay-by. Stretch her legs and fill her lungs and then decide whether it was really worth carrying on, all the way to Windward. But on she drove.

Eighteen years.

Whereas the sight of Blenthrop had disarmed her three weeks ago, this route back to Windward was as familiar as if she'd made it daily with no interval. As she neared, it seemed everything came into even sharper focus, even the coping stone still lying half hidden in goose grass at the foot of the left gate pillar. She indicated. She turned up the driveway. This was the first time she'd ever done so. She'd left Windward before she learned to drive.

You can't see the house yet. You have to follow the private road a little way on, she told herself; poker straight until the sudden sweep to the right reveals the house, sitting sedate and solemn and magnetic. Peach-pale stone, seen as so extravagant and modern in 1789, when the Jacobean manor house was demolished and the current Georgian mansion was built. For the first time Oriana noticed the peculiar sight of neatly parked cars either side of the expansive gravelled sweep in front of the house, the vehicles positioned like ribs, like fish bones. And suddenly memories of last night's cod brought with it a surge of nausea and a clammy coldness swept over her. She placed her forehead on the steering wheel.

What on earth am I doing here? This place makes me feel ill.

A sweep of memories kept at bay for so long: the day she was made to leave, the occasions she'd tried to return. The address bold in her bubbled teenage handwriting on letters she'd never posted. That day, that terrible day when she'd been fifteen.

Oriana wasn't sure how long she'd been sitting there but suddenly she was aware of an audience, and she

raised her head just enough to see two small girls
peering in through the car window. They smiled and
waved and she raised her hand half-heartedly. The
younger girl pressed her palm against the glass and
looked at Oriana earnestly, as if she felt she'd found
someone trapped, waiting to be rescued. Reluctantly,
she put the window down.

'Hi,' said the elder girl. 'I'm Emma. You can call
me Ems.'

'And I'm Kate,' said the smaller one. 'I'm five.'
She splayed out one hand for emphasis.

'I'm –' Oriana thought about it. 'Incognito' might
be prudent but they might not know the word. 'I'm
Binky.' It was the first name that came into her head.
Thank God it was two young girls she was lying to.
The name sat perfectly well with them.

'Are you visiting someone?'

'Sort of,' said Oriana, getting out of the car and
closing the door thoughtfully. Do people lock their cars
now, she wondered. She glanced at the other vehicles.
Mercedes. BMW. Range Rover. They probably lock
them.

'We live in the Ice House,' the little one, Kate,
said.

'The Ice House?' said Oriana and Kate pointed
across the cherry-walk lawn.

The shack is called the Ice House? Someone *lives*
in the shack?

'We're sisters,' said the elder. 'I'm Emma and I'm
eight.'

'Our mum is called Paula and our dad is called
Rob,' said Kate in a tone of voice which suggested

she'd had to repeat this often. But Oriana was only half listening, moving slowly away from the children, ignoring their chatter, gravitating towards the house whether she wanted to or not.

'Well, bye,' Emma was saying.

'See you later, alligator,' Kate called after her.

Suddenly, the girls were in the very periphery of Oriana's consciousness and she did not respond.

She's not very friendly, the girls concurred. We'll not be inviting her to *our* place. We'll not introduce her to *our* mum.

Eighteen years. A little over half her life. Instantly, her adulthood was condensed and reduced to a flick of light-speed separating the time when she was last here from now. The new cars – they were incongruous; as unbedded and jarring as a new and overly ornamental shrubbery might be in an overgrown garden. But the house – it was wonderfully, frighteningly, unchanged. Everything was recognizable and known. The mineralized rust around the leaking rain hopper which she always thought would be soft and slimy to the touch until she'd shinned up the drainpipe at twelve years old and found it to be hard and cold. The cracked pane in the fanlight above the front door. The chunk of stone missing from the base of the pillar of the portico, like a wedge of cake stolen. The strangulating cords of wisteria claiming the walls as their own, the defensive march of rose bushes skirting the house.

She started circumnavigating the building. Everything, denied for so long, felt forbidden. She moved lightly, quickly, holding her breath.

The familiar feel of the gravel underfoot.

The sound of it.

Tiptoe.

As in a dream, strange new details distorted the old reality. Curtains where there hadn't been, now framing the windows of what had been the illustrator Gordon Bryce's flat on the second floor. The customary tangle of flung bikes by the stone steps leading down to the cellars – but Oriana's wasn't amongst them. And no brambles by the yard. Instead, a residence now converted from the stables with an Audi parked outside on uniform cobbles.

Where do you play hide-and-seek these days then?

Oriana walked straight past her own front door at the side of the building, without once turning her head to acknowledge it. She was vaguely aware of the velvety-leaved pelargoniums in their soil-encrusted terracotta pots currently on the inside windowsills, where they'd be for another month or so before enjoying their summer sojourn out of doors. But she turned deaf ears to any sound that might seep through the gaps in the window frames. Those hateful old frames through which the icy breath of winter would slice into her sleep and the wasps in the summer would sneak in and target her.

Suddenly she heard it. The groan and creak of the great old cedar of Lebanon. She hurried ahead, towards the grounds at the back of the house and finally it came into view.

No one climbs me the way you used to, Oriana. The children are different these days. They play in different ways.

She walked quickly to the tree, crept under its boughs and up to the trunk. There, behind its protective barrier of branches welcoming her back into its fold once again, she wept.

CHAPTER SEVEN

Tick tock. Eleven o'clock. Fuck me, thought Jed, why do I *always* oversleep when I'm here? He looked around the room, once his bedroom, and wondered why. It wasn't even his bed any more; Malachy had sensibly replaced it with a sofa bed when he'd converted the room. Nothing of Jed's past was visible. A couple of Robin's small oils and four old framed prints of Derbyshire landscapes replaced the Cure and the Clash who'd once papered the walls alongside Echo and the Bunnymen. There was no sound from any of them anymore, Jed's towers of vinyl LPs replaced long ago by CD versions which themselves had since been condensed further into virtual MP3 files. The walls were now uniformly white – whereas he'd painted all five of them in different hues. Red, black, purple, navy, orange. If he lifted the new carpet, the floorboards would still bear the spatters as evidence.

He stared at the ceiling; the long, snaking crack which his eyes had traversed for so many years while music played and his mind whirred with teenage emotion, was now Polyfillaed into a slightly raised scar. The huge paper lantern shade had gone, replaced with a neat, dimmable, three-light unit. When his parents had moved to Denmark a decade ago, they had signed the apartment over to him and Malachy. Jed had persuaded his brother to take on a mortgage and buy him out so that he could purchase his own place. Malachy was thus within his rights to make any changes he wished and the room had been sensibly, sensitively converted. Jed didn't mind at all because, whatever the title deeds might say, this room was unmistakably his space and he always slept like a log here.

He showered and dressed, begrudgingly made a mug of instant coffee and took a pot of Greek yoghurt from the fridge, dolloping in honey from a sticky jar retrieved from the back of the cupboard. He thought, my brother's fridge is empty save for beer and Greek bloody yoghurt. It wasn't just a bit pathetic. Apart from the order and spryness of the spare room, the rest of the place was forlorn and dusty and the kitchen was a disgrace. And yet, of the two of them, Malachy was the together one, with the common sense and the poise and maturity, who avoided drama even if it made life dull.

'Thieving cleaner-shag aside, of course,' Jed murmured, taking a yoghurt through to the sitting room. Once the ballroom, its full-height windows flooded the room with spring sunlight, revealing just how in need of a clean they were while dust danced across the air with a we-don't-care. Automatically, Jed glanced at the piano and yes, Malachy had indeed left him a message. He hadn't bothered to check his phone: it wasn't his brother's style to text. Or to push a note under the bedroom door or stick it to the bathroom mirror or fridge. The piano had always been the place where messages were left.

J. We need food. M.

Two twenty-pound notes were stapled to the paper.

Jed grimaced at the bitter scorch of instant coffee masquerading as the real thing. He phoned the gallery.

'Where the fuck is your coffee machine?'

'It broke.'

'OK. But where is it? I'll fix it.'

'I binned it. It smashed beyond repair when Csilla dropped it when she was stealing it.'

'Oh. Shit. Sorry – I.'

'I'm kidding, Jed. But I *did* bin it because it broke.'

'Don't you have a cafetière? For emergencies?'

'No.' Malachy paused. 'I do have an old, stove-top coffee maker somewhere – but you'll have to hunt for it.'

'Thank Christ for that,' said Jed, hanging up.

Malachy anticipated the phone call which came twenty minutes later.

'You *shit*!' Jed said. 'You could have told me you don't have any bloody ground coffee *before* I searched high and low for the sodding pot.'

Malachy just laughed.

Jed was about to launch into something larkily insulting about all that Greek yoghurt, when he looked out to the garden and there was Oriana.

There was Oriana.

And Jed dropped the phone and just stared and stared while in the far-off recesses of his consciousness,

Malachy's voice was filtering up tinnily from the floor, calling Jed? Jed? You there, Jed? before everything went quiet and time was tossed in a centrifuge; the past battered, the present making no sense, the future wide open.

I am not the sort of bloke whose heart beats fast.

I will not be the sort of bloke with a lump in his throat.

I am not one to imagine things.

I am not a soft bastard.

I don't do sentimentality.

But Oriana is out there.

Jed was at an utter loss. He'd stepped back, almost tripping. Now he was rooted to the spot, looking out as Oriana came away from the cedar and into full view. He watched as she glanced up to the ballroom window and away again, up to the window and down at her feet, shyness and perhaps dread, a multitude of emotions. And Jed loved Csilla Shag Cleaner just then for thieving and leaving, and leaving the cleaning of the windows which meant that Oriana couldn't see him in there, gazing out at her.

And then he thought, but what if she goes? After all this time, and all that happened – what if she goes before I've talked to her? If she goes – was she ever really here? And then he thought, what if she's not real? What if I let her go again – for another eighteen years?

Eighteen years? Is that all? Such a long time.

And then he thought, stop thinking and get out there. And he scrambled his bare feet into his brother's docksiders that were a size too big, opened the double ballroom windows and stepped out on to the balcony.

The commotion caught Oriana's attention.

She stood stock-still while the sunlight spun gold from her hair and cut a squint across her eyes.

Jed. It's Jed.

'Oriana?' He was still on the balcony and she was still motionless. They stared and wondered, both of them, what are you doing here? How come you're *here*?

I never thought I'd ever see you again.

Jed knew the move, though he hadn't performed it for many, many years. He vaulted the balustrade of the balcony, and winched himself down, swinging against the wall of the house, grappling the descent like a crazy, out-of-practice, ropeless abseiler. The stone scuffed and grazed at his skin. He banged his knee. One of Malachy's shoes fell off. The ground seemed far away. Suspended, he wondered if Oriana might be gone by the time he'd made the descent. He remembered how she'd sing the *Spider-Man* theme at him when he'd done this manoeuvre when they were young. With the tune once more in his head, bolstering him, and a mix of clumsiness and confidence, he made it down.

Terra firma. Rooted to the spot.

'Oriana?' His voice, barely audible to him, was

painfully loud to her. And now she was turning away, moving off. No! He sprinted after her.

'Wait!'

She stopped but didn't turn. Tentatively, Jed stretched out his hand and laid it lightly on her shoulder. The wind, then, lifted her hair and wafted it over his skin, just quickly, in greeting. With great effort, she turned, not all the way, but enough. They glanced at each other, too nervous to move a step closer.

'Are you back?'

'Yes.'

'Back – *here*?'

'No.'

'I –' Jed shrugged.

Oriana raised her face, sucking her lips on words she could neither release nor swallow. 'How are you?' she asked. Formal.

'I'm fine,' he told her. And then he laughed. This was mad. Crazy. 'I'm *fine*.' He felt compelled to shake his head as if to dislodge any risk this might not be real. 'And you?'

She scratched her head. 'Just me.' She shrugged.

Jed looked over his shoulder and nodded at the house. 'Have you been in? Have you seen your dad?'

'No.' She followed his gaze though her childhood home was out of sight from here.

'Are you going to?'

He watched as she stared at the house for a long time.

'I don't know.' She fidgeted. 'Not today, though. I haven't – it's been years. It's all been years.' She looked at him, marvelling shyly. 'But you – you're still here?'

Jed suddenly felt an extreme urgency – like meeting someone on a train, for whom this was the wrong train, someone who might just jump off as soon as they could and who he'd never see again. Oriana was here, at Windward, but he sensed it was momentary and he sensed this wasn't her true destination. If it was a chance encounter then serendipity had to be shackled quickly – as if he'd have to grab her forcibly before he dared loosen his grip. He sensed he had limited time and, as such, he didn't want to waste it on formal pleasantries but feared anything intimate might cause her to bolt. He just couldn't think what to say. It was crazy. It was Oriana. It's only Oriana. It's only ever been Oriana.

'What are you doing here?' he asked.

'Here – Windward? Or UK here?' She paused and shrugged. 'Time for a change,' she said, looking again at the house. 'I was ready to come back. I didn't think anyone would be here. I assumed everyone would have sold up and moved.'

Jed thought about telling her about his parents and Denmark and the mortgage and the nice new carpet in his old room. But it struck him that, as she hadn't thought he'd be here, then she hadn't returned to find him. His hope rapidly deflated.

Don't ask about Malachy.

I'm not going to ask about Malachy.

They fidgeted with their thoughts.

'Are you OK?' he asked, genuinely sincere.

It was as if he'd said smile for the camera. He saw

how she fixed a beatific expression to her face.

'Oh, I'm fine! Fine. Just time to come back, really.' She grinned and nodded and looked around and grinned and nodded and gave a satisfied sigh. It was pretty convincing – to someone who didn't know her as well as he did, perhaps. He didn't believe a word of it.

'Anyway,' she said, 'I'd better go.'

'Wait – can I? I mean – if you're around, now – perhaps we can meet, just for a drink and a catch-up?'

'Sure,' she said. 'I'll be sure to call you!'

An unconvincing transatlantic twang to her accent. Oh he could have taken her into his arms and said shut up you silly thing. And swung her around and kissed her and said I knew you'd come back, I knew I hadn't lost you. Quick! he thought, give her your number before she changes her mind! He chanted his work number as well as his mobile to her though they came out in a tangle.

'So – you're not going in?' He nodded at the house.

She glanced there and shrugged as though it was no big deal. 'Not today,' she said. It was as though she hadn't intended to come, as though she'd just been passing and had suddenly remembered Windward was here. 'I have to go.' Though her voice wavered, she didn't take her eyes off him as she stepped close and gave him a small, soft kiss on his cheek. 'Bye, Jed. It's so good to see you.'

He watched her walk away, taking the longer route around the opposite side of the house to her old home. And then she was gone and all that was there was the house. He spied Malachy's rogue shoe on the grass, as though it had been flung off in glee. Jed looked down, surprised by his one bare foot. He hadn't noticed. Had Oriana? He cringed. But it didn't matter because he could feel the kiss on his cheek. He heard a car start, then listened as the sound of the engine faded. And then he thought shit, you stupid idiot. You didn't take *her* number. What if she never calls? What if you never see her again? Having been *this* close.

* * *

It did cross Oriana's mind that she was probably less safe to drive than if she had been ten times over the limit. But she needed to put distance between herself and Windward, so on she drove. She felt peculiar; light headed and slightly sick, hyper yet exhausted. Her throat was tight and her mouth was dry and her eyes itched with tears that she was furious about. She needed a drink of water. Perhaps she needed a drink. She drove on, thinking please be there, please be there. But the old petrol station was gone, a barren concrete slab the only remnant. She continued, heading helplessly into Blenthrop. She'd dive in, she decided quickly, buy water, perhaps walk around in a haze and then phone Cat. That was a good idea. Perhaps she'd be around this afternoon and Oriana could call on her to workshop through the headfuckness of what just happened.

The first thing she noticed was traffic wardens as though they were a newly introduced species. There was a one-way system too, which flummoxed her, but it led her to the car park by the library. It was much changed. She looked around – the little booth she remembered with the wizened old toothless man had gone. Invariably, he'd left the barrier up, but they'd never not paid. Now there were dictatorial signs everywhere. *Pay & Display.* She went to the machine and bought a ticket. At that price, an hour would be plenty.

Walking tentatively down Church Street, it felt initially as though all eyes were on her. But she knew it was doubtful that anyone knew her, and if they had known her years ago, they wouldn't recognize her today because she'd be the last person on their minds. And wouldn't most people have grown up and moved away or just grown old and died? There were a lot of pushchairs, it seemed. Pushed by parents perhaps a decade younger than she was. Changing times and with it, a new community. New housing. Self-service petrol from supermarket forecourts. She felt a stranger. She felt anonymous. She didn't know a soul and it calmed her down.

The shops were all different and yet they seemed so established that she found it hard to remember what had been there when this had been her town. Marketplace was awash with stalls selling fruit and vegetables, sickly-smelling sweets and cheap dogs' beds. A smart lorry with one side down had fresh fish on beds of tumbling ice scalpings. A van vending coffee. A stall selling crepes. A butcher yelling sausages! at passers-by like someone with Tourette's. Where can one buy just a simple bottle of bloody water these days?

Remembering that there used to be a newsagent's on Ashbourne Road, she headed there, pleased that, despite the disconcerting unfamiliarity, some things remained instinctive. Turn right. Go straight. Turn right. Oxfam! Oxfam's still here! She peered through the window but it was all changed. It looked like a proper shop, brightly lit with veneered shelving carrying fancy goods, and she wondered where in town today's teenagers went to rummage for clothes to customize. That's new – that hairdresser's. But that isn't – the kitchen shop. It has a new name but it's still a kitchen shop.

'The White Peak Art Space,' Oriana said quietly. A gallery in Blenthrop – there should always be a gallery in Blenthrop. She doubted that the old one, fusty with dingy oil paintings and insipid water-colours, had survived. To her relief, this new place appeared to be a proper gallery – not a shop selling dreadful generic pictures of sand dunes, or bluebell woods, or squirrels, or small children, all given the Adobe once-over. Nor was it full of annoying sayings on strips of distressed tin or weathered wood. It appeared to be a genuine showcase for artists, for talent; it seemed to be somewhere that Art mattered.

She looked in through the window. In pride of place, a sculpture: abstract yet compellingly figurative in essence – a surge or swoop in bronze that could be bird or fish or falling person. It didn't matter which. On one wall, a series of large landscapes in oil, compellingly globular. She knew, even from this angle and through a plate-glass window, that they depicted Baslow Edge seen from Curbar Edge and the Kissing Stones of Bleaklow. They were rather wonderful, so thickly painted she thought the scent of the oils would probably still permeate. She could make out three people towards the back of the gallery, grouped deep in conversation around a plinth on which was a smaller version of the birdman fish. Oriana stepped inside quietly and went straight over to the landscapes. They were captivating and yes, they did indeed smell wonderful. She stood and looked and inhaled and forgot she was thirsty and forgot about Windward. Instead, she was out there, on the dales, reconnecting with the comforting solitude she'd always found there and it alleviated her prior agitation and grounded her. Yes, she thought to herself, I'll just stand here awhile and get my breath back.

Malachy was too busy on the verge of a sale to notice much about the person who'd just come in. Lots of people came in to admire the landscapes by Natalie Fox. He didn't mind. Art gladdens the heart. He liked it that people thought of the White Peak Art Space as not exclusively a commercial enterprise. It was good that passers-by came in to look at paintings, to stand awhile and consider them before leaving somehow nourished. This couple, looking at *Swoop II*, had been in the previous weekend and they were back and they liked it, they really liked it, but it was a lot of money and they weren't sure what to do.

'I offer financing,' Malachy told them. And this sounded like an excellent idea because it was nought per cent and it meant that the artist had his money,

Malachy had his commission and this nice couple could own their art on an affordable basis. He went to his desk to prepare the paperwork and noted the woman very close to the paintings, apparently sniffing them. He didn't mind at all. When he'd finished the paperwork, however, he saw that she had gone. One day, he thought, one day someone will come in and buy all three. It sometimes happened like that; the unlikeliest of people suddenly turning up.

Oriana walked on and there, like an oasis in the yawing march of her memory, the small newsagent's still stood. The only thing that had changed was that the *Daily Mail* now sponsored the shop sign, not the *Daily Mirror*, but from what Oriana had deduced since her return, this switch from left to right was par for the course nationwide. She bought water and Cadbury's chocolate and possibly their only copy of the *Guardian*. The shopkeepers were new to her and had put their mark on the place with a tabletop unit containing exotic-looking pasties as well as a vending machine for coffee, tea and hot chocolate. Coffee. Coffee was a good idea. Even if it wasn't good coffee, she suddenly craved something caffeinated and hot.

Slowly she walked, so as not to spill her drink and to give herself the chance to look up and around. Blenthrop, she was back in Blenthrop and it was no big deal. The town didn't know her and the town was welcoming. With her coffee finished, she sent Cat a text, hoping to call in on her way back to Hathersage. Oriana decided to have one last look around the gallery before making tracks. The gallery, though, appeared to be empty, closed even. But Oriana thought I wonder if those people bought that sculpture? And it became a really provocative thought. How much was it? Who is the artist? But did they *buy* it? Just as she'd bought a paper and some chocolate and a coffee – had they come out on a Saturday and *bought some art*? She had to know. She tried the door and it opened.

In she went, her nose now finely tuned to the oily fragrance emanating from the landscapes. The gallery was Tardis-like; it was deceptively large and went back some way. She walked quickly over to the sculpture. A little red sticker – they did buy it! She felt peculiarly vindicated. It didn't have a price on it but the artist was called Yuki McDonald. McDonald. Maybe the form was inspired by a slippery otter playing mercurially on a Scottish loch, or salmon leaping at Pitlochry. Yuki. Perhaps the form was linked with something more symbolic from Asia – a crane or some more mythical form. She went back to the landscapes and sensed the paintings draw her in, the same sensation the dales themselves had whenever she went there – they were to Oriana as the moors were to Cathy.

I wonder how much these paintings are?

They didn't have a price. She turned to the opposite wall, wondering if anything here had a price. And, like a smack in the mouth and a blow to the heart, two of her father's works glowered at her. She crept towards them. Robin Taylor, *Depth I*. Robin Taylor, *Depth IV*. Ink and mixed media on plasterboard. Her father once told her the women he painted were imagined, that his pictures weren't portraits, they were impressions. But these women were staring at her as if they knew her, as if it was down to her to acknowledge their pain, take it on and free them. Just then, to Oriana, the White Peak Art Space became very dark indeed and she turned to leave.

Damn – I might have missed a sale.

Malachy had just come through from the back with a steaming mug of tea and a biscuit when Oriana reached the door.

'Hullo – can I be of any help?'

Usually, people automatically say no thanks, just looking, to which Malachy always says it's a *gallery* – feel free, which then leads on to varied and mostly interesting discussion about what they see when they look at art.

Just now, though, his offer garnered no response. Could be a foreign tourist though it was still early in the season. He put the mug down, took a quick bite of biscuit, wiped the crumbs on the back of his trousers and looked over towards the door where the woman had turned to stone. The tilt of her head, the whole of her. In an instant he knew who it was. Suddenly, he could no more speak than Oriana could move. The postman came in and stared at her as if she was some kooky installation. He stared at Malachy too, who was unable to take the bundle of post he was being handed.

'Well, see you next week then, Malachy.'

'Malachy as in *key*,' Oriana said quietly, turning.

The postman had pronounced his name Malachy as in *sky*.

For the first time in eighteen years, Oriana and Malachy faced each other head on.

It's OK, she said to herself. It's OK. Don't stare.

You need to look, she told herself, to see. Otherwise it's rude – and ignoring it makes it more of an issue.

But don't stare.

She noted how his hair was now delicately silvered here and there but still licked into the haphazard curls she'd never forgotten. As he approached, she caught his violet-grey eye colour striated like local Blue John. Sharp cheekbones and slim nose which always suggested an aloofness far from true.

And she had to acknowledge, for the first time, the eyepatch – a softened triangle of black protecting, concealing, his left eye; corded neatly around his head.

'You have a beard, Malachy.'

He felt his face thoughtfully. 'I couldn't be arsed to shave last week,' he said. 'But you, Oriana – you haven't changed a bit.'

CHAPTER EIGHT

'You were sniffing Natalie Fox.'

'There isn't a sign saying "No Sniffing".'

'Oils should be sniffed, sculptures touched.'

'Is this *your* gallery?'

'Yes.'

'You *own* it? It's your career?'

'Yes. You look – disappointed?'

'It's – it's impressive. Congrats. But – what about being an author?'

'A teenage daydream. But I still write. Still writing that novel.'

Silence. You don't have to stare – but it's a bit obvious you're looking everywhere but at Malachy.

'Is it?' Oriana touched her own eye, as gently as if she was touching Malachy.

He shrugged. 'It was a long time ago,' he said softly.

'But –' Oriana wasn't sure what she wanted to hear. She didn't know whether Malachy would rather not talk about it. She was unsure whether it was impertinent for her, of all people, to ask. She hadn't seen him for such a long time. And here he was, here was Malachy, changed and yet unchanged.

'I lost it,' he said in the same gentle tone. 'My eye, my sight.' He watched how she nodded but couldn't look at him.

'Sixty per cent of injured eyes become phthisical and require either evisceration or enucleation,' he continued quickly, as if medical facts made it less personal, as if being in the majority made it somehow less severe.

'I – I don't know what those words mean,' she struggled, staring hard at the floor.

'Sorry,' he said. 'Sorry.'

And Oriana thought how ridiculous it was that the word should come from Malachy. The constriction in her throat made it impossible for her to say so.

'The terms, the minutiae,' Malachy qualified, 'they're just part of my lexicon – I forget.'

Oriana glanced at him, then away, then to the door. Suddenly, Malachy really didn't want her to go, not yet, not now she was back after such a very long time.

'Beyond twenty feet, everyone sees the world as if they have only one eye,' he said. He lifted her wrist and placed her hand over her eye. Pointing for her to look at the back of the gallery, he lifted her hand off, then on. He needed to change the subject, draw her back from the past to right here, in his gallery. An extraordinary thing that they should be marvelling about. 'You're back – from the States.' It was a fact, not a question.

'Yes.'

'How long for?'

'I'm back for good.'

Just then, to Oriana, the word seemed preposterous. Life on both sides of the Atlantic suddenly seemed ridiculously complicated. Where could she run to next? Australia?

'Or for the time being,' she added.

'And are you in the area – for the time being?'

She nodded. 'Hathersage.'

'At your mother's?' He couldn't contain his surprise and it made her giggle. He had her gaze once again.

She rolled her eyes at herself and shrugged. Pathetic really. Thirty-four years old and living with her mother.

'And are you OK, Oriana? Are you all right?'

He always knew. He always knew when she wasn't.

Malachy watched as she hauled herself to her tallest and pulled the widest smile possible across her face.

'Oh, I'm *good*,' she said, with drama and drawl to her inflection.

And then the gallery phone rang. And an elderly couple came in. Followed by a father and a teenage boy. And Malachy thought this is very, very bad timing. All of it. He knew that as soon as he turned away from her, returned to the demands of his day, Oriana would disappear. In the blink of an eye, she'd be gone. That's what had happened all those years ago. Now you see her, now you don't.

CHAPTER NINE

'You look like you've seen a ghost!' Jed laughed at
Malachy when he arrived at the gallery just before
closing. 'Sorry – I know I said lunch-time. The day
ran away with me.'

His brother was just staring at him.

'I bought food though,' Jed said. 'Including ground
coffee.'

'I just saw Oriana.'

Malachy watched the colour drain from Jed's face
while redness crept up his throat.

'Oriana?' Jed looked quickly around him. '*Here?*'

'Here.'

'How did she know you work here?'

'She didn't.' Malachy paused. Jed was visibly
flummoxed. 'She literally showed up out of the
blue,' he told him. 'She said she's back from the
States and living with her mother.' Jed was speechless,
staring at her father's paintings as if they held a
clue, if not an actual answer. 'She was surprised I'm
not a best-selling author. I completely forgot to ask
her what she does.'

'Did she leave a number?'

'No.' Malachy thought about it. 'I wonder if Robin

knows.' He looked at Robin's paintings too. He turned to Jed. 'Did you pop in on him today?'

Jed hit his forehead. 'Sorry – sorry. I didn't. No.'

'I'll call in when we get back,' said Malachy.

'Will you tell him? About Oriana?'

Malachy thought about it. 'No,' he said.

'Does he talk about her?'

'Not really – sometimes he says her name, but in a disembodied way, as if it isn't connected to a person, let alone his daughter. As if he just likes the taste of the word on his tongue.'

'Did she –' Jed wondered about this conversation, how to cut it off yet know everything before he did so. 'Did she seem happy? Pleased to see you?'

Malachy thought about it. 'I'd say she seemed flabbergasted.' Then he thought about it. *Terrified* would have been a better word. 'But she hadn't changed, not really.'

'You have,' said Jed. 'She hasn't seen you since—'

'I know,' said Malachy. 'I'm aware of that.'

Jed and Malachy drove back to Windward in their separate cars, privately picking over all the tiny details. From the silt of the past, undisturbed for so long, the seed bank of memories and dormant feelings was awakened. They were both acutely aware that if they talked about her, about what had happened, they'd spend the rest of the weekend doing so but getting nowhere. They also knew there was even less point pondering her return and mulling the what-ifs of her being here. Her absence had brought them closer. Her reappearance, however, could drive them apart.

Malachy parked precisely, Jed at a hasty slant across his brother's car. His boot was crammed with shopping and they took the bags into the house. As they put the items away, they read out what each was, just as their mother used to. It gave a rhythm, a ritualization to it; a pointless family tradition that, when it was needed, carried meaning and comfort.

'Was forty quid enough?'

'Was it hell.'

'I have cash.'

'Forget about it.'

'I'll go and see Robin now.'

'Do you want me to come with you?'

'No – you're fine, Jed.'

'OK. Maybe I'll swing by tomorrow. I'll get the dinner ready – how about that?'

'Sounds good. I won't be long.'

Alone in the apartment, Jed sat down heavily. Why hadn't he said, *I saw her too*? He could have been breezy, nonchalant even. She swung by the house! We had a quick chat! Why keep it from his brother when so much time had passed and after so much had happened? But Jed knew why. All he'd ever wanted to do was to keep Oriana all to himself.

Malachy left the apartment by the inner door connecting with the interior service corridor. He never used Robin's front door. It would alarm him; Robin didn't accept visitors any more. The Corridor was like a conduit between the private worlds within the apartments and the lives in the house over the decades. From staff in the eighteenth century going strictly and quickly about their business, to the scamper and larking of the children of the artists meandering and playing for hours on end nearly two hundred years later. Nowadays, though, it was the echoes of its past that rang out the most; the newer residents rarely used it.

As Malachy walked, it was impossible not to hear Oriana squealing her way along it on a tricycle, then a bike firstly with and then without stabilizers, soon enough her roller skates, and ultimately her skateboard. Malachy smiled, conjuring her up at the far end bowling for him while he waited right at the other end in full cricket whites with his bat at the ready. Out of the gloom the tennis balls came hurtling, him fending them off as if they were missiles while Oriana called, four! six! a hole in one! rounder! And, if she caught one, bull's eye!

Teach me not to throw like a girl.

The recall so vivid it rooted him to the spot. He remembered how he'd come behind her, slipped his hand down to her wrist, tried to show her how to twist, flick. She'd tried and failed, growled at herself and stamped her feet, impatient at her ineptitude. Hurling balls here and there. It doesn't work, Malachy – I can't do it! I throw like a girl! And that was the first time he'd kissed her.

Malachy called through as he entered Robin's place, though the sombre groan of the door and echoing thunk as he closed it would have announced his arrival anyway. There was nothing wrong with

Robin's hearing but it depended on which world he was in whether he actually registered it or not.

'Hi, Robin!'

Silence.

Malachy whistled casually as he made his way from room to room. Not in the kitchen. Bathroom door open; towels on the rail, spirit-level straight. Study door closed. Malachy knocked, poked his head around. The day bed, with a tartan blanket flung back as if someone had suddenly become overheated; the swivel chair facing Malachy as if someone had only just now left it. The walls a latticework of shelves, bent and bowed with the weight of all the books and, in the spaces between the books and the next shelf, piles of papers, brochures, catalogues and magazines. The room could do with some air. And then Oriana's room. Today, he felt he did want to see in there – but what if Robin had renovated it the way Malachy had Jed's old room? What if nothing had changed and even the quickest glimpse hurled him back through time to a period during which he was happiest and at his most miserable? He took his hand off the knob, walked on to the sitting room and through to Robin's studio. He was in there, at the easel behind a canvas, and Malachy could only see his legs and the legs of the stool on which he sat.

'Hullo, Robin.'

Robin peered around the side of the canvas and stared for a moment.

'Yes?'

'It's Malachy – I just thought I'd pop in.'

'Well, fuck off.' Robin disappeared behind the canvas, muttering.

'I'll go and make you some soup, shall I?' Malachy continued. He glanced around the room. There was no sign of any meals having been taken. All the mugs that were on various surfaces were crammed with paintbrushes and palette knives, pheasant feathers, knitting needles, flat wide pencils and small branches with curled and crusted leaves still clinging on. Tea bags in dried-out little dumps on surfaces here and there; on the windowsills cigarette butts balanced upright.

'Have you eaten today?'

Robin didn't bother to answer.

'I'll go and make you some soup,' Malachy said again and he went into the kitchen, opened a cupboard and, under his breath, said oxtail, oxtail or oxtail? The interior of the cupboard was like a pastiche of an Andy Warhol screenprint.

'Nice drop of oxtail,' he called out. The pelargoniums on the sills needed water. He lifted the kettle, full but stone-cold, and gave the plants a drink. He hadn't been in yesterday and the crockery on the rack was just as he'd left it the day before. Quite possibly, Robin hadn't eaten since then. He looked in the breadbin and buttered the last two slices of bread, cutting a little mould off the crusts. He grated the last of the cheese because it was too hard to be palatable any other way. Robin had only an old-fashioned, free-standing gas cooker. With the soup heating up, Malachy lit the grill, ready to leap back as the flames licked along at ferocious speed and clawed out at him. Suddenly he remembered Oriana aged around twelve running into their apartment in floods of tears because she'd singed her fringe when grilling toast. The smell of burnt hair acrid in his nostrils even today. She'd been inconsolable. He and Jed had tried to tell her she looked fine while she sobbed and twanged off the brittle, sizzled ends. And he remembered how they had sat her down on a stool and, with solemnity and the kitchen scissors, had tried their best. Shorter they went, shorter still, until she looked like Louise Brooks.

The soup making audible phuts jolted Malachy back to the present. He popped the bread under the grill and watched like a hawk for it to brown before turning it carefully, adding the cheese and waiting until it seethed golden bubbles. He found a tray, placed on it the soup, cheese on toast, a tomato and a pint glass of cold water. He buffed the cutlery against his sleeve and folded a piece of kitchen roll into a triangle. He toyed with the idea of putting a pot of pelargoniums on the tray, but they were all encrusted with soil and Robin might well hurl it.

Malachy set the tray on the coffee table by the old sofa in the sitting room and went back into the studio.

'Bon appétit.'

Robin glanced over. 'Is it dinner time?'

'It is,' said Malachy. 'Nice bit of soup – oxtail.'

Robin left his easel and pulled himself up to his formidable height, winding turps-soaked rags around his brushes. Then he straightened his tie, smoothed the waistcoat of his three-piece suit and lightly brushed down the sleeves of its jacket. Today, Malachy noticed tiny flecks of blue, like the lightest rain, on the Harris tweed. Robin glanced at Malachy as he passed by and sat down, his teeth snatching at the toast as he crammed it into his mouth. He made fast work of it. With his spoon hovering about the soup, he stared hard at Malachy.

'Why are you staring? Why are you standing there?' His voice was sharp and belligerent.

Malachy was wondering where Robin's medication was – because it certainly wasn't in its usual place on the coffee table. 'Where are your tablets?'

'I don't know,' Robin said, as if there was no reason why he should. 'Now sod off and leave me to eat in peace.'

After a search, Malachy found the tablets in the bathroom. With one in the palm of his hand, he extended it to Robin who stared at it as if it was the first pill he'd ever seen, regarded Malachy as if he was poisoning him. But he placed it on his tongue, swallowing it down with a great glug of soup.

'I'll be off now,' said Malachy. 'I'll pop in tomorrow.' He thought of all the shopping Jed had bought. Despite the fetid air in the room and the smell of concentrated tinned soup, his own appetite hadn't diminished. He'd bring Robin some fresh food tomorrow.

'*À demain.*'

Malachy always said this as his parting remark. Some days, Robin repeated it. 'Adam Man.' Very occasionally, he laughed. Mostly, he didn't respond at all.

Malachy left the apartment, appeased. Robin Taylor was still producing great art. One could forgive him his vile temper and foul mouth. Still, some days this was easier to do than at other times. And for some people, this was far simpler to achieve than it was for others. Today was not a day to mention Oriana. And perhaps Robin should not be told of her return.

It isn't up to you.

That's what Malachy had been told eighteen years ago.

It's nothing to do with you.

That's what they'd said when he found that she'd gone.

CHAPTER TEN

Oriana couldn't help but think of Casey. Even though she'd managed to stick doggedly to her ban of permitting him anywhere near her memory for the last two or three months, she had little control over his voice ricocheting around her head today.

'Headfuck,' he'd say if he were here. 'If that wasn't one total headfuck, baby.'

And Oriana had to admit – he'd be right on that one.

She'd stilled the car. Daylight was fading. From a distance, resembling sheets of organza fluttering in a gentle breeze, the rain came sweeping over the dales in fast, cold, needle-sharp gusts. Concentrating on the sound of the weather on the roof of her mother's car while watching thousands of droplets busying their way across the windscreen provided welcome respite from the barrage of thoughts. Soon enough, though, it all became a background blur as the crux of the matter came to the fore.

What on earth was she to make of what had happened that day? The immensity of it all. Windward, Jed and Malachy too. Facts and feelings were weaving around each other like snakes in a pit, moving too fast and mercurially for her to sort through and make sense of. Ashlyn, Cat – they would both willingly wade in to help, she had only to ask. But just then, she realized that to ask meant to involve; that she'd have to confide to the one or the other as much about her present as her past. There were things she didn't want either of her friends to know, things she wanted under lock and key in a secret space. Bringing them into the open would only slice open fragile scars protecting deep wounds. A problem shared is a problem magnified. She wondered, why did I even go back there? What deluded part of me thought it could in any way be a good idea?

'Idiot is my middle name,' she said, resting her forehead against the steering wheel. 'Idiot is my middle name.' The mantra was comforting in its familiarity. Today, though, it suddenly brought Jed to the fore. How he used to love tinkering and warping the most mundane things, distorting words and situations in order to change something grave, awful even, into something ludicrous and light.

Oregano Idiot he called her when she was fretful, when she called herself an idiot, when he needed to make her feel all right.

'So your mother gave up Robbing to live with Burning Safety.'

And he had flopped back in the long grass at the edge of the mowed lawn at Windward and pulled Oriana against his chest. She'd tuned in to his heart-beat while he hummed 'The Dark Side of the Moon' on a blazingly sunny day.

* * *

Gladly she welcomed Pink Floyd into the car and played through the whole song in her head, even adding where the vinyl was scratchy and the one place the needle always jumped. But there came a point when she just had to let it fade out and she found herself still in her mother's car with the weight of the day rendering her unable to know what to do for the best. She stared at Jed's number now in her contacts lists. She opened the browser on her phone and searched for the White Peak Art Space website. She scoured it, reading Malachy's profile on the About Us tab.

Malachy Bedwell was born in Derbyshire. He is the son of world-renowned architect Orlando Bedwell and Jette Stromsfeld, a furniture designer of international standing. He was the first child to be born at Windward, the artists' collective that his parents founded in the late 1960s, with other seminal figures including Robin and Rachel Taylor, Gordon Bryce, Laurence Glaub, George and Lilac Camfield and Louis Bayford.

He credits the absolute assimilation of all arts into everyday life at Windward with his enduring passion for them.

'As a baby, my mother fed me in a highchair designed by Gerrit Rietveld. I hung my school blazer on a Louise Bourgeois sculpture and read Agatha Christie novels whose covers were original Windward artworks. The soundtrack of my teenage years was either played at home or even written there. The phone would go and Celia Birtwell would simply say, "Hullo, Malachy – is your mother home? It's Celia." There'd be a knock at the door and someone would be standing there, asking, "Is Keith here?" and we'd go

upstairs and tell Keith Richards that he had a visitor. Our cutlery was David Mellor prototypes. Our furniture was Bauhaus and beyond. We kept apples in a Bernard Leach bowl.'

Oriana looked up. I *remember* that bowl.

She remembered Keith too. And Marlon, his son. She'd had a huge crush on him. Jed and Malachy had taken the piss terribly though both their noses had been visibly out of joint too.

She read on, under her breath.

The White Peak Art Space seeks to unify the diverse talent of international artists inspired by Derbyshire. Whether they live here or abroad, whether they work figuratively or wholly abstract, whatever media they favour, our artists are united by the Peak District genius loci, *the spirit of the place.*

She felt proud of Malachy and yet strangely sad too. But you wanted to be a writer, Malachy. You and that great novel of yours. The White Peak Art Space arguably had philanthropic as well as financial value. But was it what Malachy truly wanted to do? She remembered him saying how he wanted to be the John Irving of his generation, having read *The Hotel New Hampshire* cover to cover twice in one week. How they'd all fallen about laughing! Now she felt sad, concerned. She wondered whether losing his eye had anything to do with it. She hoped not. She shuddered.

The rain had stopped and suddenly the sun was charging through and the wet landscape let off a glare; flares of light piercing through the windscreen. Headache weather.

Oriana thought, where do I go now?

Hathersage? Hathersage was no more home than San Francisco was. An image of the cedar at Windward loomed large – it was the place she'd always gone to for solace – something about shade and solitude under the embrace of the branches, the scent of the space around the trunk, the way the air was always a degree cooler than beyond the boughs, how the light from the day outside the tree was filtered into something else as it spun through the branches, the needles. It was a world within a world and for so many years it had been hers alone. In her youth, the other children had been put off it by a strange psychic who'd stayed at Windward and denounced the tree as the Place That Has Seen Death. But she couldn't go back to the tree or Windward – not with Jed there ready to leap from the balcony and her father inside the house and two small unknown girls badgering to befriend her.

The paradox struck her – she was welcome the world over; welcome at Windward, in Hathersage, she could pitch up in California tomorrow and a dozen people would fling open their doors and arms for her. Yet just then it felt that there was nowhere that was hers, not one place she could truly call home. Other people's places could never be anything other than halfway houses. She looked around her; this wasn't even her car. Those were Bernard's Werther's Originals in the cup holder of her mother's Peugeot. There was a synthetic-smelling cardboard air freshener in the shape of a smiley-faced strawberry dangling from the rear-view mirror and an oversized *Road Map of the*

British Isles in the footwell, as if her mother and Bernard took to navigating a sweetly scented kingdom on a whim any day of the week. She thought, I'd never choose this type of car for my own. And then she thought, you ungrateful cow. She felt alone mostly because she knew she was defiantly turning her back on the few who were there for her.

Cat – her childhood friend who knew so much, but not everything.

Ashlyn – her closest friend who knew so much, but not everything.

Casey. Jed. Malachy. The men she'd loved, lost, left.

She traced her finger over the shiny lion emblem in the centre of her mother's steering wheel.

'It doesn't matter how many questions there are if there can never be any answers.'

She thought, what a stupid thing to say out loud. She thought, I am not a teenage existentialist and I'm not a cod-philosophizing hippy even though I grew up with enough of them.

'I'm thirty-bloody-four and there's not a single certainty in my life.'

Oriana forced herself from looking inwards to watching how the dusk was now creeping across the moor like spilled treacle, edging its way in a slow but determined advance. Her fingertips were cold and she needed to blow her nose. If this had been her car, not her mother's, she'd have had to use her sleeve. But she looked in the glove compartment and found, as she predicted, a packet of tissues. She gave the strawberry-faced air freshener an apologetic smile. She started the engine. She wanted to be indoors, by a fire, in an armchair, on her own with a cup of tea. She wanted to be home, wherever that was. The room which opened up in her mind's eye wasn't in San Francisco nor was it in Windward but it was as well known to her as either. She started the car, made a U-turn and drove.

Django McCabe watched the headlights send stuttering beams into his quiet Saturday evening as the car made its way along the lurch and swerve of his unmade driveway. Sometimes, he experienced sights as sound and, though from inside the house he couldn't hear the car's engine, its lights were like an uninvited visitor with a grating voice asking for a favour he wasn't actually prepared to give.

'You can bugger off for a start,' he muttered, taking his mug of Bovril and heading for the utility room where he sat down and said bugger, bugger off. He thought to himself how the more social a person was in their heyday – as he had been to a legendary extent – then the more justified was a cantankerous dotage. So bugger off, whoever you are, this is my Saturday evening. I'm closed.

But the voice, when it called out, baffled him. He was expecting the brittle but strident tone of the village busybody. Perhaps the gruff hail of someone off to the Rag and Thistle. More likely, the gently melodious greeting from the vicar who had called in with alarming regularity over recent months despite Django having visited the church only twice – and once was accidental. But he wasn't expecting the voice of someone young. And female.

'Knock knock. Django? It's Oriana.'

CHAPTER ELEVEN

Cat put the phone down and looked at it thoughtfully.

Ben watched. 'Everything OK?'

She nodded slowly. 'I think so.'

'Do you want any more pizza?'

She looked at the box, in which the two remaining slices looked now to be made of the same cardboard. 'No, thanks.' She knew her husband would wrap them in tinfoil and have them for breakfast, cold.

'That was Django.'

'I gathered.'

'*Oriana* dropped in.' Cat thought about it. 'She stayed for two hours.'

'That was nice of her?' Ben was unsure why Cat appeared disconcerted.

'He said she asked to go upstairs and then she wandered around, looking in rooms and standing deep in thought.'

'And?' Ben didn't want to comment too much – the umbilical cord appeared to be syphoning off much of his wife's patience and sense of humour. If that was the case, their baby would be imperturbable and have great comic timing.

'It's just –' Cat thought about it. 'She's my oldest friend – I know everything about her.' Absent-mindedly, she pressed at her jutting navel as if trying to keep thoughts in. 'But when I saw her, it struck me that she was just ever so slightly guarded – as if there was something essential she was concealing.'

'Maybe she didn't want to say in front of Django?'

'Don't be ridiculous – Django's world famous for being unshockable.'

'I wouldn't take it personally.'

'Why wouldn't I? She's my oldest friend. God! You just don't understand!'

Ben counted to ten in his head. 'Well – perhaps she was just passing?'

Cat looked at him as if he was dense. Django lived so off the beaten track that impromptu visits always necessitated an involved detour and a certain level of planning.

'Did Django say where she was on her way to – or back from – to make a trip to his plausible?'

There was a long pause. 'She'd been to Windward,' Cat said. 'That's why it's weird. *She went back to Windward*. Just like that.' She rubbed her belly thoughtfully, as if hoping to elicit the genie from the lamp.

'And you wanted to go with her?' Ben was trying to second-guess. Cat looked at him blankly. 'Or – you wanted her to let you know she was going? Or had been?'

'You would've thought she'd've phoned me.' She felt hot, uncomfortable. 'Whatever. Doesn't matter.

I don't want to talk about it. Let's watch telly. Can I have a cuppa?'

Ben took the pizza boxes into the kitchen, Cat muted the sound on the television, randomly channel hopping while managing her thoughts. Why *is* Oriana back? Why would she go to Windward anyway? Why *hadn't* she told her – beforehand or straight after? And she thought, have we grown apart? Can friendships not last such lapses? If all you have in common is a shared past, is that reason enough to believe you'll always be as close as you were? To Cat just then, the past was neither halcyon nor troubling, it was simply a long, long time ago.

Ben made tea and thought to himself how often he had heard his patients who were pregnant complain that people treated them differently – as if growing a baby equated to diminished brain cells and the incapacity for any conversation other than about babies. They felt excluded because of some misplaced need of others to protect them from any topic anything other than bland ones. And, for the most part, they didn't like it. *My baby's stolen my identity!* one had declared. He thought about Oriana. He'd only met her a few times, when they were all living in the United States but, through Cat, he felt he knew her well enough. He remembered how, if ever he answered her call, the first words she'd always say were *sorry to bother you.*

'She'll call,' he told his wife. 'She's probably just worried about bothering you.'

* * *

In Hathersage, no one asked any searching questions. It was enough that 'Did you have a nice day?' was met with 'Yes, thanks, did you?' In fact, most of the questions came from Oriana who tactfully chose topics she knew Rachel and Bernard could answer at length. The route to Wakefield. The Bennets' house. What they'd had for their dinner. And their tea. The weather forecast tomorrow. The amount of detail that anodyne subjects warranted was surprising and insubstantial minutiae floated through the evening like musak until it was a respectable time to turn in. As Oriana climbed the stairs, she thought to herself, that's probably the longest conversation I have ever had with my mother.

It was only after cleaning her teeth, when she caught sight of herself in the mirror unawares, that the magnitude of the day that was closing swept over her again. But it wasn't what had happened or where she had been. At that moment it wasn't even whom she had seen. It was who had seen *her*, looking like *this*.

Frequently, since her return from the US, her mother had remarked how thin Oriana looked. But 'thin' implied something gently fragile, like a bird, like a Hans Christian Andersen character, something young and pretty and ethereal, waif-like. Butterfly wings and gentle breeze and dandelion heads and spun sugar. 'Thin' brought out the protective in others. But, now she looked, Oriana didn't see thin. She saw haggard. She saw gaunt grey. She saw someone to baulk at, to shy away from; to think Christ, she's aged, she looks *terrible*. What the fuck happened to Oriana? they'd say. Have you seen her these days? Old beyond her years.

'Mum!' She called out before she'd even opened the bathroom door, let alone unlocked it. 'Mum!'

Rachel's bedroom door opened. Oriana must have been in conversation with her reflection for quite some time if her mother's bleariness was anything to go by.

'What is it? Honey – you OK?'

Bernard could be heard from the gloom of the room saying everything OK? everything OK? like a daft old parrot trying to keep up with the action.

'It's fine,' Rachel called back at him. 'We're good.'

'My hair,' Oriana wailed. 'Look at it! I look hideous. Do you have a good hairdresser? Are they open Sundays?'

'You look fine,' said Rachel, agitated. 'You're a bit thin – but you're tired. Go to sleep and yes, I have a hairdresser,' and she touched her own hair as if to double-check. 'And no, they're not open Sundays.'

'They are in the lead-up to Christmas, love,' came Bernard's voice.

'It's fucking April!' Rachel seethed over her shoulder, before clapping her hand over her mouth, wondering how long it had been – truly, how many *years* – since she'd sworn like that. 'Look what you made me do!' she hissed at Oriana. 'Just go to sleep, for God's sake.' Reproach and dislike creased her face.

Rachel had never spoken to Bernard like that, never. She held his hand tightly as she lay awake, frowning into the dark. Her daughter should *not* have come back and, just then, she really resented her. Oriana was rested, fed, had a roof over her head, their home and car at her disposal and yet she looked worse now than when she arrived. Where was the gratitude in that? Into the conspiratorial darkness, Rachel let her thoughts find support. She liked her daughter less when she was troubled. In fact, she liked her less when she was in direct contact. If their relationship was to survive – or even go back to how it had been – she really did need her out of the house. Emails and occasional phone calls – that's when they'd rubbed along best. She actually didn't much like her at all – an unpleasant sensation that made her feel unwell. Distance and time could alleviate it. It had done so in the past, after all.

*   *   *

At Windward, Oriana wasn't mentioned at all that evening. Instead, the Bedwell brothers drank beer and watched sport and shouted at the teams on the television. It was innocuous and boorish, akin to watching in the pub, commentating on the game with people they hardly knew. And Malachy and Jed should have steered clear of Scotch. But the match was over and the beer was gone, so out came the Laphroaig which took the pub philosophizing to the next level as they spouted argumentatively on politics and policies, each brother taking a turn at pulling on the garb of the devil's advocate and wrestling each other for it.

Jed should have said no to whisky. He didn't have

the stomach for it, especially not after European lager and the disappointment of a two–nil defeat. Consequently, he became very drunk, very quickly and, after decimating bankers, Russian oligarchs and the Tories, he staggered off to bed mid-sentence, only to throw up later in the early hours.

Malachy heard his brother chucking his guts up. Malachy should have said no to whisky too. It didn't make him paralytic, it made him insomniac and introspective. He hadn't yet slept when Jed went stumbling to the bathroom. He'd been sitting up in bed, initially comforted by the pitch darkness making him equally blind in his good eye. Velvet black and even. He just sat in bed, appreciating the sensation of both eyes being open and both eyes seeing nothing; feeling that peculiar warmth that came with night-time silence and obscurity, nothing material to see, to imagine, to tax the eye – either eye. But then, the undeniable sense that darkness is not a constant but a flux; forms beginning to emerge as his good eye told his lost eye what they were. Mahogany chest. Flung shirt. Door frame. Right shoe. Something else – wallet. What's my wallet doing on the floor? Left shoe. Handles on the wardrobe doors that look like cartoon eyes.

Back in the present. What's Jed doing? Jed's throwing up. Dickhead.

Then –

What's Oriana doing? Right this minute? Right now, at five minutes past stupid o'clock?

She'll be asleep. Fast asleep.

Oriana Taylor back from the Land of Opportunity,

to the Country Where It All Went Tits Up. Where was the sense in that? Why had she come back? Was she running away again? It seemed preposterous that she could prefer this place to anywhere else. Perhaps she was returning simply to tie up eighteen years of loose ends into one intricate knot. Certainly she was back now as suddenly as she'd disappeared back then.

After she'd left the gallery, when the shock had subsided, Malachy had felt different all afternoon, as if he'd been imperceptibly levitated. The complexity of it all had been baffling and crazy and just a bit wonderful too. But not now. Now, in the choke of the night, alcohol tainting his blood and hastening his heartbeat, it was entirely unnerving.

He could hear Jed leaving the bathroom, shuffling back to bed with a self-pitying groan. Malachy needed to sleep, it was gone four in the morning. He thought, I don't want her in my dreams. He thought, I don't want to see her again. He thought, sleep! He thought, damn her for coming back. She had no right – however chance the encounter had been. Oh God, I really, really need to sleep. He told himself not to look at the clock. Ten to five in the bloody morning. Memories mingled with shadows, sounds with silence. It was all too bloody busy to permit sleep. He thought masturbating might help. He thought, think of some generic sex bomb. Pneumatic and faceless who you don't know, you'll never meet, you have no history with, no emotion for. Tits and ass and lips.

But ultimately it was Oriana who filled his mind.

He could taste her, hear her, feel her skin, her breath on his neck, her fingers around his cock, her body melding with his. The stretch and dip of her figure. He came. Exhausted, sleep finally crept over him. And his last thought was, how could something be so vividly real – when actually it had never happened? Not beyond those desperately grasped kisses that they'd harvested over a period of just a few months when he was eighteen and she was fifteen.

And Malachy knew he wouldn't dream of Oriana that night; he was doomed to have the rabbit dream again. Resigned, he became sleep's quarry.

CHAPTER TWELVE

As Oriana made her way downstairs on Sunday morning after a fitful night's sleep, she could hear her mother's hissing whisper.

'It's just not right! She has no business here – she *literally* has no business here. We're not doing right by her – we're *facilitating* her languor.'

Oriana thought, when has my mother ever used the word *languor*? Suddenly a memory of her mother at Windward assaulted her and she thought, my mother put the definition of languor into the dictionary. And then Oriana heard Bernard, dear Bernard, try gently to butt his way in with conjunctions that stood entirely on their own and therefore were bluntly denied all meaning. But. However. Well. If.

'She oughtn't to be here, it's not right.'

'But—'

'Not at her age – not at *my* age.'

'Well—'

'She's got to get a job! move on! move *out*!'

'However—'

'She's an *adult*. It's making me unwell, it really is. I can't have her squawking about hairdressers at whatever o'clock.'

'Mind you—'

'Mind you *what*, Bernard? *Mind you* what?'

'She's your daughter, love – and where else can she go?'

'She can find her own hairdresser!'

'I wasn't talking about hairdressers, Rachel.'

Hovering just out of sight of the kitchen door, Oriana wondered which way to go. Just then, the conundrum of whether to go back upstairs or continue to the kitchen was taxing enough, never mind where she'd go now her mother was kicking her out. She didn't want to stay – but she certainly didn't want to be told to leave. She pressed her back against the wall and thought again of Windward. Not the Windward of yesterday, but the Windward of yesteryear, where she'd grown up. A house, a place, a crazy world in its own orbit. No matter how bonkers, how unruly, how frightening, there had always, *always*, been somewhere to go. To the Bedwell boys and their beautiful serene Danish mother Jette who'd take her to school with rye-bread sandwiches and hair braided to perfection. Or to Louis for a sanctuary of stories and toast and shiny coins appearing from behind her ear. Or Lilac's where she'd be seated in the wing-back chair like royalty, presented with a plate which had a biscuit on top of a doily, and told tales of the music halls of Montmartre. And the summer when Rod Stewart kindly feigned not to notice that she spent day after day curled in the corner deep down in the beanbag while his music filled the room over and over and over. She'd received a package months later – with a seven-inch single and a message written on the cover.

You're more than the girl in the corner.

Rod xx

He'd sent it care of Louis so that she'd be sure to get it. Because Rod knew. He knew.

And Oriana thought back to the bleakest of times when nowhere at Windward would do, when the only option was to pedal herself away from the place. Vividly, she retraced in her mind the crazy cycle route, half road, half land. How she'd jostled her heavy old bike over drystone walls, negotiated boulders, forged streams and had to hoick it over five-bar gates all the way to the McCabes. No mobile phones back then, no texting to say they're pissing me off, I'm going to bike it to yours. The duration of the journey, over an hour, during which no one in the world knew where she was, what time she'd left or where she was headed. The colliding extremes of loneliness and liberation spinning her head as her feet spun the pedals. The welcome at the McCabes' – Django warm and accommodating as if it was a long-arranged invitation to tea. Cat and her sisters Fen and Pip – in a circle in a bedroom, or in the garden or around the kitchen table, listening and loving her and telling her don't worry, they're just stupid and annoying and you can stay here tonight.

She wondered if nowadays children dared to do a ride like that – that fast, that far. Was there even any need for it today – could they even be bothered? They probably just Instagrammed photos of themselves looking morose with some derogatory comment about their parents being, like, so unfair. And, just then, Oriana knew that no matter how imprisoned or squashed or unhappy or fed up or lonely or confused she'd felt when she was young, actually she'd had freedom few others would have experienced. Standing there, that Sunday morning, against the blandness of magnolia walls and gloss white skirting and the sound of her mother detesting her, she loved very much the child she'd been. She felt a familiar surge of protectiveness but also a new pride for her younger self. Rod Stewart had been right all those years ago.

* * *

In Windward, Robin Taylor hurled his palette with such force it turned into a razor-sharp Frisbee, whacked into the window frame and left its mark bloodied in smears of magenta and streaks of cerise, bruises of burnt umber. He looked back at the canvas and his objection rose in a vicious crescendo.

'No No No.'

It was as though the painting had wronged him. 'No No No.'

He pointed at it, wagging his finger with seething sarcasm. 'No, you don't. No, you *don't*.'

He walked over to the window and stamped on the palette lying on the floor.

'Fuck you,' he glowered over his shoulder back at the painting. He roared with the furious effort of hauling up the warped sash window before walking calmly back to the painting as though it was a scoundrel to be ousted from the studio by the ear. He held the canvas at one corner; it wasn't large but it was unwieldy enough, and he dragged it across the room without looking at it, like something too repellent even to be glanced at.

'Fuck you!' And he launched it out of the window.

Emma and Kate, the de la Mare girls, heard the rude word and saw the painting fall. They didn't know the man who lived in that part of the house. Just that he wasn't particularly friendly and didn't much like children or animals or women or anything or anyone other than Malachy and then only sometimes. Their mother had told them to walk around the other side if they wanted to go to the back gardens where the cedar and the willow with the rope swing were. She told them, if they saw him, to be polite and smiley but not really to stop. She told them he might say rude words and not to worry about it, to understand that he wasn't very well and rude words were part of it.

When they were quite sure that all was quiet, the sisters finally looked at each other. They felt, somehow, complicit in what had happened because after all they'd decided to go around the Other Side of the house. Currently, they were hidden in the old pigsty – which, unlike their Ice House and Mr Martin's Stables and the Corrigans' Coach House remained gloriously ramshackle and unconverted. There were rusty nails and mice, all manner of junk dumped there over the decades and something so dead and flattened it appeared to be made out of old shoe leather. Their father had persuaded their mother that it was precisely the type of place children *should* be allowed to commandeer and have as a semi-secret den. Well, a dead mouse isn't going to kill them, she'd said. Nor is a living one, he'd said.

And now, the sash window over at the house was juddered down and the shadowy figure disappeared from view, back into the mystery of the apartment. The girls waited. Then they looked at each other again before scuttling out of the sty and over to the painting. It had fallen face down just beyond the French drain. Emma flipped it over and both girls gasped.

Bosoms.

How utterly thrilling.

Quickly, they carried the painting back to the sty and propped it against a wall. Their hearts pounded at the bases of their throats, their stomachs knotted and their eyes danced – they were just old enough to grasp the illicitness of it all – bosoms in a painting that they had kidnapped, bosoms that were enough to make a grown man swear. Fervently, they explored every inch of the painting with their eyes, with their fingers. Parts of the canvas had oils so thick they had been whipped up into peaks and ridges like a storm-lashed sea. The paint was still pliable and the children fiddled, pressing with thumbs and digging with their nails. There was an area of the picture – the lady's neck – that they decided must be the fuck-you part because the paint was still fresh and tacky and the sweary man had done a bad job trying to keep within the outline.

It was like skating by fingertip – the girls swirled and tracked around the wetter paint, leaving their marks and thinking it looked better. Not perfect. It still didn't look like a nice, smooth, elegant neck – but at least it no longer looked as though the flesh had been grabbed away from the lady's throat.

* * *

'Christ.'

Jed had been in a slump on the sofa for two hours, saying nothing other than Christ. Malachy laughed at him, but privately was grateful for the ground coffee his brother had bought the day before, and he made a pot so strong that he really could stand a teaspoon in it.

'Are you staying for lunch?'

'I can't talk about food.'

'At least you've stopped talking to Jesus.'

'Fat lot of help He gave me.' Jed paused. 'Christ.'

He pressed gingerly around his eye sockets as if fully expecting to find fissures and shards. Unbelievably, his nose appeared to be straight and he still had all his teeth. The coffee helped and, after an hour, he said yes to the scrambled eggs and bacon Malachy offered to cook for them.

'I am a prize idiot,' Jed said, 'and I have only myself to blame. If I ever even mention the word *Scotch* again, you are within your rights to have me sectioned.'

Malachy laughed. His brother could always make him laugh – Jed could always bring a genuine smile to anyone: teachers ready to dish out detention, parents about to ground him, even girlfriends on the verge of dumping him. It was something Malachy had quietly begrudged him their whole lives. Not so much because it got Jed out of all manner of scrapes, but more because it seemed to amplify Malachy's diametric default. Jed the lively one, Malachy the quiet one. Jed the life and soul. Malachy the boy in the background. Jed who could get away with blue murder. Malachy who should know better. Jed the brother the girls flocked to. Malachy the brother they didn't.

But today he looked at Jed and thought, mate, I do *not* envy you your hangover.

'Stay tonight,' he said. 'You're probably still over the limit, anyway.'

Jed thought about it. Stretched. Slumped. Straightened. Shrugged. 'I'd better go,' he said, 'but thanks.'

'Don't leave it so long next time,' said Malachy.

His brother grinned. 'It's nothing personal.' Then he thought about it, about the fact that he wasn't entirely sure what Malachy did in between the times he saw him. Apart from fending off thieving cleaner girlfriends and caring for deranged aged artists. What did Malachy do when he wasn't at the gallery, or in Robin's studio? Where was he on a standard Tuesday evening, or on a random Sunday? Who was he with on any given Friday night? For Jed, Malachy and Windward were indivisible, one and the same, always there; solid, little changed, patiently pleased to accommodate him. Just then, he felt badly about this.

'Come to mine,' he said to Malachy. 'We'll go out next time.'

'I'd like that.'

'Good. I'll phone – we'll arrange it.'

'Let's.'

With Jed gone, Malachy went to check on Robin who refused to move from his chair let alone acknowledge that Malachy was even there. Malachy always thought how disconcerting it was that a human being could emanate such coldness whilst simultaneously radiating such fierce heat. He left Robin the *Sunday Times*, on top of which he placed a glass of water and the tablets. Robin's apartment seemed particularly fetid today and Malachy stepped outside and walked into the gardens, head back, breathing deeply. That afternoon, spring had finally become a tantalizing glimpse through a crack in winter, a tangible quality in the light, a benign edge to the breeze, a shy scent. He walked around the back of the house, automatically checking the pointing and paintwork around his windows which always begged for attention. These days, though, there had to be a residents' meeting to sanction anything, another to agree contractors and argue costs and a couple more just for the sake of it. Long gone were the days of an assortment of ladders and paint pots and everyone mucking in with each other's Sunday DIY tasks. The sinking fund into which he had to put money up front was a bottomless pit that seemed to produce little visible return. It pissed him off. It irked him that the original residents appeared to have less say than the new. If anything, they were kept just on the periphery of the loop and decisions were cleverly presented to them as fait accompli.

'Hi, Malachy!'

'Hi, Malachy!'

The de la Mare girls bounded over the grass to him like excited ponies.

'Guess what?'

'Guess *what*!'

Kate, the younger, was like a lively echo to her sister.

'What?' said Malachy, patting them as if they really were ponies.

'We heard him say *fuck* and there are *bosoms*.'

Priceless. Malachy looked around hoping that Paula or Rob were in earshot but their parents were nowhere in sight. 'I beg your pardon?'

'Oh – we're not swearing on purpose,' said Emma, 'we're just repeating.'

'Repeating,' Malachy said thoughtfully.

'Bosoms and fuck!' said a delighted Kate.

'Care to elaborate?' said Malachy.

'Come and see,' said Emma.

'*Come. And. See*,' said Kate, tugging at his sleeve all the way to the pigsty.

The three of them contemplated the painting in silence for some time, like art critics at a private view.

'I did *this* bit,' said Emma eventually, proudly wafting her hand at the canvas.

'No, you didn't – I did,' said Kate.

'Did *not*. You did *that* bit – see, that same colour is still on your hands,' and she splayed her own fingers for emphasis.

'Ladies,' said Malachy diplomatically. He always referred to them as ladies, never girls, and they loved it. He scratched his chin and breathed against the crook of his finger, deep in thought. It was the first time he'd seen this work and yet it had obviously been in production for some time. He recognized the subject as Rachel. Here was the Rachel he remembered. The painting was an ode to a ruinous passion so profoundly deep it imploded. The painting was a pictorial love letter because words were impotent to describe the breadth of feeling. The execution was mostly sublime – the throat, however, was simply an execution. The throat was mid-murder. Malachy thought, this painting will give me night-mares. He glanced at the girls and thought thank God for bosoms – that's the part of the painting that they'll remember.

'Can we keep it?'

'No,' said Malachy.

'But he said *fuck you* and threw it out of the window!' said Kate.

'He chucked it out because he messed it up,' Emma explained 'but we mended her neck. See? So why can't we keep it if he doesn't want it? It can live *here*.'

'Because, sometimes artists suffer for their art – they do almighty battle with their paintings and that's what makes their work so brilliant. The discord between artist and painting is what gives it the depth, so many layers, such luminosity.' The girls stared at Malachy blankly. 'It's the equivalent of your mum putting you on the naughty step. And then coming back for you.'

'I've never been on the naughty step,' said Kate.

'Oh yes, you have,' said her elder sister.

'Well – not like the naughty step, then,' said Malachy. 'It's like having a big row with someone you love and going off in a huff.'

Emma thought Malachy was using too many unnecessary words. The artist had messed up his picture. That was the sum of it, surely. He could paint another quite easily. This one had been thrown away – until she and her sister had kindly rescued and resuscitated it.

'Do you think he'll at least *like* how we've fixed it?' she said.

He'll go absolutely berserk, thought Malachy, who hoped that an ambiguous hum and a hand on Emma's head would suffice.

Into the time warp of the pigsty, Paula's voice filtered through, calling her girls to come in now, come in for tea. He escorted them back out into the daylight, around the house, along the side of the driveway, across the front lawn and through the cherry walk towards the Ice House.

'We think the painting is of that lady who came here yesterday,' Emma said.

'Sorry?' Malachy was only half listening. How on earth am I going to get that canvas back to Robin?

'The painting – the lady looks a bit like the one who came here yesterday.'

'Oh yes?' Ought I to take it to Robin – or let him retrieve it in his own time?

'Yes, the one who came in the blue car. Who had her head on the steering wheel and we thought she was asleep.'

'Of course.' I could leave it where it might have landed when he threw it.

'Anyway, she looked quite a bit like the lady in the painting. But with clothes on, of course.'

But Robin will still see what's happened to it. 'Indeed,' said Malachy. It might be prudent for me to tell him first, then bring the painting to him.

'Binky,' Kate butted in.

It was as if a guillotine had sliced off Malachy's meandering thoughts. He stared at Kate. 'What?'

'*Binky*,' she repeated.

'The *lady*,' Emma said, weary of yet another grown-up doing that annoying half-listening thing which meant she'd have to repeat it all again. 'The lady who came yesterday – who we think looks like the one in the painting.'

'A lady who came yesterday? Here? A lady who looks like the one in the painting?' Malachy stared from one girl to the other. 'What did she look like?'

The sisters glanced at each other and regarded him as if he was completely stupid.

'Like the lady in the painting?' said Emma slowly, as if Malachy was utterly dense.

'And she said her name was *Binky*?'

'The lady was called Binky,' said Kate conversationally. 'She told us. She went for a walk with your brother.'

'Hey, Malachy! Coming in for a cuppa?' Paula de la Mare was coming across the lawn to meet them.

But Malachy shook his head and walked away without even saying goodbye to the girls. He strode back to the house fast, chanting you bastard, Jed – you total bastard.

Binky.

Binky had been Malachy's dog when he was a boy. A tufty mongrel to whom Oriana had taught all manner of tricks which a slightly peeved Malachy had told her were demeaning. There'd been dogs before and after Binky – but none so special to him.

The woman in the painting was Rachel, Robin's muse, his wife. Beautiful and brittle and little more than a child when she'd come over from America for Robin. In the painting she was a little older, but still young – though her physical vulnerability was now underscored with a canny awareness of the destructive power of her beauty. But Emma and Kate had never met Rachel. And Rachel was forty years older now than in the painting. And Rachel had never given a flying fuck about Binky. So, if some woman had been here yesterday, who looked like the subject of the painting and said her name was Binky, that woman could only have been Oriana.

Oriana had come back to Windward.

She'd been here.

She'd been here with Jed.

He didn't say.

Was that before she came into the gallery? Or after?

Jed had said nothing.

Why had Jed not said?

Bastard.

Fuck him.

That is *it*, thought Malachy. Fuck him, the bastard.
Fuck *him*.

When I was . . .

When I was three I needed a haircut. If people talk about their earliest memories, invariably it's specific events which they recall. My earliest memory was not an event – it was something said about me.

When I was three I needed a haircut. I remember my father hissing at my mother, 'The child needs a haircut – it can't see where it's going.' And my mother said, 'Yes, it can.' And my mother suddenly saw me and started shouting at my father: 'She! She! She's not an It, *she's a* She, *you heartless bastard!' But I knew that she knew that I knew that she'd also called me 'it'.*

That was my earliest memory, when I was three. It remains far more cutting than what followed.

My mother hoicked me onto her hip and plonked me on the edge of the table. I distinctly remember the table that day because there were all these wine bottles on it in a perfect, accidental grouping. They were mostly but not quite empty and one was on its side. The light slicked the glass like varnish and the glass was the colour of glossy black cherries. They looked so beautiful, like a detail in a seventeenth-century Dutch or Flemish still life – like something you might spy in a corner of a Frans Hals painting – just a perfect little vignette away from the main focus of the canvas. I remember being mesmerized by these bottles; the grace and stillness a haven away from the seethe between my parents.

There's something else I recall hearing that day. Perhaps not so much a sound as a sensation – the slow ratcheting crunch of scissors against my hair and the sharp snag of any disparate strands caught around my mother's fingers. It hurt. You could, quite literally, say that 'it' hurt because when I was three, that's who I was. Everything hurt that day.

I remember Malachy and Jed laughing at me when they saw me next, ruffling my hair. Even Jette smiled. But they didn't laugh in pity, nor with derision, just with love. And then I thought that actually it wasn't too bad. I remember feeling very proud, in fact, because finally I could see where I was going.

CHAPTER THIRTEEN

Oriana was walking the streets of Hathersage like a bobby on the beat – her pace casual but purposeful. She didn't know where to go and she didn't know what to think but as walking always helped her think, she walked for hours, with no corner and no dead end forsaken. Nothing her mother said had particularly hurt her. Over the years and through a lot of therapy in the States, Oriana had done a good job accepting that it was nothing personal, that actually it had nothing to do with her at all, per se – that it was just her mother, it was just the way she was. What affronted her more now was what the hell she was going to do and where on earth, realistically, she could go.

As she passed by, she looked in the windows of letting agencies. It was rather futile – she had no intention of living in Hathersage, nor could she justify a car, so studying the particulars of property to rent in more rural areas was pointless. She did it anyway. All the agencies were closed and none was promoting little affordable cottages conveniently placed on bus routes. It was a demoralizing and stupid thing to do – like window shopping for clothes she could neither afford nor fit into. She scoured the notices in the windows of a couple of news-agents'. Room available. Flat-share wanted. Studio to let. She jotted down the numbers. Clean, bright flat, all mod cons. Female n/s wanted. She'd phone that one first.

A man answered. He said yes at the end of every sentence, preceded by a phlegmy clearing of his throat. You're a non-smoker, yes? Do you know the area, yes? Rent doesn't include bills, yes?

'Can I ask about the other people in the flat?' asked Oriana.

'There's just me, yes?'

No.

Oriana thought, I really, really don't want to flat-share with strangers. She thought how it had been different when she'd been a student – then they were all strangers in common and afterwards they chose to live together because they were friends. It wasn't the same now. It was something you just did not do in your mid-thirties.

She ordered tea and a toastie at Cintra's and, despite the owner's imploring her to sit inside, telling her spring was still some way off, Oriana chose a picnic table in the garden at the back. It was mid-afternoon and the sun was being valiant. She'd have to go back to her mother's at some point – but not until she had something constructive sorted. She dabbed at crumbs as she stared at the list she'd scribbled in the bedroom before leaving that morning:

Cat

Django

Jed

White Peak

Whom should she phone? Which one would be able to provide what she needed? She looked at the names. It was Sunday – the gallery, she remembered from the details on the website, would not be open.

Jed

Cat

Django

Jed – could she really face being back at Windward? Could she really face seeing Jed again so soon?

Cat – but her old friend was cosily married and busy feathering her nest.

Django – he was old, though, and not in good health. Actually, perhaps that was a good option – she could keep an eye on him, help. But she cursed herself for her fake altruism. She thought, perhaps I could just ask them, any one of them, if they know someone or somewhere I could go.

Who on her list was most likely to be in at this time on a Sunday – and who was most likely to have a solution for her? The two didn't necessarily tally. The names floated around the page as her eyes gauzed with tears. It's only frustration, she told herself. It's just loneliness. Really, where she most wanted to be was with Ashlyn. She'd had some of her very best Sundays with Ashlyn. Lazy lunches in Tiburon. Flea markets and hiking and an afternoon movie – Sundays were varied, a movable feast, the one constant being talking and talking; putting the world to rights with laughter, thus ending the weekend and starting the week on a good note. She looked at her watch – Ashlyn would only just be waking up. And then Oriana thought, I have enough money to fly back to California.

But she couldn't. It was impossible. The self-inflicted taunt of something unobtainable – a perfect dream that made no sense whatsoever. She focused on the names on the scrap of paper and scrolled through the contacts on her phone and took a deep breath and thought oh, just get on with it, and dialled.

'Hullo. It's Oriana.'

'Hey! How are you?'

'I'm fine – I'm good. I'm sorry to trouble you, Ben – but is Cat about? For a chat?'

'Of course!' said Ben. 'She'll be delighted.' He took the landline through to the front room and found Cat asleep.

He backed out of the room. 'You still there? She's dozing – can she ring you later?'

'OK,' said Oriana but she obviously didn't sound it.

'Are you all right?' Ben asked. 'I mean – I can wake her?'

'No no,' said Oriana, 'don't do that. I don't want to trouble her. I just fancied a chat, you know, with my old pal.'

'Thank you for visiting Django yesterday,' Ben said. 'And I know Cat would love to see you soon, too. *Herself*.' There. He felt quite proud of the way he'd handled that one.

'Definitely,' said Oriana.

'She'll phone you,' said Ben. 'It's what I call a gestational snooze. It's the legitimate equivalent of Sunday Afternoonitis.'

Oriana laughed. How she'd love to be in their home right now, all nesty and nuptial and safe and together and grown up. 'Bye, Ben.'

'Look after yourself.'

I'm trying, Oriana thought, I'm trying. And then she thought, how long does Cat sleep for? It was darkening. Nobody was out. Impending drizzle hung in the air like a low-level hum. It was dawning on her that it was unlikely she'd be sleeping anywhere other than back at her mother's that night. She looked at the list; realistically she didn't have a Plan B. She folded the paper as many times as she could and wedged it between the slats of the bench.

* * *

'I'll just be off round the block then, love,' said Bernard. 'Two shakes.'

Rachel glanced up. She'd spent the afternoon leafing distractedly through magazines and doing the crosswords in biro, rather than pencil, which meant ugly black scratchings and illegible answers, mostly wrong. 'Hmmm.'

'Two shakes,' he repeated, already buttoning up his coat. The truth was, he'd twice seen Oriana slink by the house, in one direction and then the other. He didn't worry about Rachel. Rachel he knew. But Oriana had been in his thoughts all day.

'Now,' he said to himself, quietly shutting the front

door and walking thoughtfully down the path. 'If I were Oriana and I'd been this-a-way and then that-a-way – I'd likely as not come from *this* direction next.' And off he went, feeling a swell of satisfaction when he came across her leaning like a teenager against a wall, smoking.

'I don't smoke!' she said, hastily scrubbing out the cigarette and almost standing to attention, compounding the adolescent impression.

'Well,' said Bernard thoughtfully, 'don't mind if I do.' And out from the inside pocket of his coat came a packet of Woodbines. He offered one to Oriana.

'I really don't smoke,' she told him, declining.

'Tense, are you?'

'Yes. I suppose. Sorry.'

'I understand.' His tobacco smelt of olden days and solid men.

'Doesn't she drive you mad?' The words tumbled unchecked. 'Sorry.'

He puffed thoughtfully. 'Yes,' he said evenly.

'How have you put up with it for so long?'

He considered his answer. 'A walk around the block. My smokes. The Vauxhall,' he listed. 'I like order – and she only knew chaos. So she likes my order. I'm needed and I like that.'

'And then I come back and mess it all up?'

Bernard took another suck. Oriana liked the way, after every puff, he contemplated his cigarette as if it were a thing of beauty. He was enjoying it, it had purpose, it brought pleasure. She'd wasted her money on a packet of ten that tasted vile and that she'd end up binning.

'I don't think so, duck,' Bernard said. 'But yes – she'll have seen it that way.'

'I'm going to go to Cat and Ben's. Cat – McCabe, as was – Django's girl. Do you remember her?'

'Not her – but Django, yes, of course.'

'I'm going to go there – and sort myself out from there.'

'Well – you'll not be too far,' said Bernard thoughtfully and then he looked troubled. 'I'd've liked to look after both of you – back then. I do want you to know that. But in a rum way, I know that out of the two of you, it's you who's stronger, it's you that can cope. You're the one who'll always be all right. It's only ever been that way, Oriana. It's something to marvel at.'

Oriana shuddered. Bernard's words, meant to comfort, made her feel so alone.

'Better to be able to stand on your own two feet,' he said, looking at her levelly, 'than have to be propped up by someone else.'

Oriana thought how Life appeared to be a long, steep flight of steps and while she tackled the relentless climb, everyone around her appeared to hop on and off an escalator.

'I'm Rachel's walking stick,' he said, as if diplomatically rubbishing Oriana's melancholia. 'But don't forget – Rachel's needed a walking stick since she was a young woman. Permanent, like. And that's something to be pitied.'

Oriana thought, Bernard. She thought, I had no idea. And she felt very remorseful that all these years she'd disparaged him as a dull old fart. She thought, I don't think I ever wrote 'love to Bernard' in any of my emails to my mother. She thought, I don't know when his birthday is. She looked at him; his Woodbine was almost finished and he was regarding it gratefully. He noticed all the small things as much as he was able to put the big things in their place. He was a good man. She'd missed out years of knowing him and she felt ashamed. He walked away from the pavement and dropped the butt into the gutter, treading it down and nudging it right into the corner. Not many would notice it. Few would have done that.

'Come on, pet – let's walk back together.' He crooked his elbow and Oriana slipped her arm through it. 'For the last supper,' he chuckled. 'Ham and eggs for our teas,' he said. 'That'll do you?'

'That'll do me,' said Oriana.

They walked on in affable silence, then Oriana stopped.

'Bernard?'

His open face waited.

'I just wanted to – thank you,' she said. 'For this.' She waved her hand around the time they'd just spent. 'And for being her walking stick.' He brushed it away and walked on. But Oriana didn't. 'And Bernard?' He turned. 'It's just –' She paused, then shrugged. 'I'm sorry.'

'For what?'

'For – it all.' He made it so easy for her to feel she could look at him straight. 'Me. Her. Decades.'

'Now now – let's not get all poetic and dramatic,' he said. 'It's not many who truly live the life they've chosen.'

She wasn't entirely sure if he was alluding to her

or himself. His ambiguity was premeditated, of that she was sure.

As they turned into the street and the house came in sight, it took her a couple of steps to realize he was tapping lightly at her sleeve. He was handing her something. A couple of banknotes.

'No!' she said.

'Yes,' he said, measured, almost stern.

'I have money,' she said.

'And now you have a little more.'

He opened the gate, walked ahead of her, opened the door and called through, I'm back, Rachel. Back home again.

They ate ham and eggs awkwardly. The clink of cutlery against crockery loud and jarring in the loaded silence. Oriana could barely taste the food and a glass of water did nothing to ease the constriction in her throat. She stole a glance at Bernard, tucking in to his tea and she realized, he wasn't unmindful at all. He was in the moment, enjoying every mouthful, admiring what was on his fork as it neared his mouth much in the way he had his cigarette as he'd taken it away from his lips. Oriana thought, he's parked all his worries about my mum and me and the ridiculousness of it all because there's food on the table and it's hot, eat up.

Suddenly she could taste. Salty meat, tart pineapple, crisp underside of fried egg, perfect yolk – runny on top of a firm platform. She knew she'd learned something that day – about him, about herself – to look below lightweight surface details to appreciate depth.

She did it with art all the time; now she'd do so with people, with the smaller things in life.

'Cheers,' said Oriana, holding up her glass of water and wanting very much for Bernard to sense that she was toasting him. He raised his glass, slightly baffled. Rachel's was empty and went untouched. Oriana's phone rang – it was Cat. As desperate as she was to answer it, she didn't. House rules. She was a guest at their table. And this was indeed the last supper. 'Good health,' she said.

'You do know I haven't seen your mother since – *everything*?' Cat whispered as Oriana brought her into the house.

'Look what the Oriana has brought in!' said Oriana. 'A Cat?'

Bernard laughed. Rachel looked up, sank a little and rose out of the chair as if having to shrug off a great weight to do so. She walked over to Cat and kissed her solemnly on either cheek. 'Catriona McCabe,' she said.

'It's York now,' said Oriana but Rachel ignored her.

'Hullo, Mrs, um, Rachel.'

'When are you due?' Rachel asked.

'Ten weeks – earlier if I ask Django to cook me one of his curries. How are you? You look well.'

'I *am* well,' Rachel said as if it was impudent to assume otherwise.

'Hullo!' Cat called over Rachel's shoulder to Bernard. 'I'm Cat. I don't think we ever –'

'Indeed,' said Bernard, shaking her hand, with his other hand supportively at her elbow. 'Lovely to see you – so – bonny.'

And there they stood, looking from person to person, expressions changing in authenticity according to who was smiling at whom.

'Shall I get my stuff?' And Oriana wondered why she'd asked her mother.

'I'll help,' said Cat, noticing. It had immediately evoked a barrage of incidents from their youth.

'I just can't do goodbyes!' Rachel said suddenly, actually swiping the back of her hand across her brow. 'I just can't.'

I know, thought Oriana. Oh, I know. You don't do goodbyes. You just go.

Her mother hugged her hard, spikily, too tight, no softness, no give.

'Bernard – you do it!' she said. So Bernard enfolded Oriana into the gentlest of bear hugs and kissed the top of her head.

'I meant her bags, Bernard! *Her bags*. You take them to the car.'

'We're fine,' Oriana, still within Bernard's embrace, told Rachel. 'We're good. We understand.'

Bernard again liked her ambiguity and, when Oriana looked back up the path as Cat closed the boot on her bags, he was still standing at the doorway. As they set off, she was pleased to see Bernard there still. And he waved and winked.

* * *

Ten weeks. Oriana lay on the futon on the floor of the new nursery ashamed that, in her prime childbearing years, she actually had no idea what Ten Weeks till Due Date actually involved. How long would Cat be happy for her to stay? Oriana felt slightly mortified that Cat would be the one going off to work while she'd be the one staying at home, with her feet up. That seemed a little skewed. Yet Cat and Ben had implored her to take all the time she needed.

Ben's a doctor, remember. He said you could stay. And he knows what's best for his wife and unborn child.

Under bedding that smelled fragrantly soft, Oriana looked at the paper border dancing a merry jig of pastel jungle animals all around the room. Say all the time she needed was more than ten weeks? In a fidget of tiredness that precluded sleep, Oriana tried to synchronize timetables for all of them. At Six Weeks to Go, Cat would be finishing work. Should Oriana ship out then or would her old friend be most grateful of her company at that time, of someone to help hoick her out of her chair and rub her ankles or the small of her back or iron tiny clothes and fold lots and lots of bouncy white towels? At Four and a Half Weeks to Go – that might well be when Cat would suddenly crave daytime silence and solitude. But that was probably when Ben would be most busy tying up loose ends in advance of paternity leave. So maybe that would be a crucial time to stay put? Would Cat perhaps want Oriana to stay all the way to ten weeks, just in case she went into labour and Ben wasn't there to drive her to the hospital? And what if the baby had no intention of sticking to the countdown? Say the baby came early? Really early. And then she thought, if the baby could give the parents little notice of its arrival, could the parents also give me scant notice of my departure?

She wanted to think, all in good time. But even now on her first night, so comfortable after a joyful evening during which shared reminiscing – of their pasts both in the UK and the USA – gave her a sense of solidity, the countdown had already begun.

Benign lions. Cuddly tigers. Plump bouncing elephants and jovial giraffes. Oriana gazed at the wallpaper frieze. Two by two they ringed the room, ready to comfort and guard Baby. Smiling crocodiles, with fluttery eyelashes and Hook's watch invisible but ticking, unmistakably ticking, deep inside.

CHAPTER FOURTEEN

This made Malachy's job hard. Harder than a week of slow sales. He gave each item in the portfolio a considered look, though he could have leafed through it in moments, had the young artist not been at his side, expectant. They came into the gallery unannounced, uninvited, perhaps two or three times a month, throughout the year. Some were fresh out of art college, some had been painting for decades. Sometimes, it was the relatives of artists long dead, lugging in work they didn't care for in the hope it would net them a fluke fortune. Once, a mother brought in her four-year-old's daubings. It was very much this gallery they targeted – the reputation of the White Peak Art Space having grown over recent years. Ever since all that press about David Merifield being shortlisted for the Turner Prize – a local artist with no formal training who had brought his work in on spec and who Malachy had tirelessly championed. Today, though, there'd be no prizes, no wall space – and, realistically, not much of a future – for this artist.

'I like to chew things,' he told Malachy.

Until that moment, Malachy had assumed it was

papier mâché stuck in globs to the boards. He peered closer. What *was* that? Well-masticated supermarket receipts apparently. And on that one? Enormous clumps of used chewing gum: pulled and twisted, then rolled in pencil filings and cigarette ash. Jesus, a chicken's wishbone.

'I thought you could write something like: Archie Dunfold likes to choose what he chews. Or maybe the other way around. Chews what he chooses.'

'What's this one called? Chew*bacca*?' asked Malachy sarcastically, staring at pulverized cigarettes stuck to the board with stickers saying 'Special Offer'.

'Yes, it is!' the artist said. 'You see? You *get* me. I knew it. You get me.'

Christ alive, thought Malachy. He needs to be sectioned. 'Leave it with me – I'll have a think.'

The artist started walking away backwards saying cool! cool!

'Your portfolio?' Malachy said.

'Oh – thought you just said to leave it with you?'

'No – when I said that, I meant –' Malachy thought, I do not want this person's germs in my gallery a moment longer. 'It's best if you take it with you. I've seen it – it's unforgettable.'

Oriana would be in stitches.

The thought came out of nowhere and stayed.

It's just the sort of thing that would tickle her.

It was mid-week and, while the effects of the previous weekend were still acute, they were no longer constant and his thoughts for Oriana had softened. He'd never see her again anyway – so what point was there to feel anything other than a nostalgic tenderness towards her? His feelings for Jed, though, remained serrated; so sharp he had banished his brother from his thoughts for both their sakes.

He looked over at Robin's work. People came from afar to see them. He'd had offers, some sizeable. One day, he'd accept one. He enjoyed the paintings, here on the walls of the gallery. He wasn't entirely happy that the new one – of Rachel – lingered in the spare room facing the wall. Something happened to the paint when Robin transferred it from tube to canvas, when it mutated from medium to expression, from colour to meaning, from material to ephemeral. It was an alchemy of sorts. But it generated the opposite of gold, whatever that was. Even with Kate and Emma's editing, there remained a darkness enmeshed within that work which not even the fingertips of a child could palliate.

Having tapped it against his chin whilst deep in thought, finally Malachy put his flashdrive into the computer. If there were no further interruptions from tobacco-chewing non-artists, and no more distractions of paintings in spare rooms, he intended to work on his novel. He'd had a productive evening the night before, reshaping the first quarter and introducing a new character. However, though the scene was set with a notepad and pencil to one side and a fresh cup of tea to the other, a cushion behind his back and his mobile phone on mute, the words on the screen blurred into a background pattern as a whorl of sweet recall swept over him.

He laughed out loud.

'You mad thing,' he said quietly, vividly seeing her again, as she'd been then.

Oriana had been struggling with *Hamlet* for her English GCSE.

'Hamlet is *rubbish*,' she'd been saying for months. 'He's a berk. And the play is crap!'

'Oriana – that's blasphemy.'

'He gets his knickers in a twist the *whole* time.'

'He's Hamlet – he's allowed to.'

'He just bangs on and on. And he's so morose. *To be or not to be* – well, my advice is *don't*. Don't bloody bother to bloody *be*, mate! Stop asking such pseudo philosophical questions and just piss off back to Wittenberg. Get over yourself! Get a life and for God's sake don't bloody live at home with your slag mum and evil stepdad.'

Malachy laughed now as he'd laughed then. He remembered exactly what he'd said to her.

'You know – if you had the guts – you could write that in the exam. Perhaps hold off the expletives, though. A mate of mine – did you meet Jonno? – that's how he won his place at Cambridge. He had to write an essay on courage. He put his name and candidate number at the top of four blank pages but didn't write a thing. Then, on the very last line of the last page, he wrote *This is courage*.'

'Do you dare me?' Oriana asked, looking at him askance, sparkling at the thought.

'I don't need to,' he said, slipping his hand into hers, 'you're the daring one.'

They'd walked through to the brook which demarcated the Windward boundary, taking the path the deer trod through the bluebells. *Always follow the path of least destruction* was a favourite saying of Malachy's. He said it to Oriana again that day and she laughed and biffed him and said *oh shut up, Malachy. You and your deep-and-meaningfuls.*

'I'll go easy on the swearing,' she said, 'in the essay – but I'll write it in my own way. I'll be true to how I feel.'

'Always be true to how you feel,' Malachy said.

'You sound like Polonius – *to thine own self be true,*' she groaned. 'Polonius is a rubbish character anyway – Shakespeare must've run out of ideas and resorted to churning out a bunch of clichés. *Neither a borrower nor a lender be . . . Brevity is the soul of wit* – well, old Wills didn't take note of that, did he!'

Malachy looked at her. Her face open, guileless, so very pretty.

'You do know those so-called clichés came about because of the play? They didn't exist before? Shakespeare coined them? There was, indeed, *method* in the *madness*?'

It was difficult to tell if she knew or not. They locked eyes. He came in close to her face, backed off a bit and scrutinized her expression. Did she know? Was she joshing? And then he saw it: just the most fleeting twitch of her top lip, a barely perceptible flare of her nostril. And then she laughed and punched his arm again and took his hand, weaving her fingers around his, and they walked on.

'Just write with the passion you *feel*,' Malachy told her. 'Most students will regurgitate the teacher's slant, play it safe. They don't think for themselves.

You're different. By the way, you *are* going to do English A level, aren't you?'

'Well, if I must. But I'd rather run off with the circus.' She sighed histrionically. She used to do that a lot, back then. 'Yes, Malachy, I'll be following in your footsteps,' she said. To emphasize her point, she made much of dropping his hand, dropping behind him, linking her fingers lightly over the waistband of his jeans and stepping balletically into his footfalls as they walked on.

'When do you get your results?' she'd wanted to know.

'A week before yours,' he'd said over his shoulder.

'Jed's going to get ten A-starreds.'

'I know.'

'I hate him. I'll probably get four A's. Then a B for French. C's for biology and georawful. And my maths'll be Unclassified.'

'If you pass maths, I'll buy you a present.'

'If I fail, do I have to pay you?'

'Yes.'

'How much?'

'Ten.'

'Ten quid? Ten pee?'

'Ten of these.'

And Malachy had turned suddenly and pulled Oriana close, his body pressed achingly against hers as he stroked her hair away from her face, his cool violet-grey eyes darkening with desire, holding her in an intense caught moment. The still point of the turning world – moments like these, that's what he called them, because he'd done T. S. Eliot for A level.

Dipping his face, finding her lips, brushing them gently with his until the kisses came true; instinctive, loaded, meaningful, crazy, urgent. Eighteen and fifteen.

When Malachy kissed Oriana and Oriana kissed Malachy, their age and inexperience stood for nothing. And when he touched her, wherever he touched her, the pleasure she felt sent a charge through his fingers, right through his body: skin, fibre, bones, organs. There was nothing more thrilling, more maddening, than her hands swooping over his back, holding on tight to his arms, slipping lightly down to dally over the mound swelling in excruciating desire behind his jeans.

'I love you, Malachy,' she whispered, her lips touching his ear lobe. But he pulled her hand away because the temptation, the insane feeling of pleasure locking with pain, was a bullet heading straight for regret and danger.

'No, Oriana. Not yet,' he said, enfolding her in his arms, her head tucked under his chin as he stared at the patterns on the black pine to avoid the subject that every neurone was screaming out for. 'We just can't.'

'We so *can*,' she pleaded. 'It's so stupid – sixteen! Who says! Who decides! The stupid government? Some frigid medical busybody? I'm in my sixteenth year, for God's sake. I love you. It's right. Hamlet – think of Hamlet, he was *thirty*.'

'We'll wait,' he whispered.

They clung to each other.

'Think of Ophelia!' Oriana protested. 'She was only fifteen.'

'Actually, we don't know her precise age,' Malachy corrected.

And suddenly Oriana softened. 'Well, Juliet was fourteen. And Polonius refers to Ophelia as a *green girl*. So *I'm* saying she's fifteen – and *you've* just told me that my opinion counts.'

Back at the gallery, Malachy can see it again now, so vividly – how Oriana stuck out her tongue and stropped off ahead, lightly hitting the tree trunks with a stick as she passed.

Acting her age. Fifteen. With so much ahead of her.

Sitting at his computer, staring at the screen without seeing a word of his novel, Malachy felt the disconcerting welling of the ghost tear. He rarely cried, even as a child. Jed was the one far more at ease with emotion. But since losing an eye – it was the weirdest thing. His good eye remained dry and yet the sensation of tears in his left eye – the prickling buzz of them forming, the hot oiliness of their passage from the duct down his face, the release, the relief, the physical manifestation of feeling so much – was overwhelming. He slipped his finger up under his patch. Dry. Nothing. Nothing there at all. He'd never once cried for himself, for the half-light that had been his world for almost half his life. But today, at this vividly beautiful yet terrible taunt of a past that had promised so much, the secret tears came.

Agitated and unnerved, he went to the kitchenette at the back, splashing cold water on his face, through his hair. He held on to the sink and watched the water eddy away. He felt hot, despite a thick frost still clinging to parts of the window. Spring wasn't to be taken for granted. The weather could still be harsh.

'We never did.' He dried his face, his hands. 'We never made love.'

Because just a few months later, after he gained two As and a B in his A levels and Oriana five As, two Bs and a monumental fail for maths, that's when something terrible happened.

CHAPTER FIFTEEN

Oriana confided in Cat how lacklustre she felt, how dowdy and flat. But Cat, who loved her, said she was gorgeous and sassy and not to be so hard on herself. She had been with Cat for a fortnight, she'd been back now for longer than any vacation she'd ever taken. With some embarrassment, she realized that all her working life, she'd never been away from work so long. Life was starting to feel stultifying. There was no residual stress from Hathersage, she'd given herself a break and the slack she'd cut herself was now dragging on the floor and tripping her up. It was hard to find any further justification for not doing something. After five weeks, it felt indulgent and immoral. And yet the coagulation of anxiety and apathy resulted in a sort of agoraphobia which rendered her unable to do little more than sit on Cat and Ben's sofa waiting for them to come home.

What would Casey think? Don't think about Casey. What would Malachy think? Why are you thinking of Malachy? Jed. What would Jed think? Jed would have something to say about it. He'd say, come along, foolish woman. Get your skates on and let's go for an adventure.

In her laptop there was the potential, if not for adventure, then for ventures new. Emails with contacts in her industry, letters of recommendation for her from her previous employers, her own portfolio of work. But the laptop remained resolutely switched off. She felt ashamed of her inertia, she felt unnerved by her status on paper: unemployed, homeless, single. She felt incapable of doing anything about it.

Towards the end of Oriana's second week there, Cat thought how she really was the perfect guest because she seldom left any trace of herself. Even in the nursery where, during the day, Oriana folded all evidence of herself and stacked it out of sight, while at night, there was only silence. When Cat and Ben returned from work, it was to a house cleaner and tidier than the one they'd left. There didn't seem to be any extra washing, the towel pile didn't go down. There was no longer any need to swill out dirty mugs or spoons because there was always a clean supply of both. Even Ben's mercy dashes to the garage at ungodly hours for a pint of milk or tea bags or pickled onion crisps or whatever fad was consuming Cat had become redundant.

A fortnight on, what occurred privately to Cat – with the X-ray vision of old friendship – was that none of it pointed to a particular eagerness of Oriana's to please, but rather to her absolute need to go unnoticed. This she further facilitated by deflecting attention away from herself and onto Ben or Cat or the baby. Cat thought about it; usually one felt flattered to be asked about oneself, but she might as well be asking Oriana to strip naked and stand in the middle of the street because on the two or three occasions when Cat had asked direct questions – about Windward, about Casey, about Oriana's decision to come back to the UK – she'd nimbly sidestepped answering and asked pertinent pregnancy questions instead. Bernard and her mother, however, were topics Oriana could converse on ad nauseam. It was surprising how much detail could actually be wrung from a life which appeared on the surface to be so bland. But Oriana could make bland very funny indeed. So, she made their bed and she made them meals and she made Cat and Ben laugh.

Roast chicken. Roast chicken with all the trimmings on a Friday night in mid-April. What a treat, thought Cat as she took off her coat and called through theatrically, honey! I'm home! to Oriana. But Oriana didn't call back, put your feet up, Mumma, and I'll bring you a cuppa. She didn't respond at all. The lights were on, the washing machine was mid-cycle and the back door was ajar, yet there was no sign of Oriana. Cat called out again and listened to the silence. How odd. She phoned Oriana's mobile and heard it ring up in the nursery.

'Oriana?'

Still nothing. Cat needed to sit down for a while. Her legs felt itchy and her back nagged and actually, she was simply plain tired. Anyway, if the house was empty and Oriana had left her phone here and the back door open, she'd probably darted out to pick up some ingredient urgently needed for the dish. Cat went through to the sitting room. She settled herself in a chair and felt herself being sucked into an imminent doze. She could hear Oriana's phone ring again, first an incoming call which rang and rang, then the trilling request tone for a FaceTime call. Then there was the dull thud of something like a phone being thrown. Oriana wasn't at the shops, she was upstairs. Using the banister as a mountaineer might a rope, Cat pulled herself up the staircase.

'Oriana?'

The nursery door was ajar and Cat could see Oriana crouched small in a corner of the room. She looked unkempt and distant, like one of those occasional pictures in the paper of a feral child brought up by wolves then thrust into a human environment. She was just sitting there, scrunched up and dishevelled.

Gently, Cat knocked. 'Oriana?'

She eased the door a little wider and Oriana looked up, furiously wiping away any vestiges of emotion as she scrambled to her feet, though her face remained blotched with distress.

'Oh. Hi. I must have – nodded off or something. Shit – sorry. Have you been back long? Shall I make a pot of tea?'

Her phone was Facetiming again. It was nearer to Cat than Oriana.

'It's Ashlyn!' Cat said. 'Can I answer it?'

'No, don't!'

Hoarse, desperate. It was years since Cat had heard that tone of voice from Oriana.

'But it's—'

'Leave it – *please*.'

Cat looked at her. 'What's up?' Nothing. 'You OK?'

Oriana slumped down into her corner again, her fists grabbing onto her hair either side of her temples. Gingerly lowering herself next to her, Cat tried not to emit the grunting sound that was too much of a pregnancy cliché even to her own ears. Ignoring the force field of introversion radiating from Oriana, Cat placed her hand on her friend's knee, rested her head against the wall and waited. Despite the longevity of their friendship, decades of shared secrets, she realized she hadn't an inkling what this could be about and that made her sad. She looked around the room – Moses basket, changing table, gentle hues and soft smiley images. She wished they were sitting somewhere else – this was the baby's space, nothing must sully it. No bad vibes. She nudged Oriana.

When they were children, teenagers, that's how they'd always communicated. A nudge had always led to a silent meeting of eyes. The upturn or downturn of a corner of the mouth. Nudge. A sniff or there again, a snort. Nudge. A giggle or tears. Whatever the emotion, whatever the issue, whatever the revelation, a nudge had always been both the key and the balm.

Everything's all right. Your friend's here.

Cat nudged her again, raised her eyebrow and waited. Oriana swallowed, the sound audible in her dried-out throat. The word, when it finally came, was crackled like glass shards.

'Casey.'

'Is he OK?' Cat asked. He's dead, she thought. Casey is dead. Please don't let him be dead. And then she thought, my imagination is as out of control as my hormones.

'Oh, he's very OK,' said Oriana and the sound of bitterness scorched her distress. 'He's going to be a dad.'

'Oh.' Cat thought about it. Blimey. 'That was quick,' she said. 'Some kind of gunshot conception?' That wasn't right. Pregnancy had done strange things to her vocabulary. 'Shotgun,' she corrected. 'Who is she?'

'His wife,' Oriana said flatly. 'His wife. Who else?'

Cat's confusion had nothing to do with her pregnancy and everything to do with what Oriana had told her in the past. Cat had assumed waitress, bimbo, one-night stand. Not wife. That didn't make sense. 'His wife?'

'His wife,' Oriana confirmed in a whisper taut with despair.

Cat stole a glance at Oriana. 'But – he left her for you? Ages ago?'

Oriana's eyes said it all and her voice came in a whisper. 'The truth is, he never left her.'

It took a while for Cat to digest this. It didn't taste nice. 'But when you came to Boulder – for that weekend?'

'He snuck away.'

'But you told me – you said –' Cat paused. 'You *told* me.'

'I know.' The shame of it was legible in the slump of Oriana's body, audible in the rasp of her voice.

'And in San Fran – when we visited?'

Oriana shook her head. 'He was never mine. I just – pretended.'

It was like desperately trying to chew down gristle that was too far back in the mouth. The truth, something unsavoury enough to have made Cat gag at the time, was now doubly unpalatable by being coated in a lie for so long.

'They were never even separated,' Oriana said slowly, out loud to an audience, for the first time. 'I just had him when I could. For two and a half years.'

'He had an affair for *two and a half* years?' Cat hated him.

'Don't call it an affair,' Oriana pleaded.

'What else would you call it?' Cat knew she shouldn't take it out on Oriana. Two to tango and all that. But two and a half years? With his poor stupid wife at home and poor stupid Oriana in the wings. 'But I thought –'

'He said he'd leave her.' Suddenly, in the clarity that a dreary and mundane Derbyshire evening could bring, Oriana realized how absurd it sounded. 'He said his marriage was over and I believed him.' She winced – any phrase she used would now sound risible, preposterous, hackneyed. But in the Californian sun, oh, how she'd sipped his words like a lovely Semillon from Napa until she was utterly drunk on them. 'He said he'd never met anyone like me. They married young. He told me he loved her but had never been *in love* with her. What he felt for me, he said, was *real*. He said they hadn't been physical for years. He said I made him feel alive.'

'He'd been waiting his whole life to meet someone like you?'

'That's exactly what he said,' said Oriana, deaf to Cat's tone.

'*You complete me*? Did he say that?'

'Yes!'

'Do you remember Jerry Maguire?'

'No? From school? From the States?'

'Oh God.' Cat stroked up and down Oriana's arm. 'Oriana. You of all people – you *fell* for it?'

'I wanted to believe.'

'What a –' Cat paused. Then she thought, fuck it, I'm pregnant, I'm giving myself dispensation. 'What a cunt, Oriana.'

'I kidded myself and fooled all of you and made a fool out of our friendship by keeping all this in.'

'Two and a half *years*?' Cat almost marvelled at it. 'And you clung on, believing?'

Oriana shrugged. 'I just kept hoping – because he made it all seem possible.'

'What a criminal theft of your time, Oriana. You're thirty-four!'

'I loved him so.'

'Are you sure?'

Oriana shot Cat a look that said don't you dare. 'I *loved* him.'

'You actually loved someone that behaved like that – to you, to his wife?'

Oriana nodded. 'We can't help who we fall in love with.'

'What complete and utter tosh,' said Cat. The baby was cartwheeling inside and jabbing little fists in a sort of high five for its mother. And yet Cat felt depressed that her bright and usually ballsy friend had been *that* woman. Her own pregnancy made her empathize with Casey's wife. She was flabbergasted that Oriana had trusted such a man. And, perhaps worst of all, she was angry that she'd been told nothing until now.

'I don't doubt it was deliciously intense however morally bankrupt it was. Snatched moments outside of real life. All the promises he made.'

'He gave me a dream.' Oriana was on the verge of tears.

'Oh bollocks, Oriana. He gave you drama, not a dream. And that becomes addictive – you weren't going to live the dream, you were just acting out a really shit script.' That was probably a bit harsh but a glance at Oriana's expression revealed shame but also sudden clarity. 'Is that why you came back? Was it hard? To finally let go?' Cat felt mortified on Oriana's behalf.

'Actually – no.' Oriana paused. 'There was one night – when once again he suddenly couldn't come to me and once again, I was all ready. That particular night I'd planned to perfection. He'd said he could stay – so there were candles and cooking and clean bed linen. I'd lived the details for days. Perfect – I'd made it so dreamy. I'd waxed, tweezered, buffed and I was so looking forward to it. And he texted and said can we reschedule. *Can we reschedule*, he said because you have to understand that he always had to make any text to me anodyne.' Oriana shrugged at Cat. 'I never ever had even a single X at the end of any of his texts. I just had to be content trying to read between the lines. Of texts that were phrased as if I was a work contact.'

'So was that the final straw? The night of the petals and candles?'

Oriana shook her head. 'I felt so lonely that night. I was so brimful with all this unspent passion, all this flattened hope. I wanted to be in his arms like he promised, I wanted the world to spin and time to stand still like it did when we were together. Instead I was in this interminable evening feeling utterly crap in stupid new underwear. So I phoned him. It rang and rang. I phoned him again. It went through to answer machine. I felt like I was going mad, Cat – desperate for him. I didn't want him not to see all the things I'd done that night which would have made him love me all the more.'

With the effort of admitting it, of ripping away the veil and seeing it for what it had been, Oriana's head fell to her knees and for a moment Cat wondered whether she'd passed out.

'He'd switched his mobile off,' she said. 'So I phoned his landline,' she whispered. 'He didn't even know I knew the number. I'd snuck it from his phone one night – you know, for emergencies.' She was wide-eyed now.

Cat thought, please God, tell me you didn't tell his wife. 'So you phoned his home?'

'It was really late.' Oriana nodded. 'And his wife answered and she sounded like Dolly fucking Parton and I said I needed to speak to Casey and the terrible thing – the terrible thing – was that she was just so nice. *Sure! Sure! You hold on now, honey, I'll just go get him.* I could hear her – she calls him Sugar. *Sugar – there's a call for you. Did you switch your cellphone off?* He simply couldn't believe it was me, Cat. He sounded mortified. Appalled. Hateful.'

'What did he say?' Cat patted at her chest. This probably isn't good for my nerves, for the baby, she thought.

'He said, *Oh, hi! Hi! Sure! My bad! I'll have the measurements with you first thing.*'

'What does that mean? What did that *mean*?'

'It meant get off my fucking phone and out of my fucking home, you bitch.'

They sat in a huddle in the corner of the nursery, Oriana reliving it as if it was a scar she'd sliced open, Cat as if she was at a private screening of the horror movie that had been her best friend's secret life.

'He phoned me at work the next day, asking to meet for lunch. He sounded OK – so I told myself everything was going to be fine. I fantasized he'd had a sleepless night and had finally, *finally*, left his wife. We met for lunch at this really lovely place – expensive, crowded. I thought it was a sign – why else would he take me there?'

But Cat knew why. 'Because it would intimidate you from making a scene.'

Oriana nodded. 'I worked so hard being as smiley as possible. Fresh make-up. The hope that I was exuding inner beauty as well as looking gorgeous.

And I sat down in my perfected sinuous way – isn't that pathetic? Hours – I spent *hours* home alone practising sexy ways to sit, stand, recline. I looked deep into his eyes – barging through the animosity I could see there, concentrating on the striations of his irises, boring through his pupils, deluding myself I could see straight through to his soul.' She paused. 'I remember the wine waiter came and I ordered rosé.' She paused again. 'And I happily buttered my bread roll as if this meal had no portent, it was just two loved-up people lunching.' She motioned with her hands. 'I had my bread here, and my wine here. And I had my mouth full.' She stopped, as if the imaginary bread was stuck in her throat and the wine had just spilled all over her. She brushed her hands up and down her legs. 'He had no food. No drink. He said, *It's over, Oriana. It has to be over.*' She gave herself a moment. 'He could see I didn't believe him, that I wasn't going to hear it, that I was about to say something even though I had this stupid glub of bread wedged tight in my mouth. If he'd just driven the knife in, telling me it was over, he then followed it with an almighty twist of the razor-sharp blade. *I love my wife. I love her very much. I don't want to leave her.*' Oriana looked at Cat, and continued as Casey. '*I will never leave my wife because she's who I want to grow old with. I hate myself for having come so close to fucking it up. So it's over. And I hope, if you feel anything for me, you'll respect that.*' She paused a final time. 'He put his hand on my wrist and he thanked me for saving his marriage. Whatever the fuck that meant.'

Oriana waited for Cat to say something. But Cat was speechless.

'Then he said I was never to contact him again. That I was to let him go and that I was to get on with my own life. And then he left the restaurant and I had to sit there trying to swallow the bread and not draw any attention to the fact that I had been, quite literally, left.'

'Dear God.' Cat shook her head.

'Insult to injury?' Oriana said with a sad smile. 'When I went to leave, they came after me. *Ma'am*, they said, *the check*?'

Cat and Oriana sat contemplatively alongside one another.

'When was all this, exactly?'

'Just before Christmas.'

'And he's having a baby?'

'I just found out.'

'How? You're not still in touch, are you?'

'No. Indirectly.' Oriana scrunched her hand into a fist.

'Ashlyn?' said Cat, glancing across the shadowy room at Oriana's flung phone. Oriana nodded. 'Why would Ashlyn tell you something like that? She's meant to be your friend.'

Oriana laughed softly. 'Oh, she is. It's now her life's mission to keep hammering nails into the coffin of Oriana and Casey.'

And Cat thought, hang on – did Ashlyn know the full story and I didn't? She wasn't sure how she felt about that.

'I am over him, Cat. I promise you,' said Oriana.

'That part of my life is like an old home movie which has lost its sound – the film is fuzzing and fading before my eyes.'

'You sure?'

'Yes, I'm sure. But there was something about the news – him all sorted and progressed and grown up and improved. Whilst here I am, five months on, with no certainties in my life, hoicking a battered knapsack of baggage around Derbyshire.'

'Bloody good image, that,' said Cat sweetly. 'But a bit over the top. It hurts today – but I don't think it'll feel so painful tomorrow.' She nudged Oriana, nudged her until she returned Cat's smile.

'I don't even know if it actually hurts. I mean – sure, it's a little humiliating in some ways. I was quite shocked, actually. But I know it wasn't deep love that I felt for Casey – not really. Just a neediness. There was no reality in what we had – it was all overcharged emotion and that becomes addictive. The clichéd drama of which you spoke.'

'So why so sad?'

Oriana shrugged. 'Because even someone like Casey has his life on track – doing the things he should be doing at this age, ticking off the list of appropriate timing. But look at me.'

'Is Casey why you left? Why you came back?'

Oriana exhaled. 'Actually – no. Though I suppose that's what everyone thinks. It expedited a return I feel I was destined to make anyway. It's taken so long to feel ready to come back. It was out of bounds to me, remember. For years I felt I couldn't do anything about that. But I've always needed to come back. To see – how I feel.'

Cat thought about that.

'It's strange, isn't it – I've been away longer than I ever lived here. But it's always been the place where I've assumed home to be.'

CHAPTER SIXTEEN

Malachy had trained himself to be pragmatic, not to bear grudges, to calmly turn the other cheek. The ex-girlfriend he'd been with the longest had initially loved this quality. Ultimately, it had driven her mad.

'You slept with the guy because deep down we both know it's over between us,' Malachy had told her, his voice as even-tempered as a BBC broadcaster's. 'You had sex with him because your feelings for me have changed and, subliminally or not, you want a way out.' He'd been calm and collected; she'd wept and hurled her words and herself around the room. 'It's OK,' he'd said. 'I don't blame you. I want you to be happy. Let's just – let it go, let each other go. Let's remember three great years and forget the one, not so great one.'

That had been two years ago.

Actually, at the time, her infidelity had hurt him like hell; slow-release acid in his stomach, a rusting infection in his heart and a blow to his self-esteem that made it feel as though his lung had collapsed. But Malachy had taught himself not to countenance confrontation. It was easier just to pretend to be the sympathetic pragmatist. To turn his back on it all and saunter away.

It was almost three weeks since Oriana had flown into and out of the lives of the Bedwell brothers again. There'd been no contact between any of them. Two Fridays had come and gone without Jed calling to arrange that night out for Malachy. No messages had been left from either of them. Malachy's fury at Jed's perceived deceit had dissipated and flattened into a manageable indifference. His conscience was clear and he was untroubled by barbed thoughts. He had no need to contact his brother. And his brother hadn't had time to think to call him.

Jed was busy, too busy to remember loose invitations. He saw Malachy as he saw Windward – part of his past, always there, unchanged and in a satisfying time warp. In between visits, he neither craved the place nor missed Malachy. He didn't need to; he took for granted that they were just where he'd last left them and they'd be there for him when he next wished for them. A little like a living family photo album – quietly tucked in the same place on the same shelf; there to be taken out and flipped through at his leisure, dependable always to elicit a smile, comfort, reflection, a feeling of balance.

Oriana reappearing, however, had thrown Jed utterly off kilter. She was, quite literally, a blast from the past and had inadvertently surged through his life like a whirlwind, leaving a scatter of details, memories and emotion in her wake. He'd turned his flat upside down to locate old photographs of her and, on finding them, had kept them spread over the kitchen table for days, studying them like a game of pelmanism whenever he passed. Then he'd scanned them into his phone because it felt prudent to keep her there – his phone was like a third hand, an extra lobe of his brain, used all the time. If she was on his phone then she was real, current and probable – she was connected; all she had to do now was call. As yet, she hadn't. But Jed was convinced that she would.

'You look like Janis fucking Joplin,' Cat told Oriana.

'I slept really heavily,' said Oriana, trying to pad out her hair on one side and flatten it on the other.

'That's good, but you still look like Janis fucking Joplin. Your hair has gone A-line. It's *terrible*.'

Ben tutted. Cat tutted back at him. It's how friends talk to each other, she told him.

'I'm phoning Gay Colin right now. I know it's Saturday but he'll squeeze you in. I mean, Janis Joplin was an incredible singer and songwriter and the voice of a generation and a top woman and all that. But you wouldn't want to have a hairdo like hers. Not in this day and age.' Cat phoned the salon. 'It'll do you good to get out, too. There's only so many times a day you can plump our cushions and hoover under our furniture.'

'Where's Gay Colin?'

'Pop.'

'Pop?'

'That's his salon.'

'Where's Pop?'

'He's just moved the salon to Blenthrop. It's where

Our Price Records used to be – remember? I don't know what the place was latterly. I haven't been there in ages – if I go shopping, I usually go to Meadowhall.'

'Don't let my wife bully you,' Ben said, having caught sight of Oriana's expression and assumed it was because she actually didn't mind her hippy hair. 'I'm going to get the papers.'

'Is there a problem? Do you not want to cut your hair? Are you happy channelling your inner Janis?' Cat asked. Oriana had to laugh. Cat's freak pregnancy energy came in bursts as refreshing as a tropical downpour for all who stood near.

Oriana thought, I wasn't planning on going into Blenthrop again. And she thought, Our Price was nowhere near where the gallery is. But what if we see Malachy? And then she thought, what if I never see Malachy again?

Oriana was quiet in the car, hoping Cat would somehow eschew driving the most direct route to Blenthrop which passed perilously close to Windward. In the event, as they approached and then passed the turning for the lane, Cat glanced at Oriana who was staring fixedly ahead. She didn't comment. They'd both had their fill of emotional workshopping the previous evening when they'd chucked Casey onto the pyre.

Three Saturdays ago, thought Oriana, I was here. Was that really all it was?

'Town's busy,' she said.

'We always called it Town, didn't we,' Cat recalled.

'I could've driven myself,' Oriana said. 'You could've put your feet up.'

'It's a shag that Colin's moved Pop here, really. But I wouldn't put my head in anyone else's hands.'

'And your hands and feet?'

Cat laughed. 'Cindy does the best mani-pedis – and as I can no longer reach my toes, I'm treating myself.'

Colin didn't pass comment on Oriana's hair. He merely lifted sections gingerly, as one might an old tarpaulin in a garden shed. The arch of one eyebrow said plenty.

'I can help you,' he said at length, kindly, as if referring to a catastrophic birthmark.

'I usually have it point-cut, choppy.'

'I don't need to know that.'

She liked him. He was camp and coy and his salon was chic and buzzing. Cat was in one corner, mid-manicure, infuriating the beautician by trying to gesticulate to Colin how much she thought Oriana should have cut off.

'Ignore the Catwoman,' Colin said, rolling his eyes at her. 'You're safe now.'

As he started cutting, he guessed her zodiac sign correctly and her age incorrectly, shaving off ten years. He asked about America and theorized that she'd left because of love or lack of. But he couldn't work out what Oriana did. Teacher? Journalist? Reflexologist? Botanist? His suggestions became more exotic.

'Porn star? Astronomer? Spy?'

'Architect.'

'You're an *architect*?'

'Why do you look so surprised?' Actually, Oriana thought he looked rather disappointed.

'Because I'd never have guessed.'

'Have you met many architects?'

'A couple – clients – and they seem more, I don't know.' He thought about it, scissors and comb poised. 'Serious.'

'I don't seem serious to you?'

'You look more – artsy.'

'That's my Janis Joplin hair.'

'That's gone now, duck.'

'I wear a smart suit to work,' Oriana told him.

'Where do you work?'

'*Wore*,' she corrected. 'I used to wear a smart suit. I don't have a job at the moment.'

'Would you like me to put in a word?'

Oriana thought about it. And about the list of names on her computer. The character references. The emails from old clients and her ex-boss, trying their best to help. And now Colin, flying her flag too. She thought about how she'd been feeling. She thought about the steps she could take to change that. She thought about what she was qualified to do, what she was actually really good at.

'Thank you,' she said. 'I'd be grateful.' It was out there. Finally she was doing something – about doing something.

Colin said ta da! Cat said wowzer. Oriana just said thank you, to everyone. She felt lifted.

'Let's get some lunch,' said Cat.

'Here in Blenthrop?'

'Town's no longer just greasy spoons and Chinese takeaways.'

'I think we should mosey on.'

'I need to eat.'

Oriana wasn't sure whether Cat was patting her stomach or stroking the bump.

'Can we go somewhere else – how about the Druid? Or the Rag and Thistle – we could pop in on Django after?'

'I'm craving a cheese and onion toastie,' said Cat. 'Come on.'

They were outside the salon and suddenly Oriana was disorientated, convinced that the gallery could be round any corner they were headed for.

'I can't,' Oriana said. 'Not today. Let's just go. Please.'

Cat was confused, and somewhat irked. Pregnancy should enable her to have her own way – or so Ben's deference had thus far led her to believe. 'Look – I genuinely *need* to eat.'

'I could quickly buy you a flapjack or something?'

'What the fuck?'

'Malachy,' Oriana explained.

'*Malachy?*' Cat was startled. 'Where?'

'He has a gallery here. In Blenthrop.'

'Malachy Bedwell?'

'How many other Malachys do we know?'

'He's still *here*? How did you find out?'

'I saw him.'

'*You saw Malachy?*'

'When I went to Windward,' Oriana said, her eyes constantly scanning 180 degrees. 'Three weeks ago –

the day I later went to see Django. The day before I came to stay with you.'

Cat stared, open-mouthed. 'Look, I really need to sit down. And eat something.'

'Can't you just grab a Mars Bar?'

'No!' Cat looked around. 'There – that tea shop. Can we please just go there?'

With Cat lingering over every mouthful of two rounds of hot buttered teacakes, Oriana spoke fast, rattling through the details of Windward and Jed, Malachy and the gallery.

'That's why I went to yours – Django's – that evening,' she said. 'It's the place where I always felt I could calm down.'

Cat nodded. It made sense but still she wished she'd known about it when it actually happened. 'How was Malachy?' Cat hadn't seen him for years – she'd moved to London after university. She hadn't seen Malachy since – since it all happened. Cat dropped her voice. 'How does he – look?'

Oriana gazed at the florid tablecloth but it was too bright and busy. She looked up at Cat and shrugged.

'He looks –' She thought about it, vividly recalling how he used to look and remembering the altered version she'd seen three weeks ago. 'Silvered here and there,' she said, touching the hair at her temples for emphasis. 'Filled out a little, I guess,' she said, 'his face not so angular.' She looked at Cat and whispered, 'Still handsome.'

Slowly, and with silent sensitivity, Cat covered her right eye with her hand. Oriana reached over and gently moved it to her left eye.

'Still handsome,' she said again, softly.

They didn't talk for a while.

'And Jed?' Cat said eventually.

'He hasn't changed a bit.' Oriana had to laugh. 'Honestly. I mean – he has a better hairdo these days. Do you remember when he thought he looked like Bono?'

'It was a *mullet*,' said Cat. 'He looked more like a dodgy footballer.'

'Anyway – like I said, he's still at Windward. Can you believe that? Still leaping over the balcony and shinning down the drainpipes. Still gorgeous and mad.'

Cat stirred her tea though she didn't take sugar. 'It seems so long ago,' she said.

Oriana nodded. 'All those years in between. I have often wondered about them. About Malachy. About where he went. And he's right here. And Jed – Jed hasn't left Windward.'

'It was a terrible, terrible thing, Oriana,' Cat said. 'It was a terrible thing that happened – to all of you. *All* of you.'

'It's like it happened to different people. Someone I know – but not me.'

'I think, when something happens – like that, at that age – the only way forward is to parcel it up.' Cat thought about it. 'Compartmentalize it to the furthest recesses of your conscious – and conscience.'

'When something happens – like that,' said Oriana, 'I suppose the only way forward is to leave.' They kept stirring at their cups of tea. 'One's meant to just drift away from one's childhood and adolescence – it should be gentle and blurred. But with us, the door on the past was slammed shut. Now I'm back and suddenly I find it's ajar.'

'How do you feel?'

'I'm not sure.' Oriana shrugged. 'Freaked?'

'No wonder you were too full to even consider seeing Robin,' she said. 'Two Bedwell boys in one day.'

Oriana looked at her levelly. 'Had I not seen them, it really wouldn't have altered the fact that I've no desire to see Robin.'

OK, thought Cat. OK. We'll leave that one for the time being.

They headed for home, Oriana driving. She indicated when they neared the lane for Windward and Cat didn't comment when they headed along it. She couldn't, she was holding her breath. Oriana parked up by the gateposts, switched the engine off, and they gazed up the driveway. It was unimportant that the house was not in view.

'See,' Oriana said finally. 'It's all still there.'

She turned the car and drove away from Windward. Back at the junction, she headed away from Blenthrop. A pang plunged through her body like sudden turbulence on a flight. She'd been so close. Back then, years ago. And today. She'd been so close.

That evening, Oriana went to bed early. She wasn't unduly tired, surprisingly, and there was actually good television on. But she just felt she oughtn't to be in the room intruding on Cat and Ben curled into each other on the sofa. I'm knackered, she told them.

I've seen this film a million times. I'm going to have an early night.

Upstairs, she Facetimed Ashlyn, automatically speaking in little more than a whisper. It was as if the baby was already here. This was the baby's room and new things were appearing all the time. Tiny, beautiful items which made Oriana feel the world was shrinking around her and she was a galumphing giant. At some point today Ben, or Cat, had carefully moved Oriana's laptop off the changing table, to stack folded squares of muslin and soft terry towels there. A jar in the shape of a vanilla-coloured hippo smiled out puffs of cotton wool and nestled up to a pile of minute babygros in a colour softer than cloud.

I'm fine, Ashlyn. Do you love my hair? Actually, I'm pleased you told me about Casey. I dodged a bullet there. I can't really talk now. We're about to watch a movie. Cat and Ben say hi. I'd better go. Speak soon, though?

Three days later, on the day that Ben asked Oriana if she minded staying in for a couple of deliveries, Ashlyn phoned to tell Oriana that she was engaged. This news left her more poleaxed than Casey's had.

Ashlyn's getting married. Cat's having a baby. I'm unemployed and sleeping on the floor.

Staring at the box that had arrived, at the drawing of the cot on the side, how Oriana wished her thoughts and emotions could be so neatly packaged up. And that's why she welcomed the distraction and concentration necessary for constructing the flat-pack cot.

It looked fairly straightforward, came with its own Allen key and a packet of nuts and bolts and required no other tools or fixings. To make space, she plonked her bedding on the new rocking chair which had arrived an hour earlier, and pushed it to the corner. Methodically, Oriana laid out all the components and read carefully through the instructions. They were mainly drawings, step by step. She felt strangely exhilarated. Selecting the playlist she'd named All Time Faves, she set to work constructing the cot for Cat and Ben's baby. It was going well, really well. God! Is that the time? Cat would be home soon. But the cot was almost finished. Almost. So nearly there. But not quite.

'Don't come in!' Oriana called through the door. 'I'll be down in a mo – but don't come in.'

You bastard bloody thing, why won't you fit?

I shouldn't have jammed that other plank in – I knew it ought to have fitted more easily.

'Has my rocking chair arrived?'

'Yes!' Oriana shouted back.

Cat really wanted to see it. She'd been waiting weeks for it.

'But don't come up!' Oriana yelled. 'Not yet.'

Why doesn't that bit slot in? Bloody stupid thing. Maybe it does need a shove. It's wood – wood changes, doesn't it.

Suddenly the music was getting on her nerves so she slammed it off, sat back on her knees and ripped her jumper over her head. She was hot. And very bothered. Really, she'd like to punch and scrunch the instructions and kick the cot. It just didn't make sense. She'd followed everything to the letter, and most of the pieces thus far had clicked or slid or aligned nicely into place. But this last part? It had to be faulty – it just had to be. Poor Cat.

Fit, you bastard thing, fit.

The slatted base of the whole thing was pretty crucial, Oriana knew that. It was currently wedged diagonally within the four sides.

She heard Ben arrive home. She heard Cat and him talking. Oh – Oriana's upstairs. Yes, they've arrived. I don't know. I haven't seen them yet. She won't let me up there. She says she needs a minute. She said that ages ago.

Oriana thought, shall I just give it an almighty shove?

But what if it breaks?

She pushed the cot gently, very gently.

Feels a bit wobbly. That can't be right.

She pressed down on the base with even pressure. There was absolutely no give.

She stared and stared at the instructions. Picture after picture of bolts, looking like bullets, flying towards holes. Planks called A. Struts called B. Uprights called C. As easy as ABC. Helpful little arrows pointing this way and that. They might as well have been instructions for the Tower of Babel. She stared at the page. Hieroglyphics.

There was a knock at the door. It was Ben.

'Can I come in?'

'No!'

'Sorry?'

'A minute! Just a minute or two – please.'

Oriana was irritable and cross and in Ben's bloody

nursery and he didn't like it. He knocked again and this time turned the handle and came in. Cat behind him. Oriana was sitting there, flushed and harassed. The cot for their baby was almost built, almost right but unnervingly skewed like the optically distorted drawings of Escher.

'I wanted it all ready for when you got back.'

Ben was frowning at it. Cat looked as if she was about to cry.

'Where's the rocker?' said Cat. 'Oh,' she said. 'There.' She picked her way over the scatter of instructions, over the tangle of Oriana and removed the laptop, duvet, sweatshirt and two paperbacks from the new chair. 'Look, Ben,' she said, sitting herself down and setting it in gentle motion. It bashed the wall. It was too close. But there was too much else going on in the room to move it. No space.

Oriana wanted to be miles away. Away from the stupid faulty cot, from their lovingly designed nursery, from Cat and Ben who should be admiring their new rocking chair, just the two of them.

I don't belong here. I shouldn't be here. I don't want to be here.

'I'm sorry – I just wanted to surprise you.'

'It's fine,' said Ben, who didn't sound as if it was. 'It's just – Cat and I had planned to put it together ourselves. This weekend. Easier with two.'

'Bit of a daft rite of passage – but a key one, nevertheless,' Cat butted in. 'Feathering the nest – bed for the baby – fruits of our labour. You know?'

'One of the final finishing touches. I quite like

doing things like that,' Ben said diplomatically. 'But it was a kind thought.'

He could see where Oriana had gone wrong. It was an easy mistake to make. He looked over to Cat sitting still on her new chair that was unrockable for the time being. And Oriana, sitting at his feet looking miserable. Still here, in his nursery. Still here when they had little over six weeks to go.

'Look,' he said, 'you and Oriana go and relax downstairs – I'll have a fiddle with this.'

Downstairs, neither Oriana nor Cat could really relax.

'I'm sorry,' Oriana kept saying.

'It's OK,' said Cat, who looked really tired and a bit pale.

'The best-laid plans – and all that.'

'Please don't worry,' Cat said. The baby wedged a limb under her ribs. She winced and shifted.

'Are you OK?' Oriana asked.

'Just a bit uncomfortable.'

It took Ben another hour, and his electric drill and a little wood-filler, to make the cot right. Finally, he came downstairs.

'Mrs York?' he said. 'It's done. Come and see.' He held his hand out to Cat, to help her up. Calm and unflustered. Giving her a tender kiss. His arm around her shoulder; protective, loving. Leading her back up to the nursery. Leaving Oriana where she was. Oriana shrank into the sofa. Then she tiptoed into the kitchen. She looked in the fridge and, though it was full, it was like the elements of an impossible equation. What plus what goes with what to make a nice meal? She really wanted to cook them something. She wanted to do something nice, something conciliatory. She wanted to do something *well*. But she felt hopeless and she hated it.

Cat and Ben readily accepted her excuse that she had a cracking headache and wasn't hungry and Oriana took herself upstairs. She glanced at the cot shyly. It looked perfect. She put her hand on it. It was steady. But as much as she was relieved, she was dispirited. The rocking chair was in the same place and she felt reluctant to put her mark anywhere else in their nursery by moving it. It meant that, when she put out her bedding, she was cramped between it and the cot.

She sat cross-legged, her back against the wall. She checked her phone. Ashlyn had responded to Oriana's earlier text of heartfelt congratulations.

I know! I'm all grown up! Axxx

Ashlyn now engaged to lovely Eric with whom she'd been steady for some time. Oriana thought about it. *All grown up*. It was true. A proper grown-up. Just like Cat and Ben who were expecting a lovingly planned child within a stable relationship. And, in the distant background of her life, even Casey too. Weddings and babies and mortgages and jobs. Paving a path ahead. Being able to build for the future. Embracing responsibility and acting your age.

And look at me! Just look at me!

Just then, her life seemed personified by the

scrunch of borrowed bedding laid out on the floor of someone else's room. She felt ashamed. She knew she had no business being in that room, in that house. They were saints, Cat and Ben, *saints*. They'd never once made her feel unwelcome or a burden in the way her mother had. Not even today, when she'd practically broken their baby's cot, ruined their plans and used their new chair as a dumping station.

Mi casa su casa.

But for Christ's sake I'm in the way *in their nursery*.

She had to do what was right – and the right thing to do was to do right by them. She must leave and give them their space, privacy and time to prepare for their new little family.

Oriana curled embryonically on the floor. Gradually, it struck her that her decision had little to do with altruism. Her decision to leave was not driven by her wish to afford them space and privacy. All the little gestures Cat and Ben made instinctively to one another. The sweet looks, the tenderness, the thoughtfulness, the helping hand and sentence-finishing. The cosiness. The nub of it was that Cat and Ben's life – and Ashlyn's – inadvertently amplified what she didn't have.

My life is as much a mess as theirs is sorted.

It made her feel embarrassed, humiliated. She felt a bit pathetic.

Then she thought, but that's not it. Not entirely.

She stayed stock-still, as if the knotting emotions were whispers in a strange tongue. She listened hard to how she truly felt. And she knew that the overriding emotion was pain. Pure pain. Their togetherness caused her this pain.

I have to do something about this pain.

She thought, everyone's growing up around me. I'm just this girl in a whirl of what to do.

CHAPTER SEVENTEEN

There was a slim chance, thought Malachy, that Robin might have forgotten he'd even painted it. He was sitting on the sofa, with the portrait of Rachel in front of him, balanced on his knee like a child. He'd looked at it almost daily since the little de la Mare sisters had found it and, though it was now dry and familiar, Malachy found it no less disquieting. It wasn't just the unfinished, compromised area of the neck; the painting was twisted and contorted deep beneath the surface details. The mashing of the paint around the neck simply added a heavy and dark symbolism to it. Badly executed. This woman had been badly executed. A disturbing, fucked-up, messy execution.

Malachy shuddered. Out of nowhere, he vividly recalled Rachel bursting into his home, running straight in through the never-locked door. The family had been eating their evening meal; it was later than normal for a school day because he'd had an away rugby match. He remembered that. It was dessert time when Rachel flew in. His mother's beautiful *æbleskiver* – apple fritters – a Danish delicacy, round and little and light, dusted with icing sugar. Usually chatty, his family always fell silent when eating this dish because it was just so ambrosial. But then in charged Rachel, fear and excitement, panic and delight graffitied across her face.

'He's going to kill me!'

The pervasive emotion that surged from her was exhilaration, not terror. That's how she and Robin lived their life, always scrabbling to cling to the height of drama. It was as if they dared each other to hold a precarious pose on a cliff edge. Jump. Don't jump. I'm going to jump – just you watch, you bastard.

'He loves me enough to kill me!'

How she'd hurled herself against the peace of their evening meal that night; like a bird trapped indoors, flying at full pelt straight into a windowpane.

Malachy rested the painting against the back cushion of the sofa, as if wanting Rachel to calm down, to catch her breath and think about what she'd just said in front of two young boys, one thirteen, one ten.

He went to the kitchen, not because he had wanted anything, just to be away from the painting. He sat at the table and sighed heavily through his nose as he shook his head. Loving someone enough to kill them? What tosh! That's not love! Rachel had always seemed so proud of the extremes of emotion that she and Robin could elicit from each other.

'Totally fucked up,' Malachy said out loud. 'As twisted as your neck in that painting.' He went back into the living room, hands on hips, staring at Rachel. 'Your poor daughter,' he said to the canvas. And then his voice was edged with a hiss. 'You should be ashamed,' he said, 'both of you.' He turned away from the painting, pulled instead back into the memory of that mealtime all those years ago.

Rachel had circumnavigated their table like a dervish. *He'll kill me he'll kill me he'll kill me!* She was triumphant. And there, silent in the doorway (how long had she been there?) ten-year-old Oriana looking from her mother to the *æbleskiver*. Rachel – boasting about the level of impassioned hatred her husband had for her. Oriana – gazing at the Bedwells and the plate of fritters as if wondering what it took to instil such order in a family, to achieve such a balanced mealtime, to be nourished by such home-made sweetness. Harmony – how do you build such harmony? Had Jette and Orlando designed the blueprint?

'Mum?'

Even now, Malachy remembered how Oriana's soft little voice shattered through the commotion as if it was the sound barrier.

No one else had seen her until that moment. Only me.

He thought about the extreme effort and presence of mind it must have taken for his parents to beam over their everyday smiles as if to say oh look! Oriana's popped in for a fritter!

'I *love* my parents,' he told the portrait of Rachel pointedly. 'They are good people.'

'Mum?'

Oriana's voice from the past floated back through the years to him once again.

It sounded so odd to hear Rachel being referred to directly as Mum. It was as if Oriana had her name wrong. Side by side with Jette, in his mind's eye, Malachy looks now from his mother to Rachel, from his mother to Rachel. Rachel – a *mother*?

'Go back!' Rachel had screamed. 'Go!'

So, without a fritter, Oriana had no option but to return to the man who loved her mother enough to kill her.

Malachy shuddered. He remembered how Jette had hugged him for a little longer that night, how his father's customary pat on the head had softened into a stroke of his hair.

'I don't want you here,' he said under his breath to the painting. 'This is my home now and you're no longer welcome.' He took it and left the apartment, walking through the Corridor, swinging the canvas as if it was a piece of board he was going to chuck onto the rubbish. 'You can sod off back to Robin – let him kill you, for all I care.'

Malachy respected Robin greatly as an artist. As the elderly, infirm man Robin was today, it was no bother for Malachy to look in on him, to take him the paper, heat up a can of oxtail soup, ensure he'd taken his pills. But as the man who'd caused him significant distress when he was a child, whether directly or indirectly? And as the man who'd so heinously mistreated the gift of love, of fatherhood?

The man who'd ripped Oriana away from him, from them all? The truth of it was that Malachy despised him.

'Robin?'

'In here.'

In the studio.

God, it was airless. It had been balmy all day, constant sunshine even if diluted by typical April temperatures. The windows had trapped the sunlight, drawn it into the room and expanded it. It was unpleasantly stuffy.

'You need to open the windows, Robin,' said Malachy. 'Let the fresh air in. It's been beautiful out there.'

'Why aren't you at work? Are you unwell?' Robin rose, still impressive though stooped, today in a three-piece suit of sludge-coloured wool shot through with a bright purple stripe. Today he sounded present, almost chipper. Malachy was adept at taking no notice of Robin's moods.

'I was at work all day,' said Malachy. 'It's almost seven. I shut at five at the moment.'

'What day is it?'

'Wednesday.'

'What have you there?' Robin gestured to the canvas.

'I didn't know whether you'd like it back,' Malachy said, turning it around and then casually back again, his eyes never leaving Robin's face, tuned for the slightest darkening.

'I wondered where that had got to,' Robin mused

as though it was a missing shoe. He took the canvas from Malachy. 'Let's pop you up here, shall we? See what we can do for you.'

Malachy thought, he sounds like a GP about to treat a patient for laryngitis. He thought, she needs more than a GP for that throat; she needs a plastic bloody surgeon.

'Thank you, Malachy.'

'Can I heat something up for you?'

'I've had,' said Robin.

'And your tablets?'

'And I've had my tablets.'

'May I?' Malachy gestured to a chair.

'By all means,' said Robin, who pottered around the studio as if it was his surgery. Where's my filbert brush? Stethoscope. Let's have a little look at you, shall we? Blood pressure. Palette. Let me look down your throat. Rag soaked in meths. His total focus was Rachel.

Is it not exhausting being Robin? Malachy wondered. Now as much as then? A lifetime of duress and extremes? One day, so full of venom, the next – like now – almost genial, tender even, chatty as you like?

'Keep taking the tablets,' he said under his breath. But Robin didn't hear him, Robin was communicating on another level entirely. With love in his eyes, tenderness in every flick and touch of his brush, warmth in the chosen colours, his lips moving in silent conversation – his world polarized by and devoted to Rachel.

Malachy slipped away unnoticed. Robin would

work until he had to sleep. That could well be after twenty-four straight hours of painting. He'd once asked Robin if he could install a video camera because it would be so fascinating to play it back, speeded up. The artist at work. The artist possessed. Robin had flatly refused.

Out in the gardens, Malachy walked, gulping in lungfuls of fresh air as if he'd just surfaced from underwater. He smiled at his pre-teen self – he'd taken Oriana the *æbleskiver* that night, going outside and throwing stones up at her window in their secret code to alert her. One, two. Wait. One, two. But the fritters were so light that the bag just floated back down to him well short of her arms. *Don't worry*, she'd said, *not hungry*.

You OK?

Me OK.

Idiots, Malachy said. *You can stay at ours?*

They're just idiots, Oriana had said.

Now he walked across the grass, around the house and over the drive towards the Ice House. He fancied a cup of tea with Paula. Or a beer with Rob. Or maybe, he just wanted company. As he walked, Malachy thought back some more – Rachel had left Robin not long after that. It was scandalous at the time. People were as shocked that it was Bernard she'd left Robin for, as they were horrified that she'd left her child. He was about to knock on the de la Mares' door when suddenly he paused.

He stepped away, almost staggered a step or two backwards. With sudden and startling clarity he now understood how love had nothing to do with it. It wasn't about love or lack of. Leaving Robin and choosing Bernard was Rachel making the conscientious decision to self-lobotomize. Ultimately she'd done so to save her own life.

When I was . . .

When I was twelve my birthday was unforgettable but I would do anything not to remember it. I can't recall my eleventh at all – that was the first one after my mother left. But when I was turning twelve, my mother insisted that I had a birthday party though I didn't really want one. People my age were having trips to the cinema or out for a pizza for their birthdays. But she was adamant – and she told my father it was to be at Windward because 'that's where the girl lives'. I suppose, looking back, it wasn't about me, it was all about my mother. At the time, with my mother reappearing at Windward trailing bunting and balloons, it felt peculiar to be the centre of attention. I remember how she and Bernard made trip after trip back out to their car, bringing in platters and trays piled with party food. My father stood by, watching as his ex-wife commandeered the kitchen while her new husband made awkward adjustments to this platter of crustless sandwiches and that tray of fondant fancies, or this jug of celery sticks and that bowl of Twiglets. In the end, my father just went back to his studio to paint, at which point my mother made much of an enormous sigh of relief.

And then the guests came. Nearly everyone in my class. And Malachy and Jed. And a Windward girl called Plum who was a little younger than me and her sister Willow who was a little older. Louis came down, Lilac and George too. There was no need for party games and there was no official entertainment – the tea banquet was the focus. It was straight from the pages of Lewis Carroll. We almost didn't dare eat the food, suspecting that it couldn't possibly be real, not that quantity and variety. Everything seemed so plump – the mini sausage rolls were in puffed-up pillows of pastry, the muffins were spilling corpulently over the paper cases, all manner of bright fillings oozed from sandwiches, icing had been applied to cupcakes like cement from a trowel.

But eat we did. We gorged ourselves and every time an obese vol-au-vent went, my mother seemed to pluck another from thin air and replenish the plate. It was all delicious – hyper-sweet or fabulously salty, just what we craved at that age. And the birthday cake itself – so monstrous in its extravagant confection that, when it appeared, everyone fell silent. It looked like a pile of hatboxes of diminishing sizes stacked in a precarious tower; chocolate, chocolate and more chocolate, globs of cream and huge mutant strawberries. It took both my mother and Bernard to bring it in. This year, my mother hadn't stinted on candles; they circumnavigated the haphazard tiers like flares marking the way of a magical, terrifying spiralling pathway.

They called for my father.

No singing until Robin is here. I said NO singing until Oriana's father comes. Don't touch! Be quiet, everyone – silence!

The candles had burnt halfway down by the time he came. He looked flustered. He was in rolled-up shirtsleeves. Quite something for him not to be painting in his suit jacket. He scratched at his hair while mouthing the words to Happy Birthday. I blew and I blew and, when finally all the flames were out, everyone chanted at me to make a wish. They told me to cut the cake and scream when the knife touched the bottom – for good luck.

That's not my scream.
  That's my mother.

And it was bloodcurdling.
  Almost immediately everyone in the room saw the cause.
  A woman had appeared from my father's studio and was walking across our main room as if none of us was there. And the room was vast – it had been the original drawing room of the house. She sauntered across it with no urgency, no awareness of her audience. She walked steadily past us all, towards my father, at ease with her butt-nakedness. She had small perky breasts, nipples out like bullets, buttocks creamy and round like scoops of ice cream. She had no hair on her body, which I thought was alarming as even I had just a little.
  Oh for God's sake, Rachel, my father hissed. She's my life model.
  And I thought to myself, how long has she been here, this naked lady? I had no idea there'd been anyone else in my home apart from my father and me. After my mother left my father, we were acutely aware of her absence because it brought with it a soundlessness our apartment had never known. We didn't converse much, my father and I. The quietness was private to both of us. Yet I could hear clearly the scrape of palette knife against canvas two rooms away, much as my father could hear me buttering toast for our tea. I was shocked, therefore, at the silence of real nakedness going on behind the closed door of my father's studio. It

*was more shocking to me than my mother's hollow scream
on my twelfth birthday.*

When I was thirteen, I had two birthdays. Mum and
Bernard were off on a cruise so they had to rush through
my birthday a week early. They picked me up from school
and took me into town for supper because my mother still
harped on about never stepping over the Windward
threshold as long as she lived. Or 'over my dead body'
she'd say if she was being even more dramatic and morbid.

I was hoping for a radio-cassette recorder – Malachy had
one. Every Sunday, he let me and Jed sit in his room and
'watch' the Top 40 on the radio. That's how I learned which
bands were cool – if Malachy recorded it, I knew it was
worth memorizing the lyrics and the tune by heart. I couldn't
decide whether it was art or science – but it was visually
impressive – Malachy's perfected method of pressing the play
and record buttons at precisely the moment the DJ stopped
talking and the song began, releasing his fingers an inspired
millisecond before the music faded and the presenter barged
in again. 'You can borrow the tapes any time you like,' he
told me. I did borrow one, not that I had anything to play
it on – I simply wanted it in my possession, just so that I
could imagine what being a bona-fide teenager must be like.
That intriguing brown ribbon containing the music that
made life OK. If Malachy thought I was mad, he didn't say.
Jed did, though. I was never offended that Jed laughed at
me. It always felt rather wonderful to be so audibly the
subject of someone's happiness.

When I was thirteen my mum and Bernard didn't buy
me a radio-cassette recorder for my birthday. I thought they
had – because the box looked about the right shape. But

it was a set of stuff for the bath. My mother called it a
coffret *and the French accent she used curdled with her*
slightly anglicized American one. Bernard said to me, I had
no idea you wanted a radio-cassette recorder, love. My
mother looked aghast. Well, that's news to me, she said.
But we all knew it wasn't so we pushed the food around
the plates for a bit. This is far more useful, she said, running
her fingers over the display of bubble bath and lotions as
if I was horribly spoiled and ungrateful. Did she truly
believe that tablets of bath salts were more useful to a
thirteen-year-old than the music of a generation?

Malachy made it better. 'What'll she buy you next year?'
he said. 'Scented drawer liners? A frilly shower cap?' He
put his arm tenderly around my shoulders and gave me a
squeeze.

And that was the moment that it felt different. That was
when I felt it.

I'd known Malachy and Jed for ever and we'd always
roughhoused and linked arms and poked each other and
ruffled each other's hair. But that day, Malachy's touch felt
different from before. And different from Jed's.

At thirteen, there was no way I was having a party –
not after what had happened the year before. But I knew
Jette had spoken to my father who then told me I could
invite a gaggle of girls for the afternoon. I hadn't a clue
whether there was a model in his studio, naked or clothed.
I didn't intend to find out. I had no need to – Malachy
lent me his radio-cassette player and a tape of the current
Top 40, abridged for coolness – a seamless medley with no
DJ banter. Cat was there; she bought me leg warmers. She
told me Django had laughed at them, offering to cut the
sleeves off one of his Peruvian pullovers instead. We

convened in my room, five or six of us, and it wasn't about it being someone's birthday. There was no cake, no balloons. It didn't matter – it was all about being together. It was about singing. And leg warmers.

'These are from my mum.' Malachy came by just to deliver a plate of fritters from Jette.

Who is he! my friends wanted to know.

What's his name! How old is he! Oh wow – who is he!

He's Malachy, I told them.

And it was then that I thought to myself, he's Malachy – and he's mine.

CHAPTER EIGHTEEN

When Oriana considered how hard she'd found it working out where she'd go from her mother and Bernard's in Hathersage, deciding to leave Cat's lovely home was bizarrely easy. It surprised her that the decision of where she'd go was so simple. She had no job, she had already dipped into her savings. Her future, in some ways, was currently wholly dependent on her past. Really, she had no alternative other than to return to it.

'Are you *sure*?' said Cat, trying her best to wrap her arms around Oriana, despite her bump holding them apart.

'Sure sure.'

'You can stay.'

'I know.'

'But are you sure you want to go *there*?'

'Sure sure.'

'Well, you know where we are.'

'Cat,' said Oriana, 'I know you'll always, always be here.'

'But when will you go?'

'Well, I'm hoping the weekend,' said Oriana. 'I'm going to phone him now.'

'You haven't asked him yet?'

'No.'

'Well, if there's any problem – or if you change your mind, or if it doesn't work out, or if you miss us – you know you can stay here.'

'I know,' said Oriana, starting to well up. 'I don't know how to thank you.'

There were two numbers to choose from but Oriana opted for the one most likely to be answered on a Thursday afternoon. And so she dialled. It was a woman's voice that answered.

'Kidson Hazel Meade, good afternoon?'

She put Oriana through.

'Jed Bedwell.'

'Jed?'

'Yes?'

'It's me.'

'Hullo, me.'

'It's – Oriana.'

Silence. 'Oriana?' Stillness. *'Oregano?'* Laughter. 'Are you serious? Hullo!'

'Hullo. I hope it's OK to call you at work?'

'Of course! Christ! I'm – I mean. It's great to hear from you. I assumed – well, I hadn't heard from you.'

Oriana thought about it. 'I've had so much to sort out.'

'It's OK. That's fine. It's just good to hear your voice.' Oriana could hear him smile as he spoke. 'It's good that you phoned. How *are* you?'

'I'm well – thanks, Jed.'

'I'd love to see you.' Jed looked around the office, open plan and buzzing. How could no one sense that something glorious was happening to him? 'I'd really love to see you.'

Oriana thought, make it happen. It was a favourite phrase of Casey's – finally she'd commandeered it with no thought for him.

'Jed, you can say no. It's just – I was wondering, hoping, that it might be OK with you if I came and stayed. Just for a while.'

It was Christmas. It was his birthday. He'd won the lottery. It was the best day ever and the first day of the rest of his life.

'Of course it's OK, Oriana. Of course it's OK.'

'Are you sure?'

'Sure sure!' said Jed. And Oriana suddenly remembered it was his phrase, not hers. 'When?'

'This weekend? I can borrow Cat's car – I don't have much stuff.'

'Cat McCabe?'

'Yes – long story.'

'Cat McCabe! God, we have so much to catch up on.'

'I know.'

'Years. And *years*.' Jed paused and laughed. 'Fuck!' It was amazing, bizarre. 'Fuck! It's going to be great!' People were looking at him now – but his colleague was tapping his watch and pointing at the meeting room. 'I have to go,' he told Oriana. 'I have to go – I'll call you later.' He paused and softened his voice. 'And I'll see you very, very soon.'

* * *

190

Oriana stared at the phone for some time, as if it had become a small plaque commemorating her considerable achievement of making a decision and getting on with her life. Wasn't she just taking skeletons out of closets, dusting them off and interring them decently?

'And Jed said?'

But Oriana was deep in thought and didn't hear Cat.

'And Jed said let's eat bread and let's get wed and go to bed and call our red-head baby Ted.'

'What?' Oriana looked over at her.

'And wear boots of lead,' said Cat, 'and have a horse called Ned.' Oriana frowned. 'Jed?' said Cat. 'And Jed *said* . . .' God, this baby was making her insane.

'He said yes.' Oriana didn't look as sure as his answer.

She and Cat stared at each other; a flitter of silent but obvious questions reverberating between them.

'Just be –' Cat thought about the best word to use. '*Aware*.' Oriana tipped her head to one side. Cat continued. 'I mean, I don't know what his life is like these days but I'm just saying you've been elsewhere for all those years but he's stayed here.'

Oriana nodded because she knew what Cat meant. 'I remember when you and Ben lived in Colorado you once said to me how physical distance gave emotional distance from memories and feelings.'

'But Jed's never left. And now you're back here. You mulled over it for months, but to Jed you've returned as abruptly as you disappeared.'

'I will be *aware*,' said Oriana. 'And cautious. And careful.'

'And sensitive.'

'Yes,' said Oriana, thinking of Jed. 'And sensitive.'

'You know he's probably still holding a torch for you?'

'Don't be daft.' But she remembered the fullness of his gaze back in the garden weeks ago.

'And you,' said Cat. 'And Malachy.' She regarded Oriana, concerned. 'Are you *sure* you want to go?'

Oriana nodded and told herself don't you dare bloody cry, you'll set Cat off and she won't be able to stop.

'Sure sure,' she said. 'It's all part of it, isn't it? Coming home.'

Jed arrived back at his flat quite late. The client meeting had been a storming success and the team had gone out for drinks afterwards. He'd drunk a lot but his head remained clear, the adrenalin causing the alcohol to give him a buzz, not a blur. What a day. What a day!

He jiggled the key in the lock and said turn, you bastard thing, *turn*. Then he thought to himself, where the fuck is the spare key – Oriana will need her own key. He thought, I'll get another cut for her – and I'll have to show her how to jiggle it. Then, as the lock finally eased with a satisfying click, Jed thought, I can afford to have a new lock altogether, one that doesn't stick and make me swear. Why don't I just do that?

He opened the door. And suddenly it struck him.

Oriana had phoned him at work; her call had been diverted to the main switchboard and then redirected to his desk phone.

I said I'd call her later – but I still don't have her number.

And then he realized something else.

She said she's coming at the weekend – but how does she know where I live?

CHAPTER NINETEEN

'I'll bring the car back later,' Oriana told Cat. 'It seems wise to drop some of my stuff there today – then you can take me tomorrow and it'll be more relaxed. You could even come in.' Oriana's voice had a caught crack of tears in her throat belying her outward smile.

'At least I have advanced pregnancy to blame for being an emotional fruitcake,' said Cat, tearful. 'You're just –'

They shrugged at each other.

'Nervous,' Oriana admitted. 'Now it's come to it.'

Cat put her hand on Oriana's arm. 'It's OK. You're brave and you're beautiful and you're making a good decision.'

'I'm *really* apprehensive, actually,' Oriana said.

'I'll see you after work.' Cat looked at her watch. 'I'd better shoot.' She paused. 'Can't believe you're leaving me.'

'Stop being so histrionic,' Oriana laughed.

In Cat's car, Oriana sat awhile. She thought of nothing, just immersed herself in the calm environment of a stilled car. She was in transit again and it felt like a bubble, a place of suspended time. She was all by herself but she felt safe and not alone; a benign no-man's-land between the life of Cat and Ben and the brave new world of Jed. She was ready. She started the engine and drove away.

If he's there, he's there, she said to herself. I'll deal with it.

Windward seemed to be completely empty; she could sense this as soon as the house came into view from two-thirds of the way along the drive. It was peculiar because she'd never known Windward to have no outward signs of life. Today, she had to acknowledge that Windward wasn't the Windward she'd known. When she'd lived there, it was a place of work, a hive of activity, a melting pot of creativity as well as home to like-minded if disparate souls. It had been like a tangle of colourful yarns somehow knitted into something beautiful and useful.

Compared to that Saturday of Oriana's first visit – when it felt more normal because there were children out and windows open and the sounds of families – today, on a Friday, Windward was deserted. Few cars were around. It was anomalously quiet. She sat in Cat's car and waited a moment or two before stilling the engine.

'People have gone to work,' she murmured. 'That's what they do these days. They only live here.' She thought about it. If that was the case, they only really had a slice of Windward. She recalled the estate agent's particulars which Cat and Django had shown her. What was the shoutline? *'Windward is an exclusive, peaceful and orderly place to live,'* she quoted to herself. Little did they know! No mention had been made of the fact that two of the original pioneering inhabitants were still there. People don't want bohemian these days. They want order and anonymity. They want luxury and solitude after a stressful day at work. They want containment and no spillage. They want to forget the rest of the world. And these days they pay big bucks for the privilege.

The facts and figures of Windward were too extraordinary to be forgotten – and yet few would actually know them. She could still recall vividly Malachy and Jed's father telling them how he'd negotiated rent of £16 per month which was a bargain, even then. And then, in 1973, they'd all chipped in and bought it for a song. £35,000. And now Louis' apartment was for sale for £400,000 and mysteriously had three bedrooms and two bathrooms. What a vulgar insult to those lovely proportions! What daft bugger would pay that for it? Some stressed-out soul with enough money to buy sanctuary, to buy back their sanity.

'I digress,' Oriana said out loud. 'I'm just stalling. Come on, woman, *come on.'* She got out of the car. Stretched. Breathed deeply. 'Welcome home.'

At some point she really would have to go past her old home; she'd need to look up at the windows and, if necessary, acknowledge the person inside. But, for the time being, she didn't have to go to that side of the building and she could justify that she wasn't avoiding it, she was simply taking her stuff to the Bedwells'. The entrance to their apartment was at the front of the house, probably one of only three doors currently never locked. Standing with her bags and suitcase a step or two away from the car, Oriana regarded the building. Despite all the changes to the place, visible or otherwise, Oriana could so easily conjure up the inhabitants of old. How she needed them just now. She was suddenly frightened – the circumstances of her abrupt departure reared caustically from her memory and disrupted the calm she desperately needed to accompany her arrival today. Under her breath, she spoke an affectionate roll call to guide her slow passage towards the front door.

Louis who wore cologne and who declared that all children were revolting though every Windward child felt unconditionally adored by him.

Lilac who'd danced at the Café de Paris, George the composer and their son Rafe, the oldest of all of us, who could play every instrument in the world.

Plum and Willow – daughters of Laurence Glaub, novelist, and his actress wife what's-her-name. What *was* her name? Mousy woman always in the garden. Patty!

Zoot the musician whose real name was Bob – offering friendship and sanctuary to Ronnie and Rod and, for that one summer, so they'd been told, Jimi too.

Gordon Bryce, illustrator extraordinaire of cutting-edge bespoke book-jacket designs for Agatha Christie and Sylvia Plath and Elaine Dundy.

And the Bedwells – architect Orlando and furniture designer Jette, sons Jed and Malachy; the family at the very epicentre of Windward physically, intellectually, parentally.

As she made her way to the great front door, the cast, as vivid now as they had been then, danced around Oriana with the tribe of all the waifs and strays who'd ever convened at Windward. Passing the Corinthian columns, they took her up the grand stone steps, under the temple-like portico and all the way to the majestic double doors. And there they left her. This part was down to her. She placed her hand on the wood and, for a moment, cast a wish deep into the grain.

Look after me.

With her hand on the scalloped brass doorknob, she took a deep breath and pushed the door open. It creaked out exactly the same dissonant scale she remembered from her childhood. And then she was in.

The vestibule. Everyone always enjoyed lingering over that word, emphasizing the invisible 'Y'. Vestibyool. It was amusing to give the area such reverence when it was always a dumping ground for boots and bikes and dead or dying houseplants people forgot to take to the compost heap. There was only one bike today, two pairs of wellingtons, a pair of trainers and two mismatched walking boots. A pile of newspapers in a green tub, glass and plastics ready for recycling in a black one. It needed a sweep.

Inside for the first time in so many years, Oriana really noticed the travesty of the stud wall almost directly in front of her, denying from view the beautiful staircase which rose in one wide sweep before splitting off into two. It had been one of the quirks of the commune – to divide the building so radically and yet amiably. Had Orlando Bedwell, such an esteemed architect, really agreed to so drastically compromise the integrity of the original design, to slander the Georgian architect's vision? But what was it that Jette had told Oriana – a concept that, at the time, had seemed so pioneering to a teenager? Even today Oriana could quote her verbatim.

It wasn't about ownership, my love – it was about sharing. You have the staircase, we'll have the ballroom. In the late sixties it wasn't about tradition, it was about the New and the Now.

The New and the Now. How she'd loved Jette.

Oriana stared at the inner door that would lead straight into the heart of the Bedwells' home. How much of Jette might remain? What degree might be covered up, torn down, remodelled? Suddenly, she wondered if she herself was prepared for change, for the New. She opened the door and entered.

With a sigh of relief, Oriana stood in the kitchen and saw how Jette's Scandinavian eye had provided a legacy as tasteful and functional today as it had been then. There had been no reason to change much at all. The units were still milky grey, the worktop the same scrubbed maple. Even the kitchen table remained, with the mismatched chairs that encircled it as perfect as the different personalities that make up a family. Oriana noted a mug and a plate with toast crumbs beside the sink. And washing-up yet to do from last night and the night before, by the look of things.

She walked on through to the hallway and put down her bags. The bathroom was unaltered though today it seemed cold and unused. No towels on view, no bath mat. No loo roll. Opening the door to Malachy's childhood bedroom, Oriana found little more than stack after stack of paintings. Perhaps he stored the overflow from the gallery here. Jed's old room was completely changed – a sofa bed, a rowing machine; but she couldn't resist lifting the edge of the carpet. The floorboards remained spattered with the paint, black and red, purple, navy and orange. It made her smile and that enabled her to ignore two small oils by her father on the far wall.

Back into the hallway, ahead of her, the *pièce de résistance* of the Bedwells' place. The tall, arched double doors were ajar and, with a deep breath, she pushed them wide open. The ballroom. The original ballroom with its flamboyant proportions, intricate plasterwork, exquisite full-height windows, balcony and sublime bay at the far end. She looked around. It was greatly changed and yet the spirit of the place, so indelible in her memory, was untouched. The piano was still here and one of the vast draughtsman tables. Originally, although there had been three of these desks each busy with drawings and designs, none had ever encroached on the space. The same purple velvet sofa remained, about twice as long as any normal sofa, in need of some repair these days – just a throw or couple of scatter cushions would suffice. She thought to herself that perhaps she'd provide them, like a moving-in gift. She noted new items of furniture too, paintings she'd never seen, a state-of-the-art sound system and a very large, black, glossy television. There was a navy-blue pullover slung over the arm of the Eames lounger, a pair of suede moccasin slippers with the backs trodden down. Another dirty plate with a blackened banana skin on it.

'It's all a bit dusty,' Oriana said quietly, running her fingertip along. She wondered how often Jette visited. Ten years ago, when Oriana had last asked her mother about Malachy, Rachel had told her that Orlando and Jette had moved back to Denmark. *Do you have an address for them? No, I don't. Where's Malachy? I don't know.* Even if her mother had known, Oriana doubted that she'd have told her.

She went to yank up the sash windows and open the balcony doors to let the fresh air in, but she was momentarily transfixed by the sight of six pieces of yellow film, each covering random sections of glass. Quickly, she stepped out onto the balcony and back into the memory of Jed clambering over it and grappling his way down to see her a few weeks ago. She looked out and gazed at the cedar, her cedar. Then she turned to the room again and opened the door along the back wall into what had been Jette and Orlando's bedroom. Here was the biggest change. It was obviously still the master bedroom but now – yes – it had an en-suite shower room. She laughed.

'I remember you two coming back from rugby or football and your dad hosing you down outside, midwinter,' she said to a photo of the brothers aged around nine and twelve. 'I remember your mum berating the fact that in an apartment this size, there was only one bathroom.'

Oriana stood awhile with her memories, challenging herself on this crazy thing she was doing, trying to make a sensible present out of an insane past that happened right here at Windward. She was gasping for a cup of tea. Back in the kitchen she opened cupboard doors and drawers to orientate herself. She was quite appalled at how disorganized it was, and how relatively barren. The contents of the fridge were shocking. Beer and butter, unwrapped cheese, pots of Greek yoghurt and two jars of chutney. There was just about enough milk for her tea – but a sniff at it made her pour it away and drink the tea black. She sat at the table and made a shopping list. If she was going to stay here, she couldn't spend all her time captivated by reminiscences. She had to make it work. She'd need to ensure she was useful, thoughtful and generous – as she'd been at the Yorks'. If one ignored the cot incident. It prompted her to phone Cat.

'I think I'll stay here tonight and drop the car back with you tomorrow – is that OK? I just want to do a shop and unpack. Maybe cook something. I think that would be nice. He obviously doesn't look after himself particularly well.'

'Have you seen him?'

'He'll still be at work – I guess he'll be back around six?' She looked at the kitchen clock which had stopped. She looked at her watch. It was just gone five.

'Don't worry about the car,' Cat was saying. 'I've

decided Ben can be chauffeur from now on because I can't fit comfortably behind the steering wheel anyway. And his car has Isofix for the baby seat.'

'So I'll see you tomorrow – I'll phone you in the morning?'

'Bet you stay up all night rampaging down memory lane,' Cat said. 'Say hi from me.'

Oriana liked Cat's little car. She wondered if Cat might even lend it to her for longer – on account of its being unable to Isofixate, or whatever it was that babies required. Heading for the Sainsbury's between Matlock and Blenthrop, she pulled over halfway along the drive to let a car pass, on its way home to Windward for the weekend. She didn't notice the driver. She didn't know it was Malachy.

CHAPTER TWENTY

I'm sure there was milk.

I *definitely* had milk.

The kettle had boiled, the tea bag was already in the mug and Malachy wanted his customary cup of tea. He continued to look in the fridge, on every shelf, convinced he could will the milk to appear. He laughed at himself, closed the fridge and opened a cupboard door, rooting around for a jar of coffee whitener and reading the label to see if it would do for tea.

No.

Fuck it, he'd have to have coffee at a time when really, only tea would do.

How can coffee whitener have a sell-by date? Thinking about it, when was the last time he'd used it? He unscrewed the lid. It was still sealed. He couldn't actually remember buying it but as the sell-by date itself was almost two years ago, that was hardly surprising. He thought back to which girl he might have been with at the time. Who was the coffee drinker? Who might have bought it? Who might have been fed up with him running out of milk or having milk past its best? He laughed at himself again.

'Any one of them!'

None had been relaxed about Malachy's relaxed attitude towards food freshness or pantry management.

He broke through the foil seal, sniffed the contents and spooned out the slightly crisped, congealed powder.

'Who needs Starbucks,' he said. And then he noticed the cup and saucer on the kitchen table and all thoughts of coffee were shelved. He never used that cup and saucer, he'd forgotten he even had them – they must have been right at the back of the cupboard. On closer inspection, it appeared to be a third full of black tea. He put his hand against the china. Lukewarm.

'What the fuck?'

He looked in the sink. Just the items of overdue washing-up. He looked under the sink and there, in the bin, the rinsed-out carton of off milk. He looked again at the cup, felt it once more, observed the chairs, gazed about the kitchen. But there were no further clues.

'So where are you, Goldilocks?' he murmured under his breath, leaving the kitchen. 'Hullo?' Silence. 'Who's been sitting in *my* chair?' But he knew the place well enough to know it was empty.

He'd never given a girlfriend a key – they'd never needed one because he'd never locked a door in his life. So who was it? Who'd returned? And why? Perhaps it wasn't a girl but a bloke. Was there someone who bore him a grudge, who was lurking behind a door ready to cosh him? Some tough guy who steeled his nerves with tea in a china cup and saucer? Shit – whose woman did I steal? But he knew the answer to that – no one's. It had never been Malachy's style.

Walking through from the kitchen, he then came across the luggage. A suitcase, a holdall, a laptop case, a couple of carrier bags. No identifying tags on any of them. He peered into the open plastic bags without disturbing the contents. Clothes – just jeans, it seemed. Trainers – quite small. An iPad. A couple of paperbacks. Crime fiction – who did he know who read crime fiction?

'Am I stupid? Someone breaks into my house and I'm too polite to rifle through their things to find out who they are?'

Still, he couldn't bring himself to open the case or holdall and it never crossed his mind to switch on the iPad. He looked in at Jed's old room and the bathroom. No further signs in either. He went through to the ballroom and saw the windows were open. Had someone seriously climbed up to the balcony to let themselves in? If so, it can't have been anyone who knew him very well. He went through to his bedroom. Who's been sleeping in my bed? But there was nobody there. He sat on the sofa and waited. What else could he do?

As Oriana breezed her shopping trolley up and down the aisles, she wondered about Jed and what he liked to eat. Apart from beer, blackened bananas, stale cheese and off milk. She thought back to all the delicious dishes Jette had made, the spectacular Danish feast on Christmas Eve of roast pork followed by their traditional massive trough of *risalamande*. Invariably, everyone was too full to really want any rich rice pudding but nevertheless they always wielded their spoons as though it was war and gobbled it down praying for someone to find the whole almond as soon as possible. Oriana found it one year and won the marzipan pig. She'd eaten her prize there and then, fearing it wouldn't taste quite the same away from Jette's incomparable domain. Once back home, though, she had thrown up spectacularly. Which Christmas had that been? How old was she then? She remembered that only her father was there so her mother had already gone. But both boys had been there too. It was coming back to her – there'd been laughter and togetherness that evening; even her father was amiably chatting about Cocteau and Picasso and Ivon Hitchens having a model who'd once posed for Matisse. She'd sat by Jed who'd squeezed her hand under the table and all the while she'd looked over at Malachy, on tenterhooks for the electrifying moments when their eyes might bore into each other. It struck her that it was the last Christmas. Before it happened. The last Christmas that they were as they were, all together.

Oriana found herself standing stock-still in the personal hygiene aisle of Sainsbury's, absent-mindedly staring at condoms. She shook the assault of memories from her head and moved on, selecting toothpaste and loo roll and shower gel and shampoo-conditioner. As she continued to fill the trolley, she thought about the night ahead, of tucking down in Jed's old room, a stone's throw from her childhood home, spitting distance from her father. It would be decidedly strange. Maybe she should buy some sleep aid. But she chose to add two bottles of red to the trolley instead. Perhaps being drunk was the better option.

'I really have to get a job,' she winced under her breath, pushing her credit card into the reader. But she didn't begrudge spending her dwindling funds on resuscitating Jette's kitchen.

Malachy heard the door open. He remained where he was, sitting on the sofa. He hadn't moved. There were no lights on and it was almost dusk now. Whoever it was wouldn't know that he was there. He wondered what to do next. And whether it was up to him to do anything at all. Maybe he should stay right here – just as his father had, stern and displeased, on that sole occasion when a teenage Malachy had returned three hours late and blind drunk.

Lights went on. The person went out again, then returned and did this twice more. They weren't venturing beyond the kitchen. Cupboards were being opened and closed. Malachy could hear the jostle of shopping bags, the clunk of them being brought in, plonked down, unpacked. He'd never ordered a supermarket home delivery. In fact, he mostly avoided supermarkets. What the fuck? Enough. He was waiting no longer. He slipped his eyepatch back down and ventured out of the ballroom to find out just who was in his home.

Oriana froze at the sound of footsteps. She had assumed Jed wasn't back from work yet. Frantically, she looked around and felt dismayed – she'd wanted everything neatly put away and supper cooking for when he arrived back. The place looked ransacked. Quickly, she brushed her fingers through her hair, gave her cheeks a little pinch, cleared her throat and prepared to trill ta-da!

Malachy?
  Oriana?
  Here?
What are *you* doing here?

Malachy couldn't actually say anything. He was flummoxed and surprised and delighted and irked and the emotions blended into a swirl of dumb-foundedness that rendered him unable to blink or think, to swallow or speak. Synapses and nerve endings flared inside him, yet he was incapable of twitching a muscle.

Oriana, in comparison, was in full flight mode and she gasped, staggering backwards and crashing into the stove.

'What are you doing here!'

It was her visible shock that released Malachy's vocal paralysis, even if he was still stuck motionless in the doorway.

'I think it's me who should be asking *you* that,' he said.

'I'm just waiting for Jed – I've done some shopping.'

Wildly, Oriana gestured around the kitchen before

her arms dropped to her sides, leaden. Her face was flushed and her eyes couldn't stay still.

'Jed's coming here?' Malachy took his phone out of his back pocket and checked the messages. Nothing. He hadn't heard a word from Jed since the weekend they'd both seen Oriana almost a month ago.

'Yes?' She wondered why Malachy looked so surprised.

'That's odd,' said Malachy. 'He didn't say.'

'Does he have to?' Oriana asked, relaxing a little at Malachy's bewilderment, even glancing in a bag on the table to check if the contents needed to go in the freezer.

'Sorry?'

'I mean – was *he* expecting *you*?'

'Jed? Expecting me?'

'Yes – was he expecting you to be here too, then?'

Malachy frowned, tipped his head and regarded the surreal scene playing out in front of him. Oriana was in his kitchen and as confusing as everything else was, the fact remained that Oriana was actually *right here* – in his kitchen. Though bizarre, there was nothing wrong with that. Now as then, whenever Malachy saw Oriana, he was helpless not to soften and that was not a bad feeling to have.

'I live here,' he said. Oriana was in his kitchen with bags of shopping. Those were her things out there in the hallway. Jed was some abstract part of the equation but he wasn't here now and for the time being he didn't matter. It was as perfect as it was peculiar. It was irrelevant what any of it meant and that nothing made sense. Just imagine that all of this is quite normal. Go with it. See where it takes you. Oriana's here.

'I live here,' he told her again. Now able to move, he stepped towards her, so close that the fabric on their sleeves brushed. Malachy looked into a bag. Pistachio nuts. Sun-dried tomatoes. Fresh garlic and chillis. Olive oil. An aubergine. He looked at Oriana; she was so close he could count every eyelash.

'*I* live here,' he said a third time. 'Not Jed.'

He shrugged. He started to unpack the items and put them away into the cupboards of his kitchen. He was naming them under his breath as he did so, just as Jette used to do.

It made no sense. Oriana sat down heavily and stared at the surface of the kitchen table, her hands in her lap, shoulders a little hunched. The teacup was there from earlier, from when she'd first arrived, when it had still been Jed's home, when everything seemed simple and straightforward and all she had to do was nip out to the shops and make a nice supper for them both. Malachy had put the rest of the shopping away. Now he was holding up one of the bottles of wine and proffering it to her; his expression a gentle question mark. Oriana nodded. He poured two glasses.

'Pistachio?'

He opened the packet but she just continued to gawp.

'I prefer cashews myself,' he continued blithely. 'Though actually, with red wine, I favour the classic,

211

ready-salted crisp. But I don't think you bought any.'

How could he banter as if there was nothing out of the ordinary about Oriana stocking his cupboards? It did strike him as decidedly odd that he could feel so calm, so light, about her being here. Oriana, however, was so bewildered she could not theorize, she could only run through known facts out loud.

'When I came, a month ago, Jed was here,' she explained slowly. 'He was on the balcony, I was on the lawn and he came down to see me.' She paused and racked her mind for precise memories. 'He did not say that he did not live here.'

Malachy thought about it. 'Did he say I lived here?'

Oriana frowned, trying to remember. The cacophony of the current jumble rendered the conversation with Jed so faint, she could barely make out even the gist of what had been said. It seemed as distant a part of her past as any.

'He did not say that you didn't.'

Malachy nodded. It made sense to him. The triumvirate of Jed, Oriana, Malachy – why should the years have resolved the complexity?

'Is he coming here – to collect me?'

To Malachy, she suddenly looked like a child left behind, forgotten, at the end of the school day. And then he remembered how she had indeed been that child on more than one occasion. *I'm just going to collect Oriana*, his mother would say, putting down the telephone. *Robin must be busy with his painting*.

Malachy looked at her today. 'I don't know if Jed's

coming,' he said. 'I haven't heard from him.' He
paused. 'Shall we call him?'

'Call Jed?' Oriana said.

'Yes – we can phone him right now.'

They looked at each other. They could indeed
phone Jed. It would be easy enough to do so, logical
even. And Jed would breeze through the confusion
and call himself a stupid bastard and say I'll be right
over! crack open the beers! And he'd come and take
her away.

Oriana and Malachy glanced into their wineglasses
and then returned their gaze to each other. For all
they knew, he was already on his way. If that was
the case, then they had only the loaded moments
from now until then. Why hasten them with phone
calls? Why, after all these years and all that had gone
before and all that had happened, why would they
cut short this sacred portion of time that was being
gifted to them? Why consign the present to the past?
Why not just sit awhile with each other in the kitchen
and just be?

CHAPTER TWENTY-ONE

'Did you come in through the window, by the way?'

'Of course I didn't come in through the window. I used the front door.'

Oriana's indignance made Malachy laugh.

'What's so funny?' she asked, curious but not offended, not really.

'The funny thing is, you didn't even make my list of possible intruders,' Malachy said. 'The fact that it might be you never crossed my mind.'

'I told Jed that I'd be here tomorrow – that I'd have Cat's car. I assumed he wouldn't mind me dropping stuff off earlier, you see.'

'But he doesn't live here.'

'I didn't know that. He didn't say.' Oriana paused and helped herself to more wine. She looked over at Malachy who was making patterns out of pistachio shells. She didn't speak for a while. 'Where *does* he live?'

'Sheffield.'

Sheffield. I'm going to live in Sheffield. Stainless steel and the Supertram. Joe Cocker and Jarvis Cocker. A. S. Byatt and Malcolm Bradbury. Heaven 17 and the Human League. ABC and the Arctic

Monkeys. *The Full Monty* and *The History Boys*. And Meadowhall. Sheffield Hallam and Sheffield Wednesday. And Hillsborough. Hi, I'm Oriana Taylor – I live in Sheffield.

'It was a peculiar concept – that I was coming back here to Windward to live. But to think I'm going to live in Sheffield –' She paused, trying to absorb this huge new fact. Reluctantly, she conceded that, however bizarre the thought of living in Sheffield, ultimately it was far more plausible than Windward. Windward, from where she'd run away so often, the home she'd ultimately been banished from, the one place she'd never expected to return to.

'Are we going to eat?' said Malachy, gently butting into her runaway train of thought. 'I *can* cook, you know.'

Oriana brought herself back into the kitchen. For however long this evening might last, she was here, at the Bedwells', alone with Malachy.

'Sour milk, manky cheese and beer?' she said. 'That won't get you onto *MasterChef*.'

Malachy flicked a pistachio shell right at her. She giggled. It was good to hear. Her face was bright and he could barely look.

'I will cook,' she said. 'It's the least I can do.'

'Can I help, at least?'

'I'm good,' she said. 'It's all under control.' Just then, the meal was about the only thing in her life to be so.

'I'll just take a quick shower then.' Malachy made to leave the kitchen, stopped at the doorway and turned to face her. 'OK?' It had nothing to do with the shower.

'OK,' she nodded; a distracted smile.

'You OK?' he persevered, the chosen phrase, his tone of voice, the way he looked at her, rocketing both of them back to years ago.

She thought about it. 'Me OK.'

Alone in the kitchen Oriana knew it was useless trying to compute the last hour into any kind of logic. At some point, Jed would come. Explanations, reasons, excuses, whatever. And then he'd be taking her to Sheffield to live. She could no longer remember whether the point had been to stay at Windward, or whether it had been to stay with Jed, or whether it had been not to contact Malachy, or whether it had been simply to leave Ben and Cat's. As complicated as all of it should have been, it wasn't. Standing in Jette's kitchen with the comfort of so much that was remembered, and with Malachy's quiet calmness washing over her, Oriana discovered how this sudden and extreme disorder was not cacophonous but just a sweetly melodic middle eight in the strange song that was her life. A hiatus. An intermission. The bridge that would link yesterday to tomorrow.

The New and the Now. Those words had been Jette's mantra and here was Oriana standing in her kitchen, embracing them for all their permutations. She had a meal to prepare and Jette's culinary skills to channel and, just then, Oriana felt suddenly so safe that she soared.

Thank you, Jette, for your home within my home – now, as much as then. For the example you set and the love you gave. I've thought of you often. I am sorry.

'Need any help?' Malachy was back. Jeans and a Ramones T-shirt and the moccasin slippers, his hair a little damp.

Oriana handed Malachy a replenished glass of wine. 'No, thank you,' she said. 'Everything is under control.'

Penne with aubergine, roasted peppers, garlic, lemon juice and one finely chopped, red-hot bird's-eye chilli. As she checked the sauce, she found herself wondering if Malachy would be wearing his eyepatch were she not here. She wasn't ready to confront the alternative and she wasn't ready to ask him.

'It smells great,' he said, peering over her shoulder and into the pan.

'Thank you,' Oriana said, ducking away to search unnecessarily in the utensils pot because she couldn't breathe with Malachy so close.

'OK – so I am going to pop in on Robin now,' he said.

Oriana stopped her rifling.

'I look in on him most days,' Malachy explained to the back of the statue that she'd become. 'For his pills. And oxtail soup.'

The sauce was making a sound similar to bubbling volcanic mud.

'Does he know you're here?' Malachy asked.

'No.'

'That's fine,' Malachy said. 'I won't be long.' And just before he left, he laid his hand on her shoulder. 'I understand.'

And Oriana knew that he did.

Malachy ate fast. Her father's undeniable proximity had curdled with the scent of the cooking and quite taken away Oriana's appetite, but she forked single penne slowly into her mouth to be sociable. Malachy was already helping himself to seconds.

'What do you usually eat?' Oriana asked him. 'When you're on your own. Just manky cheese?'

He shrugged. 'Mostly I just grab something on my way home and eat it on my lap as I drive.'

'Like what?'

'Sandwich?'

'For your *tea*?'

'Sausage roll?' Malachy said. 'Sometimes I pop into Sainsbury's and buy a hot rotisserie chicken.'

'And you eat that in your *car*? As you drive?'

Of course he didn't. But he was amused that Oriana was so appalled at the concept. He was happy to find how naturally it came to take advantage of her gullibility. He always used to do this for his own amusement and, despite her protestations, she always loved it, they both knew that. 'It comes in a useful polystyrene box,' he teased her. 'Sometimes I go for noodles, though. Those come in a cardboard container. It's only fractionally messier.' He looked at her. She appeared horrified. 'Finger food,' he shrugged. 'Saves on washing-up. This is the first time I've used cutlery in ages.'

'Malachy,' she said and she shook her head. She wanted to ask him, why aren't you married? Why don't you have someone here for you? Why are you all alone at Windward eating from boxes with your fingers? How long has it been thus?

'Oriana,' he said. 'I'm joking.'

She thought, you could always bloody do that. Tease me, wind me up to the point of roaring frustration but then always placate me and make me laugh.

'Are you vegetarian still?'

'God, no,' she said.

'My mum worried about you when you were – she said alfalfa was for livestock.'

Oriana laughed. 'I remember that! She said something about lettuce being for rabbits. And you said I was practising to be a Bunny Girl and your mum cuffed you and I had no idea why.'

'I was hoping you wouldn't remember that,' said Malachy.

'I've been remembering so much,' said Oriana quietly. 'Things I didn't even realize I'd forgotten.'

'I told them,' Malachy said. 'That I'd seen you. That you look so well. That you've changed so little.'

Oriana looked at her plate.

'They were pleased that I'd told them,' he said, putting his hand gently over hers. 'Honestly.'

'Do they come over?' Would she ever feel able to see them again?

'Most Christmases,' Malachy said. 'But they always stay at Fischers – Baslow Hall – these days.'

They'd finished eating; Malachy's bowl scraped clean, Oriana's still half full.

She looked at her watch.

'Half past nine!'

Much at the same time as Malachy, she sensed Jed was unlikely to turn up that night.

'More wine?' He tipped his head. 'You can stay, you know. Your stuff is already here. Jed will come at some point and you'll be on your way to Sheffield.' They looked at each other. 'But you can stay tonight – if you like.'

How to answer? A simple thank-you would do. Why was it so difficult? She found no assistance in the swirls of the wooded tabletop. There was no meaning to be gleaned from the configuration of her leftover pasta. Malachy's expression, as straightforward as it was also unreadable, was nevertheless benign. You can stay tonight – if you like.

'If you're sure that's OK.' She'd previously told Cat she'd be staying. But that was before Jed's place became Malachy's home.

'I'll clear up,' said Malachy and he stood and collected the plates and it was all decided. Nothing was a problem. Everything was fine. Stay the night – nice and simple. Don't drive home in the dark. Have another glass of wine.

'I'll help.'

'You cooked,' he laughed. 'You get to go through and sit down.' He gave her the wineglasses and the bottle while he ran a sinkful of hot water.

In the ballroom Oriana considered where to sit. There were so many options. The vintage Eames lounger, surely now something to look at, not use. How she'd loved cosying into that chair when she'd been young; the scent of leather, the luxuriousness of it. She gave it a squeeze as if it was Orlando's arm. Lovely man. She could recall him sitting there, smoking a pipe, wryly contemplating the general careening of Windward children that regularly took place in the ballroom.

The window was still open and the room was cold enough so she went and closed it. She caught her reflection in the windowpane. For hours she'd been on the inside, looking out, and suddenly she saw herself as she'd be seen – Oriana Taylor, aged thirty-four, shoulder-length hair, jeans, Converse trainers, American football-team top. She observed how she was; standing there, absolutely there, right in the middle of the Bedwells' ballroom. It was the strangest concept. I. Am. Here. And yet, she could just as easily have been teleported back through the decades as fast-forwarded to the present, because there was a blurring of the distinction between the Oriana of today and of way back then.

She curled into the massive old sofa. She felt surprisingly at ease. The wine had undoubtedly helped but actually it had more to do with Malachy. Whereas Jed would have been bouncing off the walls, twirling her about, saying mad things, filling every moment with energy and exuberance, Malachy was simply washing up. After all that had happened, all the time that had passed, the things that had been done, the things that had never been said, he had very simply welcomed her home.

* * *

Really, he could leave everything to drain, that's what he normally did. Malachy looked at the tottering pile, soapsuds making a slow slither like melting snow. But he took a tea towel and started to dry anyway, making the process unnecessarily methodical and thorough. Then he decided he'd put everything away. And then he looked around and wondered where else he could wipe. And then he had to acknowledge that this had nothing to do with new-found house-pride and every-thing to do with feeling suddenly shy of the girl in the ballroom. He stood in the kitchen and listened. There was only silence. He thought, has she gone out of the window? He thought, has she left? Have I lost her before Jed comes to take her away again?

'Malachy?'

But she was still here. And, as he went through to the ballroom, he noticed her bags were no longer in the hallway.

He wasn't entirely sure where to sit either. Oriana appeared to be partially absorbed into one end of the vast sofa. If he sat at the other end, they'd be like figurines at opposite ends of a mantelpiece, formally placed and somehow disconnected. Instead, he chose his father's lounger, close enough to be in reaching distance of her.

'I wasn't sure if it was just for show these days,' Oriana said of the chair.

'Charles Eames would turn in his grave – chairs are functional.'

'It's a design classic.'

'It's a chair.'

'It's an heirloom!'

'*It's. A. Chair.*'

She laughed and he grinned. Her phone buzzed through Cat's response to her hasty text. 'Poor Cat's been having kittens wondering if I'm OK.' She glanced at the message.

WTF! Malachy not Jed? SHEFFERS?! FFS! OMG!

'When's her kitten due?'

'Six weeks or so.'

'Here's to Cat,' said Malachy, raising his glass. 'I liked Cat.'

'You fancied Pip.'

'I did not,' Malachy said.

'You did so!'

'I snogged Fen when I was about fourteen. Bet you didn't know that.'

'Of course I did,' said Oriana. She raised her glass. 'Anyway, here's to Ben – he's the tomCat.' As she took a sip of wine, she wondered about something. She looked at Malachy quizzically.

'Do *you* have children, Malachy?' It was quite possible.

He smiled into his glass. 'No,' he said, 'I don't.' He looked at her. 'Do you?'

She shook her head.

'Been married?' he asked.

She shook her head. 'You?'

'No.'

It was so bizarrely plausible that both might have had children, might have married. Time had not stood still, after all.

'Girlfriend?' she asked.

'No – not right now.' He thought about it. While

223

he didn't mind Oriana asking and while he was happy to answer, how much did he actually want to know in return? 'You?' he said, after a pause.

'*Girl*friend?' she said, with mock surprise.

'Bloke – you idiot.'

She shook her head but, he noticed, not without reddening a little.

'Is that why you came back?'

'What – to find a bloke?'

He looked at her levelly. 'To get away from one?'

She thought, how does he know? And she thought, because Malachy knows me. She thought, and I changed country. Like I did once before.

But then she realized something. While she was sitting right there, with Malachy, she knew that she hadn't left the United States because Casey had left her. She'd left because she'd always known that at some point she would be destined to return here. Whether she wanted to or not, whether she admitted it or not, whether she liked the place or professed to hate it, ultimately Windward had pulled her back at a time when she was free and open to return. She'd had no idea that she'd find Malachy there. And now she was here, with him. Privately, she thanked all the stars on that spangled banner she'd been waving for the last sixteen years.

It struck her how Casey was a fraction of the man that Malachy was. That the feelings she'd had for him were risible against the depth of love she felt for Malachy. She was caught – not wanting to waste time talking about Casey, but wanting only to be honest with Malachy. When she'd confided in Cat, digging up the details was like gutting a fish. It was messy, unpleasant. This evening that she'd had so far with Malachy, the night that stretched ahead – why would she actively sully it? Why not ensure that every moment – and they were passing fast, it was already gone eleven – was filled with goodness, not detritus?

'His name's Casey,' she told him. 'He was married. It went on way too long. I regret it.'

To Malachy, it seemed to make sense. He thought about how to respond. 'Were you in love?'

'I liked to think so at the time,' she said. 'I'm very clear that I was deluded.'

He considered it. 'Idiot woman.'

'I know.' She winced.

'Idiot woman.' The repetition was underscored with kindness.

Oriana looked up from her lap. 'I'm sorry.'

He didn't understand.

'I'm sorry that I haven't come back with wholesome adventures to recount.'

'I'm just glad you're OK,' Malachy said. 'Sometimes, adventures are overrated.'

'Aye to that,' said Oriana and she leant forward and touched her glass against his.

Into the small hours they talked. They shared and swapped and informed and listened. There was so much to say, so much to learn; so many years to account for. Sometimes, they simply fell silent and just sat, holding empty wineglasses and each other's gaze, fleeting smiles underscored with long-term tenderness and desire. They talked about themselves and questioned each other, sensitively, impudently. They discussed random things; Tories and Republicans, the rules of American football, whatever happened to Judd Nelson, whatever happened to everyone who'd ever lived at Windward. Do you remember? Yes, I remember. Impossible to forget.

It was very late. Oriana shivered and Malachy passed her the navy pullover she'd seen earlier. She put it on. It smelt good. They sat a while longer, not ready to relinquish each other's company for something as sensible as sleep. Malachy stifled a yawn and rubbed his forehead, slipping his fingers under the ribbon of his patch, a swift swipe right under it. Oriana was consumed by a surging need to go to him, to offer her cool fingers for the purpose, to heal what had been hurt. If it was possible, she was more desperate now than she'd ever been, just to try to make it all a little bit better.

'Malachy?'

He looked at her. 'I'm fine,' he said.

'It's just –' Her voice cracked. 'Are you –'

'It's OK, Oriana,' he said. 'Let's not.'

It was the first time that entire evening that it was suddenly glaringly noticeable that he wore an eyepatch, that he was blind and disfigured behind it. Earlier that evening, when she'd first seen him, what had struck her most was that Malachy simply hadn't been Jed. She hadn't noticed his altered looks at all.

'It's just.' She tried again. 'I don't even know. No one would tell me. And then I was gone.'

He didn't want this conversation now, he didn't

want her to ask, to know, because, quite selfishly, he wanted to keep the night unblemished and beautiful. But the more he looked at her, the more he knew that out of everyone, Oriana had a right to know.

He leant forward, cupped his hands around hers. He spoke softly.

'At first they hoped to save it – my eye. Not my sight, that had gone – that they knew. But it's preferable to keep the eye – to eviscerate, to take away the damaged contents but leave the scleral shell intact. Movement remains good, prosthetics are extraordinary. The problem was that my eye then became phthisical – wasted, dead – which brought the risk of sympathetic opthalmia. After trauma, the good eye can go blind too.' He could feel her recoil into herself, and he held her hands a little more tightly. 'It's OK, Oriana. They were brilliant. Ultimately, they had to enucleate – to take the eye completely – but they saved so much else. Muscles were reattached to the implant and then they –'

He noticed how she was nodding and nodding, her head bowed. He watched a tear cling to the tip of her nose, then drop. Funny really, that he was the one making the soothing 'there-theres'. Would she feel better if he told her about the brilliant ocularist, about the bits of rib bone ingeniously used to rebuild the fractured outer orbital section, the titanium mesh that made his surgeon a genius sculptor too? He could reassure her once more that, beyond six metres, everyone sees the world as if they have one eye. But he sensed it was best to leave it there. No more tonight. Tonight was about discovering that their closeness had been deepened, not widened, by time. Tonight they were together again, just the two of them, in the world within the world that was Windward.

'Does it hurt you?'

'Not any more.'

'If I wasn't here – would you,' she stumbled. 'Would you not wear the patch?'

Malachy nodded.

'Is it because it's me?' she asked in a whisper.

He smiled gently and leant right forward. 'It would be like you seeing me naked,' he said, catching her gaze and holding it. 'Very stark naked.'

Tentatively, he brushed strands of her hair away from her face, tucking them behind her ear, liking how they flopped forward again. He ran his fingertips lightly over her cheek, along her jawline, before turning his hand so the back of it stroked her so gently that she wasn't sure whether he was actually touching her.

Then he stood, offered his hand to Oriana and pulled her up. She felt unsteady, woozy with wine and tiredness and emotion.

'Come on, sleepyhead,' he said. 'Time for bed – it turned tomorrow three hours ago.'

But they hovered. Fixing on Johnny Ramone's name on Malachy's T-shirt, Oriana placed her hand lightly on his chest, stood just a little on her tiptoes and slowly kissed his cheek while his hands found their way to her waist and he kissed her back. There they stood, immobilized by the weight of not knowing what on earth to say or do next.

Eventually, Malachy nodded over his shoulder

towards what had been his parents' room. 'I live *that* way now.' It was as if he was about to walk miles in the opposite direction.

'And I'm in Jed's bed.'

Instantly, she regretted it. No matter how innocent the faux pas, or how many years had passed, and though the words shouldn't have had an ounce of meaning or a wisp of symbolism – they did. They were the crash of cymbals that ended their night. She felt him retreat before he'd taken a step.

'Sleep well, Oriana.'

I'm in Jed's bed.

It was irrelevant that this particular piece of furniture was new. She turned her back on it, went to the window. There was nothing to see in the pitch blackness of the dreamless hour. With silent tears slicing a stinging path down her face, Oriana lifted the duvet from the bed and made herself a cocoon on the floor.

CHAPTER TWENTY-TWO

Jed thought, if I don't go now, I'll either not make it home alone, or not make it home at all. He thought, I really must go. Oriana's coming tomorrow – I need to go home *now*.

'Don't go!' The girl was tugging on his shirt. 'That's so boring!' He wasn't sure what her name was; he wasn't actually sure whether she'd told him or not.

'I have to go,' Jed laughed, removing her hand. She was extremely pretty but absolutely blitzed. For a split-second he cursed Oriana for intruding into what was a sure thing. And then he chastised himself for trying to compare the incomparable. It was all very flattering – and there'd been no one since he'd broken up with Fiona – but did he really want to have sex with this girl? If Oriana wasn't coming tomorrow, would he really be tempted? He hoped not. He took his leave of all these people he really didn't know and scanned the bar to say goodbye to the people he did know, those he'd come in with. Friday nights were one ridiculous cliché, he knew it and yet he was a willing member of the cast. However sincere the intention was to make it just a couple of drinks with colleagues, the liquid in their glasses on this one night of the week always diluted their willpower. Jed observed them now, scattered around the bar like a handful of peanuts flung accidentally from a bowl. Mostly drunk and unforgivably oblivious to how much time they'd devoted to their swift half after work. He was one of them. He had to leave.

The fresh air hit him like a slap around the face, sobering him up enough to realize how much he'd had to drink. He jumped in a cab and at last was headed for home.

'Doing anything nice over the weekend, then?'

'A friend's coming to stay.'

'Oh, yeah.'

'An old, old friend.'

'That'll be grand.'

'She's lived abroad for many years.'

'Oh, yeah – she's a "she" then, this friend?'

'Yes.'

'And "just good friends", is it?'

Jed glanced at the driver's eyes, reflected in the rear-view mirror, which were assessing him with a knowing smirk.

'We'll see,' he told the driver. 'Time will tell.'

Inside, Jed sat awhile on his sofa with a pint glass of water, rotating two Nurofen tablets between his fingers like worry beads. His mind was full, jumbled with thoughts. It wasn't about the proximity of tomorrow, it was about what lay ahead. Tomorrow he would be ready for her – the cleaner had come today and his flat was spruce. The supermarket would be delivering in the morning so the fridge and cupboards would be full. He had no other plans apart from to settle her in. But once she was here, unpacked, orientated – then what? What happens the day after tomorrow? Or next week? He should phone Malachy – phone his brother and say guess who phoned me and guess what. But that could wait.

He swallowed down the ibuprofen and refilled the water glass. He was determined not to have a hangover when he woke and he'd damn well sit up, sipping water until his head felt truly on top of his neck again and the room was steady around him.

What does she like to eat? What does she have for breakfast? Is she a tea or a coffee person? Does she still eat jam straight from the jar? He looked around. She'd like all the books. But he would put all those back issues of *Stuff* and *GQ* in the recycling tomorrow. She'd recognize the little bronze sculpture of the boxing hares that used to stand at the centre of their kitchen table.

'Does she want this place as a hotel – or to make it home?'

He looked over to the CDs and DVDs crammed along the shelves in the two alcoves. I bet she's stayed loyal to Rod and Bruce. He wondered, how much stuff is she bringing with her? His shelves had no space left. He stood, pleased to find the ground was now firmly under his feet. He went over to the DVDs. Has she seen *The Wire*? Shall we watch *The Sopranos* back to back? He pulled out his copy of *Spaced*, wondering whether it was shown in the States when she lived there. He could envisage the two of them relishing evenings in with their teas on their laps, watching boxed sets and laughing at the same things.

'Is she coming here because she needs a place? Or is she coming here – because it's me?'

He went through to his kitchen, small and shiny and open plan with the sitting room. It was still unbelievable that Oriana had even asked – and yet the reality of it was imminent. He ran the cold tap and drank directly, the ice-cold tributary which trickled down his neck making him shudder off the final linger of alcohol. In bed, a little while later, he tried to read. The words didn't bounce around the page, he was pleased to find, but his mind darted this way and that.

'Sorry, mate,' he said to Bruce Chatwin, closing the book and letting it drop to the floor beside his bed. 'Just stay where you are on your Black bloody Hill and I'll come and find you again soon.' He switched off the light and stared at the dark nothingness while his mind tried to tidy away the tumble of thoughts and emotions so that he could sleep.

The sound broke through Jed's dream and turned from being some kind of klaxon at a foreign fair he was at with Oriana, back into his door buzzer. Scrambling from sleep, he hopped his way to the front door whilst pulling on boxer shorts and a sweatshirt. Don't go, don't go! he chanted. I need you like you wouldn't believe.

'Come up!' he called into the intercom. 'Third floor, door on the left – take the lift!' He kept his finger on the button whilst peeling his ears for the clunk and rumble of the lift. Only then did he relax.

Jesus Christ, he said to himself, if I'm this jittery for shitting Sainsbury's, what am I going to be like when it's Oriana?

He hadn't realized how excessive his online shop had been until he found great difficulty finding space for everything. He hated aubergines, yet he'd ordered two. He'd bought new shampoo, conditioner and shower gel though the bottles he already had were mostly full. He'd bought a four-pinter of milk which he could barely cram into his fridge, and a litre of olive oil in such a tall and fancy glass bottle that he had to lay it on its side, and then it protruded too far for the cupboard door to shut.

'I cannot believe I ordered capers,' he murmured, looking at the peculiar little green beads. 'I cannot believe I ordered capers solely because I read somewhere that they're an aphrodisiac.' He laughed out loud and called himself a stupid soft bastard, while wondering if he could risk leaving the *tarte au citron* out of the fridge.

He thought, I wish I'd asked her what time she was thinking of coming. He thought, I wish she'd phoned again just to confirm. He thought, I assume it was Mel on the front desk who gave her my address. He thought, if the MD finds out, he'll fire her. And Jed thought, have I time to nip out for the papers? He thought he probably did, so out he went.

It was one of those sublime, full spring days which kid you it's still cold and crisp but within minutes the sun is seeing off layers of clothing. With his sweatshirt tied around his waist, Jed walked fast to the corner shop for the Saturday papers. He bought two Bounty bars too, because they'd always been Oriana's favourite.

It's the coconut thing, he remembered her saying when she progressed on to Malibu. *It's not the fact that it's booze – it's the fact that it's coconutty. Like an alcoholic Bounty bar.*

On his way home, Jed went via the off-licence and bought a half-bottle of Malibu. Sprinting up the stairs to his flat, he suddenly wondered whether Oriana would absolutely hate all these reminders of her past. Once inside, he consigned the bottle and the chocolate bars to the top of his bedroom cupboard. Then he sat down with the papers and a cup of strong black coffee and he rested from the barrage of thoughts and plans. He drank his coffee and he read the newspaper. And he waited.

CHAPTER TWENTY-THREE

Malachy wondered if Oriana wanted coffee or tea. On his way to the kitchen, he'd hovered by her door and listened. It was so quiet it was quite possible she'd gone. And yet there was a peculiar warmth and calmness to his home that morning and he knew she was still there. Fast asleep at Windward for the first time in God knows how many years.

He boiled the kettle and also set the little coffee pot on the stove top, grateful to Jed for having bought ground coffee and telling him it would keep fresher in the freezer. The scent and the sound of it brewing were uplifting. He made a cup of tea and a cup of coffee and took them along the corridor, placing both on the floor outside the door. He knocked.

'Good morning, Miss Taylor,' he called through, to no answer. He knocked again, this time with a spry rhythm.

'Morning, Taylor!'

Still no reply. He opened the door a fraction. The bed was empty. When did she go?

'Morning, Bedwell.' The sleepy voice drifted up from the mumble of duvet heaped on the floor.

He was alarmed. 'Did you fall out of bed?'

'No,' she said. Her face appeared, like a cartoon creature resurfacing after hibernating. Her hair was mussed and her cheeks were flushed. She was blinking and her face was in a scrunch.

'Is this some weird yogic-Californian-thang? Sleeping on the floor?' Malachy asked. He was still on the threshold, him and the two cups.

She laughed a little. Yawned and stretched her arms up out of the swaddle. 'Yes,' she said, 'it's a Yogi-Bear-den-theng.'

'I made you coffee,' Malachy said. 'And I made you tea.' He paused. 'Take your time. There's no rush.'

He glanced at his watch as he went back to the kitchen. He'd be leaving for the gallery in little over an hour. Oh, that he needn't go. Oh, for an assistant. He'd probably sell nothing today – it was a beautiful day and people would be out in the dales, marvelling at spring, just as they should.

Malachy saw that Oriana had bought croissants. Would she mind if he had one? He had to admit to himself that, despite the serendipity of it all, despite the closeness and intimacy they'd shared last night, these croissants hadn't been bought with him in mind.

Into the kitchen she padded.

'Sorry – I couldn't resist,' he said, through a mouthful of flaky crumbs.

'May I?' Oriana asked, mindful this morning that she was in Malachy's kitchen, not Jed's.

''Scuse fingers,' he said, passing her a croissant.

She spread a little butter on one half. 'I bought jam.'

'You did?'

'The jar you had in the cupboard had charming green fur on it.'

'Adds to the taste.'

She raised an eyebrow and then went to the cupboard. '*Confiture*,' she said, reading the label.

'Bless you,' Malachy said, as if she'd sneezed.

She giggled, relieved, at ease. Her fear, walking to the kitchen minutes ago, was that he'd be aloof with her this morning. Not want her there. She dipped a spoon into the jam and dolloped it straight onto the buttered side of the croissant. Malachy watched as she loaded the spoon again, and this time put it straight into her mouth. He grinned.

'What's so funny?'

'Nothing,' he said, remembering her sitting in various Windward kitchens over the years, spooning jam directly into her mouth. 'Would you like more tea?'

'I need to teach you how to make coffee properly,' she said, walking to the stove to brew a fresh pot, calm and relaxed. The kitchen had once again become a shared space, as it had been last night. They continued with their breakfast in affable silence for a while, passing butter and croissants, passing time. Can I have the milk, please? More jam, dear?

'Oughtn't you to be getting to work?'

'Not just yet,' said Malachy, who was at the sink, his back to her. 'I'll just do the washing-up. I don't want you leaving here thinking I'm a slob.'

She watched him as he did the dishes, liking the way his cotton shirt caught over his shoulder blades, liking how his sleeves were rolled up to just above his elbows. She liked the way the ribbon of his eye-patch wove through his hair as if in an intentional rhythm. Over under, over under. He was wearing dark-wash jeans. On his feet, his moccasin slippers. She'd quite forgotten the chill of the floors in the apartments at Windward. It had confronted her this morning and she could feel it still, through her socks. It was as nostalgic as it was unpleasant. She curled her toes and tucked her feet around the legs of the kitchen chair.

'I'm not going to see my father,' she announced, as if Malachy had posed the question.

'I understand.' He turned to her, drying his hands, unrolling his shirtsleeves and buttoning the cuffs. He paused. 'I suppose I'd better get ready now.'

'It's a beautiful day,' Oriana said, gazing out of the window. 'I might go for a walk around the gardens.'

'And then?'

'I want to say hullo to Lilac,' she told Malachy who was looking at the day outside.

'And then?'

'Well – I'll have a tidy-up, I think. If you don't mind.'

'And then?'

'I need to return Cat's car.' She frowned at him, not realizing he was perversely torturing himself to hear her say, and then I'll phone Jed.

Malachy paused. Was she going to call Jed or just trust that he'd turn up? Would it be the brotherly thing to phone him, perhaps?

'And then?' he said.

'I'm not going to see my father, you know,' she mumbled. She raised her eyes to his and Malachy saw that Jed was far from her mind.

'I understand.' He regarded her. 'But say he sees you?'

Malachy was pushed for time. In his mind's eye, he taunted himself with a long snaking queue of wealthy art lovers, waiting impatiently for the gallery to open. But he didn't want to leave, not just yet. Time just then had a desperate quality – as if nothing could be achieved. Coming out of his bedroom, he found Oriana hovering in the ballroom, pretending she wasn't.

He wanted to say, you can stay here, you know. You don't have to go. But something strangled away his words and he wasn't sure whether that something was raw emotion or pure common sense.

And she wanted to say, perhaps Jed won't turn up. Maybe I'll still be here when you get back.

'I'd better be off,' he said. Why prolong it? What could be said? What could change a thing? The sharp light of day had somehow vacuumed all that time last night and trapped it within a dreamlike orb now floating around like a thought that couldn't be caught. All that had been said, all that had passed between them, was incarcerated in a crystal ball which had no future to tell.

'Bye then.' He shrugged, satchel over his shoulder, hands thrust deep into his pockets. 'You take care of yourself, Taylor, you tinker.'

His soft words, used so often in her past, caused

a sharp shard of flint to wedge in her throat. She couldn't make a sound. She couldn't even say goodbye. Malachy waited for her to respond but all he had to go on was the speechless scramble emanating from her eyes. He had to go. He walked past her, his sleeve brushing hers, just as it had last night, in the kitchen, when she couldn't breathe, right at the start of the evening. She thought back – those hours and hours they'd had. They were now locked in some memory box, confined to the Past. This was the Now and the New. Years on. Separated lives.

He looked back into the room when he reached the doorway but Oriana was turned away from him, gazing out at the day beyond the ballroom. She heard the front door close.

If this was a movie, I'd run right now. I'd run after him, I'd skip down the steps, I'd catch him just as he was about to step into his car. And I'd put my arms around his neck and draw him to me; we'd fold into each other, as close as close can be. We'd stand there, with no need for words. I would hold and be held. And he'd know – everything I could ever say, everything I've always felt – it would flow out of me and into him. Silent soundwaves of truth.

But she stayed where she was. There was no point leaving the ballroom; it wasn't necessary to tiptoe to the kitchen and look out of the window to make sure. She knew that Malachy had already left.

'Oh God – I'm so so sorry.' Paula de la Mare rushed up to Oriana who, after walking to the great cedar to compose herself, had then gone to the front of the house to sit on the front steps and have a think as so often she had, her back to a pillar warmed by the sun. Today, though, she wasn't thinking of anything really. The sunlight on her face felt good enough just to close her eyes and raise her chin towards it, and the air around her still had that soft spike of spring chill that made it so fresh and cleansing.

'*So* sorry – have you been waiting long?'

Oriana looked down to see a breathless, apologizing woman at the bottom of the steps. 'Me?'

'I'm Paula,' the woman said, 'de la Mare. No relation – though the main house was home once to poets and writers and all sorts of artists. Anyway, I'm here – to show you round.'

Oriana wasn't really sure what to say or how quickly to interrupt her and point out the mistaken identity.

'Come on,' said Paula. She jangled a set of keys as if they'd open a world of possibilities. Oriana stood like one in a trance, letting herself be led along by Paula's friendly stream of chat about how sorry she was to have kept her, that time always flies on a Saturday, that she'd lost half an hour already but that there was no rush. They were perilously close to her old front door but Paula strolled straight past and on to the entrance to the interior corridor.

'It's a sort of communal space,' Paula said. 'But private too. It's difficult to explain. Think of it as a covered pathway between apartments. Have you been looking long?' She turned. Oriana had lagged behind.

In fact, she was standing still and mesmerized, having a long look, lips parted, as if she couldn't believe her eyes.

'There is another door – but you'll find this entrance more *serviceable*.' Paula thought, I'm sick of this – bloody estate agent phoning me to say, can you just open up for a viewing? Paula thought, why do they keep sending people so obviously unsuitable?

'Are you OK?'

'I know this smell,' Oriana said quietly. 'I *know* this smell.'

Paula couldn't really detect any scent, fragrant or otherwise, though if she really analysed it, perhaps the York flagstones and old walls gave off a tinge faintly reminiscent of church.

'Anyway,' she said, 'I'll just unlock and leave you to it.'

'Unlock?'

'The apartment.'

Suddenly teleported to the present, Oriana stared at her. 'Whose apartment?'

Paula frowned. What were the estate agents thinking? Had they actually met this woman? Anyone less likely to buy the Coopers' apartment they'd be hard pressed to find.

'Number four.' Paula smiled politely, walked on a few steps and put the key in the door.

'*Louis'* flat?' Oriana quickened her pace. 'This was Louis' flat.'

'Geoff and Helen *Cooper*,' Paula said, holding the door open so that Oriana could enter.

Oriana looked over her shoulder at Paula, her

expression a beguiling mix of excitement and dread. 'I don't know the Coopers,' she said. 'But I knew Louis Bayford – who lived here from 1966. I lived here too, you see. I was born here. I grew up here.'

While Paula was absorbing the facts, Oriana was already walking ahead. She knew the route off by heart but today it thrilled her. When she was little she thought nothing of it – it was simply the way to Louis'. Today she appreciated every footstep: a narrow passage, quite poky, suddenly turning sharply, delivering her right to the base of the elegant staircase. For the first time, she truly appreciated the audacity of the Bedwells' blunt stud wall separating the grand front hallway of the house from the staircase. It was daring, it was outrageous, it was even a little subversive. The Bedwells in the 1960s, leaders of the cult of the New and the Now, proposing that the features of a house were subservient to the personalities who dwelt there.

And it was so very Louis to have opted for the staircase – up and down which he could sweep with maximum theatricality and flounce. Dearest Louis with his powdered, bouffant hair, his eyebrows subtly plucked so that they arched superciliously, his hips-first walk – or 'mince' as he liked to call it. Louis, who gave Oriana sanctuary and pulled pennies from her ears and told her that she could rule the world. It was Louis who informed her that her name had been a nickname of Elizabeth I – and that Oriana was twice as golden, three times as feisty and infinitely more beautiful.

Dear Louis – I'm here again, I've come back.

She was already climbing the stairs when Paula caught up with her.

'I'm sorry,' Paula said, 'but who exactly *are* you?'

'I'm Oriana Taylor.'

'As in *Robin* Taylor?'

'Yes.'

'You're his –?'

'Daughter.'

'And you've come to view number four?' What Paula wanted to say was, he has a daughter? That man is a *father*?

They'd reached the top of the stairs and were both a little breathless; the flight was misleadingly steep despite the landing and the return halfway up. How on earth had Louis managed for all those years?

'I haven't come to buy Louis' apartment. I don't really know what I'm doing here. I'm sorry if I misled while you led me here. I stayed at Malachy's last night,' she said. It acted like some kind of code word and Paula visibly relaxed. 'We go way, way back,' Oriana continued, running her hand lightly over the polished mahogany banister. 'It's all been a bit weird. I haven't been back for so long.'

She and Paula looked at each other. They were around the same age. Oriana liked Paula's style; her boots, the way her eyes emphasized her smile. Paula sensed a connection; what she really fancied was a cup of tea and a long, long chat with this woman. They were standing on the landing in front of the main door to the apartment.

Paula smiled at her warmly. 'After you, then,' she

said, sweeping her hand theatrically to usher Oriana ahead.

But Oriana couldn't do it. Wave after wave of imagery cascaded over her, billows of recall so vivid that tears sprang to her eyes. All that Louis had given her. And she never said goodbye. Oh, to have five more minutes, one last cup of tea, to hear a few final words sweet or salacious. Suddenly, she was acutely aware that behind that door, none of it remained, not a whisper of Louis. The apartment had been commandeered and remodelled without a thought to him. She recalled the property particulars in the newspaper that Cat had shown her. Even from the small grainy photos, it seemed that the transformation of the place she'd known was a travesty and nothing to marvel at. Nothing to see – because it was all nothingy. She didn't want to see a glossy kitchen and hi-spec bathrooms running roughshod over the bohemian opulence that had been Louis'. If it wasn't Louis' any more then whatever the intervening years and a lot of money had done to the place held little interest for her.

Paula's eyes, though, were glinting with anticipation. She tipped her head towards the door and smiled. It was as if, through Oriana, she might step back in time to a Windward she couldn't imagine. But Oriana shook her head. She shrugged and shook her head again.

'I don't want to,' she said. And before Paula could cajole her, Oriana was walking slowly down the stairs, brushing a tear away.

As they walked along the Corridor, she added

further details to the vivid portrait of Louis for Paula. They were a step away from daylight, from leaving the interior and the secrets it held.

'I learned to ride my bike in there,' Oriana said, gazing back. 'I skateboarded and roller-skated and did bowling practice with the boys.' She didn't tell Paula about her first kiss with Malachy. 'We ran up and down like mad things. All the Windward children did. It's one of the wonders of the Corridor – you can't hear a thing that goes on there, from the apartments along it. It's at the heart of everything – yet afforded us our most private times there.'

Outside, the women stood awhile at the side entrance until Oriana walked on, setting the pace at a thoughtful stroll while she and Paula talked easily. An invitation was made for Oriana to visit Paula's home in the converted Ice House – Paula keen to hear Oriana's memories of the shack long before it was remotely habitable. Back at the front of the house, a couple waited – the bona-fide appointment for number four.

'Tell them about Louis,' Oriana said.

Paula gave her arm a squeeze. 'Don't you worry,' she said, 'I fully intended to.'

'Tell them about the throne.'

'And the ostrich feathers. And what happened in Marrakesh.' Paula laughed. 'I'll tell them everything.'

'Louis Bayford,' said Oriana.

'Louis Bayford,' Paula repeated.

CHAPTER TWENTY-FOUR

Jed would kill him – Malachy could imagine the accusation. Why didn't you phone me? As soon as you knew the mix-up – you should've called. But Malachy appeased himself – he was entitled to kill Jed anyway, for concealing Oriana's previous visit to Windward. And if Jed was too stupid or too pre-occupied to have worked out where Oriana was headed, then it was his own fault. Malachy thought, why deny her the chance to spend time at Windward, which is what she wanted to do, in spite of every-thing. And he thought, why shouldn't I have her to myself for one night only – considering she's going off to live with him.

After a surprising surge of visitors mid-morning, the gallery was quiet now, at just approaching lunch-time. They often did this – came through Blenthrop supposedly to stock up on food and drink for a walk on the dales, only to be waylaid by the more unusual shops, of which the White Peak Art Space was one. One time, a couple in walking boots, gaiters and with maps in plastic pouches around their necks had come in and spent an hour and £3,000 on a bronze by Matt Birch. This morning, though Malachy hadn't made a single sale, experience and a hunch said that two of the visitors would contact him at a later date, by phone or email, and he'd sell to one of them if not both.

Has she gone?

Is she still there?

What did she do this morning?

Whom did she see?

He looked at his phone and scrolled through to 'O', staring at the numbers she'd given him as if she'd been reduced to a barcode. He hated phones, he hated text messaging and he hated seeing the population obsessed by these gadgets glued to the palms of their hands, walking gormlessly along with their thumbs in some unnatural yet evolutionary crook hovering over the screen.

But has she left or is she still there?

* * *

Jed looked around his flat. There was nothing left to tidy, sort out or rearrange. Actually, it all looked a little odd to him – like visiting a known place in a dream. His world was just slightly off kilter. Deep down, he sensed that Oriana would bring either balance or chaos. He wasn't sure which. He'd welcome both. He'd have to wait and see.

He went to the kitchen and ate a late lunch right over the sink so as not to spill crumbs anywhere. He gulped it down fast, anticipating the doorbell at any moment and not wanting a gob full of clagging ham-and-cheese sandwich to impede his planned and expansive welcome. Half an hour later, heartburn set in. His body felt as if it was imploding and, hunched, he limped to the bathroom for antacid. He gave himself a long look in the mirror. Despite a haircut the day before and a long shower and good shave this morning, he didn't look good. His eyes were slightly sunken and a little red from the discomfort; his face was pale. He looked at his hairline and cursed it for having receded, even at a mercifully slow pace, since his teenage years.

'Pull yourself together, mate,' he muttered at himself. 'It's only Oriana.'

Of all the people he'd ever known, Oriana was the one with whom he'd felt most at ease and most alive. No one he'd met since had inspired such feelings of heady levelness. Those teenage years when the two of them believed they were pioneers, that they alone had the answers to the most complex questions the universe could ever throw at humankind. Back then, they could talk through entire days and into the early hours while they sorted out the problems of the world, solving poverty, finding a solution to the nuclear question, tearing down the greenhouse effect, pulling the ozone layer tight closed again, saving the whale and fighting for peace. All the while, limbs entwined, fingers knitted.

Jed smiled kindly at himself. 'I believed I knew more about the human condition than any poet, any philosopher.' He laughed. 'I could have lectured the world on What Love Means.'

He felt better, looked around the bathroom: no bristles in the sink, plenty of loo roll, toilet seat wiped and lid closed. He was ready for Oriana to walk back into his life. He was as prepared for this as he'd been unprepared for when she left. It was as if he knew, he always knew, that she'd never be gone for good. She was always destined to return. Fate had decreed it – you're not given a love that vast without being enabled to bring it to fruition.

Back in the sitting room, Jed flicked on the television. There was an old John Wayne movie playing. He had his phone to hand, a glass of water within reach, the Saturday papers neatly folded at his side. While he waited for Oriana, John Wayne was there to show him what it is to be a man. Everything was ready. Jed waited.

*   *   *

Back in the Bedwells' apartment, Oriana wondered what to do. She'd been curled up on the sofa with a cup of tea for a while, thinking about Louis, looking around her, grateful for so many reminders of the Bedwells' place as it had been, as well as appreciating the changes of the New and the Now. She intended to visit Lilac but found herself feeling quite nervous about it. It would be all right if there was some magic guarantee that she'd find nothing changed but she had to acknowledge that Lilac was now in her eighties. Malachy had warned Oriana that since George's death, Lilac's feistiness had been smothered and her *joie de vivre* was these days sung in a minor key. Oriana anticipated that to confront the changes in Lilac would be far harder than seeing Louis' flat modernized – and she couldn't even bring herself to do that.

She walked around the ballroom, wondering if Malachy ever said 'come in to my ballroom' to a girlfriend. No, it wasn't Malachy's style, not even in an ironic way. Jed, though, would have lots of fun with it. Where *was* Jed? Had he forgotten? It was almost two in the afternoon. Should she phone? She'd wait a while longer. She came to the tilted draughtsman's table and sat at it, sweeping the back of her hand over the vast surface area. It had been a while – tables like these were uncommon these days – but this was undoubtedly her domain. You could put Oriana behind such a desk, anywhere in the world, and she'd know what to do.

* * *

Lilac Camfield was distracted from John Wayne swaggering around the television screen by the sight of the doorbell. She quite liked the discordance of the senses in old age. She couldn't hear the doorbell so her son had rigged up a contraption that lit a light bulb when anyone pressed the buzzer outside. She could see John Wayne on the screen at the other end of the room but she couldn't read the *Radio Times* right in front of her. She couldn't remember what she'd had for breakfast but she could recall the precise taste and texture of a millefeuille she'd had for tea in Paris fifty years ago. There was John Wayne – over there, in the far corner of her room. He was very cross. She knew this because he was bellowing in her ear via the enormous headphones her son had given her so she didn't deafen the neighbours with the level of volume she required these days. Ingenious! A long length of wire suctioning out the sound from the Box and delivering it right into her lugholes. Her granddaughter had told Lilac that the headphones made her look like a pilot.

'A *who*, darling?'

'A *pilot*, Granny – a man who flies an aeroplane.'

Lilac sincerely hoped that there were female pilots flying planes these days, otherwise Amelia Earhart and Amy Johnson had taken to the skies for nothing.

Oh, the doorbell! She'd quite forgotten! The light bulb was winking and blinking while John Wayne was shooting and killing. What an exciting afternoon! Is someone at the door? I wonder who on earth that can be? What day is it? Lilac removed the headphones and, on the second attempt, levered herself out of her chair. She went to the front door, able to hear the bell as she approached; the persistence of which, rather than annoy her, was of some comfort.

'Oh hullo, Oriana,' Lilac said. Because it seemed like yesterday. It all seemed like yesterday.

For a while, sitting opposite each other, Lilac and Oriana just looked at each other in awe. Lilac's expression was one of pure pride; Oriana meanwhile marvelled at how small Lilac was. Did all people shrink this much or had Lilac been granted some Lewis Carroll magic? The clock gently counted off the seconds, its mellow tock seeming to stretch time a little longer than normal. Oriana looked around; there were fewer trinkets than she remembered.

'Where are all the bits and bobs, Lilac?'

'They are in homes across Derbyshire,' Lilac laughed, with an expansive wave. 'I gave them to the cancer shops, dear.' She paused. 'One doesn't need stuff – not at my age.' Oriana thought of some ship, currently transporting the bulk of her own belongings, most of which she didn't really need either.

'They were so pesky to dust.' Lilac interrupted Oriana's thoughts. 'I'm a little clumsier than I was – there again, why should someone in their dotage fret about dusting?' Lilac caught her eye and took it upwards, to the corners of the ceiling where glitter hung in the cobwebs.

'To throw glitter at the cobwebs is far better than dusting the cobwebs away,' Oriana told her. Lilac smiled graciously.

'Rafe – you remember Rafe, don't you? He's forever saying, Mother – let me. He came in with a feather duster once – it made him look like Louis. You remember Louis, don't you?'

'Of course I remember Louis. And I haven't forgotten Rafe either,' Oriana said. 'I always thought he was so – exotic. Because he was the oldest of us kids and he went off travelling and came back with a beard and tattoos and so many stories.'

'He's a dull old accountant these days, my dear. But kind – I am lucky. He's very kind. He has a family – I have two grandchildren. My favourite is my granddaughter Ruby because she reminds me a little of you.'

'How old is Ruby?' Oriana asked, now sitting very close to Lilac, holding her hand.

Lilac looked momentarily confused. Then she smiled mischievously. It was the same as the cobwebs – if age dared to impede her movement or her memory, call its bluff. 'About this big,' she declared, gesturing at a height appropriate for a child. 'However old that is.' Lilac paused. Oriana thirty-four? Did Oriana tell her she was *thirty-four years old*? 'How long has it been, Oriana?'

'A long long time.'

'George died.'

'I know. I'm so sorry.'

'Louis died too. You came to the funeral.'

'I did.'

'But you didn't stay.'

'I know – I'm sorry.'

'You couldn't.'

There was no accusation, no blame.

'No,' Oriana said. 'I couldn't.'

'Have you seen him?'

Lilac's bluntness was something that Oriana always found refreshing rather than confrontational.

'No,' said Oriana. Lilac's pale eyes did not leave her face, travelling over her features like a well-worn route. She'd always been one of the few people in Oriana's life with whom she felt she could be transparent. Time had not altered this.

'I can't, Lilac. I don't want to.' Oriana shrugged. 'Even now I'm here, I feel absolutely no need to. I'm used to being estranged. It's been years – he made me leave when I was so young. That's what they'll say in the obituary, I suppose. *Robin Taylor had one daughter, Oriana, from whom he was estranged.'*

'How terribly morbid for such a lovely afternoon,' Lilac said with her eyebrow raised archly. 'And my dear – I wasn't referring to your father, but to Malachy.'

*   *   *

Robin was eating tuna straight from the tin, forking it into his mouth while looking out of the window. He needed to rest his eyes from the canvas where reality stared confrontationally at him from the surface, while meaning was enmeshed and trapped deep behind it. Gazing outside helped because outside, especially at Windward, depth and meaning were boundless. There was no surface, just layers and layers of colour and texture and sound and scent.

He watched her as she mooched around. He knew exactly which route she'd take, where she'd stop, the pace of her walk, what would catch her eye. He knew she wouldn't look up. He knew this had nothing to do with there being so much else to occupy her gaze. He just knew she wouldn't look to the windows of the place in which she'd grown up. As Robin watched Oriana, he thought of all the women he'd ever painted, and he thought of all the women who'd ever been in his life. He looked again at Oriana – it should be so simple. There was nothing to her – she had even features, a neatness to her figure, a containedness that kept the surface details in check and the workings behind them under control. Robin continued to look at his daughter who was currently sitting on one of the old giant olive oil urns which had been specifically positioned and placed on its side by Randall Peterson during one of his stays at Windward. Robin thought how odd it was that out of all the women he'd ever known – even Rachel, about whom he felt such searing intensity – it was Oriana he found most difficult to paint.

CHAPTER TWENTY-FIVE

She's at Windward.

Jed stared at Malachy's text message. He felt at once relieved but humiliated too. And he felt very, very stupid. Of course Mel on reception wouldn't have given out his home address. Of course Oriana would have headed for 'home' – because she had no reason to believe anything other than that's where he lived. At Windward.

When Malachy's text first came through, after momentary immobility Jed had charged around his flat, ricocheting off walls, trying to work out the order in which to do things. Then he sat down heavily, swamped by the weight of his brother's words. At first, he read them as accusatory, as if Malachy had deleted *you idiot* from the end. Then, they became a declaration, underscored with alarming permanence. *She's at Windward*. Full stop. Malachy, who hated texting and was always as brief as possible, had taken the time to add a defining full stop.

Now Jed's mind was a tumble of questions. How long had she been there? And why hadn't Malachy told him sooner? And why hadn't Oriana made contact as soon as she'd realized her mistake? But the fact remained that she was there because of him. He had to concede it wasn't her mistake to make. She was the mistaken. He'd misled her – straight back to Malachy.

Say she doesn't want to live in Sheffield?

And then he thought, just because Malachy's told me she's at Windward, does it follow that she'll want to leave and come with me? He pondered this quietly for a while, before concluding that surely Sheffield was preferable to Windward, for Oriana of all people.

And then he reread Malachy's words.

She's at Windward.

The bluntness was akin to that of a kidnapper. It was a challenge, as if there was a ransom. *That* made most sense of all. So Jed set off to rescue her.

It was four o'clock when he hared up the driveway. Oriana didn't hear him. But when the front door opened and wasn't closed again, she knew it was Jed. Quietly, she stepped down from the stool behind the draughtsman's desk at which she'd been sitting since returning from Lilac's. She walked quickly through the ballroom absorbing, as if by emotional osmosis, all the details as she went.

'Oriana?'

'Just coming.'

They came across each other in the hallway. Jed's hair was in haphazard soft spikes of frustration and the provenance of his flushed cheeks was the same. But his smile was expansive and there was tenderness and relief in his eyes that made it easy to be welcomed into his hug.

'Daft bugger,' he said into the top of Oriana's head and she wasn't sure to whom he referred.

'Where's your stuff?'

'In your old room.'

'Did you stay the night?'

'Yes.'

'Here?'

'Yes – *here*.'

'Where here?' He said it casually.

'In your old room,' Oriana said.

And then Jed heard this as he'd first read Malachy's **She's at Windward**. With the silent *you idiot* at the end.

'Shall I take you to your new room, then?'

'In Sheffield?'

'Yes.' He looked at her. He didn't expect her to jump for joy – but a grin or just a glint would be good. 'You'll love it,' he said. 'Time for a change,' he said. 'For something new.'

Oriana thought, he's right. She thought, Malachy and Jed always knew what was right for me. It was just so peculiar that their theories were usually diametrically opposed. Sheffield. Somewhere new. That in itself had to be a good start.

'I'm intrigued,' she said.

'Sheffield – the City of Intrigue,' Jed said, gesticulating as if it was written in lights. They collected her bags and headed out.

At the front door, though Oriana knew she had everything, she was suddenly acutely aware that one thing was missing. She hadn't forgotten to take something with her, she'd forgotten to leave it behind. A goodbye.

'I'll just be a moment,' she said to Jed. 'I need the loo.'

Back in the apartment she stood halfway along the corridor in the silence and wondered how she could ever have thought that the space had been Jed's. Malachy was everywhere.

'Goodbye, Malachy,' she whispered. 'Goodbye.'

'So we're dropping Cat's car back at her place first?' Jed was standing by his, when Oriana came down the front steps.

'That's right,' she said. 'We're invited in for a cuppa. You'll love Ben.'

'Lead on, lady, lead on,' said Jed, hopping into his car. He popped on his sunglasses and placed his phone in a cradle on the dashboard. He turned on the engine and music bounced about inside the car like beads on a drum. While Jed crunched his car over the gravel in a seventeen-point turn, Oriana looked back at the house.

Windward wasn't just the building. Windward wasn't held up by pillars and pediments. Windward wasn't defined by a ten-acre plot. Windward wasn't a place, it was the *genius loci*, the spirit of a place. Every new footstep was merely covering a previously trodden and more important path pioneered years ago. The fancy cars now parked in gaudy neatness? They belonged to *visitors*, Oriana decided, not residents – regardless of how much money they now paid to be there. Curtains at windows and sleek new kitchens were temporary, as removable and crushable as doll's house furniture. Front door locks were a laughing matter; they were inessential.

All around her, on this beautiful day as spring turned into early summer, in the leaves and through the breeze, from each nodding bluebell and the glint off every single blade of grass – everything spoke of the living history of Windward. The moss-matted pots in the shrubbery and the lichen-licked statuary on the lawns, the spurt of the fountain and the gnarl of the fencing – they all told of who'd been who and what had happened when, in this world within the world. The soul of the place was in the details; seen and unseen, man-made or intrinsic. It sparkled in the glitter thrown at cobwebs, it lived on in the secret kisses hidden by corridors and it was epitomized by the breathless wonder of following the sweep of an old queen climbing the staircase.

CHAPTER TWENTY-SIX

She's gone, Malachy thought to himself as he turned in to the driveway. She's gone. He could sense it. Just as animals can sense a gathering storm, so Malachy detected the flatness in his home, the return to monochrome, the sound of silence. He sat in his car outside the house for a while letting a conga line of memories encircle him. Jed and Oriana and Louis, Lilac, George, the Glaub children Plum and Willow – they all danced around him while Rod and Ronnie provided the music and Patty Glaub directed and Gordon Bryce captured it all in his scratchy line drawings. And away they went, the memory-makers and past-stealers, down the long driveway and away. Malachy tapped his fingers lightly on the steering wheel, grabbed the Chinese takeaway from the passenger seat and walked towards the building. At the last moment, he changed course and went around the side, to Robin's.

'I thought it would make a change from oxtail soup,' he said, raising the takeaway bag as an explanation.

Robin peered from behind his canvas and stared hard at Malachy. 'You bought me a takeaway meal?'

Malachy shrugged. 'I fancied it.'

Robin continued to eye him levelly. 'She's gone, you know.'

Abruptly, Malachy focused on Robin who had returned to painting, humming tunelessly, casually.

'You saw her?'

Robin looked around the side of the canvas again. 'Yes.'

'She came to see you?'

'No.' Robin sighed as if Malachy was boring him. 'I just saw her outside, whilst she sat in the midst of one of her daydreams.'

Malachy said nothing.

'Well,' said Robin lightly, 'she's gone.' He paused and when he picked up, his voice was lower, softer. 'I didn't need to see her leave to know she's no longer here.' He paused again. 'And that's why you're here too. With your food in paper bags and cardboard boxes. You don't need to go into your home to know that she's not here, do you? And you don't want to go into your home because you know she's gone. That's why you've brought your meal for two here – of all places.'

'Do you want to eat?' Malachy wasn't sure whether Robin was trying to empathize or rile.

'No.'

I don't either, Malachy thought to himself. He stood up and made to leave. At the door, Robin called after him.

'You can put half in the kitchen,' he said. 'Children starving in Africa and all that.'

Malachy had no appetite and left the entire contents of the bag in Robin's kitchen.

* * *

Home was as it always was. Calm and welcoming but, just then, it was a restaurant with nothing remotely tempting on the menu. He didn't know which room he wanted to be in – none appealed. He looked in the newly stocked cupboards and fridge but nothing sparked an appetite. He was too tired to read, too restless to watch television, too distracted to write his novel, too introverted to call anyone and say hey, let's meet for a drink. He didn't want a shower to wash away the morning just yet. It was pathetically early to think about going to bed. It was Saturday evening and this alone irritated him. The pressure of the one night of the week when one oughtn't to be pacing around, harangued by the reverberating echo of solitary footsteps and crowded thoughts.

His blue pullover was on the arm of the sofa. He was just about to pick it up and put it to his nose when he stopped himself. You're a ridiculous sad fuck, he thought. And then he thought, this time yesterday this time yesterday this time yesterday. The proximity of it quite set his clenched teeth on edge. He thought, I can't stay here all evening. This is all wrong.

He hovered outside Lilac's front door, clearly envisaging her watching the television, her enormous headphones on and a dainty glass of Harvey's Bristol Cream to her side. Oh, to sit alongside her, invisible. He'd happily just sit there and lip-read Saturday-night television, take comfort from not being on his own in a room goaded by ghosts. Lilac, he realized, was the only one left who would know how he felt. But was that fair on Lilac? She'd want to busy about, to fuss over him, to make him tea, to fan out ginger biscuits on a doily on a china plate. She loved her television: 'my programmes' she called them, as if they'd been commissioned exclusively for her and were beamed into her home only. She was old, she was to be protected from worrying. And she'd worry about Malachy, if he let her.

He slunk down the wall until he sat with his back to Lilac's door. *Just going to see Lilac*. That's what they used to say, all of them. They'd say, *just going to Louis'*. But they'd say, *just going* to see *Lilac* – as if Lilac was more than a person, she was a colour, a soft filter on the world.

It struck him that with Lilac, they never went to talk to her; they visited her because they wanted to be read like an open book. *You have X-ray vision, Lilac*, he once told her.

'Don't push her away,' she'd told him years ago, when he'd gone to see her, to fiddle absent-mindedly with the ornaments on her windowsill. He remembered the feeling – comforted and alarmed.

I'm not pushing her away.

She just wants to give. Don't shrug your shoulders at me, Malachy.

It's a timing thing, Lilac.

I was married at nineteen.

We don't do that these days. Anyway – she's fifteen. That's just stupid. And anyway – Jed wants her.

Come and sit down.

And after it happened, Lilac went to see Malachy. In the hospital and when he convalesced at home.

She just sat beside him and patted his hand. She knew everything already and she didn't need to tell him that.

The pipes in the house suddenly groaned out their cracking great yawns, as if they'd been waiting for the commercial break in Saturday-night television to do so. It brought Malachy out of the then and back into the now. He stood and rang Lilac's doorbell, estimating to the second the process from her seeing the warning light to her opening the door.

'Well, hullo, Malachy dear, have you come to see me?'

'I have indeed – unless you're entertaining?'

'Just the Prime Minister and a few hangers-on,' she said.

It was banter they'd repeated often over the last decade.

'I'm having a sherry – care to join me?'

At this hour, he could ask for tea, he could ask for a glass of water, but she'd bring him sherry, he knew that.

He toasted her health and took a sip. It was as hideous as it was settling; like Gaviscon on heartburn.

'Well!' Lilac declared. 'Oriana popped in this afternoon to see me.'

In a sly instant, she assessed Malachy's reaction. She did love the way everyone always thought her a batty old fruitcake. Being of diminutive stature, she'd been able to play the little-old-lady card for many years – and it was a role she relished. It won her the patience and kindness of others and amused her no end. Malachy's response to Oriana's name was immediate, as if the twisted vines of a fairy tale paralysed him before he thrashed his way out.

'Yes,' he said. 'I found her.'

'Don't you push her away this time,' Lilac chided him. 'Don't you push her away.'

'She's gone, Lilac,' Malachy said kindly, as if Lilac was deluding herself.

'Well, fetch her back,' she objected, as if he was the silliest boy in the world.

Back home, he was finally ready to eat. He did think about the Chinese food he'd ordered and wondered whether Robin had touched it. He didn't really know why he'd bought it, it was his least favourite cuisine. He'd been seduced by nostalgia, not the menu. It had been thoroughly exotic when they were young and Oriana would eat with her fingers, unaware of the way she cooed in delight as the tastes hit her mouth. Today, he'd bought it even though he knew she wouldn't be here when he returned. He'd bought it because it was something concrete to enable him to say I remember, Oriana, I remember.

He piled a plate with slabs of bread, tomatoes, onion marmalade and Stilton and took it into the ballroom. He sat down, flicked on the television and chose what Lilac had been watching. A chill seeped over to him and he glanced at the open window. For a split second he thought, maybe – just maybe. But pragmatism slammed the thought down. He ignored the window. There was a plate of fresh food on his lap and Bruce Forsyth on the television and everything around him could sod off for a while.

He continued to watch whatever came on next. He refused to check his phone for text messages – he detested the enslaved, conditioned need that he witnessed all around him. People came into the gallery to look at paintings and ended up glancing away from what was on the walls to the graffiti of abbreviated nonsense on the screens welded to the palms of their hands. What would he find anyway? Jed saying Cheers! I've got her now. Oriana saying Hi I'm in Sheffield. Oriana saying Thank you, Oriana saying Goodbye. Or the wretched screen saying nothing at all.

It was cold now and Malachy was tired from the late night last night and the tumult of emotion that had begun early yesterday evening. He reached for his pullover and put it on, unable to do anything about the scent of Oriana woven around every thread. It was fragrant and awful in equal measures; a comfort and a tease. He'd wash it tomorrow, but tonight he'd sleep in it. He went over to the window and pushed it down hard. It sent a wave of cold air through the room and caused a flap and a waft somewhere behind him. He turned in the direction of the sound and noticed a little white triangle, the edge of a piece of paper, jutting out over the edge of his father's desk. So often he'd thought of moving that table out, perhaps storing it in the communal area in the bowels of the house. Orlando told him to chuck it but Malachy would never part with it though it hadn't been used in years. The last time it had paper on it was when his father had sat behind it. Malachy went over and looked. He took his hand to his mouth to keep his voice from exposing the surge of emotion.

Oriana had drawn two views of Windward.

The back elevation and the view from precisely where Malachy now sat; from where she'd sat, for God knows how long earlier that day, waiting to see where life was going to take her. Her architectural drawing had always been extraordinary – he remembered his parents murmuring about it when she'd been young and the Windward children would while away Saturday afternoons or whole days in the holidays right there in the Bedwells' ballroom. Gently, he traced the lines with his finger as if running them over the walls themselves, Oriana's hand under his. Though the drawings were purely linear and in black pen, he could feel where stone became wood, where space became glass, where sun came in and brought warmth.

Robin never liked the way she drew; that detail and precision controlled her style while colour and emotion dictated his. Use your heart! he'd shout at her. Don't draw what you see – paint what you feel! And yet, as Malachy gazed and gazed at the drawing, everything Oriana felt about Windward was delineated and demonstrative. This was the building she'd loved and hated, that she'd left and returned to. It was massive and steady, it was cold and welcoming. She knew it off by heart though she was a stranger to it now. And there *was* heart in the drawing; it beat life into it and it rose out of it.

The love was right there, just under her signature.

Oriana
x

She'd made her mark.

CHAPTER TWENTY-SEVEN

Jed vividly remembered his mother gently scolding him when Binky the dog arrived on Malachy's birthday. Binky was a very small wire-haired terrier, possibly too small, probably because she'd been taken from her mother a couple of weeks too early. Jette had bought her from the farmers' market, from a man on the fringes who had a squirming litter in a crate. The puppy was unsteady and shy and the family watched as she took one faltering step forwards before taking two slinking ones backwards. Malachy was pensively sitting on his knees right beside the cardboard box Binky had arrived in. His father sat quietly at his desk – a pencil behind his ear, his spectacles low on his nose. Jette was standing motionless between the windows, smiling benevolently at the scene, her long slender arms folded loosely. But Jed couldn't stay still; Jed was keen to welcome the newest member of the family even though the puppy was for Malachy. Jed bounced and laughed and rolled on the floor and offered Binky a succession of things to play with. He tickled her and scooped her up and kissed her. His mother had chided him – not because Binky belonged to Malachy, but because Jed was not being helpful.

Let her come to you, Jette said. *If you fuss over her too much, you'll push her away. Let her find her feet; leave her alone for a bit.*

Watching Oriana now, finally in his flat, he remembered his mother's words. Today, it was as hard for him as it had been all those years ago. His instinct was to flap around her, offering tea or coffee or juice or water. And biscuits or toast or some fruit. And to sit or stand or give her the guided tour. And to read the papers or watch TV or choose a DVD. And play music or the radio or just chat. To talk and talk about all the history they'd shared and all the things they'd done since. To stay in or go out. But he allowed Jette's words to guide him.

Don't fuss. Let her come to you. Don't push her away. Not this time. Not again.

It was excruciating though, just being a passive observer. He watched as Oriana thoughtfully circumnavigated the room, passing and pausing at things he was screaming inside to talk about. She was perusing his CDs. He wanted to say do you remember? Do you remember the crush you had on Damon Albarn? Has she got to 'S'? Has she seen that the Stones and Springsteen and Stewart are all waiting for her? Do you remember Rod and Ronnie coming to Windward?

How could any of them forget?

Eventually, she came full circle. Finally, she turned to Jed.

'It's lovely here,' she said, smiling. 'Cup of tea?'

'Do you still like Bounty bars?' It tumbled out. His mother would be tutting, saying hold off! a rich tea biscuit will do!

But Oriana laughed. 'I haven't had one in years.'

'I have one – I bought it this morning. Would you like it?'

She was grinning, really grinning. Her eyes were crinkling. 'You shouldn't have – but yes, please.'

And when he darted off to the bedroom and belted back with the chocolate bar, she laughed again and asked if he had a whole stash of confectionery in there. Yes, he said, in case we fancy a midnight feast. And she said, oh! a midnight feast – brilliant! And it was then that Jed relaxed. As he watched her reconnect with the sickly sweetness of syrup-clogged coconut and chocolate, he thought to himself – see how happy she is. He thought to himself – she's going to love it here. He told himself – I'm going to ensure that she never wants to leave.

CHAPTER TWENTY-EIGHT

'I'm getting shooting pains where the sun don't shine and it feels like my fanny's going to fall out. Stop *laughing*.' Cat glowered at Oriana though the sparkle in her eyes contradicted her protestation. 'And when I walk, it looks like I've cacked my pants.'

Oriana was on Cat's sofa, doubled up in mirth.

'Bitch,' Cat muttered. 'Oh – and I'm also really, really temperamental.'

'Bless you,' Oriana laughed, wiping her eyes. 'Bless you.'

'I thought maternity leave would be all about wafting around the house, folding babygros and towels – everything soft and fragrant,' Cat continued. 'It isn't. It's about me going "oof" every time I sit down; it's about me burping a lot. It's about me reading magazines and pregnancy books and changing my mind.' She looked sorrowfully at Oriana. 'I've changed my mind, Oriana. I've decided not to do this – not to give birth. I'll just look obese for the rest of my life. Fine by me. But there's no way on earth I'm going through labour. No way.'

Oriana held up the four fingers on one hand to signify the weeks of Cat's pregnancy remaining. Cat held up four fingers too, but in a double-handed two-fingered *fuck off*.

'You'll be fine,' Oriana told her. 'You'll be brilliant at it.'

'I don't want Ben seeing me all inside out.'

'Your husband's a doctor.'

'That's irrelevant.'

'Your husband loves you very much and this is a much-wanted baby. Anyway, he doesn't have to go south.'

'Say I bellow like an ox and poop on my baby?'

Oriana shrugged. 'My mother mooed – everyone at Windward heard her. And all the little children mooed at me.'

Cat raised an eyebrow as if to say, I rest my case. Then her face softened. 'Have you been back again? To Windward?'

Oriana looked down at her lap and shook her head.

'Have you seen Malachy again? No? Spoken? Texted, then?'

'I did text,' Oriana said thoughtfully. 'A couple of weeks ago. On my first night at Jed's. I sent Malachy a message saying – well, just saying thank you. And stuff.'

'Define *stuff*, please.'

Oriana took her phone from her back pocket, scrolled through and located the brief exchange between her and Malachy. She read it out loud to Cat.

Hey. Just to say . . . thank you. For so so much. It all seems like yesterday to me. Oriana xxx

'And?'

'Well – he sent a reply a day later.'

'Saying?'

'Not much – he doesn't really do texts. He's so funny when he talks about his absolute hatred of the humble mobi.'

'But what was his response to your text?'

Cat watched a paleness course through Oriana's eyes as she read out his reply.

Thats ok Malachy

'That's *it*?'

'No punctuation, even. I told you – he doesn't like texting.'

'Have you phoned, then?'

Oriana shook her head. Cat thought about it quietly. What on earth was Oriana doing?

'And Jed?'

'Jed's Jed,' said Oriana warmly. 'He's really easy to live with. His flat is in a great part of town – quite near the Botanical Gardens. He's introduced me to some lovely people, taken me to some cool bars and restaurants. He orders supermarket deliveries and the flat is always warm.'

'Wow, he'll make someone a lovely wife,' said Cat and Oriana wondered whether the mistake was intentional. 'Does he have a girlfriend?'

'No – he's hilarious about the ones he has had. He has me in stitches.'

Cat nodded thoughtfully. 'Has he made a move on you yet?'

Oriana baulked. 'Don't be stupid.'

'It's not stupid.'

'That was years ago, Cat.'

Cat raised her eyebrow.

'Years ago,' Oriana stressed. 'Another life entirely.'

And Cat thought to herself, have it your way for the moment, Oriana. Because she thought back to two weeks ago, when Oriana had dropped her car off and brought Jed in for a cup of tea. And she thought back way beyond that, to the years ago to which Oriana now referred so lightly. It was still plain to see. Jed had never fallen out of love with Oriana and it was both deluded and insensitive of her to ignore the fact. And when he told her so – and it would be *when*, not *if* – it would hit Oriana as forcefully as when that lump of stone parapet fell off the roof at Windward in front of all of them, smashing to the ground, pulverized beyond repair.

'I'm going to Blenthrop on Saturday,' Oriana changed the subject.

'Oh?' Cat's first thought was for Malachy. Her second was Windward.

'Got to keep Janis Joplin at bay,' Oriana said, lifting a tress of her hair for emphasis. 'And when you took me there last time, Gay Colin mentioned his clients who are architects.' She paused and smiled. 'Here's you, on maternity leave – here's me, finally truly ready to work again.'

Gay Colin told her she really needed her colour doing. Oriana told him she could barely afford the cut and blow-dry. Much to her relief, this led him on to asking whether she had a job – and whether she'd like the contact details of his architect clients.

She left the salon with great-looking hair and two email addresses.

The route between Sheffield and Blenthrop took her nowhere near Windward. And the car park was in the opposite direction from the White Peak Art Space. In her hand, a piece of paper that might solve present financial burdens and pave the path to continued success in her career. In her bag, the keys to Jed's car which he'd generously put at her disposal. Tonight, he was taking her to Greystones – Richard Hawley was playing a one-off there. He said he'd bought the tickets ages ago – when he was still with Fiona. Yesterday, she'd been invited along to his after-work Friday-night drinks. He'd bought her a bag of chips at two in the morning and made her a mug of tea when she woke up.

'I should go back,' Oriana said quietly, walking off in the direction of the car. 'I said I'd cook before we head out.' She stopped and carefully put Colin's piece of paper in her wallet. 'I will send emails this afternoon.' She fidgeted with her hair and looked around her. She knew no one. This wasn't her town any more. Sheffield was her city now, she lived in a different county altogether. South Yorkshire. Blenthrop, in Derbyshire, was simply where her hairdresser was and, like Cat, she wouldn't put her head in anyone else's hands. She looked at her watch and thought of Jed. She retrieved her phone from her bag. He'd sent a text.

Yo Janis! When are you coming back? Jxx

He'd even found emoticons of a pair of scissors, another of a girl with her hands in her hair. Oriana thought, life is good. She thought, I'm having fun. She thought, I desperately, desperately want to see Malachy.

There was no dread lacing the adrenalin which propelled her in the opposite direction from Jed's car. Just anticipation. She wasn't going to bother with texts. She was just going to turn up. She was only a few yards from seeing him again. Moments. Just footsteps away. There's the gallery. She hadn't thought of any clever phrase to announce herself. She wondered if perhaps she should. Quickly though, she scuttled right past the door, a momentary glance computing that there were people in there and Malachy was bound to be amongst them. She walked back to the newsagent's on the corner, the one with the coffee machine, and loitered there for a while. Her mind racketed over pithy things to say but the words tumbled around into Double Dutch. Twice, the shop owner asked if he could help her. Twice she mumbled something about being fine, just looking. Eventually, she thought that a hot cup of coffee would be the perfect ice-breaker, so she bought two. Lingering a little way along the street, Oriana waited until she noted a couple leave the gallery. And then in she went.

He wasn't alone in there; he was deep in conversation with an older man. The man was being expansive in his arm gestures while Malachy humoured him, nodding seriously. He'd told Oriana, at some crazy hour a fortnight ago, that he'd perfected his salesmanship. It's about respecting people's bullshit, he'd said. When people contemplate art, they say mostly ridiculous things. But if you want them to buy art, you must let them know that actually, their opinion is as valid as the most eminent art critic's. If art inspires them to talk, then it's fulfilled its promise.

What's the most stupid thing anyone has ever said? Oriana had asked.

Malachy had put on a posh accent. *I'm looking for something – a sculpture – Picasso meets The Simpsons.*

Then he nodded in the direction of Robin's paintings.

Your father's work tends to stun the viewer into silence, he'd told her.

Here he was now, listening attentively to the man with arms like a windmill. Had he seen her? Was he on the verge of making a sale? Should she back away, perhaps? She sipped nervously at one of the coffees – it was the one with sugar that she'd ordered for Malachy but the sweetness, from which normally she'd recoil, was comforting. And he glanced over to the front of the gallery because he'd noticed someone enter. And suddenly, for all he cared, the man with the rotating arms might have a million pounds in his pocket but Malachy could no more listen to him than he could deliver his spiel about monthly instalments. Oriana was standing just there, with a cup in each hand, like a statue of Justice and her scales. Malachy experienced chaos and balance, exhilaration and caution, delight and apprehension. If anything tipped, she might leave.

He held up a finger. One minute, he mouthed. She nodded, her head slightly coy to one side, brandishing the cups as if they were the only reason for her reappearance.

Her father's art, not for sale, on the wall opposite her. She realized she was looking at his work now without flinching. Could she remember these being painted? She couldn't. She went over to them and stood very close, regarded the date. She'd have been in her mid-twenties, just graduating from the School of Engineering at Stanford University with her degree in architectural design. Did her father know she'd been the top-scoring student in her year? That she'd been granted a full needs-based scholarship because the department needed a student as gifted as her? Come to think of it, did her mother know?

'Oriana?'

Malachy startled her back into the present. She'd been miles away, years away, back in California. She jumped and the spilled coffee ran in a zip-like scorch along her hand.

'Ouch,' Malachy said for her, taking the cups, walking to the back of the now empty gallery, calling over his shoulder, let me get you a tissue. 'Here,' he dabbed the wetness from her skin and frowned at the growing redness there. She saw how his eyebrow puckered above his patch with concern. He looked at her and she looked away quickly, guiltily even, as if she'd been caught staring right at his disability. 'How does that feel?' he asked. 'Sore?'

She shrugged. 'Ish.'

'You ought to run it under the cold tap,' he told her, his hand gently at her shoulder, leading her to the sink in the tiny kitchenette behind the stud wall at the back of the gallery. He turned on the tap and, standing behind her, so close that she could feel his breath through her hair, he took her wrist and let the peaks-cold water rush silkily over her skin. There they stood, not moving, though her hand was now freezing and his back was aching with the effort of keeping his body from pressing against hers.

He encased her hand in a tea towel, holding it between his. He told her to count to ten, for no other reason than to enable him to stay right there with her, to preserve the loaded silence, the closeness. Back in the gallery, they sat opposite each other at his desk, the surface busy with a scatter of brochures and artists' details, pens and a laptop, various forms and a box of tissues, a glass of water, an uneaten chocolate bar. But nothing distracted Oriana or Malachy from sipping their coffee while wondering who might speak first and what they might say. Only the arrival of a visitor interrupted their genial silence. Malachy rose.

'Don't go,' he whispered. 'Stay awhile.'

She watched him. She thought, I could spend all day watching him. Just like I used to. Those times he didn't know. And those times that he did.

* * *

She stayed in the gallery for over two hours. When people came in it was like the DJ interrupting the songs that they'd listened to on Malachy's radio cassette recorder on Sunday afternoons at Windward during their youth. And, just as he had been back then, so today Malachy was equally expert at cutting out the extraneous so that nothing interrupted the music. He noticed her hair – it's flicky, he said, it suits you. She liked his shirt. It was denim and well worn and worked well with his faded black jeans. She took a private snapshot of the base of his neck, where his collarbones met, the subtle suggestion of chest hair. So vividly could she recall how their differing heights had enabled her head to tuck under his chin, how she could raise her face so that her lips could kiss precisely this part of him. Did he remember that too? She looked over to him. Busy busy with his working day. He probably didn't want to remember. She thought, why would he? It was probably the last thing he thought about because it was the furthest thing in his memory. Was there anyone who was less likely to want to revisit the past?

'I'd better go,' she said. Her phone showed three unread texts, all from Jed – and a missed call from him too.

Malachy made a gesture that was half shrug, half nod.

Why don't you just say don't go! Oriana desperately tried to telepathize as she rose to her feet. Just ask me to stay. Tell me to wait.

But he didn't. He just nodded. No shrug. Just nodded as if he agreed, yes – you'd better go.

'See you next haircut,' he said lightly. He was standing, his hands in his pockets.

'OK,' Oriana said. 'It's a date.' And she cringed because it was such a stupid thing to say. And it wasn't a date. It was just Malachy saying something polite and jaunty.

They stood and looked at each other and she so wanted to kiss him. She'd be happy enough to place just a small one on his cheek. Had she, he would have taken his hands out of his pockets and put an arm lightly around her waist and kissed her back. But someone came into the gallery and it marked the end of their soundtrack for that afternoon.

Jed knew that haircuts didn't take that long – not even a really good cut by Gay Colin. And instinctively he knew why Oriana was late, he knew where she'd been. But he didn't want to ask. He didn't want it to sound the way he knew it would sound. He didn't want to say, it's too late to cook now. He didn't want Malachy between them. Instead, he welcomed Oriana back with a barrage of chat and cups of tea and come on! let's go into town now! Let's eat Mexican and have a drink before the concert starts.

Nothing like sharing nachos for spilling the metaphorical refried beans.

'I went into the gallery and had a chat with Malachy.'

That must be the chilli that's making Jed choke. Yes, that's what it'll be.

'How is my older bro'?'

'He's fine.'

'Was it busy? Is business good?'

'He sold a print and a few cards while I was there – but there was a steady flow of visitors.'

'That's good.'

'Yep.'

'We should get him over – for a drink. Invite him to ours, cook him a meal. Take him out.'

And when their eyes locked, just for a moment, they knew that it was the most stupid suggestion because it was the last thing that any of them would want.

'I haven't seen him in ages,' Jed mumbled between hasty mouthfuls. 'I must give him a call.'

Oriana swigged almost all her margarita in one.

The Richard Hawley gig was enthralling. Oriana loved his music, finding it wonderfully strange that the artist she'd first discovered in California was actually from the city in which she was now living. Everyone danced and sang and grinned at each other. Greystones was hot and sweaty and the atmosphere was perfect.

'That was the *best*!' Oriana enthused as they fairly bounced down the street late, late that night. 'Amazing!'

'Awesome,' said Jed.

And back at the flat they sat on the floor with their backs to the sofa like students, drinking white wine that should have been chilled, listening to

Richard Hawley on CD and talking. Talking about nothing in particular, Oriana would have termed it. Shooting the shit, would have been Jed's take.

Richard Hawley had not played 'Don't You Cry' live earlier that night. But the song rang through Jed's flat now. For Jed, it was simply just another superb track and he didn't connect it to how contemplative Oriana had suddenly become. He didn't realize it was the reason that her energy was slinking away and she was deflating a little before his eyes, like a soft toy squeezed a bit too hard.

'You OK?' he asked tenderly, touching her cheek with his fingertip. His hand dropped down, lightly coursing along her arm, to her wrist, to the hand she'd spilled the hot coffee on earlier that day. He wove his fingers through hers. 'Hey?' Might she lay her head on his shoulder like she used to? Might that lead on – like it once had?

'Just tired,' she said. It was a lie, but he didn't hear it because she kissed him. He didn't acknowledge that it was just sweetly on the cheek as she said goodnight. It was a kiss. It was a kiss.

'Just really tired,' she said as she stood up.

In bed, she nestled deeply into the duvet, pulling it up high like a child hiding from monsters in the cupboard. Richard Hawley's lyrics continued to reverberate in her head. Not just in her head – she could hear him drifting through from the sitting room, where she'd left Jed with a kiss on his cheek, a glass of warm wine in his hand and the CD on repeat.

In separate rooms they were both listening to the song again. The relevance of the lyrics now striking both of them. The years and years between them and what had happened. And so it was a lonely futility that marked the end of their day.

> *He knows that she's so sad*
> *She knows the goods turned bad*
> *He knows that she's so sad*
> *She knows the clocks don't turn back*

CHAPTER TWENTY-NINE

'Oriana?'

It was her mother and it came as a total shock. She had barely thought of her since she last saw her almost two months ago. They'd spoken just the once in that time, which was back to the regularity of their contact when Oriana had been living abroad. Now her mother's voice brittled right through her, threatening the spring in her step created by the job interview she'd just floated out of.

'Mum?'

'Where are you?'

Oriana was in the centre of the city, off Tudor Square. 'I've just had a job interview. I think they really liked me. It's an amazing company.'

'Yes, but *where* are you?'

'Sheffield.'

'You're in Sheffield.' It was a statement underscored with immense irritation.

'Yes.'

'For God's sake.'

'Sorry?'

'What are you *doing* there?'

'I just told you? About the amazing job interview?'

Oriana saw the Winter Gardens ahead of her and walked there quickly. Peace amongst the plants, just what she needed. And oxygen. Her mother's voice had a toxicity similar to carbon dioxide.

'Sheffield.' Her mother sounded appalled. Did she hate the city – or the fact that it hadn't crossed her daughter's mind to update her on her whereabouts?

'Yes,' said Oriana. It was sad, really, that she hadn't thought to inform her own mother about this change in her life.

'Well, could you get yourself *out* of Sheffield. All your stuff is here.'

Oriana racked her brains for what on earth she had left at her mother's. A pair of jeans perhaps? Was her presence so negatively intrusive that her mother wanted them out of the house? Oriana wished it was Bernard who'd phoned her. Why couldn't her mother have had a histrionic flounce and said to Bernard you phone her! You tell her to come and get her jeans!

'I'm pretty sure I took everything, Mum.'

'Oh yes – oh yes! You *took* everything, didn't you!' The sarcastic hysteria in her mother's voice rose like the spikes of an ECG. It was the same tone she used to use with Robin and it hurt Oriana's ears. 'There is a truck blocking our road,' she continued. 'And it's brought *everything* from the United States.'

Oriana sat down heavily, aware of the irony that she was surrounded by thorny, twisted plants. All her stuff. Shit. The same welling emotion struck her now as it had then, when the truck had trundled off out of sight with the essential pieces of her life.

Fragments of Oriana in a plain crate, sailing the ocean to find her again. She'd given away and sold so much – but there were a few key items that she'd never part with. She was defined by every weft of the vintage patchwork quilt, each turned corner of a book's page, every dovetail joint in the investment pieces of furniture she'd saved hard for. How often had she given herself a good talking-to in that oversized mirror with the gesso frame? And escaped into the benign landscape of the oil painting she'd picked up at the Flea? And her Specialized bike that she'd ridden miles on? And the desk at which she'd studied and drawn and shaped her career?

'What am I to do?' Her mother's wail brought her back to the present. 'We can't have it here! We have no storage! This isn't bloody Windward, you know!'

And then a thought surged through Oriana like the perfect wave, lifting her up and over her mother's squallish angst, delivering her to a place where everything was calm, magical and as strange as a fairy tale.

'It's OK, Mum,' Oriana said. 'Can you tell the driver to wait just five minutes? I need to make a phone call.'

Malachy had rewritten Chapter Seventeen many, many times. Chapters Sixteen and Eighteen were fine – he was very happy with them. But Chapter Seventeen just wasn't right. The prose was clunky, the dialogue unconvincing, the leaps in plot pretty ridiculous. He sat back in his chair and thanked the Lord that it was quiet in the gallery and no visitors could see him tearing his hair out, hissing *for fuck's sake* at the laptop screen while stabbing at the keys as if that would teach the words a lesson.

'Yes?' he answered the gallery phone, irritated.

Oriana was a little taken aback. She'd left the spiky plants for a more genial area of soft and feathery ferns. Malachy's fractious voice made her coil into herself, like a frond of bracken by which she sat.

'White Peak Art Space – yes?' He spoke as if to a hoax caller. Or an imbecile.

'It's me,' Oriana apologized.

There was a momentary pause.

'It's Oriana.'

'I know it's you.'

'Are you OK?'

'Just pissed off with my stupid novel.'

Oriana had to smile. Had there ever been a time when Malachy's novel had caused him anything other than extremes of emotion? She thought back to what he'd told her when they'd talked late into the night. That, for him, it wasn't about getting published, it was about telling the story. Rejection slips from publishers had bluntly extinguished his teenage dreams of being Derbyshire's John Irving. Selling art had been something he'd been good at during his university vacations, when galleries were happy to employ him because customers wanted to buy from him. What he'd assumed to be a secondary career choice had soon become the sensible thing to do. But if his business brain was in the gallery and art was in his heart, writing his novel still nourished his soul. And sometimes tortured him too.

'It'll be all right,' Oriana told Malachy. 'Just read one of the chapters you *do* like.'

Malachy nodded at the phone, temporarily soothed by familiar advice she'd dispensed verbatim so regularly a long time ago. Now, as then, she wasn't wrong.

'Thank you,' he said, as if it had been him phoning her for advice.

'I need a favour,' she said quickly, worrying he was going to end the call. 'A hulking great huge one.'

Malachy wasn't sure whether he was flattered or unnerved. It wasn't about Jed, was it?

'A crate of my belongings has just turned up in Hathersage, outside my mother's house. She's popping hernias as we speak.'

'You want to store it in the cellar?' It was said so matter-of-factly that it dispensed with the concept of it being much of a favour at all, let alone a liberty.

'I'm in Sheffield. I just had a job interview.'

Malachy nodded at the phone again. 'You want me to close up the gallery? And nip back to Windward? And unpack your worldlies for you?' He paused. 'You want me to leave my novel mid-chapter? Forgo all potential sales today?'

'No!' Oriana was appalled. 'I just wanted to know if it was OK, in theory. I need to phone them and rearrange the delivery. I won't trouble you – you needn't be there. There's not a huge amount. I just thought –'

He smiled. She was still just as easy to wind up. 'It's fine, silly. It's fine.'

Oriana unfurled a coiled finger of bracken. Malachy calling her silly had always been a comfort in times of duress. 'I'd better go,' she said. In her mind's eye, her mother was stamping and stropping and cursing her daughter this very moment. 'Thank you, Malachy. And reread your good chapters. Bye.'

'Bye then.'

The shipping company took Oriana's crate away, with an arrangement to deliver two days later, on the Friday morning. Her mother didn't want to speak to her.

Jed wasn't keen on lending Oriana his car. Yes, she could drive him in to work and collect him. But what he really wanted was to prevent her going to Windward at all. If she went there, all the public-relations work he'd done promoting the merits of a new life in Sheffield might unravel. If she went there, she might clamber about her memories the way she used to clamber up and around the cedar. And she used to spend hours and hours doing that. Who might she want to be when she surfaced? And if she went to Windward, would Malachy be there?

It was over three weeks since she'd moved into his spare room, but he hadn't once told her how he felt – still felt – about her. He hadn't made a move on her. He'd come so close then retreated, spending wakeful hours in bed, turned on by her proximity, frustrated by his fantasies, silently and urgently powering his semen out of him so that he might at least sleep.

And he'd steered clear of even mentioning Malachy. It wasn't so much an elephant in the room as a can of worms in the corner. If he could just keep the lid on it, he could establish and cement all that the present held for the future and make the past seem redundant.

'I'll pay for a tank of petrol,' Oriana said, hugging her hands around her cup of morning tea.

'No no.' Jed brushed away her suggestion as he swept the spilled flakes of breakfast cereal off the table and into the palm of his hand. 'It's fine. Just drive carefully.'

Then he looked at her directly and she saw all the steel in Sheffield shoot through his eyes.

'Maybe you'll see your father when you're there.' It was below the belt but, he felt, a legal move. You hate Windward, remember? You hate it.

'Malachy?'

He didn't appear to be at home though the scent of toast was still fresh in the kitchen and the kettle was hot.

'Hullo?'

Oriana walked through the apartment, calling out softly every few steps or so. Her drawings of the house had gone from the table in the ballroom. His bedroom door was closed. The navy pullover was still over the arm of the sofa. On various surfaces there were used mugs yet to be taken into the kitchen. Next to the Eames, the newspapers from last weekend were in a scatter on the floor. She went back into the hallway and opened the door that connected with the cavernous interior corridor.

As she headed for the cellar, she thought about

the stories she'd shared with Paula as they'd walked back from not quite going into Louis'. It was as if drifts and details still lingered, whispering at her as she walked. Some to step over, others to turn towards. The bounce and thwack of green tennis ball against willow bat. The skid of roller skates and the tumble of limbs in the ensuing crash. The puff on a spliff, the echo of giggle and snorts. Hiding a folded five-pound note in crumbled masonry and seeing who'd find it first. Forgetting where it was. Remembering weeks later and feeling rich. And it was here – right here – where he kissed me.

Does Malachy remember this when he passes this point?

How long ago did he decide that he'd rather forget?

There was no door to the cellar, just oversized old hinges where once there had been one. There was light down there, the weak but warm glow from old bare bulbs which illuminated little but created a whole cast of strange ominous shadows. The unmistakable smell of chalky dampness seeped up the deep stone steps. Carefully and slowly, Oriana descended. At the bottom, she stood stock-still and just looked around. Monsters under dust sheets and piles of ghostly crockery. A table with a velvety layer of dust, two candelabra laced by cobwebs and a chair at one end pulled out a little as if Miss Havisham had just left. Boxes and crates marked with names long forgotten and others not known.

'Boo!'

Oriana leapt. 'Oh, for fuck's sake!' She hit Malachy

and clung to him and laughed at herself and cursed him.

'Sorry,' he said, 'I couldn't resist.' In the half-light of this shaded world of what had been forgotten and what was there to be kept, Malachy's face was like a charcoal portrait. He could feel her penetrating gaze and he turned away from it, quickly touching the ribbon around his head. He had thought about not bothering with his eyepatch; it was dark enough down here that shadows would provide protection – for her as much as for himself.

It was so dusty. He cleared his throat.

'There's plenty of space – as you can see. Do you want to clear yourself a specific area?'

She looked around, peering into the gloom. She was relieved to see that there was no new order; no individual plots. However closed off and privatized the apartments above might now be, however formally delineated the car parking, down here in the cellar it was as gloriously disorganized and communal as it ever had been.

'I'll just fit in and around everyone else,' she told him.

'What time are they arriving?'

'About ten-thirty.'

'Are you sure you can manage on your own?'

'Yes – absolutely.'

'Because I'd better head off to the gallery now.'

'I know. Go. You go. I'll be fine. It's not like I have to lock up when I leave.'

'Why are we whispering?'

'I don't know.'

Might you kiss me, Malachy?

No. I'm going to turn away now. I'm going.

'How's Jed?' Malachy's normal voice, and the blunt timbre of his brother's name, sounded abrupt now they were out and in the Corridor.

'He's fine,' said Oriana. 'He said he'd call you about coming to Sheffield for a drink.'

'Sure,' said Malachy and, as they walked, he hated himself for wondering have they? Are they? Perversely, he threw an image into his mind of them together, Oriana and Jed; together as they were today, and as they had been when they were fifteen.

Oriana stopped at the place where Malachy had kissed her, willing him to stop too, for the significance to hit him, for him to retrace his steps and join her. To recreate the stuff of dreams and what memories had been made from. But he just kept walking.

'Malachy?' she called after him. Finally he turned. They were a few yards apart but she didn't want to leave that spot. She swept her hands out in front of her, all around her, as if to display where she was. She didn't have to say, remember? Do you remember? Do you know where this is? Malachy's heart heaved and surged and hurt. She was looking at him beseechingly, as if shyly pleading with him not to forget. He looked at her and let his breath go.

'Come on,' he said, though he only mouthed it. He held out his hand. '*Come on.*' She walked slowly over to him, a little downcast, slipped her hand into his and let him lead her back out into the daylight.

* * *

The central sash window rattled as the lorry rumbled across the driveway and round to the side of the house. It could have been a tank for all the noise it created and the commotion it left in its wake. There were people whistling and shouting, there was the clang and slam of metal chains and vehicle doors, the blunt honking signifying the lorry's reversing, the vulgar hiss of air brakes.

'Some of us are trying to bloody paint!' Robin yelled out of the window.

Was someone moving in? Moving out?

'Oh dear God,' he cursed. 'What in the name of Christ is going on?'

He went through to the kitchen and looked out of the window to see a small forklift truck trundling down a ramp off the lorry. Above the din of the engine, three men were shouting as if they were fresh from Babel. With a groan and a wail, the lorry seemed to lower, like an elephant sinking to its knees.

'How can I paint? *How can I paint?*'

Robin hammered his frustration at the window, banging until finally the men looked up. There they saw an old man with furious hair thumping at the glass, raising a clenched fist at them. They could see how his mouth was twisting around all manner of inaudible abuse. They put their hands to their ears as if to say, speak up, mate! We can't hear you! So he struck at the window and swore and brandished his fist while the men grinned at him in good-humoured joshing.

'What is going on?' Oriana came around the side of the lorry.

'Some old boy's getting his knickers in a twist,' the foreman laughed. But that particular old boy was now stock-still at his kitchen window, his arm still raised but immobilized. Similarly, Oriana faced the men in a frozen gawp before slowly turning and lifting her gaze until her eyes locked with Robin's. She wasn't sure if she was holding her breath or whether she just couldn't breathe. She was unable to move. While the men, oblivious, unloaded the crate, Oriana and her father stared at each other.

Robin's fist slowly unclenched. His wrist rotated and, like petals unfolding, his fingers fanned out and his hand moved from side to side. A small gesture of greeting, like a splice of turquoise sky through storm clouds.

As Oriana directed the men where to put what, as she drove back to Sheffield, as Jed chatted away in the pub that night, she thought of the missed moment with Malachy in the Corridor. But as she lay in her bed and felt her body soften into slumber, she could think of only one thing.

My father waved at me.

And I waved back.

CHAPTER THIRTY

It struck Oriana that, when she'd been living at Cat's, she'd experienced an agoraphobia of sorts; not wanting to go out, preferring to stay in, to hunker down and hole up. Perhaps it had something to do with Cat's place being very much a home. Initially this had been a great comfort to Oriana, having left hers in the United States and then finding the antithesis to exist at her mother's. Eventually though, Cat's set-up rubbed a newly exposed nerve in Oriana so raw that it became untenable, too painful, for her to stay. Every framed photograph dotted here and there at the Yorks' could have been – perhaps should have been – of Oriana. Oriana and husband. Oriana and husband at jolly family get-togethers. Mr and Mrs on holiday. And with friends. The long, healthy history of Mr and Mrs. And the pride of place to the scans of their unborn child – from kidney bean to Baby Suckathumb in extraordinary ultrasonic images. Cat's home was testimony to someone who was just like Oriana but who, unlike Oriana, had made clear decisions and wise choices, got her life together and was enjoying its bounty. It didn't make her love Cat any the less, but it did amplify the disappointment she felt in – and for – herself.

At Jed's it was different. It was a lovely flat in Nether Edge, paid for with wages that could comfortably cover Ocado deliveries, nights out and the top Sky package. Everything worked and it was clean. It had mod cons and home comforts. But it was impersonal. In essence, it was a decent two-bed flat that Oriana suspected looked just like this when Jed bought it and would remain so for the next owner. It was Jed's place, but almost a month later it wasn't Oriana's home. Even though she had nowhere specific to go, it felt indulgent to be lounging indoors while she waited for news from the job interview, or *that* phone call from Cat which was imminent, or one from Malachy which would never come. It wasn't the sort of interior for lolling anyway. It was a little like a hotel and, as such, she felt obliged to leave for most of the day.

Therefore, when Jed left for work each morning, Oriana wasn't long behind him, not least because, after a week of rain, the weather now was fine. A balmy spring was truly established – in the air, in everyone's step. Walking the mile and a half to the Botanical Gardens was a pleasure that didn't diminish and it had become something of a daily ritual. It's *free*, she'd told Ashlyn. All our museums are free too. And Ashlyn thought to herself, when did that happen – when did my friend feel so British again? In the fifteen years she'd known Oriana, she'd only ever heard her employ the third person when speaking of her birthplace. *Their* museums are free.

Now *their* museums had become Oriana's and Ashlyn thought she'd better plan a trip over there, to see what all the fuss was about. She thought about her honeymoon. And how fun it would be to visit the United Kingdom. And that mythical place Windward which, from Oriana's tales, had to have been the best place in the world to grow up.

On a bench, in the sun, *The Times* read, cappuccino drunk, Oriana closed her eyes and raised her face. Is today the day when Cat and Ben's baby will come? Is today the day that she'd land herself a job? There was an air of anticipation that made her fidget on her bench and, much as the sunlight on her face felt lovely, she couldn't stay there. She checked her phone. Nothing. Not even a text. If she texted Ashlyn, she wouldn't receive it till she woke up six hours later. She'd already sent a message to Cat who'd sent back one saying no news. If she texted Jed, he'd send a jaunty barrage back – which sometimes she liked and sometimes she was irritated by. Dear Jed. You're like a puppy.

If she texted Malachy, she knew not to expect a reply. Just then, though, she longed to see him. She wanted so much to tell him about the wave that had passed between her and her father. She wanted to tell him how odd it was to see her belongings again, how strange it was that they were now on English soil, stranger still that they were at Windward. She wanted to show him some of her things. The painting. The Shaker rocking chair. Each had a story to tell, fleshing out the years of her history which he'd missed. Had he liked the book, she wanted to know.

Had he remembered it? Had he even seen that she'd put it there, on the piano in the ballroom, when everything was safely in the cellar and she was about to leave? It was a tome on Louis Sullivan and the Chicago School and it had belonged to his father. Orlando Bedwell had given it to Oriana when she was fourteen. He'd seen her drawings, her potential. You'll like this chap, he'd told her. You'll like this chap.

She checked her watch. It wasn't even time for elevenses. And Oriana thought, what shall I do with my day? She phoned Cat as she walked out of the gardens, heading for Ecclesall Road.

'Are you in labour?'

'Still heavy with child.'

For the past fortnight, all their calls had started thus.

'Shall I come and see you?'

'I'd love that.'

'I'll get the bus.'

'I'll see you in ten years' time, then,' said Cat. 'No doubt I'll *still* be waiting for Baby.'

Later, though feeling a little queasy on the return journey, Oriana was left with a good impression and analysed the route map at the stop. She could travel to Blenthrop direct. She'd had no idea! And Hathersage with one change. And even slightly circuitously with a hike at the end, to visit Django.

The fresh air was welcome after the lurch and sway of country lanes and city traffic, so she mooched the long way back to Jed's, looking in the shop windows along Eccy Road. There was a rare and welcome 'local independent retailers' feel to the area, the occasional generic coffee chain appearing to be trying to butt in on conversations between close friends. She was just thinking how she hadn't been down this far when she saw a shop that stopped her in her tracks. Helpless not to approach, she felt a numbing pressure throbbing in her head.

With a nice shoe shop on one side and a boutique on the other, the gun shop stood between the two like a bodyguard. The exterior was spruce yet old-fashioned. The window display, the title *Gunsmiths*, announced a family business, established and proud. Part of the high street for over thirty years. *Everything for the shooter!* More than the weaponry on show and details of ammunition stocked, it was that exclamation mark that made Oriana baulk most.

When I was . . .

When I was little I hid my father's gun. He had quite a
few but the one I hid was the only one in working order.
It was an old Winchester and it had belonged to my
maternal grandfather who I'd never met. It was the only
thing of any value in my mother's dowry. The rifle was
an early twentieth-century Model 1890 and it was, my
father used to marvel, the first ever repeating slide-action
.22. It was the gun of choice for shooting galleries, hence
its nickname, which my father loved – Gallery Gun. Very
occasionally, he used it for shooting pigeons from the
window. He was a poor shot and rarely nabbed a thing
though the Short .22 was perfect for small game like
squirrels and rabbits. I always felt guns were a terrible
paradox – sculpted polished wood so beautiful and warm
to the touch for something designed to kill in cold blood.
Some of my father's muskets were decorated with filigree
silverwork that gave the pieces a jarring femininity in
brutal contrast to their function. Those didn't work,
though. Those were just for show. When they were little,
Malachy and Jed used to pick them up and shout bang! Just
the once I remember my father spinning a fanciful yarn
about the provenance of two of the pistols, who'd owned
them and what duels for justice and land and women had
been won with them. We knew it was fiction but, back when
we were small, fiction wasn't a lie, it was a parallel world.

Two actors once stayed the whole summer at Windward. They were fabulous thesps, friends of the Glaubs, with lines to learn for performances at the Crucible which never materialized. Our summer break was spent in an imaginary amphitheatre on the lawn, watching them rehearse with their exotic props. I can't remember if it was an existing play or whether they were improvising. It was a Restoration comedy of sorts. They wore breeches and garters and used our black felt-tip pens to draw beauty spots on each other's faces. And they always had a daily duel. We children loved the daily duel. We loved that their guns went snap! with a puff of pungent smoke from the powder charges of potassium perchlorate, sulphur and antimony sulphide. What compelled us most was that heart-stopping moment when we all wondered whether the man down was really shot. The victor standing over him in contemplative triumph. Is he dead? Even the birds and the insects were silent as we waited. Is he actually dead this time? The relief when he rose and smiled! The applause we lavished when they both took a bow! They had lived to die another day!

They let me do the shooting once.

Good aim! said Malachy when I pulled the trigger and down fell the actor instantly, as if his body was suddenly devoid of its skeleton. For a split second when my hair might well have turned white, I did wonder if I'd killed the actor. But up he leapt and thanked me profusely for felling him so convincingly.

That summer, I said I wanted to be an actress when I grew up.

Don't be stupid! said Jed. You're way too shy.

You can be anything you want, said Malachy.

I know, I said. When you're an actress you can pretend

to be anything you want. I spent a long time wanting to be an actress and thinking of which roles I'd most like to try.

Apart from that one rifle, the rest of my father's guns were defunct as weapons but had a second innings as props for a series of his still lifes; an extraordinary run of nine paintings called La Mort. *As detailed as Chardin; with chiaroscuro as accomplished as Caravaggio. Nine intricate oil paintings of the spoils of war or the rewards of hunting, of the elegance of country traditions or the barbarism of the aristocracy – however you wanted to look at it. A classically composed still life, painted nine times. Two rabbits and a partridge, a pair of leather gloves, a silver tankard, two rifles beside them on a mahogany surface all set within a richly panelled interior. The first rendition was so fresh I remembering touching the surface convinced that the pelt of the rabbit would feel soft, the partridge still warm. The implosion started in the second canvas. By the ninth, the decay and decomposition were so horrible I didn't want to get too close. Robin Taylor,* La Mort. *The distortion of beauty and life, of survival and sport; confrontational and pioneering, long before Damian Hirst or Sam Taylor-Wood even thought of art as a career.*

That day at the Bedwells' – the day my mother came haring through the place shrieking he's going to kill me! He's going to kill me! That was the day that I hid my father's Gallery Gun.

CHAPTER THIRTY-ONE

Cat's baby girl arrived a week later, five days late; the very same day that Oriana was offered the job she'd given up hoping for. It was the distinctive day when suddenly late May makes it plain that as June is next week, spring may as well finally become summer, and a warm and benign fragrance danced on tiptoes in the air. Bluebells were long forgotten in the sudden tangle and burst of the summer flowers, like a riot of children released at the end of term. It was Good News Day for Oriana and though her world was a small one, she wanted to share it with everyone she knew. Ashlyn was FaceTimed. Oriana and Django spoke by phone in sentences left incomplete by emotion. She even phoned Hathersage and knew the day was blessed indeed when it was Bernard who answered and marvelled with her in his own level way by adding an appreciative eh! to the end of each sentence. A baby girl, eh! An architect at Stone & White, eh!

'I did find a bus route from me to you,' she told him. 'But now I have a job, I may not be visiting for a little while.'

'Now you have a job, perhaps you'll be buying yourself a little runaround,' said Bernard.

She composed a text to send to Malachy but sent it to Jed instead. Why hassle Malachy when he's already said how he hates texting? She wondered, if she worded it more like a conversation, with proper spelling and punctuation, might he be happy to receive her news? She realized, however, that though it was important to her that he knew, it was his response she longed for. She thought herself slightly ridiculous for having to quell a stomach full of butterflies when she phoned him instead.

'White Peak Art Space.'

'It's me.'

'Hullo.'

'It's Oriana.'

'I know who "me" is.'

Her own pause infuriated her. 'I just wanted to phone because I know you hate texts.'

'You OK?'

'Oh yes – I'm more than fine. How are you?'

'I'm fine too.'

'I just thought I'd phone because Cat had a baby girl. This morning.'

'That is wonderful news,' Malachy said, soft and contemplative.

'And also – I got that job.'

His voice changed from thoughtful to energized. 'Oriana – that's really terrific. Well done.'

'I just thought I'd phone you. I reckoned you'd like to know. About both.'

'Absolutely.'

'I know you hate texts.'

'I do. I don't much like phones, full stop.'

'I can take a bus all the way to Blenthrop.'

'What – now?'

Frantically she looked at her watch. She could – if that's what he was suggesting, she'd be delighted to.

'Oh, you mean simply that it's possible. That's good – you should do that some time,' Malachy had already continued. 'Congratulations to Cat and to you.'

'Thank you.'

'Does the baby have a name?'

'Annabel.'

'And do you have a job title?'

'Well – architect.'

'I love that,' said Malachy quietly. She'd done it. It struck him now how this was the grown-up Oriana. And that she'd made it. They'd all made it, in their own ways, despite everything. 'I'm proud of you.'

She heard him the first time. 'Sorry?'

'I'm proud of you,' he said again.

Fanbloodytastic! Jed's text bounded in. **I'm taking you out to celebrate tonight. Come and meet me from work. Champagne'll pop like never before. Jxx**

Malachy looked at the work phone. Apart from that one text sent when she moved to Jed's, Oriana had only ever used his work number. That afternoon, he wondered about that. Was it like the *vous* and *tu* in French? Had his dislike of phones inadvertently caused her to feel constrained and formal? Why hadn't he told her that it was irrelevant whether or not he hated mobiles when actually, to have contact with her by whatever means was good. He thought about buses and how protracted the trundle of the

route from Sheffield would be. He thought about
the crate arriving from America – how lengthy and
circuitous a reason it had provided for Oriana to
make another visit to Windward. He thought about
the hassle of borrowing other people's cars.

I haven't made it easy for her, he thought. I haven't
once said to her, hey, why not come over? Why not
come for dinner? For Sunday lunch, for a stroll, for
a chat, for a plunder of photo albums and a rummage
through the kitchen cupboards?

A visitor to the gallery interrupted his intense
consideration.

He sold a screen print and the framing costs on
top.

'Will it take long?'

'Shouldn't do.'

'OK – will you let me know straight away?'

'I'll phone you as soon as it's in.'

It struck him he hadn't once phoned Oriana since
she'd given him her number. He thought of Oriana's
single, shy little text trying to sneak past his own
stubborn and vociferous eschewal of phones.

Today her oldest friend had given birth and Oriana
had her career back on track. And she'd wanted him
to know.

He stared at the message box on his phone. How
much reading between the lines did a text message
carry? That worried him. He wanted nothing to be
misconstrued. His relationship with Oriana had
always been searingly honest and he was concerned
that this might be upended by a few words entrusted
to the ether. With Oriana, unlike with any other

woman, any person in his life really, it had always been that what he said was all that she could have. He hid nothing, he'd always ensured that everything he'd ever told her had precise meaning that could never be doubled. He couldn't bear to run the risk of that happening now.

Malachy looked at his mobile for a long while. He had to concede that actually, little had to do with him disliking gadgets. To text Oriana was to talk to her afresh, to establish a new conversation based on the present. He'd never forget how they'd been, what they'd said and the way they used to talk to each other. Perhaps it was time to see if they really could communicate now. When it came to Oriana, he had never hidden what he felt but he knew that he had stopped himself recently for fear of what might happen if he started. Just then, it struck him that it was time to confront that fear instead of pretending it didn't exist. Still, there was a great difference between his door being unlocked and him flinging it wide open.

When Malachy's text pinged through to her phone, Oriana was singing while darting around Jed's flat, her wet hair turbaned in a towel as she prepared for a night out to celebrate. She didn't hear the message arrive; she was running late due to finally being able to speak to Cat by phone. The utter joy to effuse together directly! The excitement to be able to visit tomorrow!

'Where's my bloody key?'

Oriana ricocheted around the sitting room

checking surfaces plainly bare just in case the key had miraculously materialized.

'Oh well, Jed'll have his.'

It was only while she was waiting for the bus and thought to text him that she was running late, that Oriana discovered she didn't have her phone with her either.

Her phone had slipped down onto the floor, nestled out of immediate sight between bed and chest of drawers. And so Thomas Hardy was to be played out in a flat in Sheffield. Like Tess' letter to Angel, so Malachy's two texts to Oriana wouldn't be found when they were most needed, when they could change the course of things and shape history in a better form.

When I was . . .

When I was really quite young I learned how to switch off a little part of me.

CHAPTER THIRTY-TWO

'It suits you.'

'Oh God – it's ages old.'

'Not your clothes.'

'Oh!'

'Have some more champagne, girl. I meant, friends having babies and you landing prize jobs – *that's* what suits you. You're glowing.'

As Oriana glided into the buffer of chilled champagne, so her blush was quelled back into a glow. Throughout the evening, she'd been accepting congratulations on behalf of Cat by a group of smiling, drinking people who'd never met her friend. And these same gregarious people, whom she barely knew, had repeatedly chinked her glass and raised theirs to toast her new job. At the beginning of the evening, their familiarity surprised her and she wondered if they just wanted a reason to drink. Soon enough, it didn't seem to matter. There was a buzz and an energy because it was Friday night and any old excuse would do – that the newbie amongst them had a new job *and* a friend with a new baby was perfect. While she floated through the evening on a swell of compliments and champagne, anchoring her all the while was Jed.

Whenever her glass was emptying, he refilled it. Whenever the conversation flowed away from her, he guided her back in. If there was an in-joke, he gave her access. Whenever she looked at him, he was already smiling at her.

'This is a nice bunch,' she said to him. 'I liked the lot we met up with last week at the Stag too. And those guys at the pub quiz. And of course your work chums.'

'I'm lucky.'

'You know loads of people,' Oriana marvelled. 'Mr Popular. I can count my true friends on the fingers of one hand.' It was something she'd always felt proud of. Jed, though, gave her a look of condolence.

'I'm lucky,' said Jed. But then he wondered, out of all the people who liked him, how many truly knew him? Was there anyone in the world who knew him as well as Oriana did? Probably only his brother.

'More champagne anyone?'

Oriana watched as Jed was thanked and patted and cheered. He looked over at her, her cheeks flushed, her smile wide, her eyes simultaneously sparkling yet glazed with champagne. He glanced at his watch; the evening started so long ago but the night was still young. He perused the table: bottles of champagne, some empty, two still full; shiny-faced revellers having a great time all thanks to him. His back was slapped and his good health constantly toasted. There was a girl with them tonight – Kathy – with whom he'd had a brief dalliance. She was still keen even now, when it was so obvious to everyone that he only had eyes for Oriana. Jed looked at Oriana and at the people sharing his evening and at the table groaning with glasses and he thought to himself, I'm a pretty good catch.

The cold of the early hours hit Oriana as much as the smell of kebabs and chips which clung temptingly to the air.

'Oh God, I am drunk,' she wailed at Jed. 'You bad man. You bad, bad man.'

'You can't be that drunk,' he reasoned, taking her arm and linking it through his as though it was necessary to steady her. 'Because if you were, you wouldn't have walked past the takeaway, you'd be pushing your way to the front.'

'True,' said Oriana.

'Do you want a kebab?'

'No, thanks.'

'Did you enjoy it tonight?'

'I had a brilliant time.' She thought about it. 'I had a brilliant day.' She thought about her job and how much taller she felt after the phone call than before, how she felt older now but no longer half as old as she had been feeling. This morning she'd felt a little ragged, faded. Now she felt talented and bright. 'I feel – capable.'

'Capable?'

'I'd been feeling anything but. As if whatever I might design would surely collapse.'

'Now you'll be paid to design skyscrapers.'

'Residential,' she qualified.

'Mansions, then.'

She giggled.

'What's so funny?' he asked and in one simple move, his arm was now around her and travelled swiftly from her shoulder to settle at her waist. Within two paces, she had her arm around his waist too. Walking was just too jolting otherwise. 'What's so funny?' he asked again, slowing right down. Stopping, giving her a little squeeze. 'Eh?'

'Not *funny* per se,' she qualified, pulling away to stand, hands on hips, to think about it. She was pleased to discover that the buttons on his shirt were no longer levitating above the fabric as they had appeared to do when they left the bar. 'Not *funny* – just every reason to laugh.' She looked at Jed, wonderment wrinkling her nose. 'What a day! I got a job. But Cat had a *baby*!' She paused. 'She gave birth today. She's a *mom*.'

Jed put the key in the door and opened it

'You just said "mom",' he said casually over his shoulder.

'Fuck off!' she said, jogging after him and into the lift. 'I said "mum".' She pressed the button for the third floor.

'You did not!' He looked at her wryly. 'You said "mom". Yank.'

She bashed him lightly on the chest and he caught her wrist and held it, his eyes completing the net he'd encircled her with.

'We're all grown up,' he said and his tone of voice had changed from larky to a murmur. The resonance of his words hung thickly like humidity in the closed air of the lift. He didn't let go, of her eyes or her wrist. He slipped his fingers through hers and led her to his flat.

The mess he made of fitting the key to the tricky lock and jiggling it open, the clumsy removing of shoes, the slinging of coats, the sudden running of noses that the warm interior caused – nothing intervened on the overriding sense of anticipation.

He was very close.

When did you get so tall, Jed? When did your cheeks develop that smooth scoop? The crinkle at your eyes? The width of your neck and the breadth of your shoulders?

He stepped closer, one hand lightly at the base of her back, the other holding hers again. For a suspended moment in which she had plenty of time to think but none to act, Oriana knew he was going to kiss her. Her power of reasoning was immobilized. As his face came closer and her focus blurred she forgot about who she was and whom she loved because all that mattered was the sensation. Sometimes, the cerebral is unrelated to the physical. Sometimes it's just better to feel than to think. Sometimes the exhilaration of the moment outweighs the risking of the long-term. Sometimes it's all simply down to the pursuit of pure pleasure.

A portion of fries after dieting. A pillow after a long sleepless journey. Sheepskin boots after a day in high heels. A stilled car after hours on a motorway. Closing the front door at the end of a shit day. That's what kissing Jed was. It was something not tasted for a long, long while and never had it felt more timely. The last person she'd had any intimacy with had been Casey though it was months before the end of the relationship when he'd actually kissed her like this. But she didn't think of that, or of Casey, or Jed, or even Malachy. She was, quite simply, present. She was just kissing for the joy of kissing and grabbing at all that it gave. The thrill of another's lips moistened, and the flick of someone else's tongue, the actual taste of their desire for her when for so long she'd been desired by no one. Hands travelling over her body, the buzz between her legs, fingers through her hair, the sound of someone wanting her: hastened breathing, a burgeoning sigh.

Like fries after dieting it probably wasn't a very healthy idea but as with anything denied for so long, the temptation was to gorge. How she might feel afterwards had no place in her conscience right now. Jed took her hand and led her away from the thought and into his bed.

Clothes were shed at the same rate as inhibition, what was normally concealed came into the open. Jed didn't want to tell her how she'd changed because he wanted what he'd long dreamed of: continuity. He wanted this Oriana to be exactly the same as the one he'd lost his virginity to almost two decades ago. Over the years in between, he'd recalled vividly every dip and sway, the hue of her nipples, the shape of her belly button, the feel of her legs. Now, almost everything was just slightly altered. Undulations were a little more pronounced, arms thinner, hips that bit wider, legs like a woman not a girl, breasts fuller, stomach softer. What hadn't changed was the silkiness of her skin and as Jed's hands swooped all over her, so he could conjure again how it had felt all those years ago.

The feel of a man. The broadness of shoulders and sense of safety being in strong arms. Oriana folded herself tight within his embrace and buried her nose in his neck, returning to his mouth every now and then. She couldn't work out if she was hot or cold but she could feel herself shake as hands stroked her thighs, her nipples were sucked, fingers probed inside her tantalisingly gently, eliciting her wetness and desire. Her eyes closed and she let him push her onto her back. As she felt his mouth brush and kiss and taste and bite, she couldn't have opened her eyes had she tried. Lower he went until he was licking up her inner thighs, kissing at her while pushing her legs open. His nose nudging, his tongue flicking, his fingers joining in the play until it felt as though he was drinking her in when she orgasmed. The pulsing pleasure enveloped her in wave after wave, transporting her far from where she was and where she hoped to be. Her body took over, and greedily. And then she opened her eyes and in the darkness of the room everything was glaringly clear.

That's not the sound I make when I come.

I am crying.

I am awake.

I am present.

I am here.

I don't want to have sex with Jed.

* * *

She tried to push him away, she tried to pull her thighs together, she turned her face away from his and used her hands to lever his chest off hers. But she couldn't say a word because her throat was tight with tears. He thought, is that the noise she makes when she comes? It sounded unfamiliar but he couldn't remember back to when they'd been young and inexperienced, he couldn't remember what sex between them had actually been like. He'd embellished the memories to such an extent that the fiction was more real. However, the musky scent of her was in his nose, his mouth was full of the taste of her and the need to be inside her was so strong it felt as though his entire being was flowing into his cock.

'For so long,' he murmured. 'For so long.'

She was sure she said no. She could hear herself yelling it inside her head. But the realization that she couldn't be heard was terrifying. Clamp your legs shut, she screamed at herself. Turn away! Push him off. The paralysis and panic were worse than quicksand in a dream.

Her legs were being spread, her mouth had been plugged with tongue, her breast was being kneaded, her hair was grabbed as he pushed up into her. And that was when a little part of her switched off and closed down.

Everything went black and deep and silent. The only thing she could feel was the stinging slick of one fat, silent, oily tear. Into her head came Malachy and, at the sight of him, finally she let go; she wilted and she wept.

It was precisely then – when her body went limp, just seconds before he realized she was crying – that Jed stopped abruptly. He pulled out of her and flicked on the light. She was facing away from him, curled in a muddle, the prominence of her spine a tattered, curved ridge. Jed watched her body shake. What had he done? What on earth had he done? Had he hurt her? Did she not like it? He hadn't been rough, had he? He'd been immersed in his desire for her – but he hadn't meant to hurt her. He would *never* hurt her.

And then it struck him. Did she not want it? Had she said no but he hadn't heard? Had she tried to resist? He pulled the sheet tight around him, suddenly ashamed of his stridently hard cock. Should he touch her? He reached a hand tentatively for her shoulder and laid it there as gently as he could. What damage had been done?

'Oriana?'

He could detect the extreme effort of keeping her sobs to herself.

'What's wrong?'

He tried to cuddle up and spoon lightly against her, to make her feel safe the way he had once been able to, but he felt her stiffen and then slink away.

'Oriana?'

'I'm sorry,' she whispered. 'I'm so sorry.'

Didn't she want him? Was that what it was? After all they'd shared, all those years that had passed since, and now this extraordinary opportunity to pick up where they'd left off – did she simply not want him? He looked at the way she'd folded herself up. She was in the brace position as if she was plummeting.

He wondered, has she changed her mind? And then he wondered, or was it me who made it up for her?

CHAPTER THIRTY-THREE

When Oriana sat beside Cat, next to the clear plastic cot and dropped her head and cried, Cat beamed and felt quite proud that the birth of her daughter could move her friend so.

'It's just I am really really happy for you,' Oriana said, her face a blear of tears and snot.

'Thanks,' Cat said. She wasn't quite sure if the baby was latching on. It hurt. There were no nurses around.

'I don't know what I'm doing,' she said to Oriana.

Oriana looked at her. 'Neither do I.'

They smiled at each other, at the baby, at Cat's boob, and then they both started to laugh.

'Can I help you?'

'Have you done this before?'

'Isn't it like hanging a picture? Don't we have to just hook the baby on somehow?'

'I honestly don't know. Yesterday, the midwife helped.'

'Shall I go and find someone?'

'Good luck with that.'

Cat winced as the baby chomped down, unaligned.

'Ouch,' said Oriana. Then she had a thought. 'Try holding her like a rugby ball?'

'Surprising as it might seem,' said Cat, 'I've never actually played rugby.'

'It's just I recall at Windward – do you remember Plum and Willow? When their baby brother came, there was a lady with a long silvery plait and skin as smooth and brown as a conker. I don't know who she was or how long she stayed but I do remember her placing the baby – like *this*.' Gently but authoritatively, Oriana changed the position of Cat's baby, facing her little body the other way, supported by a pillow.

'Yes – this is how it's meant to feel! I am being milked!'

'Does it hurt?'

'Sort of, but I think it's meant to feel like this – not like that.' Cat looked at Oriana. 'We'll make a midwife out of you yet.'

'Well, it's a nice offer,' said Oriana. 'But I've already accepted another job.'

Cat was thrilled to hear about it; it took her mind off the stinging yomp of the baby suckling. 'Shouldn't you look a little more over the moon?'

'I am,' said Oriana, her little finger tight within the baby's grip. 'It's just – other stuff.' She glanced at Cat who was eyeing her suspiciously.

'You have to tell him how you feel, Oriana,' Cat said earnestly. 'You need to go to Malachy and tell him what he means to you.'

'How did you know it was Malachy?'

'Are you nuts? It's always been him. You need to bring it to fruition. It's been years and years in embryo. It's ridiculous.'

'Why would he feel the same way?'

Cat gave her a look. 'Even if, after everything, nothing comes of it – you still need to release the tumbling truth that's caught up inside you.'

'I never loved anyone like I loved him.'

'Don't put him in the past tense.'

'It's too complicated.'

'That's an excuse. A stupid one. You're not a teenager. You're a grown woman. You deserve exactly what I have. You'd be bloody good at it.'

'Something happened with Jed,' Oriana said, casting her eyes down.

'Something's always happening with Jed,' said Cat. 'He's that type of boy. But Malachy's the one for you.'

'It's just – I don't know. It seems to me that I bring chaos and cause a mess wherever I go.'

'You're being way too melodramatic,' said Cat. 'Jesus.'

'Sorry.' Oriana thought back over the years. 'They never gave me the chance to say sorry.'

'Seems to me you have that opportunity now.' The baby had slipped off Cat's nipple in drunken oblivion.

They sat in silence gazing at tiny brand new Annabel who spun warm threads of calm and contentment around them.

'It's just that yesterday Jed and I – well. Sort of but not really. There was alcohol. And I was emotional. And I closed my eyes because I was being kissed and ravished and I liked the feeling. Then I opened them – and I really didn't want to be there. It was awful. Just awful.'

Cat stared at her levelly. 'In a peculiar way, it will be easier to rectify your friendship with Jed than develop your relationship with Malachy. But when did you ever take the simple route anywhere?'

Oriana let Cat's words hang in the air.

'Oriana – it seems to me that despite a massive detour via America, your destination was always Windward.'

When Django arrived, Oriana took a back seat – literally moving to an orange plastic chair in the corner of the ward. It was good to be alone with her thoughts. She would clean up the mess she'd left in Sheffield, it wasn't impossible. The situation was awkward but not caustic. It was like a bowl of cereal spilt before the milk's poured in. Annoying but a small mercy to be thankful for. Last night with Jed – what might that jeopardize? Must Malachy know? She shuddered, though, when she thought of Malachy. How to get close to him, when being close to him was all she'd ever wanted? And what if he didn't reciprocate? If he didn't feel the same? Because, after all, why should he?

She read again the texts he'd sent last night which she'd found this morning. She knew she was feeling over-emotional but still she thought there was a certain predictable tragedy that she hadn't come across them at the time. That's why she hadn't shown them to Cat. Fate, it seemed to her, had a horrible way of intervening in her relationship with that man. It was as if some greater power was saying, time and again, no, not him, when every fibre of her being contradicted that and said only him. No one else.

She watched from afar as Django took the baby into his arms, saw how Cat's field of vision had polarized around what was important in her life, what now defined her. Mom. Mummy. There were hundreds of words for it in every tongue known to Man and yet not a single word could really encapsulate it.

She would speak to Malachy. She would speak to Jed. She prayed that Jed, whom she did so love, would understand what she said even if he hated the sound of it. And she'd have to prepare herself that Malachy, whom she loved so deeply, might tell her what she dreaded. She would have to acknowledge that the truth is the only thing worth listening to because truth, unlike lies, has a future.

When Ben arrived and his world with Cat and his daughter closed the door on all visitors, Django and Oriana left together brimming with emotion. There was a waft of gauzy rain coming rhythmically from the distant dales like shallow breaths and, against the sunshine and warmth of the early afternoon, even the modern hospital buildings were licked with gold, the cars festooned with pearls, the puddles filled with gemstones.

'What a day,' said Django. 'Will you come back with me? For a cup of tea or a glass of something? Strangely, for one so happy and content, I don't want to be on my own.'

The McCabes' house was home. Oriana sank into the cavernous sofa and sat in amicable, thoughtful silence with Django, sipping peculiar herbal tea and gnawing into hunks of a strange cake that was both rock hard and super sweet. They felt replenished and relaxed, so conversation came easily. Sheffield and bus routes and new jobs and babies and the ins and outs of keeping prostate cancer in check. And do you remember this person and that person? And the parties. Oh, the parties. And that terrible teacher at school with the vast grey teeth. And Fen's news. And Pip's. And all about California. And yes, Django had heard about the debacle with the cot. And don't you worry – it was related in only an affectionate way. And the baby! Oh, the beautiful beautiful tiny little soul. How grown up you kids are. How old I am become.

'I saw my father.'

'I know.'

'You do?'

'He told me.'

'You've seen him too?'

'Yes. I do. Every now and then. I dig him out, brush him off and take him to the pub. To the Rag and Thistle where there are folk far more cantankerous than him and the beer is much more bitter.'

'Really?'

'You're surprised.'

'I thought he never left the apartment.'

'Never? Of course he does! He takes a taxi to Bakewell sometimes during the day. But mostly he paints when it's light and surfaces after dark. And once in a while he phones and tells me to pick him up and I do.'

'I never thought –'

'It's quite amazing, isn't it, that your parents' generation can make decisions and plans and maintain a life of their own where you don't feature.'

'I never figured in my parents' lives.'

They let it hang in the air like smoke after a firework.

'That's not strictly true,' Django said. 'Shrug all you want, my girl – but that's not strictly true.'

She was never going to agree on that one.

'But my father told you that he saw me?'

'He told me you waved.'

'He waved first,' Oriana said defensively, wanting it known that the mythical olive branch was not her idea.

'I meant "you" plural.'

'Oh.'

'He's an awful man, Oriana. But I say that with cautious affection. Not much – but some. And he's old. And alone. Apart from Malachy.'

Malachy. For hours she'd had respite from thinking of him. Now he might as well have been standing right there in the room on the flagstones, arms folded, waiting for her soliloquy, his response concealed. Even the image was too much for her to confront.

'You're not going to tell me you play Bridge with my mother and Bernard, are you?'

Django laughed and shook his head. 'I haven't seen her in years. How is she?'

'The same. I haven't seen her myself – since I stayed at Cat and Ben's. It seems to me there's a silent pact not to see each other more often than when I lived abroad – regardless of proximity.'

'Wise,' said Django but Oriana heard it as 'why' and continued.

'Some might think that sad,' she said. 'But I don't. It's enough. My relationship with my mother has never altered. Nothing that's happened has worsened it. No sudden deterioration. Nothing to workshop, nothing to improve. An acceptance that it is what it is because it's always been as it is.'

Django stroked his goatee rhythmically. He didn't have to say out loud, *whereas with Robin* . . . Oriana could see the words were on the tip of his tongue and she loved him for keeping them there just then. Over the years, her sadness and anger and fears and frustrations had been given voice in this house. Tonight, there was wisdom in the silence.

'Why don't you stay here tonight?' said Django.

It was so tempting. Oriana could go upstairs and find rooms that she knew off by heart, that would guarantee her a safe and potentially dreamless sleep. She knew how to run the bath, to handle the taps with the sensitivity of a wartime code transmitter, fine tuning the flow so that the temperature was even. It would be so lovely to stay, so easy. She wouldn't have to think about a thing. She could have one of Django's epic Sunday breakfasts tomorrow, perhaps catch a lift and visit Cat again.

And then what?

She looked down and found she had plaited all the strands on the tartan throw. She remembered how all of them – Cat, Fen, Pip – had at one time or other done this. Worries about boys, school, friendships; moodiness was always lessened by plaiting the strands.

'And what does the magic blanket say?' Django broke through.

Oriana unravelled them, smoothed them straight again, ready for someone else's angst. 'I ought to go.'

'You are welcome any time, Oriana. Not as a guest – as family.'

She was so tired, so emotional. She brushed a fast tear away quickly. And another.

'Where can I take you?' Django asked.

'Please could you take me to Windward?'

CHAPTER THIRTY-FOUR

'Are you sure?'

'I'm fine.'

'You don't want me to take you all the way up? To wait?'

'No – honestly.'

'But say he's not in?'

Oriana looked at Django, grateful for the ambiguity, not wanting to name 'him'. She wanted to be dropped at the bottom of the drive, she said, because she fancied a stroll in the fresh air. Django knew it was more to do with a desire not to be seen.

'Well, if you're absolutely sure,' Django said, a little reluctantly.

'I'll be fine,' Oriana said. 'Thank you – and congratulations, Gramps – what a day!'

He could detect the effort behind the exclamation mark but he respected her request and drove away.

As was typical at that time of year, early summer and late spring were still at loggerheads; a fine day earlier gave way to a decidedly brisk evening. As the light changed with night beckoning, so the benign breeze of the afternoon had now churned into something less clement. The driveway at

Windward was a quarter of a mile long and Oriana still remembered how to make the walk longer or shorter. There had been times when she'd dragged her heels along it, meandering from side to side, taking the hump of the bends to clock up a few precious extra yards. On other occasions she'd cut every corner, sticking to the underside of the curve and saving herself minutes. Tonight she kept clearly to the middle, her footfalls providing a rhythmic base under the wind's freeform song which gusted about her. One more bend and then she'd see it. It would come into view at this time of night, its lumbering silhouette pierced with lights shining inside, like a candle within a skull. But she couldn't see it yet and the indistinct light, typifying dusk slipping into night, was comforting.

She stopped a while by the lime trees and spoke under her breath. She'd memorized her plan of action but she felt fortified by repeating it. I'll knock. If there's no reply, I'll just go in. If he's there, I'll simply say hullo. I'll try to keep it warm and friendly and just see where it leads. If it doesn't lead where I hope, I'll just go. I'll go to Lilac's. I'll make out that is where I was headed all along, at 9.30 on Saturday night.

By the time she was crossing the turning circle in front of the house, she'd managed to make the journey there last almost ten minutes longer than normal. She'd just passed the Ice House where she knew Paula and the de la Mare family lived. They had pleasant uplights making their trees glow, breathing warmth into the brickwork that counteracted the chill night air. The Ice House, known only as the shack, a ruin, to Oriana, now looked like the stuff of fairy tales. One day, she'd accept Paula's invitation and knock on the door. She thought about it, imagined taking little Emma and Kate on a tour of the building she'd known. But all this was just procrastination. She had to walk on, heading for the main house which, just then, looked so different from how it should.

When she was young she knew absolutely who put the lights on when and where. It was as if each resident was standing at the window waving to her. Sometimes, they had. She was a familiar sight in those days, taking solace in the gardens if she didn't want to be in her apartment. Tonight, Windward looked very different. It was difficult to tell who was at home because luxurious curtains were shutting off the inhabitants from the world, or the world from them. Privacy was being brandished as a purchasable right these days, whereas when she was growing up at Windward, privacy had seemed peculiar. Tonight, no one would know she was there – because they were unaware of anything outside their windows. Oriana would have the night to herself and it made her feel at once safe yet also isolated.

Is he in?

Why wouldn't he be in?

How will he react?

Instead of knocking first, instead of just opening the door, Oriana hovered. Long before she came to the door, she could sense he was there but she was aware of something else too. Voices and laughter. It was both perplexing and chastening. She chided herself – what right had she to assume that he'd be there on his own just waiting for her to waltz in? The world doesn't stop turning, time doesn't stand still, life goes on regardless of Oriana Taylor. A little unsteady, she took a wide and stumbling route right around the building, edging her way along the garden to her cedar tree which afforded her an unparalleled view of the back of the house. She could see quite clearly from here that Malachy wasn't alone.

The windows to the balcony off the ballroom were open and someone was having a cigarette out there, their glass of wine glinting every now and then. From where she stood, Oriana scanned the apartment; there didn't seem to be anyone else in the ballroom but from the opened windows of the kitchen assorted voices and various conversations drifted pleasantly into the night like the different aromas that make up a great meal. Slumping a little against the trunk of the tree, Oriana was struck how the intervening years had made a massive difference to absolutely everything. Malachy had established his own life and how could she have been so deluded as to think that he might have saved a space for her? Malachy was a man in his late thirties now, not a boy. He had silver flecks in his hair and crinkles around his eyes which spoke of the history he'd amassed long after she'd left his life. He had his own life, his own business and it was none of hers.

And she was honestly thinking of pushing into his life tonight and telling him that she'd never stopped loving him?

Was she really expecting him to say my darling! I've always loved you too!

A happy ever after? With Malachy? At *Windward*? Was she out of her tiny mind? It was all preposterous.

She thought, I am in the middle of the fucking gardens on a chilly night. She thought, I have no means of getting home. She thought, I have no home. She couldn't bear to think of Jed, what kind of a day he'd been having, of having to see him again and confront it all. She thought, I could go to my father's. And then she thought, what difference does a single wave make? None. And actually, she didn't want to go to her father's. And of course she wasn't going to disturb Lilac. She was in her dotage and should be allowed to while away a Saturday night wearing her massive headphones with Bruce Forsyth or John Wayne for company, nodding off in front of the television without being disturbed by the endless and depressing dramas that Oriana had brought to her door throughout her life.

Her feet were cold. She needed to keep moving. She needed to walk, to keep walking, all the way back to Sheffield. She could make it some stupid epic hike; she'd accept no lift, no help. It might take her the ten days between now and her new job starting. See the lone walker! She's made it to the A61! No one knows where she's come from and no one knows where she's going – least of all her. Perhaps she should just sod the job and keep on walking, all the way to John o'Groats, then trudge into the ocean and swim the Atlantic back to the United States. She was cold; she really ought to go.

She glanced at her watch. She'd been out here, ruminating, for forty-five minutes. Malachy's buddies were probably on the cheese course by now. She started to walk across the lawn, just putting one foot in front of the other, thinking how the lawn had never been so rolled and even in her day. It had been tussocky which had made playing It or rounders or British Bulldog or even Kiss Chase all the more challenging and exciting.

The smoker had gone in some time ago but look! he's back again, with a replenished glass of wine and having another cig on the balcony. He wouldn't see Oriana. He wouldn't know where to look. Just then, she felt like the most invisible thing in the world and far from being empowering, it simply served to highlight how inconsequential she felt. And then her phone rang out. The signal had returned almost as soon as she left the sanctity of the cedar, and emails and voicemail alerts trilled through the air while the screen lit up like a beacon. Her cover was surrendered; the man on the balcony had clocked her, a nameless person just coming into view in the moonlight.

Just look like you live here, she said to herself. Just mooch and mosey as if you're a resident out for a stroll.

'Malachy – there's someone in the garden.'

Don't worry, Oriana said to herself, Malachy won't be surprised. It's just a resident out for a stroll.

But Malachy was surprised because mostly, these days, the Windward occupants holed themselves up at night, shutting the door on the outside to enjoy all the interior trimmings their wealth bestowed. Supersized Internet TVs in prime positions on walls where once paintings created at Windward had hung. Music from MP3 files filling the rooms more perfectly than the bands who'd jammed in them. Mood lighting more atmospheric than the moon, deeply luxurious sofas far more comfortable than garden benches and tree stumps. They did still pick blackberries – because the fruits that freckled the hedgerows were far plumper and sweeter than those in prepacked M&S punnets. But it was too dark for that and anyway, it was a good two months too early. Malachy went to the balcony and looked. He could see no one.

'I must be seeing things,' his friend said. 'This Bordeaux's good.'

'You're on your third glass, Rob,' Malachy laughed. 'Come on – Paula's pudding awaits you.'

'I do love a double entendre,' Rob said.

'Your wife has baked the dessert,' Malachy said, as if talking to a simpleton. 'Come on. There's hot sauce.'

'Double entendre,' said Rob hopefully.

Malachy looked out over the garden again. There wasn't anyone there. But that's because no one knew how to hide as well as Oriana, to blend into the background as expertly as she could.

Then the rain came. What had been gentle drizzle that afternoon was now prosaic, cold and fast. Once she would have danced and laughed and been ecstatic to be soaked to the skin. Just then, however, it seemed predictable that if her plans were a washout, it might as well just go ahead and piss it down on her parade. She wasn't entirely sure what to do next. She could see the lights on in her father's studio, but nowhere else in her old home, and she didn't want to continue the wave anyway. Lilac's apartment was dark. She found semi-shelter under the overhang around the side of the building and checked her phone. Two missed calls from Jed. Two texts as well.

Where's you? I hope you're ok – walking?! Thinking?! Let's do some talking. So sorry if in any way I did something wrong. Love you]xx

And then, a couple of hours later:

Have you gone??]x

She thought, if only Jed was the bona-fide baddy in a fictitious adaptation of her life, how much easier it would be to set the record straight. But he wasn't and he'd done nothing wrong. And tonight, she could only hide away from him much as she was currently hiding from the rain and from her father and from Malachy with his kitchen full of friends and cheer. She couldn't call Cat. She absolutely wouldn't be dragging Django out. There wasn't the signal to FaceTime Ashlyn. She didn't have the money for a taxi anywhere, she didn't even have a number for a cab firm anyway. She shuddered to think how her mother would react if she called for Bernard to pick her up. This was the first time in her life that she'd been at Windward with no place to go. She'd always been able to leave her own home for someone else's. The Bedwells' had never been closed to her. But tonight, in the modern age and the real world, in the rain, it was.

She stood there for over an hour, huddled into a zone where she focused on nothing. While she listened instead to the sound of the weather, she tuned in to the feel of the night, the sight of how leaves became trampolines for raindrops and the ground lapped up being wet. And then, one by one, Malachy's guests left. From the shadows, Oriana watched as two cars headed off, and Paula and her husband, the man from the balcony, returned to their dwelling. Was there anyone left? The notion struck her like a punch of lead hitting her stomach. He'd told her he didn't have a girlfriend – but had that changed? Or maybe there was someone he wouldn't classify as a girlfriend, just someone who was a casual thing? Stealthily, she took a route well known to her, sticking to the shadows though it provided little shelter from the rain. As she went, she saw the kitchen lights were still on. She wondered if Malachy was clearing up, whether he was washing dishes or sitting down and munching on leftovers. She backed into the garden, trying to see in. The rain was making her blink a lot. It was hammering down now. It didn't feel as cold as before, the wind had dropped. The audible squelch with every footstep she took made her realize that her feet were soaked.

The ballroom was dark. Did you mean to leave the kitchen light on, Malachy? Did you forget to turn it off before you went to bed?

No, you idiot girl. I'm standing on the balcony getting wet but you haven't thought to look over this way.

He watched her and wondered why she was here, why she was outside instead of inside. For a moment, he wondered whether the front door might be locked but he knew it wasn't. He wondered whether Rob had been right – whether there had been someone in the garden earlier on and whether it had been Oriana. And did that mean she'd been here, all that time? Outside in the rain? When did she arrive? How did she get here? What did she want? Was he meant to do something? Did she even want to be found?

'How's the weather down there?'

Slowly, Oriana turned to her left and looked up at the balcony.

'How's the weather down there?' he said again. 'Up here, it's pretty damn wet.'

She couldn't think what to say. 'It's raining.'

'You don't say.'

She watched as Malachy tipped his face up to the sky as if suddenly working out that's what this wet stuff was.

'It's raining up here too.'

'Oh.'

He watched her. She was standing still. Almost still. She was doing that thing she'd always done when she was deep in thought, or out of sorts, not knowing quite what to do and trying out different ideas. She was staring down at her shoes, raising the toe of one, then the other, as if her feet were giving her this option and that, and she was working out which thought fitted best.

'Oriana,' he called in a tone which knew how to bring her back to the present.

She looked up and over at him.

'Would you like to come in?'

'You look like the Lady in the Lake who's been in there a bit too long,' he remarked, opening the door. She stepped inside and he closed it behind her. 'Or Ophelia.' His comment, wryly made, flung both of them back through the years to feisty spats on the merits of *Hamlet*.

'Still think the play's full of clichés,' Oriana muttered. She looked up at him shyly. He wasn't as utterly drenched as she was but still his cotton shirt clung to his torso here and there, his forearms were damp and his hair was licked wet.

'Come on,' he said. 'Let's get you dry.'

He watched – he heard – as she battled with the soaking laces of her Converse trainers and squeaked her feet out of them, her socks pulling off a little as she did so. She took them off too. And Malachy thought, I remember your toes. I remember your toes. And he had to turn away from the sight of them and a charge of barefoot memories. Running in the gardens. Padding in and out of each other's homes. Lolling and listening to the radio, or a band. Or watching the television, or someone rehearsing. Holding her feet between his hands and playing This Little Piggy when they were far too old for that but when they were all alone, with no one around, and they could fold into each other and this little piggy went kiss kiss kiss all the way home.

'Come through,' Malachy said, walking ahead, away from such stirring emotions. 'I'll get you a towel.'

With the towel he gave her some jogging bottoms and a sweatshirt and a pair of socks. By now she had started to shiver.

'I don't have any lady's knickers,' he said and he saw how she was too cold, too wet and too exhausted to banter back.

Oriana stood in the shower for a long time, motionless, just letting the comfort of hot water replace the discomfort of too much rain. She didn't want to get out, to get dry. She didn't want to wear his clothes because they'd smell of him. She didn't want to move time forward to when she'd have to say all she'd come here to say. She spent a long time, wrapped in the towel, sitting on the edge of the bath, staring at the pile of clothes. Eventually, feeling chilled again, she dressed. His clothes were much too big of course, but she rolled up trouser legs and sleeves and sat down again, burying her nose in the neck of his top.

'Have you drowned?' He knocked.

'I'm fine,' she called.

When she appeared, swamped in his clothes, Malachy thought she looked like something that had shrunk in the wash.

'I made you cocoa,' he said and she saw he was

holding two mugs. 'Mum's recipe – remember?'

She hadn't forgotten. Hot chocolate in the States had never tasted quite right.

'Come on.' He led on through to the ballroom. By the time he'd shut the balcony doors, she was curled in the corner of the sofa just as she had been a few weeks ago. He took his place on the Eames, resting his mug on the footstool, on a make-shift coaster of the Louis Sullivan book she'd left for him.

'You saw the book,' she smiled.

'Yes.'

They blew on their drinks and sipped.

'Congratulations on your job,' he said. 'That's great news.'

'Thanks.'

'When do you start?'

'The week after next,' she said.

'Looking forward to it?'

'Yes.'

And Malachy remembered how, when Oriana had so much to say, she could manage only one word at a time. He also remembered just how he used to be able to extract it from her. He took quick sips of the chocolate, as if to swallow down the memory and keep the technique at bay. If she had something to say, he wasn't sure whether he wanted to hear it.

'What's the time?' she suddenly said. He recalled how she'd use this as an avoidance tactic. It had happened often. He'd tell her the time and she'd say oh! I must be going. And off she'd disappear. He glanced at his watch and he knew she'd be going nowhere tonight.

'It's tomorrow,' he said.

She looked worried.

'Do you want me to drive you to Sheffield? I'm probably just under the limit.'

'OK.' Her response was rushed and unsteady.

They stood up, holding their mugs which were still over half full. 'I'll get my keys then,' he said and he left the ballroom.

She stood where she was, cursing herself for her timidity.

'Ready?' he was calling.

She shuffled off, skating her feet slowly over the floorboards because she'd trip over Malachy's socks otherwise. He was standing near the front door. He had shoes on already and he'd put on a long-sleeved top over the T-shirt he'd changed into. He stared from her soaked trainers to his socks on her feet.

'Do you want a piggyback to the car?'

'OK.'

'Do you want to take the hot chocolate with you?'

'OK.'

'Shall we go then?'

'OK.'

Malachy opened the front door.

'I'll bring the car round then,' he said and he started to walk down the stone steps. For Oriana, time suddenly did the opposite of standing still – it rocketed forwards at breakneck speed giving her an inkling as to what would happen, and what wouldn't, if she didn't do something about it instantly.

'Malachy,' she said, and the tone she used was the same as the one he could employ. They could say each other's name and break through a thousand thoughts, scratch out any to-do list, stop time from ticking; a tone of voice that said wait, listen, please, it's me.

He turned. And then he came casually back up the steps, as if returning for something forgotten. He could feel her eyes steady on his face but he didn't look at her; he busied himself instead, patting the pockets of his jeans, doing anything to ignore the pace at which his heart pounded. And then there was nothing to do but turn slowly and face her.

Oriana placed the mug on the floor and stepped towards him, stepped in closer still, raised her arms and put them across his shoulders, around his neck, like the softest scarf. Then she turned her head and rested her face against his chest and held on for dear life.

For a while, Malachy just stayed as he was, being held again by Oriana. She didn't seem to want anything from him, she seemed only to want to give. He could feel her melding into him, bodies softening so that dips were filled and curves fitted. He felt a breath leave him slowly, like sinking into bed at the end of a day. And it was then that his arms were ready to hold her. One around her shoulders, the other around her waist. There they stood; gently.

'I am so so tired,' she said because she thought she might very well fall asleep standing up soothed by the soundtrack of his heartbeat. His reply was a hum of sorts. God knows where holding her had taken him but he wasn't quite ready to leave there yet.

Oriana felt as though she was teetering on the edge, somewhere between sleep and wakefulness, between all that had happened and all that could be, between yesterday and today, between being fifteen and being now. So much had happened in the last day. So much had happened over the years – the times when they were together, the years they'd been apart. She was full of emotion and devoid of strength. She was in Malachy's arms again, the safest place she knew, the place from which she'd been ripped. She was aware that when she let go she'd either fly or fall and until she let go, she had no way of knowing which it would be. But she would have to let go at some point very soon, because everything else was crumbling under her feet. She was standing in Malachy's socks but it wasn't his floor beneath her; it was memories and ideas and her history and words spoken and things never said, and feelings – decades of feelings. She was sinking into American soil and she was balancing on a corner that was for ever England. She was in the midst of the lonely terrain of no-man's-land knowing what she had to do, wherever that might lead. In a moment, in a few words, she'd be walking either on razor blades or on a cloud for the rest of her life.

She let go.
She let go.

'I love you, Malachy,' she said, loud and clear. Words she'd never regret, never take back.

And then she started to float and she started to fall; there was nothing beneath her feet at all and she had no way of knowing which way was up.

When I was . . .

When I was a kid my parents pretty much let me do what I wanted. I never had to ask permission. I just did as I pleased because they were rarely interested in what I did, let alone in stopping me. I could easily have bunked off school – for weeks on end. I could have started drinking or smoking young. I could have been a right little tart. I doubt they'd've reprimanded me. But I didn't do any of those things. I don't know exactly where my sense of right and wrong came from because there was no code of ethics accompanying my family crest. If my mother was in one of her self-obsessed slumbers – when she'd lie in bed as if she'd been flung there, limbs akimbo, hair in a tangle, eyes glazed – I knew I had no hope of her driving me to school. And if the studio door was shut, my father was painting, and pulling him away from a canvas was pointless; he'd be a hazard on the roads. So I'd find some breakfast and double-check I had everything and I'd magically appear by the Bedwells' car moments before the family emerged for the school run.

The first time I did it, I saw the look that registered momentarily on Orlando's face. It was surprise of course – but concern and pity too. But I saw him correct it quickly.

'It's just your car is a bus,' I said to him. 'Your car is the Windward School Bus.'

He smiled benevolently, as all grown-ups tend to do at

a child's banal chatter. But I was insistent. He couldn't open the boot for us to shove in our bags because I was standing there, tapping on the letters of the car's make.

'See,' I said, 'Subaru.' I pointed at them again back to front. 'U r a bus!'

'All aboard!' said Orlando and after that, if I wanted to catch the Bedwell Bus, I didn't even have to ask. I was never late.

I was never late with homework either. I liked studying, I liked the glimpse into all the possibilities the world held for me, all the ways I could make it in life.

How old was I? Nine perhaps? It was primary school. For secondary school we all trudged down the driveway for the official school bus. Apart from Willow and Plum who were home educated. I didn't envy them one bit – what kind of an education would I have received if it was left up to my mother and father? Well, by default, I learned what wasn't right, what was wrong.

I loved going to my friend Jennifer's house. It was so ordered and precise and her parents were so strict. We weren't allowed a biscuit until we'd had a piece of bread and butter, after which we could choose one plain biscuit and one chocolate one. Everything had to be eaten at the table. Homework was done immediately, after which we could watch John Craven's Newsround *and possibly* Blue Peter *on the television. Then play time. Then supper. Then bath, bed, reading. Lights out, please. No talking, Jennifer – I mean it.*

Jennifer loved coming to Windward as much as I loved going to her house. But we always made sure it was the Bedwells' that she was dropped off at and collected from. Jette obliged because she was pleased to enable me to have

Freya North

a friend over. I was sworn to secrecy about my home, otherwise Jennifer's parents would never have let her come over. You're so lucky, she'd say. You never have to see your parents. I really envy you, she'd say. They never tell you what to do. You're never told off for a single thing.

I was though. Twice. There were two occasions when my father went ballistic and I had to do as I was told.

My mother had already left. She phoned one day, wanting to speak to me. I always knew when she was on the phone if my father answered it. He softened; he became not so tall and not quite as angular. It was the only time his voice betrayed a clue to his Welsh upbringing and his few words came in a gentler, more musical tone. He never said much – just 'hullo' and then 'I'll get Oriana for you'. But it was obvious what the sound of her voice meant to him, what it did for him. He'd pass the receiver to me and he'd hover while I was on the phone, his face a picture of regret and longing. At the time I found it irritating and pathetic. What I loved best about being a teenager was that suddenly I was pretty much the same as most of my friends – we all groaned about our embarrassing nightmare parents.

'It's your mother,' he said that time. 'On the phone.'

'Yeah and?' I was doing my homework.

'It's your mother,' he said, 'and she's phoned to speak to you.'

'Tell her I'm busy,' I said.

'I'll do no such thing.' The sound of his vitriol made me look up and I saw how he'd clutched the telephone to his chest, right at his heart, as if protecting my mother from hearing, from me.

So I had a good shout. 'I am doing my homework! I do not want to speak to my mother!'

354

'Hold on,' he said into the receiver, as if giving her instructions on how to weather a gale. He put her back against his heart.

I stood up, flounced over to him and snatched the receiver.

'What!' But there was silence at the end of the phone. 'Hullo hullo?' I looked at my father. 'Psychotic cow has gone!'

And that's when he told me off. 'How dare you!' he said. 'Go to your room,' he said. He was suddenly enormous and strong and dark and glowering and powerful and authoritative. And he was also quite right. As I walked away I heard him talking.

'I'm so sorry,' he said. 'It's her age. I'm so sorry.'

I turned. He was talking into the receiver. To this day I do not know whether my mother was still on the line or if she'd gone when I thought she had.

He saw me. 'Go to your room. Now.' He turned his back on me.

I did as I was told.

I hated that contradiction – someone who, for the most part, barely noticed me, suddenly becoming all authoritative and laying down the law in a home where there'd been no rules.

The other occasion was when he sent me away from Windward. Banished me. I railed and begged and cried, but he told me that I had no say in the matter. I was to go. He said so. There was absolutely nothing I could do about it.

CHAPTER THIRTY-FIVE

Malachy woke early and lay gazing at the window as morning made its way into his bedroom. He hadn't closed the curtains when he'd gone to bed, he hadn't undressed. His belt buckle was now digging into his stomach. The duvet was in a scumble. Oriana was in his arms. As he stroked strand after strand of her hair, so he pulled his thoughts through his mind. He thought years back to the arrival of an elderly lady who would live at Windward for a couple of years. All the children thought she was a witch for a while because she was pointy and stooped and moved around the grounds in a stealthy sweep; gathering things in a black basket, catkins and teasels and pine cones and little twigs and bits of bark. She also lived all the way upstairs, right at the top, and she had a spinning wheel. Jed had reported back on this when he'd climbed to the ramparts and hung like a bat to spy in to the room. One of the smaller children had asked her outright, *Are you a witch?* And suddenly all of us had gathered round.

'No,' she said and she was quite forlorn to disappoint them so. 'I'm afraid I'm not.'

'But you have a spinning wheel.'

'And you look like a witch.'

Malachy smiled at the memory of Jed saying that – amiable and cheeky with his butter-wouldn't-melt face. They'd gone up with her, all of them, and she'd shown them how she carded the fleece and slowly coaxed it through the wheel into wool. While she spun, she talked, story after story coming through in the same easy rhythm. Spinning yarns, quite literally. Thereafter the children called her Granny, at her invitation. Now Malachy sells her work at the White Peak Art Space on behalf of her estate. Geraldine Shaw. She lived until she was 101 and she spun till her dying day.

He turned his head from the window and looked at the Geraldine Shaw wall-hanging which faced his bed. *Dovedale, 1996*. It was five foot high and four foot wide, a landscape woven from hand-spun wool, enlivened with felting and threadwork, a little quilting here and there. Some seed pods. A few ash twigs. Flicks of limestone and a kingfisher's feather. It encapsulated the spirit of Dovedale more than any photograph he'd seen.

The analogy was blatant and it was helpful. Geraldine spinning; turning fleece into wool. Malachy teasing Oriana's hair through his fingers while he worked through the bale of thoughts crowding his mind. Geraldine and he, turning the raw into something of worth.

He'd done a lot of listening last night, after he'd done the knight-in-shining-armour thing. He smiled about that now but at the time it had been quite alarming; the way Oriana had wilted just as soon as she'd told him she loved him. He'd cosied her into her favoured corner of the long purple velvet sofa but he hadn't taken his customary place on the Eames. He'd sat right tight beside her, very close, holding her hand, watching her, wondering about breaking the silence. In the end, she did it for him.

'That was a bit melodramatic of me,' she said shyly.

'Straight out of Brontë,' Malachy said, sitting upright, letting go of her hands.

'Please stay,' she'd said, reaching for him.

So there they'd stayed.

'All this stuff,' Oriana said. 'All this stuff they always bang on about.' He waited, but she didn't qualify it. Then she giggled at Malachy's obvious confusion. 'That one should have various partners, live together before you marry,' she explained. 'Try before you buy. First love is a myth. All that.' She held out her hand and he took it. 'We never even slept together,' she said. She thought about it. Did she regret it or marvel at it? Did he? Was he relieved? 'Despite my advances.' That made him smile. 'I suppose you were right,' she said. 'And in the long run – did it matter?' She thought about it. 'No,' she said. 'It didn't matter – because here we are. Because it's you. It was you. It's always been you.'

Malachy took Oriana's hand to his mouth and pressed his lips into the valley between her knuckles. It was still acutely vivid – in his head, in his body – the amount of self-restraint he'd had to call upon during those years when his body ached for her and he denied himself what he craved.

'People might say it's all extremely naive and

fanciful,' Oriana continued. 'But –' She left her sentence hanging. He saw that her eyes were now shot through with tears. 'It's you, Malachy,' she said. 'For me – it's only ever been you. I never stopped. I never stopped.'

It took some time to find his voice. 'And here you are,' he said and she watched as his smile coursed its way all over his face and over to hers.

He'd taken Oriana into his bed. She was almost drunk with emotional exhaustion. He'd cocooned her in the duvet while he had lain on top of the covers, propping himself up on his side, stroking her hair as she drifted in and out of slumber. He wished he had her way with words. Call yourself a novelist? Tell her!

'Sleep,' he'd whispered. 'I'm here.'

He thought about it now. How beautiful she'd looked in the suffused light. She'd placed her finger against his lips. 'You don't have to say anything,' she'd said.

'Can I tell you that I'm actually quite cold?' he'd said.

And she'd unwrapped herself from her duvet burrow and cloaked the covers around them both. There they lay, facing each other; just looking, no further words necessary. He didn't feel himself move towards her, he didn't sense that she'd brought her face closer but the tips of their noses touched and their lips brushed together. When he'd begun to kiss her last night, eighteen years of his life had evaporated in a superfast rewind. He'd been back where they'd started, and all the shit that had happened and all the time that had passed since was made sense of. Kissing her last night was so complete, so sustaining, that it didn't need to lead on. It was lovemaking and communication in its finest and most basic form. It was enough. They slept awhile.

She'd woken him. He could feel her kissing his cheek, the corner of his mouth. He could feel her fingertips stroking his jaw, his neck, running through his hair. She traced his nose, his eyebrow. She breezed her hand gently over his forehead, her fingers touching the path of the ribbon of his patch while her lips were on his. And then she slid her finger under the ribbon and she lifted it up and off and away. He didn't look at her. She needed privacy despite the darkness. His heart banged against his ribcage. He felt naked and vulnerable. He'd never felt like that with other women. This is what I look like without my patch, he'd say quite conversationally. Are you ready? See? The pitting and the crevasses and the scarring – it looks worse than it feels these days. And that's not my eye at all, it's a scleral shell over a hydroxyapatite implant. And it moves, but not very well and sometimes not quite in sync with the other eye – which still bugs me. But no more operations. And the patch? I don't like attention. And I like it that small children take me for a pirate instead.

Now, another hour on, he was awake and she was sound asleep and his belt was still digging into his flesh but he didn't want to move. He thought back to the times when he'd wondered where she was. He could have tried harder to find her. He had allowed himself to be fobbed off with the same old story: 'She's in America.' He had allowed himself to be persuaded that this was best for Oriana. In turn, he'd told himself that she was better off without him, or that he was better off without her, that if he loved her, he ought to let her go and if she loved him she'd find her way back to him and all that Richard Bach bullshit. Lying here now, he was quite content to eat his words. It was on the wings of Jonathan Livingston Seagull – or his modern cousin, Virgin Atlantic airways – that Oriana had come right back to him. He now knew why he'd stayed at Windward when he so easily could have left, why he took out a size-able mortgage to release Jed from his share. Windward was in his name; it was his home, his nest. It was feathered and ready and had been for years.

* * *

Jed knew Oriana hadn't come back last night. He didn't really need to wake up to know this. The knowledge had permeated through his dreamless sleep like noxious gas. Now awake, he didn't need to leave his room and check on hers to know it was empty. He knew why she wasn't here and he also knew where she'd gone. And he just couldn't bear it. It was exquisitely painful. He curled up in his bed. It wasn't fair. There was nothing wrong in what he wanted, he was driven only by love and devotion and the belief that you're not given a dream without the power to fulfil it. It wasn't fair at all. He knew that sounded petulant and stupid

– but he felt that way and, for a while, he'd damn well wallow in it. Then he'd get dressed and do something about it.

* * *

'Morning, sleepyhead.' Malachy smiled as Oriana opened her eyes and blinked herself into the here and now.

'What's the time?' she said with a stretch.

He smiled, thinking back to last night, to the same question asked. This morning, in his bed, rested and restored, she simply wanted to know what the time was.

'It's almost ten.'

He was looking at her, grinning.

'Please don't look at me,' she said, pulling the covers up to just under her eyes. 'I'm all creased and crumpled in the mornings.'

'Bollocks,' said Malachy. He leant forward and kissed her forehead. 'I've got an *eye* for a pretty girl when I see one,' he said. For a moment, Oriana was appalled by the inappropriateness of his comment. But then he grinned. 'Beauty is in the *eye* of the beholder,' he said. 'In my case – quite literally.'

She punched him lightly on the arm and told him he was terrible. She looked at him steadily, seeing in fine detail what she'd felt for in the darkness with her lips and her fingertips; the area where his left eye had once been. He was letting her see him starkly naked and beautiful.

'You are much changed,' she said quietly, touching

the scars gently. Then she smiled. 'But there again – so am I. We all are. That's age for you. You're braver than me, Malachy – I don't intend to let you see my cellulite.'

He laughed, really laughed.

'But we're still you and me,' she said.

'And still, we've never had sex,' he said, leaning forwards and kissing her.

'I have morning breath!' she protested, pulling the duvet up to her forehead. 'Go away!'

Malachy gazed at the top of her head, worked out the shape of her beneath the covers. He didn't give a fig about cellulite, whatever that was. He saw his eye patch on the bedside table. Sunday morning. This is what his average Sunday mornings would now be like. And it was just lovely.

'Breakfast?' he said. 'Bacon and eggs?'

'Starving,' came her voice and her face reappeared. She thought about the cake hewn from rock that she'd had at Django's, the last thing she'd eaten. She thought of Cat. And yesterday. Was all that really only yesterday?

'Cat had her baby.'

'I know,' he said.

'Every now and then, the notion returns to me and I swoop inside.'

'Would you like one?'

'Yes, please,' Oriana replied as if he'd just asked if she'd like one egg or two. 'Boy first.'

They looked at each other. Everything that had been impossible was now not so.

'Leave it with me,' he said and he left the room.

Oriana was so deep in thought, lulled into far-off daydreams by the herald of a beautiful day which was now streaming in through the window; Malachy was so engrossed by the sizzle of coordinating breakfast for two when mostly he cooked for one; that neither of them was aware that Jed had careened his car to a stop outside and was making his way up the steps.

Jed paused at the front door. He knew this feeling of determination very well; it was a quality that had propelled him to achieve all that he had. A first from Cambridge. A fast scaling of the career ladder. The flat he wanted. The busy life. I ask for one thing only, he said under his breath. I ask finally for just this one thing. His mother's words drifted into his head. *Bange hjarte vandt aldrig fager mö.* Faint heart never won fair lady. Well, the fair lady was in there and he was prepared to fight for her. He was armed. He turned and looked back at the driveway. He breathed in through his nose and out through his mouth. Then he opened the door and went inside. Oriana's Converse trainers were on the mat, stuffed with newspaper, the laces removed and currently hanging over the old shooting stick that had always been propped in the corner as though it was some kind of buttress.

Malachy wasn't in the kitchen but breakfast for two was already laid. Bacon, eggs and hot buttered toast. Henderson's Relish. Tomato ketchup. Salt and pepper. Steaming mugs of tea. Two pieces of folded kitchen paper, cutlery placed on top.

Jed walked on through the apartment, quietly

opening the door to his room with hope in his heart – for everyone concerned – that he'd find Oriana in there. But she wasn't. He looked in to the ballroom and saw his brother, his back to him, heaving up the great sash windows. The balcony doors were already open.

Some would call it a gentle breeze that tickled its way into the room but suddenly to Malachy it was an ill wind. He turned and found Jed leaning against the wall, casual as you like, as if he owned the place; his arms crossed, staring at him with a look far worse than hatred: detachment.

'Look –' It was all Malachy could think to say.

'I can see!' Jed said. 'Did you fuck?'

'Jed – for God's sake.'

'Did you? Did you *fuck* her?'

'Jed – I'm warning you.' Malachy glanced at his bedroom door, knowing it was impossible for Oriana not to have heard.

'OK – I'll rephrase it. Did you have sex, shag, bang, copulate, fornicate?'

'No.' It was important to Malachy that Jed heard him. 'No.'

'You slept with her, didn't you? You fucking slept with her.'

'Yes, Jed – we slept together in that we went to sleep together.'

'Right! Right!' said Jed facetiously. 'That's why her clothes are all over the place in here?'

Malachy looked around. It was true. They were in here. He'd hung them over the radiators to dry. At the time it had seemed logical because they were wringing wet. Now it seemed daft – the heating had been off for almost a month. 'She was wet through.'

'You talk such shit, Malachy. I've never been able to work out how so many people have fallen for the shit you shovel out.'

'Jed – you need to calm down.'

'I am calm.'

'No, you're not.'

'I've just come to collect what's mine.'

'What?'

'I've come to collect Oriana. She lives with me. She chose to live with me.' Then Jed enunciated it as three distinct and desperate sentences. 'She. Chose. Me.'

There was silence. In Malachy's bedroom, Oriana had flattened herself against the wall. She wanted to be a million miles away. She wanted to be anywhere but here; America, Hathersage – anywhere.

'Leave her alone,' she heard Malachy say.

'Why don't you just go fuck yourself,' she heard Jed say. 'You've always done this to me. I *hate* you for it.'

'Me!' Malachy's voice was raised. Oriana had heard it raised only once before, eighteen years ago. It was a sound she never wanted to hear again. She charged out of the bedroom and into battle.

Jed pointed at her but kept his eyes level on Malachy; his voice raw. 'Out of your bedroom and in *your clothes*?' Then he looked at her in disgust. 'Why didn't you say?' he asked her. 'What kind of a heartless bitch are you?'

Malachy wasn't having that. 'That's enough.' He

walked to his brother and took him by the arm, to lead him away from Oriana and make him go. Jed snatched his arm away and pushed Malachy hard who shoved him back immediately. A side table was knocked over and a lamp crashed to the floor.

'Please stop it,' Oriana whispered, covering her face with her hands. 'Please, boys, please.'

Envy, years old, brand new, cut through Jed like a serrated knife while a lifetime of keeping quiet erupted out of Malachy as they fought. Hurling insults, they threw punches and blasted each other across the ballroom.

'Stop it!' Oriana cried. 'Don't! Just stop!'

'For fuck's sake, Malachy,' Jed yelled up close to his brother's face, pointing his finger straight at the eye that could no longer see.

'She fucking *shot* you!'

It was as if the shot rang out again. The same deafening, life-changing sound. They all stood motionless and silent as the damage done seeped around them like spilling petrol, Jed's words hanging like the touchpaper, perilously close.

'Go to your room, Oriana,' said Robin, suddenly amongst them. 'Go to your room, now.'

CHAPTER THIRTY-SIX

Oriana walked through the Bedwells' rooms and out into the internal corridor, along it and up to her old connecting door, in a daze. She didn't soak up the nostalgic scents along the way, or stop for memories to play back like scenes from a favourite film, nor did she note what was new, what had changed. She was going to her room, just as she'd been told, heading for there directly with no time for detours emotional or otherwise.

The door into the Taylors' groaned just as it always had and the spherical brass handle was just as loose, the dent exactly where it had always been – an odd flaw, the exact size of some man's peculiarly strong thumb. It was a strangely comforting sight and, as she looked at it, she recalled one day in midwinter. Everyone was using the Corridor rather than brave the bitingly cold weather outside; Oriana had stood by her door and asked each man who passed to place his thumb in the indent. They all obliged but none of their thumbs fitted. Sometimes, living at Windward had something of the fairy tale about it. Not all fairy tales are happy and light, most are peculiar and dark. But they are all magical.

She shut the door behind her and, for the first time in eighteen years, she was back in her childhood home. The smell hit her immediately. She hadn't noticed it when it had been part of her every day, but now it struck her forcefully and she inhaled deeply, not knowing if she liked it, just needing to reacquaint herself with it. Brushes and turps and oil paints and the cloying smell of size used to prepare canvases. She was nowhere near her father's studio but his art was in the air. She looked around the kitchen; everything was in its place. The cooker was the same, there was still no toaster but now there was an electric kettle. She rubbed her wrist, feeling again the scorch of steam that had been par for the course when making a cup of tea. The pelargoniums were still on the windowsill, in bud now. This year he was late putting them out on the doorstep where they'd provide a slightly forlorn fanfare to the home. She went on, into the main room with the same wooden table at which she'd sat to have her impromptu haircut and her disastrous tea party and all those breakfasts she'd had to see to for herself.

Here and there, dried-out tea bags stood like small brown islands in the midst of a stained sea. A cigarette butt standing upright, smoked down to the filter and left to extinguish on its own. She and Jed used to dare each other to sniff them; the most disgusting smell in the world. She'd double-dared him once to eat one. And he had.

She walked all the way around the table, trailing her hand along the surface as she went. The same kinds of things were on it today. An old newspaper. A bottle of wine down to the dregs. Another cigarette with a little ash around the stem like silver leaves around a miniature tree trunk. There was a piece of paper with her father's indecipherable coded hand-writing. Also, an array of disparate objects that could marry up for a visually provocative still life. All these things, mostly so divorced from reality, from what was normal for a tabletop in a family home. Just then it was like contemplating museum exhibits and it gave Oriana a similar, pensive calm. But she kept walking, taking in the view from each window, knowing how each pane gave a slightly altered vignette from the one before. On she went to the door which was ajar at the far end, to her father's studio.

You were never, ever allowed to go in there if the door was closed and Robin was working. But on the occasions when he wasn't, when it was open, you were free to enter. She tiptoed in now, as she had then, as if not wanting to startle whoever was being brought to life behind the surface of the canvas. In works in progress, the subjects always seemed so new to the world, as if they'd only just been released, as if giant rocks had been spliced to reveal them, to liberate them. And then, when the paintings were finished, his subjects always exuded this worldly experience, this innate knowing, as if they carried the secrets of the universe and it was the viewer who was so newly formed.

Today there was a man she didn't recognize, gazing at her pleadingly, to hasten the return of the artist to free him, so that his life would be completed. Using the edge of her little finger, she lightly touched the surface. It was still wet. She looked at the tiny purple mark on her fingertip; it was like a blood blister. She rubbed it on a cloth. Her finger now smelt of turps. Everything smelt of turps. It didn't surprise her that all around the room, canvas after canvas, board after board, her mother's face stared out. She sat on the stool by the easel and tapped her fingers rhythmically on her knees. Don't look at me like that, Mother. I have every right to be here. But she couldn't relax in this space, not just because her mother's eyes were upon her wherever she looked, but because this wasn't where she should be. *Go to your room*, her father had told her. *Go to your room.*

Walking back through into the hallway, Oriana glanced in at the study and sensed that was where her father now slept, by the look of the day bed and tomorrow's shirt and tie on a hanger, balanced on the bookshelf. When he'd suddenly shown up at the Bedwells' he'd been in his three-piece suit, he'd been working. He was as smart when he went to work as any businessman. And just as hard-working. It was Sunday after all. Art doesn't close for the weekend. How loud the fury at the Bedwells' must have been, to have been audible here, to have compelled him to come. Outside her bedroom, Oriana stopped; she bowed her head and stood a moment longer before opening the door and stepping inside.

She gasped.

Why had he done this?

Was he mad?

Eighteen years and he hadn't changed a thing?

The same bed linen. A black Tempo felt pen at an angle on the desk beside a collection of books in an unstraightened stack, like a precarious staircase from *To Kill a Mockingbird* on the bottom to *The Catcher in the Rye* on the top. She always used to arrange her books like that. If their spines were aligned she feared the stories would blend. Scout would be in Holden's world and that just wasn't right. In a parade along the skirting, all her vinyl LPs and singles. She crouched and flicked through them. Songs not heard for almost two decades coming in and out of her mind. The disc sent especially to her from Rod. An LP signed by some long-forgotten band called Saturn Returns. Hadn't they stayed at Windward? Hadn't they practised at the Bedwells'? One of her favourites – Alec Guinness reading *The Waste Land*. Lilac and George had bought that for her birthday. *You'll like his voice,* they told her, because she was far too young to understand the poem. In fact, she never had a clue what any of it meant but the timbre of the actor's voice and the rhythm and flow of the words were significant to her. She flipped up the lid of her record player, plugged it in, gently dabbed a finger on the needle for the affronted hum that would tell her it was on. She slid the record out of the sleeve, her middle finger and thumb remembering the stretch from hole to edge. As Alec Guinness came into the room so Oriana went and lay down on her bed. So much ugliness this morning after so much beauty. It was horrible. Horrible. If she stayed here long enough, could she too become frozen in time? To a time before she shot Malachy? To a time before Jed came into this very room and found her with him?

I have single-handedly fucked up the lives of so many.

Who the hell do I think I am that I thought I could return?

But where was the sin in the love that flooded out of her for Malachy and the tenderness flowing from him for her? All night in his arms. His fingers through her hair. His heartbeat steady. Bacon and eggs? Yes, please. Would you like children? Yes, please.

And Jed. Generous and warm, and inspiring such affection in her. Over recent weeks she knew how she'd ignored the fact that the light which beamed from him shone directly from the torch he still held for her. Deeply ashamed, she turned away from the thought and faced the wall while Alec Guinness told of Mrs Porter and her daughter and Oriana joined in washing their feet in soda water. If Jed had only said out loud how he felt, what he wanted – if only he'd taken a punt and declared his feelings – then she could have let him down gently.

No.

It was brutally unfair to pin any of the responsibility on Jed. In fact, it was cowardly.

She'd known how he felt – even if she didn't want to admit it, even if she made excuses for it, she'd known. It was obvious as soon as he appeared when she'd first come back to visit. Vaulting the balcony and shinning down the wall, one shoe off and one shoe on. She should have done something about it, something for him, much much sooner. It was bad enough realizing she had now lost one of the best friends she'd ever had. It was mortifying to think how she'd severely damaged another Bedwell boy in the process.

But life is about letting go. Life is about adapting, about changing course. A stream keeps flowing even if inclement weather forces a change for its path. Love is about forgiveness. And love is about hope.

Look at you, Oriana. You said you'd never return. You said you didn't care. You said you hated him. But you're in your old bedroom and you're comforted to be there. And your father just stepped in to help, he was there to protect you.

CHAPTER THIRTY-SEVEN

Oriana's watch didn't make sense to her and the clock in her room had stopped goodness knows when. Could it really have been only an hour or so since Malachy sat on the bed and took the piss at his own expense for having just one eye? An hour since Jed returned and their worlds, individual yet intertwined, were flung into a maelstrom? And her father at the Bedwells', doing what? Umpiring? Counselling? Was he standing there, a hand on each boy, keeping them apart while they flailed to get at each other? Was he even there still? Perhaps he'd returned. Perhaps he was painting.

The clock in the sitting room was ten minutes faster than Oriana's watch. The one in the kitchen read the same time exactly. There was no clock and no Robin in the studio. What was she meant to do? Just stay in her room where she'd been sent? Into a wasteland of her own making with only Sir Alec for company.

> When lovely woman stoops to folly and
> Paces about her room again, alone,
> She smoothes her hair with automatic hand,
> And puts a record on the gramophone.

She put her watch to her ear and listened to it ticking. She had to go. She had the biggest part in all this anyway, there was no resolution without her.

Back at the Bedwells', straight through the apartment to the ballroom, three faces were already trained on the door for her entrance. Her father, sitting in Orlando's chair like some stand-in patriarchal invigilator. Jed and Malachy at opposite ends of the sofa, sitting forward both of them, their hands clasped in their laps. She felt the eyes of the three men focus on her while she stared at the legs of the piano and wondered why they ended in the shape of claws. How long would they let her just stand there saying nothing, mesmerized by furniture? They'd give her as long as she needed, it seemed. They were waiting for her, they'd all been waiting such a long time.

Over the years, she'd perfected soliloquys, amassed a whole volume of them – what she'd say to Malachy if only she had the chance. She'd honed feelings into stanzas of beautiful poetry and shaped memories into epic prose. Now was her chance. Gradually, her gaze travelled over to him, stopping on the way briefly but directly at Jed, then at her father.

And when it came, she didn't need her script. She walked over to Malachy, dropped to her knees, sat back on her heels, her hands resting suppliant in her lap.

'I'm so sorry,' she said. She looked up at him. 'I'm so sorry.' Then she sank into herself and wondered if she'd ever stand up again.

* * *

She felt a hand touch the top of her head, laid just lightly over her hair as if in blessing. And then it stroked down and another joined it and they cupped her face and tipped it up. Malachy was holding her steady.

'It was an accident, Oriana.'

His thumbs smudged away her tears and she closed her eyes, blinded.

An arm around her shoulders, a body close to hers. Jed's voice soft on her ear.

'It was an accident,' said Jed.

When finally Oriana opened her eyes, she was with the Bedwell boys again, deep within their fold and safe. They sat together for a long time, saying nothing more.

Robin broke the silence.

'Oriana,' he said. 'A word.'

And he left the Bedwells'.

She looked up at Malachy.

'Go,' he said. 'I'll be here when you come back.'

When I was . . .

When I was fifteen . . .
  When I was fifteen.

When I was fifteen I changed everything for everyone.

Our exams were done, term ended early and Malachy finished school for good. And though the anticipation of results slightly sullied the summer, August felt a way off and we knew what would be would be. I wrote a cracking essay on Hamlet *and if I didn't get an A I would personally storm the examiner's office and demand to know why. If Jed didn't get straight A's then everyone who knew him would be in that examiner's office declaring him insane. Malachy deserved to achieve the grades he hoped for because he worked hard and it was harder for him as he didn't have Jed's natural super-intelligence. I didn't want to think of Malachy getting his results, because they'd take him away from me, to Bristol University which was his first choice. If he didn't win his place there, he'd still go to York. Or Birmingham. He'd still leave. I knew I wasn't prepared to lose him, to let him go.*

That summer we just wanted to be on English turf. All those weeks since winter, when we hadn't dared step outside because we had revision and checklists and stacks of books and so much homework. Months on end when we didn't hang out with our friends, when we were cooped up and stressed out and quietly wondering what the fuck it was all about anyway. So the Bedwell boys didn't go with their parents to Denmark and Malachy was left in charge because everyone trusted him. My father wasn't interested in where I was that summer – but when was he ever? He was painting a triptych which obsessed him and made me cringe. The Agony and the Ecstasy *it was called and I really didn't want to see my mother like that or know that my father had those kinds of feelings for her. I went into the studio only once during that period and I rolled my eyes as my stomach turned. Gross, I said to everyone. Oh my God – it's just gross. Sex, we believed, was not for anyone over twenty-five.*

We spent most of our time outside. There was no place like Windward on a summer's day. Private and so beautiful. We lolled because we were kids and schoolwork had meant no lolling for such a long time. We'd meet at the back where, because of the position of the house and the angle of the sun in high summer, there was a section of lawn that was never in the shade. We were practically woven to the grass, lying there, listening to Malachy's radio cassette recorder which we had to stuff with new batteries on a weekly basis. I read my way through the American greats that summer – For Whom the Bell Tolls, Of Mice and Men, Flowers for Algernon, On the Road *and* The World According to Garp.

Jed decided he'd start smoking and he had this thing for some brand called Raffles which came in a black packet. Malachy drank beer. I had a new bikini. I wasn't concerned with how I looked; I just loved it that I could feel the sun on so much of my skin. Jed had stupid Garfield swimming trunks. *Malachy wore denim shorts. We were all brown as hazel. Bob, the ancient gardener who'd come with the house when our parents moved in, mowed everywhere else but never asked us to move. He mowed all the way around us. It meant we had this lovely large circle of long grass and it was our island. If you looked out over the lawns at night, it was like gazing at the shadow of the moon.*

I lay between the brothers, chattering with Jed but all the while electrified by Malachy's presence. I longed for him. I looked forward to when Jed cycled off to buy cigarettes or when he stayed over with friends. Then I had Malachy to myself. Out in the garden, side by side, eyes closed. I'd sneak a look at him but he'd always open one eye before long which I'd immediately shy away from. When Malachy looks at you, he looks into you. But he kissed me less often during that summer. It frustrated the hell out of me. Couldn't he see me for the growing woman I was? I'm in the sixth form now, Malachy. I don't wear school uniform any more. I'll be sixteen soon enough. I tried to think it was because Jed was around so much but I knew it wasn't. I knew Malachy was pulling away, I knew he'd be leaving Windward. I knew that he was preparing to go. I knew that I'd lose him.

When the A level results came through, the Bedwell boys threw a party at the behest of all their friends. It was logical – Jette and Orlando were still away, they had the apartment to themselves and Windward was the perfect setting. Our GCSE results were still a week away but that was the summer when any old excuse for a party would do.

'I did it, Oriana,' Malachy repeated while I was filling his bath with ice for the beer. *'I got the grades. I'm in.'* He was sitting on the closed toilet seat, holding the piece of

*paper as if it was a screen showing him the rest of his life.
I went over to him and sat on his lap and he held me
tightly and we kissed deeply and desperately and I thought
to myself this is the beginning of the end.*

*At the party there was beer and cider, a ridiculous rum
punch and boxes of warm white wine. There were cigarettes
and joints and hash cakes. There was Acid house and
grunge and Neil Young and Springsteen – always
Springsteen. We had our arms in the air and the world in
our hands.*

*The ballroom was heaving with people I didn't know. I
finally found Malachy out on the balcony. He tried to hide
a joint from me but I raised my eyebrow and said I'm not
a child you know, and I took the joint and sucked hard. I
hated the head rush. We stood, side by side, our bare arms
touching, goosepimpled by the connection and the middle-
of-the-night air. We looked down on our circle of grass, we
looked across to the cedar, we looked at each other and our
fingers wove together. He didn't need to kiss me. And he
didn't.*

*What are you doing? said Jed who was suddenly with
us, staring at our hands long after they'd disengaged.*

Nothing, we said. Just chilling.

*He stood with us, me in the middle, the love of two
brothers encircling me like vapours.*

*Are you coming back in? Malachy asked me but I didn't
want to say the joint had made me feel nauseous, that I
needed to stay outside, focusing on the steady silhouette of
the cedar. So I just said I was going to hang out with Jed.
I let Jed hold my hand. It wasn't unusual, he often did.*

'You know he's shagging Charlotte?' Jed said.

'I'm sorry?'

'*Charlotte – who left school last year.*'

'*The scary one?*'

'*Yeah. You know he's shagging her?*'

'*Malachy?*'

'*Yes, Oriana – Malachy.*'

No, I did not know that. And I didn't believe Jed.
Malachy would have told me. He told me everything. But
Jed turned my shoulders and I saw inside; I saw Malachy
sitting on the piano stool being straddled by scary Charlotte,
her tongue inserted into his mouth like a slug, his hand
moving around inside her shirt.

What was I going to do? What was I going to do? I went
home in a huff, that's what I did. I curled up in bed with
a bucket on the floor and when Jed tiptoed in and climbed
in beside me and spooned next to me and cupped his hand
over my breast and pressed against me and kissed my neck
I didn't object, I didn't move. I couldn't.

When I woke in the morning, Jed was propped up on
one arm, smiling at me.

'*Oregano,*' he said, '*you snore.*'

He helped me avoid Malachy for the next few days by
keeping me busy and keeping me with him. He took me
fishing all day and we crouched around at dusk aiming at
rabbits with my father's old Winchester which I'd purloined
for all those years without him ever commenting. We caught
lots of fish but we always missed the rabbits, accidentally-
on-purpose. And all the while Malachy lazed on our circle
in the sun, listening to our music, reading and sleeping as
if he'd never noticed we'd been there in the first place and
didn't miss us now we weren't. I was too humiliated, really,
to tell Jed how crushed I felt. Jed's chatty warmth and his
tactile attentiveness were a distraction and a positive antidote

to Malachy's reticence and rejection. I did notice that Charlotte was never around and that Malachy was always at Windward but I said to myself who cares?

Our GCSE results came the next weekend. I was chuffed, I'd excelled at what I loved, and failing maths was almost cool. I wanted to tell my father but he was in the studio, door shut. There was a knock on my bedroom door and in came Malachy. I turned away from him but he wasn't going to let that stop him. He took the slip of paper from me and absorbed the facts and figures.

'You flunked your maths pretty spectacularly,' he smiled. 'But you'll retake it and I bet you'll get a B.'

I shrugged.

'Well done.' He was beaming, he was proud. He came and sat beside me. 'Clever girl.'

'Where's Jed?'

'Gone to get fags.'

I wanted Malachy to go. To stay. To go.

'Did he get his straight A-starreds?' I asked.

'Of course.'

'Is he ecstatic?'

Malachy thought about it. 'I'm not sure really – he could have done them with his eyes closed last year. Where's the sense of achievement if you haven't had to strive for something?'

'Your parents are going to be cock-a-hoop,' I said.

'Does your dad know?'

'No – he's working. I'll tell him later.'

'You've been avoiding me all week.'

I couldn't answer that. He nudged me. He nudged me again. And then he put his arm around me and kissed the side of my face so gently again, again and again, slowly,

slowly, while he stroked my neck, my arms. My Malachy
was back and I didn't care what the consequences were,
I just wanted to stay in that moment. We crumpled onto
my bed and kissed each other's faces and wrapped our
arms and legs around each other and pulled each other
in as close as we could. We took off our tops and basked in
skin against skin. I could feel him harden and strain
in his trousers and, just fleetingly, he swept his hand up
between my legs and pressed his fingers against me. We
lay together and rolled and rocked and he was on top of
me and we moved and kissed and writhed and something
extraordinary started building in my body. And suddenly
Malachy was fumbling with his flies and breathing hard.
I was so ready. This was how it should be. It was going
to be perfect.

And then he pulled away. 'We can't.'

I reached out for him. 'We can. I want this. I love you.'

He shook his head. 'It's crazy. You're fifteen! I'm going
to university. It's just – impossible. Ridiculous.'

'Please don't say that.'

'I'm sorry.'

'You have nothing to apologize for.'

'You'll thank me, Oriana. One day – I promise.'

'Don't say that. That's rubbish. Malachy – please.'

'Don't you see? If we – made love –' He couldn't finish
the sentence. 'I want to,' he said, hoarse. 'It's just not the
right time, Oriana. It would be wholly wrong.'

'Are you shagging scary Charlotte? Is that why?' I think
he laughed as much at my accusatory tone as at the concept.

We lay beside each other again while our bodies tried to
make sense of the come-down. We lay together and just loved
one another, tiptoeing fingers up and over the landscapes of

each other's bodies as if committing the routes to memory should we ever find ourselves lost. I knew Malachy was right but what he said conflicted so strongly with the physical and the emotional, that denial seemed an insult to the veracity of those feelings.

'I love you,' he whispered to me with a glazed gaze. 'I love you.'

And that's how Jed found us. Semi-naked, wrapped up in each other with the word 'Love' hanging in the air like a neon banner.

He had a cigarette behind his ear and it tumbled off as he turned and stormed out.

'Shit,' said Malachy and he dressed quickly and left.

And I lay there thinking that everything sucked and everyone was going to get hurt but I never imagined that in ten minutes' time the hurt would be so cataclysmic.

The noise coming from their apartment. The crashing and banging and yelling. It was more unbearable than any of the furious rows my parents had ever had.

'What's going on?' My father had stormed out of his studio and appeared to be ricocheting off the walls in our hallway. 'I'm trying to paint!'

'It's OK,' I said. 'It's the boys – they're just scrapping. I'll go. Here.' I gave him the paper with my results. 'I flunked maths. Sorry.'

Even the deadening flagstones of the Corridor and the monumentally thick walls couldn't absorb the sound of the fight. I rushed to be there and found myself in the midst of such uncontained hatred that I didn't know what to do. I watched, I felt. Jed punched Malachy square on the jaw and sent him flying but he hurled himself back with an empty bottle in his hand and thwacked Jed hard on the

385

side of his skull. As Jed staggered and swayed, Malachy spat blood on the floor.

'Fuck you,' Malachy said. 'Just fuck you, Jed.'

Malachy rarely swore. I always felt a bit childish if I did so in his presence. Those words from Malachy enunciated his hostility more than any strike. But the moment of separation re-energized them and they ran at each other again with a combined roar, hurling one another against the walls.

I was terrified and desperate. I needed the Bedwells to be the family full of love and support and solidity. I depended on them to be so. They needed to exemplify the opposite to my family. This wildness I was in the midst of, the primal hatred and violence and baseness, was more than I could handle. It had to stop. The noise, the blood, the damage and the despising had to stop. If it was me who'd started it, I had to stop it. But they couldn't hear me shout. They weren't listening to me at all.

People say that when terrible things happen, it's as if the protagonists have been flung backwards momentarily, held in abeyance; then the action proceeds in slow motion towards the impending disaster which is at once known yet unavoidable. This is not so. It does not happen like that. Time went into overdrive that day and moved too fast for any of us to sense what lay ahead. My father's rifle was on their mantelpiece, left there from one of our futile rabbiting attempts. I ran for it. I wasn't aiming. There was no time to put it to my shoulder, though that rifle alone was heavy enough on a teenage girl's wrist and that was before the kick. I just grabbed it and raised it, and the sun struck through the middle pane of the upper section of the second sash window to the left of the balcony and blinded

*me the moment I shot into the air. I couldn't see a thing.
I never saw that Malachy had stood up while Jed remained
down. I was shooting into the light to make them stop and
in a split second, that stupid rifle that couldn't kill a bunny
maimed Malachy for life.*

That's what happened. That's how it happened.

That's what happened when I was fifteen.

*Eighteen years later, I have finally accepted that it was an
accident. Because Malachy told me so and Jed corroborated
it and it was only the three of us there, back then. And
the three of us are here again now.*

CHAPTER THIRTY-EIGHT

Malachy and Jed

It was hard not to be transfixed by the space that Oriana had left when she'd gone. If they imagined that she was still here, sitting between them, then they could keep their focus on her and not have to adjust it to take in the wider picture bespeckled with overlapping details of what had happened that morning. Eventually, the rumble of his stomach caused Malachy to stand, to look at the time and say Jesus, it's almost midday, to glance at his brother and ask if he'd like tea.

'Please,' said Jed and he stood and stretched and yawned and slumped back down on the sofa.

Malachy looked at the cold breakfasts, forlornly curling on the plates. Had they only been made this morning? It seemed longer than that. Time was playing tricks.

'Jed,' he called, 'do you want to eat?'

In the ballroom, Jed was looking over to Oriana's wet clothes. He wondered, what kind of crazy adventure did she have yesterday?

'I'm starving,' he called. 'Thanks.' And he stood

up and crossed to the windows and smoothed the yellow film back flat where it had peeled away from one of the windows. The middle pane of the upper section of the second sash window to the left of the balcony. He checked the film on the panes to the right and the left of the neighbouring sashes, up a little, down a little. He remembered his father studying the passage of sunlight for hours each day while Malachy convalesced, hovering with the pieces of sticky-backed coloured coverings as if poised to refract the rays before any further harm was done. He remembered how his mother would run her eyes over the six coloured panes for months afterwards, as if they were notes forming a dissonant tune she could never quite memorize.

Malachy returned with sandwiches filled with cold bacon and eggs. They didn't taste too bad and they were much needed. The brothers ate in silence and gulped down the tea.

'Refill?' Malachy asked.

'Looking back, she and I were hurled together by what happened that day.' Jed regarded Malachy. 'During that time when you were down at Moorfields and Mum and Dad were with you most days.' Jed wanted to continue but he wasn't sure how; he gave up stumbling over his words and put his head in his hands. 'The drifts of news we scavenged were getting worse and worse.'

'I remember so little,' Malachy said. 'I remember nothing of it happening.'

'She cradled your head,' Jed told him, looking up at him again. 'She was so brave because it was terrifying and you looked terrible but she didn't stop talking to you.' He paused. 'Your hand over your eye. The blood. Your head in her lap,' said Jed. He pointed. 'The copper shell casing just there. The rifle flung – over there.'

Malachy considered it. In some ways, he felt lucky to remember so little. 'You must have been beside yourselves.'

'I called the ambulance. I didn't know what to say. Suddenly, Robin was here and he couldn't speak. And Lilac. Others – I can't tell you who. It was oddly quiet. Just waiting. I think people probably prayed. But all the while, Oriana talked to you. You know it took her two days to realize how badly sprained her wrist was from the kick.'

'As bad as it was for us,' said Malachy, 'for me, for our family, it was beyond awful for that girl. She was a kid. She believed we were all she had.'

Jed nodded. 'I want you to know that I did tell Dad it was an accident. And Mum. Even Robin. And they all said "I know" and they all said "That's beside the point." I did say "Don't blame Oriana" but I don't know if I said it enough. If I'd said it more, maybe Mum and Dad could have stepped in to stop her being sent away.'

Malachy had been through this privately again and again over the years; he knew the logical answers to every question, the reason behind every action, the provenance of every emotion that all of them had experienced. He shook his head.

'There wasn't anything you could have done. Or me, come to that. It was going to be impossible for her to stay,' he said. 'Mum and Dad told me that Oriana was going. I pleaded with them too, Jed. I heard them in the hospital room saying *Windward's imploding*. They blamed themselves. All the grown-ups blamed each other. By sending Oriana away they were taking responsibility, assuaging their guilt, telling themselves they were doing the right thing for everyone. Boarding school on the South Downs – it came at the right time and even if what happened hadn't happened, it still would have been the best for her, I suppose. Windward – me, you – she was fragile, Jed. I don't think we truly appreciated that. Had she stayed – who knows what would have happened.'

'Is that why you didn't sleep with her? You thought it was wrong, damaging, because of her age and her vulnerability?'

'Partly.' Malachy looked at him. It would be easy to nod and be done with it. But he shook his head. 'Actually, that wasn't the main reason. I was – desperate – to. It's why I fooled around with crazy Charlotte, I was so – pent up.'

Jed seemed surprised. 'Charlotte? I thought that was a rumour? I thought you didn't?'

'Well, I did. And yes, I lied to Oriana – but don't you go blowing my cover. It's what she needed to hear at the time. I needed her to let go, I needed her to hate me a little and not want me so much.'

'Are you crazy? If I'd felt that kind of desire from Oriana, I'd've never jeopardized what we could have had. Why did you do that? Why did you deny yourself that? Just because on paper she was fifteen?'

'Partly,' said Malachy. He wasn't sure whether the truth would harm his brother by hurting him further. He wasn't sure how to temper the truth without lying. He sensed that there was only today to bury the past; by tomorrow it would already have calcified, immobilizing things unsaid into fossils that would stare out and goad, encased for eternity. 'I was leaving. I was eighteen.' Malachy paused. 'I couldn't take her with me, Jed.' He shrugged, his face softened. 'But I knew it didn't matter because I was always going to come back for her. Always. That's why. Do you see? That's why.'

'Were you living in a Dickens novel?' Jed said and a note of admiration struck through the ridicule. He took their mugs and plates back into the kitchen, tutting under his breath. He put his hands either side of the sink and allowed his shoulders to slump. When Oriana had returned, he'd been flooded with the thought of him and her picking up from where they'd left off. If he smothered her with love and provided her with all the accoutrements of a great life, she'd never need to think *what-if* when it came to his brother. Just now, he had to concede that he hadn't actually taken her feelings into consideration at all; he'd been too busy thinking about what he wanted, assessing what he was capable of achieving. He needed to admit defeat in a battle with Malachy that his older brother had no idea he'd even been part of, let alone won. Malachy had always had this overriding conviction of destiny with Oriana. And much as Jed felt adored by Oriana he had to accept that he'd sensed all along that her love was solely for Malachy. And that realization in itself, for someone who'd achieved so much with so little effort, was a sharp and humbling lesson for Jed.

'I didn't want her just because you did or because she wanted you,' Jed told his brother quietly, returning with fresh tea. 'It wasn't a challenge. It was deeper – it was personal. Those were *my* feelings, *my* desires, *my* own hopes and dreams. I had to pursue them. All I'd ever heard was *Jed can achieve everything he sets his mind to*. It gave me a skewed sense of what was possible, what I was entitled to, what was success, what was failure.'

'I know,' said Malachy. 'I realize that.' His voice dropped and he looked over to Jed. 'I'm reluctant to ask, but I feel I have to.' He paused. 'When you two –' He tried again. 'When I was in hospital – that's when you two –' He looked at Jed. 'How is that even possible? Coming so soon after –?' He wasn't angry, just utterly baffled.

Jed thought back to that time – twelve days of hermetically sealed togetherness. That was all. Adults running in circles wondering what to do and, incredibly, not noticing the two teenagers clinging to each other. His parents, mostly in London. Robin away from Windward in crisis talks with Rachel, or locked in his studio. Jed and Oriana safe in a new world they'd discovered the route to together; a place where you could forget about everything else. There were details that Malachy didn't need to know, Jed told himself. Partly because he wanted to keep them sacred, partly out of respect for Oriana, partly out of sensitivity towards his brother. Earlier that day he could easily have spat the details in Malachy's face. The sounds she made, how frantic her passion was, all those firsts for her and for him. How clumsiness and fumbling gave way to an ecstatic flow. Condoms and cunnilingus and blow-jobs and this way and that way and all day long.

'You know – we were beyond terrified, Malachy, by what had happened and what was happening. We didn't know if you were going to be OK. No one told us. Often, there was no one here. We cleaned your blood from the floor. We eavesdropped on people saying *blinded* and *further surgery* and *facial reconstruction* and *no, he won't be going to Bristol this year*. We were thrown together, Malachy. We literally clung to each other. We were right in the path of the hurricane and we had to hold on to each other to stop ourselves from being flung, torn, destroyed. So, you see, the physical – it just helped. It took us away from pain and panic. We could get lost in sex.' He glanced at Malachy. It was difficult to tell what his brother was thinking. 'It wasn't about love,' Jed said. 'It wasn't about togetherness. It was neither lovemaking nor was it shagging. There was no shared emotion, no profound meaning, nothing momentous that we discovered together. It was where we escaped to, it was somewhere that fear and guilt couldn't infiltrate.'

Malachy stared down into his tea. Of all the days that his brother could have brandished damaging details, this was the one. But Jed hadn't and for that he was grateful. He observed Jed who looked crumpled by it all. The memories of that day and the aftermath. The dashed hopes of today.

'It's OK,' Malachy said. 'I know you didn't do it to spite me.' The more he thought about it, the stranger his conclusion. 'Thank God she had you during those days. Thank God you found a way to cope.' How bizarre did that sound? Not so bizarre. 'Those days were as dark for you as they were for me,' Malachy said. 'Dark days.'

Jed scrunched his eyes tight shut and grabbed the mug hard to stop himself shaking. 'On day nine the police came. I honestly thought they'd come to take her to jail. She was beside herself. It was that doddery old PC – do you remember him? But he came to interview Robin, about licences and certificates and lockable cupboards – all the rules that would have accidentally bypassed a place like Windward.' Jed paused. 'And then her sixteenth birthday came and went. Nobody noticed. She said nothing. I only remembered late that afternoon.' Malachy's head was now in his hands. Jed cleared his throat. 'And then she left the day before you came home. Day thirteen. Robin frogmarched her out – there was a taxi waiting to take them to the train. Two suitcases. She'd come in to me in the small hours. *They're making me go away, Jed*, she'd said. *No one will help me stay. Not Lilac. Not Louis.*' Jed looked at Malachy imploringly. 'There was nothing I could do, Malachy.'

'No one would tell me the name of the fucking school,' Malachy said.

'I stood on the steps and she banged on the minicab window and she yelled out, *Tell Malachy tell Malachy tell Malachy.*'

'Tell me what?'

'I don't know.'

'But you never told me that.'

Jed looked ashamed. 'I promise you part of me just didn't know what I was meant to tell you.'

They sat silently with their thoughts.

'When you were little – out in the orchard – of all the stunted twisted trees you could just have stood on your tiptoes and picked the fruit from, you always, *always* tried for the apple or pear just beyond your grasp. You'd jump and leap and you'd clamber along precarious branches. You would not be appeased by any other fruit on any other tree, even if they were bigger or riper or easier to have. That's why there are so many photos of you climbing trees, Jed. Mum and Dad used to say *There goes Jed, lured by the golden pear*.'

Jed remembered. He brushed away a tear. He glanced over at the cabinet in which were the albums containing those very photos.

'I remember,' he said before falling silent again. He didn't really want to say it out loud. It would mummify his past and define his future if he did. But hadn't he been through enough? Hadn't they all been through enough? He looked at his brother. 'You say you were always going to come back for her – but look what happened, Malachy. Oriana came back to you.'

Oriana and Malachy

Robin had said he wanted a word – but when they left the Bedwells' and came back into the apartment,

Robin had gone straight through to his studio and shut the door. Oriana knew Jed and Malachy needed time together alone. But it left her standing all on her own, in her childhood room for the second time in one day, and it was beyond bizarre. She put the LP of *The Waste Land* back in the stack, moved *Flowers for Algernon* to the top of the pile. She was still in Malachy's clothes and she looked at the few garments of hers remaining in the cupboard. One day, she'd try them all on. But today wasn't a day for snow-washed jeans or the particularly virulent Acid-house top. Today, the past was like a vast museum and she was fatigued by all the exhibits on show, all the history and cross-references that accompanied everything. She straightened her bed covers and left her bedroom, closing the door quietly behind her. She walked lightly through to the sitting room.

At the far end, the studio door was shut. And she thought to herself, so bloody what. She thought to herself, for somewhere like Windward which prides itself on its open-door policy she'd been shut out too many times and for too bloody long. She didn't bother to knock; she just went straight in.

Robin wasn't working. The man on the canvas was still trapped. Robin was standing in the middle of the room, looking at the portraits of Rachel. He knew Oriana would come in. And now she was there just behind him, while Rachel was right in front of him. His child. Their child. Their grown-up child with a piece of her mind on the tip of her tongue. He could pre-empt and deflect all he expected to hear her say but, just then, an overriding feeling of sorrow and shame left him speechless and somehow open.

In Oriana's big book of soliloquies there were a fair few she'd composed to her father. But standing there in his airless studio, staring at his back, she couldn't recall a single one. What she did know was that the animosity that had made her estrangement seem vindicated, that had set the tone of all those speeches in her head, had dissipated today. There just didn't seem much point having such strong feelings for someone like him.

'You wanted a word?'

'Not any more,' he said, without looking at her.

And she thought, what is the point of a confrontation if the net result is something you don't really want? It's just not worth it. It wasn't as if there was a relationship to resuscitate because there hadn't actually been one in the first place. So why waste breath? Robin didn't want a showdown either, it seemed. He didn't even want the paltry 'word' he'd asked her for half an hour before.

'Well,' said Oriana, 'I'll be going then.'

And she left, quietly closing the studio door behind her.

'Off to the Bedwells',' Robin said to himself. The phrase so familiar, so forgotten, now back again and known by rote. It caused him to drop his brush and it fell to the floor, smudging vermilion onto his brogues.

Malachy was watching television when he looked up to see Oriana's face appear around the edge of the door. She saw that Jed had gone. He returned his gaze to the screen but opened out his right arm. Into the room she padded, over to the sofa to curl up beside him. She took his arm and fitted it closely around herself. And there they sat.

'What did your father want?' Malachy asked her.

'Nothing.'

'He said nothing?'

'Not a word.'

'He's a mad old bastard,' said Malachy.

And then it struck Oriana forcefully. She stood up from the sofa and paced the room. 'You're right, of course,' she said. 'But do you know something? I didn't actually mind him being a mad bastard.' She was pacing the room, agitated. 'I grew up accustomed to it, I was inured to it.' She thought about it. 'My mother – she was more outwardly unhinged. But Robin – he was utterly consistent in his introversion and indifference.'

'Don't make excuses for him,' Malachy said. 'You were just a little girl.'

'Malachy – I've only ever felt loved by you. Similarly, I always felt that to Robin I was an odd, strange little thing – a funny little curiosity he sometimes forgot was there. He wasn't cruel, he just wasn't interested.'

Malachy wondered if this analysing was wise after the day she'd already had. He thought perhaps she was better off on the sofa, his arms around her, watching the television.

'So these last eighteen years when I cut him off – they had nothing to do with the first fifteen years of my life. Nothing at all. They are instead a direct consequence of that one day, that Thursday right at the start of September, the day before you came home from hospital. How could he, who had eschewed all natural parental responsibility for all those years, suddenly become so strident and lay down the law and send me away?' She was staggered, indignant. 'Where did he suddenly get this new-found authority to do that? How dare he rip me from my home!' She paused. Malachy could see she was shaking. 'There was a gun in the house!' she whispered as he went over to her. 'We were just kids!' He put his arm around her. 'Bang! My childhood ended abruptly and my home and the people I loved most were taken away from me.'

Malachy rested his chin on the top of Oriana's head. They stood very still, very quiet.

'They left me with no one,' she sobbed. 'How could they do that?'

'There are no answers, Oriana,' he said. He thought hard. 'But look what you've done, look how far you've come. Look at where you are. You've made it back, unscathed and extraordinary. You're here. You're back home with me.'

Jed and Oriana

Jed was not expecting to find Oriana in his flat when he returned home from work the next day. The White Peak Art Space was closed on Mondays and, though he tried not to think about it, he had to concede that if he was Malachy, he'd spend his entire day off in bed with her. But here she was, with supper cooking away.

'Hi,' he said, looking at her quizzically. Could he kiss her hullo?

'Hi.' She looked different. He knew she looked different. Radiant and contented.

'I didn't –' I don't know how to finish the sentence.

'Is it OK with you – if I stay?' Oriana asked. 'Till I sort out a car? Would you mind?'

Jed put down his keys and loosened his tie, rolled up his sleeves, went to the fridge, opened two beers and gave one to Oriana. 'Of course it's OK, Oregano. Of course it's OK.' He put his arm around her and gave her a squeeze.

'My stuff is here,' she said. 'And I start my new job next week. And – it's all *new*. But you're my old Jed.'

'Enough of the old.'

'You know what I mean.' She chinked her bottle against his and he heard her swallow down a strange sound. 'Jed – I didn't mean to toy with you.' She was red and teary. 'I should have been more honest. I'm deeply sorry.'

He held her tightly. 'Don't apologize for any of it,' he said. 'I understand. I – I'm a bit embarrassed. But I know something – I've realized something.' He paused, wondering how best to put it into words. 'How else do we sift through our dreams and work out which can make it into the real world?'

'And Malachy,' she said. 'It's just – what happened between you and me the other night.' She paused. 'Back when we were fifteen.' Her head dropped.

Jed held her close. 'It was between you and me,' he said. 'It was ours.' He thought about his brother. 'No more hurt,' he said.

When Oriana looked up at Jed and saw how his eyes were glistening with emotion, a little bruise pressed into her heart. He saw it.

'It's fine,' he told her. 'I'm cool – I'm a bloke.' She watched him think. He looked at her and he nodded and smiled. 'And it's not all sad, you know. I was thinking about it. I have my brother back. And my best buddy too – who rode her way out of the Wild West and back into my life, Windward Ho.'

There wasn't much more to say. All that was left to do was for Jed to clink his bottle against Oriana's, smack her bottom and collapse on the sofa, finding a rerun of *Top Gear* to watch on TV.

'What's for tea?' he called.

'Chilli,' Oriana said and she added salt to the water and set the rice to boil.

Oriana and Robin

Oriana was back at Windward the next weekend. Jed had brought her and, despite Malachy's invitation to stay awhile, said thanks but no thanks – I'm off to the pub with my mates. Jed knew there'd be a time when he could, when he would again dump his bags in his old room and plonk down on the purple velvet sofa and say to Oriana and Malachy, let's get a curry in. But not just yet.

Paula and Rob had Malachy and Oriana over for Sunday lunch and Oriana marvelled at the conversion of the old shack into the Ice House, a lovely home. She understood now how the regeneration of Windward was essential to its survival – how houses, like people, have different periods in their lives. The Windward of today, with all the changes, somehow gilded the past and kept it pristine and distinct. The halcyon years. There'd been a golden heyday and people who had a connection to it were blessed. The de la Mare daughters, Emma and Kate, whom Oriana had met on her initial return, told her that if it was OK, they'd rather like to call her Binky. Malachy told them, that's a dog's name. But they were having none of it.

With a plate heaped with leftovers, Malachy and Oriana strolled back across the lawn. There were the Sunday papers still to be read and so much left to talk about, to explore and discover.

'I'd better take you back,' Malachy said. Evening was drawing in and they were in bed, dangerously sleepy. 'Big day for you tomorrow.'

The first day at her new job.

'Excited?'

'You know I am,' Oriana laughed. 'It's all I've been talking about.' She stopped. 'Will you meet me from work one day?'

'Of course.'

'Good.'

'Did you phone Bernard?'

'I did,' said Oriana. 'He was chuffed to bits to be

asked to look out for a little second-hand runaround for me.'

'And did you speak to Rachel?'

'Only briefly – she seemed relieved that it was Bernard I'd called for.'

They were on their way out, putting shoes on by the front door, when Oriana caught sight of the plate of leftovers from Paula on the kitchen table.

'Will you be eating that, do you think?' she asked him.

'Jesus – you're not still hungry, are you?'

'No,' she said, 'I'm not. I wasn't thinking of me – but perhaps –'

Malachy looked at her. He knew he could help her by finishing the sentence. But he let her work the words out and into the open.

She shrugged at him. 'I thought I could run them over to my father. While, you know, you bring the car around.'

Malachy kissed Oriana on the forehead. 'I'll see you at the front,' he said.

It would have been quicker, from the front door, to go to the side of the house. But that wasn't the known route and what Oriana had found that she liked so much was rediscovering and retracing all that was remembered. It was like finding footprints in the sand and discovering that they were your own after all and no one else's. So she took the plate, went back into the house and through the internal door to the Corridor.

And her thumb was still too small for the dent in the doorknob.

And her childhood home was still silent, and a bit dark and gloomy, and pungent with turps.

Robin wasn't in the study. Or the sitting room. And the studio door was closed. He was in there, she could smell the fresh oil on canvas. Today, she'd respect that the door was shut. She cleared her throat and waited. There was no response. She looked around. This place needed a good tidy-up. Finally, she put the plate down on the crowded coffee table and walked away. As she passed the kitchen, she remembered the pills so she filled a glass with water and returned to the sitting room, placing it alongside the plate. The pills were on the mantelpiece so she put them on the tray, then changed her mind and propped the packet up against the glass. That was better. He wouldn't miss them. She walked away. She walked all the way back to the internal door. And there she stood, her forehead resting on the wood, muttering oh for God's *sake*! under her breath over and over.

Robin was tired and the light was going. He'd finish now, he decided. He cleaned his brushes and wiped them. He lit a cigarette and assessed the day's work. Sometimes, he thought he heard his subjects talking to him from beyond the canvases. Rachel especially. But that wasn't Rachel's voice.

'Dad?'

He listened again.

'Robin?'

He looked around his studio and tapped the flat of his hand against his ear as if to dislodge the trick which a spectre or just old age might play.

'Dad?'

She hadn't said that word for such a long time. She never called him that to his face. She only ever referred to him as her father.

'Dad?'

The studio door opened and Robin appeared. He sucked at his cigarette and regarded her thoughtfully from behind a safety screen of smoke.

'I brought you some supper,' she said. 'Beef,' she said. 'Potatoes. Peas. Yorkshires.'

He continued to pull on the cigarette. It was so dim in the room with no lights on; the dying light from outside cast him into one stretched shadow. God, her father was tall. She'd had every right to think him a towering, glowering giant when she was little.

'The food is cold,' she said, 'but you can just heat it up for ten minutes or so.'

The cigarette was almost finished. Robin turned and placed it upright on the windowsill, a little cylinder with its amber top travelling down in a warm glow. It gave Oriana an idea for a building design.

'Thank you,' said Robin.

'That's OK,' said Oriana. 'And your pills are here.'

He nodded, noting them leaning against the glass of water.

'Well, I'm going to go now,' she said.

'It was nice to see you,' he said. 'Thank you.'

Oriana looked at him. She still couldn't see his features clearly but his voice – calm today, soft even – drew the picture of his expression. But she knew, too, how he was just as likely to have been in a hurling foul temper. Next time, he might well be. It wouldn't surprise her. She'd deal with it. There was nothing that could surprise her at Windward, she knew the place inside and out.

Robin could see her quite clearly. Evening light washed such silk-subtle tones over a face as lovely as hers.

'Anyway,' she said. 'I'll pop in again – some time.'

He nodded.

'But I'd better go – Malachy is waiting.'

And she went, with an awkward half-wave which Robin found easy to mirror.

Robin thought he'd rather like the leftovers hot. He took the tray through to the kitchen and lit the gas oven. He placed the plate inside, shut the oven door and set the timer. What had Oriana said? Ten minutes or so. He went back to the sitting room, flicked on the table lamp and took his pill. And there he sat, listening out for the ping from the kitchen to tell him that his supper was ready.

EPILOGUE

Rachel never returned to Windward but, that following year, Jette and Orlando did. It was strange at first, Oriana nervously tiptoeing into the ballroom when they arrived, as if the very sight of her might hurt their eyes. But they were quick to welcome her back into their fold, to say to her, we never blamed you, Oriana, we blamed ourselves. Our dream, our idealized world of Windward – it imploded one summer and we weren't there to prevent it.

'What kind of parents did that make us?' Orlando said.

'Dad –' said Malachy.

'But look at you!' Jette marvelled, taking Oriana's hand. 'Look at what you've achieved – the life you've led.'

'And look where it's brought me,' Oriana said. 'Look where I am.'

Jed visited more and more, sometimes hanging out with Oriana on Saturdays when Malachy was at the gallery. Occasionally, he brought a girlfriend with him and Oriana loved the way Jed always introduced them.

'This is Oriana,' he'd say. 'And this is my big brother.'

It was difficult sometimes to remember which name went with which girl, who was in and who was on her way out. But after a while Angie was the only one mentioned, the only one he brought to see them, and she was the one who often answered his landline at home when Oriana phoned for a chat or to make plans.

Cat and Ben often came over too because a rug on the lawns at the back, or the shade of the cedar, made Windward the best place in the world for a baby to be. Django's health dipped but levelled again and twice Robin had asked Oriana to drive him over so he could visit.

Robin never came to the Bedwell apartment again. The only sound that he heard, if he heard any at all from there, was laughter floating in through his studio window like dust dancing in sunlight. Just little drifts of two lives rubbing along happily, day to day.

Malachy or Oriana popped in on him a few times each week. Usually, it was on some pretext or other – but invariably it was just to check he had food and to nag him to remember to take his medication. He had shouted at Oriana the other month and flung a loaded palette to the floor, but he'd noticed how she just rolled her eyes as she turned to leave. And she'd still switched on the oven on her way out. And propped his damned pills by the bastard glass of bloody water.

*   *   *

Then Ashlyn said she was coming to visit and Malachy wondered why Oriana seemed so reflective about this.

'You've hauled me in on your ridiculous Face-offs or whatever you call that thing you do with your iPad,' he'd said. 'I feel like I know her – certainly I know how you feel about her – but you don't seem that thrilled that she's coming. Do you still feel bad that you didn't go over for the wedding?'

'No,' said Oriana thoughtfully. 'No, not that.' It had been a small wedding in Hawaii, after all. 'It's more to do with the fact that she really wants to come *here*. That's why I feel bad.'

She was sitting at Orlando's old desk, 'doing homework' as she liked to say. Malachy walked over to her, glancing at the drawings of Windward that she'd left for him all that time ago. The closest thing to a love letter he'd ever had, now framed and on the wall just above where she currently sat.

Malachy pulled up a stool. 'Why do you feel bad that she's coming here?' He looked around. 'Don't you love this place? Do you want to redecorate or something? Is it shabby? Is that it? It looks pretty spruce to me, now that we have Maggie cleaning once a week.'

Oriana smiled at him, touched his arm. 'This place is perfect.' Why was he wearing his patch inside today? Did he realize?

'Well then, why are you being mad and looking all forlorn?'

'I lied.' She shrugged and she said it so conversationally that Malachy was at a loss how to respond.

'I was evasive and careless with the truth.' Oriana took her pencil and put it behind his ear, then brushed her legs as if smoothing away crumbs. 'Remember when I first came back – how I made out that my life in the United States was amazing?' She paused. 'Well, when I was out there, I spun this huge psychedelic web of intrigue and fibs around Windward.' She shook her head at herself. 'I made out it was all Julie Christie and Keef and Rod and lark after lark after lark.'

Malachy thought about it. 'It was Ronnie too,' he said. 'And you were very special to Rod.'

'I know. I know all that.' Her voice was a little choked.

Malachy thought, I can help her. It's my duty to help her.

'Oriana,' he said, 'you're not likely to say to a bunch of new friends that your father has a personality disorder and your mother's psychotic and that something God-awful happened when you were a teenager.'

'For years, I kind of put my entire childhood into fancy dress,' she said quietly. 'I layered all sorts of embellishment and disguise over it.' She sighed. 'They all wanted tales of my liberated upbringing. All the far-out hippy-dippy freedom I had.'

He took the pencil from behind his ear and twiddled it fast between finger and thumb so that the faceted sides disappeared and it appeared perfectly cylindrical. Life with Oriana was about smoothing those sharp edges for her, one by one, slowly and surely.

411

'It wasn't *freedom*, Oriana,' he said quietly. 'You were pretty much forgotten and had to fend for yourself.' He took her hand. 'That's not liberation – that's practically neglect. And it's OK not to tell people about that part – even people you love as much as you love Ashlyn.'

'It's a bit dishonest,' Oriana said.

Malachy shook his head. 'You know why it's all right not to tell? Why it's fine to dress it up a little differently, or put a rainbow cloak around it?' She looked so ashamed and it hurt his heart. 'It's OK because they were never part of it,' he said. 'It's OK because the people who were with you then are still with you now. Me. Jed. Cat – Django. Lilac. We hold your past in our hands and we know it's as precious as porcelain.'

Oriana looked up at Malachy.

'It's true,' he said and he tucked her hair behind her ear. 'It's true. There's no deceit in not telling everyone everything that ever happened to you.'

Oriana stepped away from the table and into Malachy's arms.

'You're so wise.'

'That makes me sound old.'

'Well, how do you think Lilac feels?'

'She loved her birthday cake – and the sing-song.'

'I can't believe she's leaving Windward,' Oriana said.

'Nor me. I just can't see Lilac in an old people's home,' Malachy said. He'd worried about it greatly since she'd told him of her plans – or rather, Rafe's plans for her.

'But she'll be nearer her family,' Oriana said. 'And not so far that we can't visit.'

'I know,' said Malachy, but he didn't seem sure.

'She'll take her headphones and her remaining trinkets,' said Oriana, 'and wherever she goes, she'll take a little Windward glitter with her.'

Rachel never came to Windward, though Oriana took to driving to Hathersage every couple of months. Bernard liked to give her little car the once-over – check the oil, the tyre pressure, top up the screen-wash, hang a smiley scented strawberry on the rear-view mirror, pop a packet of Werther's Originals in the cup holder. And, really, that's why Oriana liked to go. She'd stand on the pavement while Bernard tinkered and they'd chat. Sometimes, they strolled round the block and had a quick smoke. Not often.

Malachy didn't always accompany Oriana to Hathersage. When he had first seen Rachel again, after almost twenty years, he'd had to quell an insane urge to blast her for all the torment she'd caused him, never mind Oriana. He wanted to say – do you have any idea what your behaviour did to a young boy? How often I was unable to sleep? How I'd go to my parents and beg them to lock your door to the Corridor because I was scared I'd wake and find you ranting in my bedroom? How I'd slip out of our apartment at ungodly hours and run along the Corridor to check that your door was in fact *unlocked*, just in case Oriana needed to escape to ours?

He wanted to say to her, have you any idea how

much I hated you for disturbing – and I mean *disturbing* – my family on countless occasions with your conceited lunacy and self-obsessed drama? He wanted to ask her – why couldn't Oriana have lived with you in Hathersage after all? What was that all about? She's your daughter. You didn't step in to stop her being sent away. You never thought about her, only yourself.

But Malachy found he liked Bernard. He did have vague memories of him from the past but the reality was fresher, brighter, not least because Bernard's affection for Oriana was palpable. Malachy liked to listen to them both witter on; Bernard asking her so many questions about her job and trying hard to understand the answers which tumbled from her in an effervescent stream like a can of shaken soda.

Just the once, early on, Malachy was able to orchestrate time alone with Rachel. He insisted on clearing the table, insisted Bernard and Oriana went through to the lounge to relax. Rachel was expecting Bernard to bring the dishes into the kitchen.

'You're not thinking of coming to Windward any time soon, are you.' There was emphatically no question mark at the end of Malachy's sentence and his voice was low and steady. He could sense her rising indignance. There was a wildness in her eyes and the colour rose from her neck but drained from her face in the way that he remembered only too vividly. But it didn't upset him today. Today, he was the grown-up and he had control.

'You're not coming back to Windward at all,' he said.

She looked affronted, victimized.

'Give over, Rachel,' Malachy had said, seeing right through her. 'Windward is Oriana's home. This is her dance.'

Ashlyn and Eric spent a glorious week of their honeymoon at Windward. Ashlyn seemed to know the place as soon as she arrived. Robin was on spectacular form swearing at canvases and telling his daughter he wasn't *an exhibit for bloody Yanks to gawp at* – much to Ashlyn's delight. There were the traditional local well-dressings to see and Chatsworth to visit – which required much persuasion that no, Ashlyn, this wasn't built for a movie. They all came to meet the honeymooners: Jed, Cat, Ben, even Django resplendent in something smock-like from Guatemala. The ballroom. The balcony. The art inside and out. The cedar tree and the cellar and the long, legendary Corridor. When Ashlyn and Eric returned to the United States, they took with them tales and details that corroborated all of Oriana's stories about Windward.

'Thanks for being such a great host,' Oriana said to Malachy.

'It was a pleasure,' he said. 'Anyway, we'll honeymoon in the States and get our own back.'

Oriana smiled to herself. It wasn't the first time he'd alluded to such things but she'd bide her time and wait for him to find the right moment. He flopped down onto the sofa and she cosied up next to him. He ran strands of her hair through his fingers, thinking.

415

'I love our life,' he said.

'I do too,' she replied.

That night, for the first time since he couldn't remember when, Malachy had the dream again. In the woods, with Jed – as they are now but in their teenage bodies. It's dusk. Here's the rabbit. He's running off, the bugger. Stopping now, turning and facing Malachy. Delicate eyes and soft silver pelt. His lope-long ears rigid and erect as though he's flicking Malachy the 'V'.

Where's the gun? Quick! Look at the little sod, he's stock-still. The perfect target.

Where's the gun?

And where's Jed?

Jed's not there.

'Malachy?'

But Oriana is.

She's lying in the grass next to him, arm against arm, sun on their backs, blades of grass tickling their legs.

'Bless him!' Oriana whispers to Malachy as they look at the rabbit and the rabbit looks at them. Looks at them for a long time before skittering off and away.

There is no gun.

There is only Oriana.

'Malachy,' she is saying. 'Malachy.'

He woke.

Oriana was stroking his face, saying his name. 'You were dreaming,' she said. 'You OK?'

Disorientated, Malachy sat up. 'I'm fine.'

He put the light on and smiled at her. 'I'm fine,' he said. He laughed a little. He leant over and kissed her.

'Go back to sleep,' he said. And he left the bed, pulling on clothes in a hurry.

'Where are you going?' Oriana asked. 'It's the middle of the night.'

'I'm going to finish my novel,' said Malachy. 'The ending's just come to me.'

ACKNOWLEDGEMENTS

Sincerest thanks to Team North – especially my wonderful agent Jonathan Lloyd and my talented editor Lynne Drew. Grateful thanks to the supporting crews at Curtis Brown Ltd (especially Lucia Rae) and HarperCollins. Mary Chamberlain and your fine-tooth comb – thank you.

In terms of research for this novel, my gratitude goes to Professor Anthony Bron, Piers Hernu, Immy de Cordova, also the Pursers and Mark Daniels at Marden Hill.

I'm so grateful to my lovely readers for the banter on Twitter and Facebook. You're such a loyal and warm bunch – the extended family of my characters. Your support is extremely precious to me – thank you all.

On the home front, the book just wouldn't have been finished were it not for my friends and family. The Pegg People, the Pottery Ladies, The Cucumber Girls, J6 Mums – you're very dear to me, thank you. Ma and Pa – as ever, heartfelt thanks.

My much cherished coven: Jo Smith, Maureen Pegg, Amanda Abbington, Mel Bartram, Jane Sutcliffe, Leslie Dunn, Sarah Henderson, Kirsty

Jones, Clare Griffin and Lucy Smouha – I just really, really love you.

Most of all though, for their patience, computer skills, coffee-making and bath-running abilities, noise, energy, bonkers sense of humour, general craziness and bottomless pit of affection – my deepest gratitude goes to my beautiful children Felix and Georgia.

In memory of Liz Berney 1968 – 2005

www.freyanorth.com
www.facebook.com/freya.north
@freya_north

READING GROUP QUESTIONS

Do you think Windward can be seen
as a character in this book?

Who is your favourite character in this novel? Why?

Why do you think Oriana comes back?

Bernard is a very different character to the others in
the book – what do you think his role in the book is?

What role do the older generation – Django, Lilac,
Robin, Bernard and Rachel – play in this book and
what did you feel about the way they were portrayed?

What does this book tell us about friendships
versus family relationships?

Would you recommend this book to friends?
What would you say when you pressed it
into their hands?

Q&A WITH freya north

I asked my loyal readers on Facebook to fire questions at me... Here are my top eight. Thank you so much for joining in – the response was amazing and, if I had more space, I'd happily have answered all of you. Join me at facebook.com/freya.north where I love interacting with my readers.

HELEN MITCHELL – What is your favourite word in the English language and why?

Discombobulate. I make sure I use it in every book I write... Why? Because it winds up my best friend Jo Smith. I never tell her where it is – so she always sends me a fantastically sweary text when she comes across it.

EILEEN BEASLEY – Was there ever a criticism that nearly stopped you writing?

It took me five years of rejections from agents and publishers alike before I found my wonderful agent who, twenty years on, still represents me. There was plenty of criticism – rarely was it constructive. On the contrary, it just spurred me on. The one I remember most was a publisher saying, "You can't start a book like this!" (Sally starts quite raunchily...) and I just thought well, if one person's saying I can't – there must be someone else out there saying why not! Go girl!!

ANNE MACKLE – What three things would we be really surprised to know about you?

I am brilliant at building fires. I went to school with fellow author Jane Green and we scored the lowest marks possible in our Maths exam. I won a dressage competition on the day of Princess Di's funeral. My friends say I should keep my crush on Laurence Llewelyn Bowen secret – but I'm loud and proud about that one...

SARA SCOLES – Have you ever wished you could go back and rewrite the endings of any of your stories.

Never. I don't plot or plan my novels – I just start with Chapter One and let the book unfold organically... A strange thing always happens towards the natural ending of a novel – I suddenly experience this surging, euphoric sense that the end is imminent. My fingers skitter over the keyboard trying to keep up with my train of thought and then suddenly

– the closing sentence, the final full stop and I sit back and think that's it. It is done. I have never changed or even tweaked an ending – it's the part of the book about which I am always utterly convinced.

TRACEY HALL – Do you have a tattoo? If so what and where?

I do indeed – a cheeky little gecko in a cheeky little place…

PRUE NICHOLS – How has *The Way Back Home* changed you? What has it taught you about yourself or life?

Writing this novel had a profound effect on my self-belief – at times I had none at all. It was the first time in my career that I was stricken with Writer's Block so severe that it made me pretty ill. I think people assume that if commercial fiction is 'easy' to read, then it must be easy to write. Not so. I put my heart and soul into my novels and for months, I honestly thought that I had no books left in me, that I'd never write again. It was terrifying, as I am the sole provider for my two children. Most frustrating was that I KNEW the story – I just could not access it; it remained just beyond my grasp. I felt desperately ashamed, I felt a failure but I dug very deep and, somehow, the book was written. When I read the book now, there are vast passages I cannot remember writing. So *The Way Back Home* taught me to have faith in myself and just to keep going, no matter how bad things might seem.

ALEXANDRA JAMES – Is there anything specific you wish to say to your readers?

Yes! I'd like the opportunity just to extend to all of you my heartfelt thanks. Many of you have been loyal to me in and out of the years – there is no seal of approval more precious to an author than a happy reader. I love being able to interact with you on Twitter, Facebook and by email. I truly feel you are like the extended family of my characters. Thank you.

HAYLEY COOPER – How do you fit in writing a book with family life?

Sometimes, Hayley, it's more a case of how I fit family life into writing a book. It's very hard. I'm a single parent and I have to be very disciplined to maximize the hours between the school runs. I say I'm not going to write at weekends or on holiday – but invariably I have to. My children always press 'send' when I email my final draft to my agent – they want it out of the house! As proud as my children are of me, I heard my daughter Georgia saying that if a child of hers ever wanted to be an author, she'd tell them not to be.

THE STORY OF WINDWARD

Two years ago, friends moved into an apartment in a glorious Georgian mansion in Hertfordshire. I went to visit...

"This place is amazing," I said.

"It was an artists' commune in the 1960s and 1970s," my friend told me. "Come and meet Mark, he was born here. He has the apartment that still has the original ballroom."

"A ballroom?" Who one earth has a ballroom in their flat? Ding! A novel was taking root and I'd only been there ten minutes. I was led along an old interior service corridor, crumbling plaster on the walls, huge worn flagstones underfoot; off which were old doors to what are now separate apartments.

And so Windward – the old house at the centre of The Way Back Home – came to be. Much more than simply a building, the house became a leading character in the novel. It was to be an artists' commune and the novel would feature the families that had lived there.

But I didn't want it to be all bonkers artists wafting around in kaftans to the sound of a tambourine. I wanted characters rounded enough to illicit a strong response in the reader, whether it was fondness or dislike. I wanted to infuse a little unease, tension, secrets. Why should a commune be all peace and love, Man? I thought about grownups who should have been more responsible and kids who would have to grow up fast. I wanted love and rivalry, deprivation and plenty, cold and warmth, estrangement and desperate closeness to fill Windward.

I thought back to the summer when I was fifteen – that heady, edgy time when there's a constant vibration between feeling emancipated and mature – and so often vulnerable and disempowered. Exams are over. School's out. We felt we could rule the world even if our parents told us we were still kids. I recalled the summer when I was fifteen. It seemed so carefree, as if it had been put into the calendar simply to provide fun for my friends and me after an eternity studying for exams. We had the sun on our backs and the world at our feet.

But what if something changed the course of the lives of the teenagers at Windward? What if something happened the summer they were fifteen – that summer that should have been theirs for the taking? What if you were suddenly exiled from your childhood home and then, eighteen years later, you came back?

THE TURNING POINT

Coming soon from Freya North

Over one short weekend, when Canadian musician Scott Emerson and British children's author Frankie Shaw meet by chance, a profound connection is made.

Their homes are thousands of miles apart: Frankie and her children live by the coast of North Norfolk while Scott's roots lie deep in the mountains of British Columbia. It's a miracle they even meet and, against all advice, they decide to see where this might go.

Over oceans and time zones, they make sacrifices and take risks, discovering along the way the truth about love and family. For the first time in a long while, it seems life could be very good.

But fate has a tragic twist in store, one that could destroy all that was believed in and hoped for.

Poignant, engrossing and moving, *The Turning Point* is a novel about the importance of seizing happiness and trusting that love will always find a way.

READ ON FOR AN EXCLUSIVE EXTRACT

SCOTT

Alone in his truck on an empty stretch of road in the middle of Thompson Country, Scott cursed out loud though no one could hear him. For the previous half an hour, as he drove from the belly of Kamloops and through the entrails of its suburbs, his phone signal had been off and the radio had played crystal clear everything he wanted to hear. His own personal playlist, beamed telepathically back through the radio, providing company and a soundtrack to the three hours remaining of the journey home. And now, as the road climbed and the scenery most deserved a rousing score, the music had gone and, instead, the cell-phone networks were polluting this immaculate part of British Columbia. His phone rang, his voicemail beeped, his phone rang again, his voicemail beeped. The sound wasn't dissimilar from some god-awful plastic Europop. A barrage of text-message alerts now chimed in like a truly crap middle eight before the calls started again. The phone was in his bag, in the footwell. Whatever risks Scott had taken in his life, he'd only ever driven with two hands on the wheel and both eyes on the road ahead. He pulled over. What, for Christ's sake, what?

The voicemail icon with its red spot as angry as a

boil. The envelope signifying text messages bursting with four unread. Missed calls. Managing his phone was the only thing in life that Scott was prepared to multitask, because to minimize the time spent on it, was time well spent. He accessed the voicemail whilst clicking into the texts. Before he'd heard a thing he knew what was wrong from Jenna's two words:

I'm fine x

But by then, a recorded voice was filling the car with the details.

'Hi Scott – it's Shelley. I've been trying to contact you – Jenna's had a seizure. She's OK now but it lasted near enough five minutes. She hit her head, she has a concussion so they've taken her to Squamish just to be sure. It's just gone two. You have my number so feel free to call me.'

Scott only vaguely listened to the later messages, all from Jenna's friend Shelley repeating the information in different tones of voice: tired, upbeat, reassuring, pseudo-medical. He stamped on the gas and drove fast, without looking at the view and with the radio off. There was no quick route. Too many mountains in the way.

When he opened the door to the hospital room, Jenna was still sleeping. Four hours later she woke, groggy and bashful. She always looked that way after an episode – not that she had any control over them. They had lingered over her life, a storm cloud, a menacing smudge on an otherwise blue sky and she never sensed when they were about to cover the sun.

'Neil Young, Jimmy Reed, Prince,' said Scott.

She looked at him as if to say, Really? I have to do this now?

'Joan of Arc,' she said. 'Dickens and Dostoyevsky.' She knew why he did it, this roll call, to make her feel less ashamed, less alone. She was part of a club, a member of epilepsy's renowned society – but it irritated her.

Actually, Scott did it to gauge her responsiveness.

'They glued me,' she said lightly. 'See?' Her finger hovered tentatively over the dark maroon splice above her brow.

'Very Harry Potter,' Scott said, thinking to himself that if he was a religious man he'd want to thank God for medical glue, for the fact that she was OK. But he wasn't a religious man because he just couldn't reconcile a God figure smiting someone so beautiful, so vital and harmless, with such an affliction. He sat down and put his hand gently over her wrist.

'I'm sorry,' she said. 'It just happened.'

He hated the obligation she felt to apologize. He hated God for that too. Why burden the victim with guilt as well?

'I know, sugar, I know.'

'I thought we had the meds pretty much sorted.'

Quietly, they both felt suddenly foolish for having had so much hope in the new drug.

'You're booked in for your EEG next month?'

Jenna nodded. 'Can I come home tonight?'

'Doc says tomorrow.' Scott looked at her and assessed in a glance the new scar she'd be adding to her collection. And then he shrugged, his signature gesture when he'd assessed all the pros and cons in a split second. Jenna had suffered a seizure but see, she's back.

'It's been a while,' he said, 'since you had one that's ended you up here.' He tucked her hair behind her ear. But Jenna didn't nod and he found he couldn't look at her. 'Tell me it's been a while.'

Jenna could do neither half-answers nor white lies.

'They've been, you know, *manageable*. And, as you say – they haven't put me in here for a good while.'

Scott was appalled. 'Why didn't you tell me?'

'Because you'd react like this? And blame yourself? And worry too much?'

The accusation was fair but it irked him.

'I kept a note – so I can discuss it with Dr Schultz next month.'

'You should have told me.'

She looked pale and exhausted. 'No driving for me, I guess,' she said. 'That's another six months wasted, hoping for normality.'

They both thought of her little red car in the driveway at home, which had hardly moved in two years.

Back home the next day, Scott settled Jenna into the armchair and built a small fire though it was May.

'I can cancel England next week,' he said.

'Are you crazy?'

'They can do it without me.'

'No, they can't – you won't let them anyway. You *have* to go,' Jenna said. 'That's what they pay you for.'

'The team there is great – they know me, I know them.'

'I'm not having this *thing* do this to me – to you. You have to go. It's your career. You need the money.'

They sat and reflected quietly, independently, together.

Scott went to the kitchen and took something out of the freezer. This *Thing*. Jenna's epilepsy was indeed just that – an incendiary entity that would grab her when he wasn't there, that would fight him for her when he was. All these years and he was no closer to finding any peace, any acceptance that this affliction held Jenna hostage right in front of his face and he just couldn't rescue her. A long time ago, he'd decided that if he couldn't rescue her, then he'd be right there with her, alongside her in captivity.

He rooted around for potatoes and onions, he clanged pans against pots, he clattered cutlery and muttered inanities under his breath but loud enough to fool Jenna if she was listening. All the while, he tossed the concepts around, like a juggler throwing machetes. It didn't necessarily follow that though she'd had a bad seizure another would recur any time soon – so if he did cancel England next week, say she was fine? And then, say the next time she *wasn't* fine when he was abroad? But how many times had there been recently that he hadn't known about? She'd said a couple – did she really mean only two? And define 'recently' Jenna. How long are we talking about?

England. Would she come with him? But she had work. Anyway, she wouldn't want to – she'd been there and done that and they both knew he'd have little time for anything other than sleep and work. Her life was here. If only the thing would do them both the courtesy of some kind of schedule, better warning signs, softer landings. But when had it ever done that? The only predictable thing about most of her seizures was just how unpredictable they were. Scott thought about it as he sliced and chopped and steamed and fried. There was no magic solution, no cure, and still it made him furious.

Jenna was dozing when he went back through with a tray of food. He lifted a strand of hair that he felt was too close to her new wound. He had no appetite. He pushed his tray to one side and kept watch while she rested.

I'll always be here. I'll never leave you, baby. His oath was as solemn now as twenty years ago.

FRANKIE

Alice Alice Alice.

Frankie paused. She'd been here before, waiting for Alice. There was little point expending emotion on it. She'd just chant Alice's name again, in case she was creeping up on her, unseen.

What are you up to this time? Frankie asked quietly. Where are we going, youngling – you and I?

She thought she could hear her, in the distance. A snatch of a giggle, the arrhythmic scamper of small footfalls over twigs and leaves, the sound of joy that propelled a leap into the air.

Alice? Are you coming?

Frankie! Frankie! Can you hear me?

Sort of, but you're very muffled. Come closer, you little minx. Come closer so I can catch you.

Can you see me, Frankie? I'm *here*. Look!

Yes! There you are! Hold on – wait for me.

And then the back door opened with a creak and closed with a slam and all that Frankie had to show for her day was a stark, staring whiteness. A blankness that was as confrontational as it was empty. A sheet of white paper, with absolutely nothing on it.

'Hi Mum.'

'Hi darling.'

'Are you Alice-ing?'

'I thought I was.' Frankie smoothed the paper in front of her as if it was as creased as her brow. It wasn't. It might as well have been ironed flat, such was the pristine sharpness to the edges, as if potential paper cuts were its *raison d'être*.

'Haven't you done *anything*?'

'Almost.' Frankie looked at her son and glanced away. 'No.'

'Mum,' Sam sighed.

'It's so hard –'

'– there's no crisps.'

It was this that was the cause of Sam's concern, and it made Frankie flinch. Just then no crisps was worse than no Alice.

'Have crackers,' she said with forced brightness, 'with butter. That's what I had for lunch.' She gauged her son's response and she thought, when I was thirteen, would I have dared roll my eyes at my mother? And then she softened. My son with the hollow legs. 'I'll make them for you. Homework?'

'Chemistry and maths.'

'How awful.'

Sam thought about it glumly. Then he perked up. 'I can show you how to do a mind map on the computer – it's the best way for organizing ideas. It can cure your Writer's Block. I swear on my life.'

Frankie looked at Sam, looked at the pages in front of her, woefully devoid of a single word or image. Her body felt compressed and inert from the effort of spending all day creating nothing.

'OK, but you still have to do your homework.'

'I'll do it later. This'll only take me ten minutes to show you. It will change your life. I swear to God.'

'Sam – if I can plan my next book in ten minutes, *I'll* do your homework for you.'

'Sick! Promise?'

'No.'

He rolled his eyes at her. 'Can I just check Instagram?'

'No. And don't roll your eyes – it makes you look like you're having a fit. And that's not funny.'

Forty minutes later, Frankie was still flailing about with the technical demands of on-screen mind mapping. Her son truly wondered whether she was pretending to be so thick or whether it was an avoidance tactic because she didn't actually want to do another Alice book. One time, he'd watched her clean the inside of the dishwasher rather than write.

'Sorry darling – about the crisps.'

'Annabel will be far angrier than me. You promised her, remember.'

For a hideous frozen moment, Frankie could not move.

'Oh shit – not again.'

Listening to his mother fulminate her way through the house, tripping over her own shoes strewn in a doorway, hunting for keys tossed goodness knows where that morning, Sam thought to himself that resurrecting the swear jar might be a very good idea indeed. He and his sister would be rich in a matter of days.

Frankie backed her car from the driveway. Today, it infuriated her that she'd bought a house with a driveway but with no space to actually turn the car. Every day, it cricked her neck. Added to that was the headache of being really late already and now she found she was going to need to wave and wait and wave again at Mr Mawby. The elderly farmer next door was manoeuvring his tractor from the road into his yard as cautiously as if it was a Ferrari he wanted to keep pristine. Oh God please don't get out of the cab, please don't come over. Get back in the cab, Mr Mawby. No time for a little mardle today.

It did occur to her that she hadn't had time last week either.

'Hi, Mr Mawby, hi.' She wound down her window but kept her car creeping along. 'Are you well? Mrs Mawby too? I have to go – I'm late for Annabel.'

And Mr Mawby thought, When will that girl slow down and bed in?

Over the last few months, it had struck Frankie that the sharp bends on these empty and stretching country lanes were every bit as taxing as heavy traffic in the city she'd left nine months ago. As she drove, she suddenly felt nostalgic for the crafty back-doubles she knew off by heart around the roads of North London. There didn't seem to be any short cuts to Annabel's school. Or perhaps there was a clever route she didn't know about because she wasn't yet local enough.

Even from a distance, she could see that Annabel was glowering at her. One of the few children in After School Club and now the last child in the playground.

'I'm so so sorry,' Frankie called out in general, as lightly as she could, as she approached. 'Oh dear.' She was so out of breath she couldn't even swear under it. 'Mrs Paterson, I am so sorry – I was writing. And the time – it just . . .'

'That's all right, Miss Shaw. Annabel and I were having a very interesting conversation.'

Frankie didn't doubt that.

'Good afternoon, Annabel.' Mrs Paterson said goodbye with a formal handshake.

'Good *night*, Mrs Paterson,' Annabel said.

'Sarcasm is the lowest form of wit,' Frankie told her daughter as they walked to the car.

'That's what Grandma says,' said Annabel. 'I don't know what it means exactly – but I do know that you say *oh God I sound just like my mother* like it's the worst thing in the world. So I wouldn't say that one, if I were you.'

Sometimes, thought Frankie, there really is nothing you can say to a nine-year-old who has all the answers. She took Annabel's hand, persevering until, after snatching it away twice and then turning it into limp lettuce, her daughter finally furled her fingers around her mother's.

'Not much more than a year, then it'll be better. When you and Sam are at the same school, same bus.'

'But I don't want to leave my school,' said Annabel quietly.

Frankie looked at her. 'You like it here, don't you?'

'Yes,' Annabel said. 'I've only been here two and a bit terms but I like it much more than my old school. In fact, I hardly ever think about London.'

'Nowadays we have the sea,' said Frankie.

'And a big garden,' said Annabel, 'and a room of my own.'

'I'm truly sorry I was late, darling.'

'Sometimes I really hate Alice.'

'Why? What happened? Shall I speak to Mrs Paterson? Hate is a terrible emotion.'

'Not Alice in my class, Mum. *Your* Alice. She's like this stepsister or something. It's like you favouritize her. What's for supper?'

'Baked beans, chips. Tomato and cucumber. Possibly.' She paused. 'I didn't have time to go to the shops. I was working.'

'Does that mean there are no crisps?'

'I'm so sorry, darling.'

It was Annabel's forlorn silence, the way her little fingers slackened as if sighing, that made Frankie feel suddenly useless at everything. She knew Annabel blamed Alice. But Frankie had no one to blame but herself.

'Come on – let's go via Howell's and I'll buy you two packets and one for tomorrow.'

But then she realized she'd come out in a rush without her purse. And she wondered, does nine months living here warrant credit at the local shop?

Alice & the Ditch Monster
Alice & the Ditch Monster Hatch a Plan
Alice & the Ditch Monster Brave the Storm
Alice & the Ditch Monster Save the Day
Alice & the Ditch Monster Go for Gold
Alice & the Ditch Monster Halloween Howls
Alice & the Ditch Monster Wonder What the Fuck
They're Going to Do Next.

Children quiet in bed, one asleep, the other reading. A glass of Rioja to hand. The paper is still stark white and glaringly empty in front of Frankie. It's raining outside and it shouldn't be. All that relocation research done quietly in Muswell Hill over a two-year period